LILAC

A NOVEL

A.A. BARTON

First Edition

ISBN: 979-8-9934868-0-2
ISBN: 979-8-9934868-1-9 (eBook)

For more information, visit: www.aabartonauthor.com

For Carole and Cheryl.

Though no amount of time would have been enough,
you still deserved more.

Table of Contents

CHAPTER ONE 1
CHAPTER TWO..................... 8
CHAPTER THREE................. 14
CHAPTER FOUR 21
CHAPTER FIVE.................... 31
CHAPTER SIX..................... 39
CHAPTER SEVEN................. 49
CHAPTER EIGHT................. 55
CHAPTER NINE................... 64
CHAPTER TEN..................... 75
CHAPTER ELEVEN............... 83
CHAPTER TWELVE.............. 90
CHAPTER THIRTEEN............. 96
CHAPTER FOURTEEN........ 102
CHAPTER FIFTEEN 108
CHAPTER SIXTEEN............ 112
CHAPTER SEVENTEEN....... 120
CHAPTER EIGHTEEN 127
CHAPTER NINETEEN 140
CHAPTER TWENTY 151

CHAPTER TWENTY-ONE 165
CHAPTER TWENTY-TWO 179
CHAPTER TWENTY-THREE 185
CHAPTER TWENTY-FOUR....... 196
CHAPTER TWENTY-FIVE 209
CHAPTER TWENTY-SIX 216
CHAPTER TWENTY-SEVEN 221
CHAPTER TWENTY-EIGHT 234
CHAPTER TWENTY-NINE........ 241
CHAPTER THIRTY 246
CHAPTER THIRTY-ONE........... 253
CHAPTER THIRTY-TWO........... 258
CHAPTER THIRTY-THREE........ 264
CHAPTER THIRTY-FOUR 270
CHAPTER THIRTY-FIVE........... 274
CHAPTER THIRTY-SIX.............. 280
CHAPTER THIRTY-SEVEN........ 286
CHAPTER THIRTY-EIGHT......... 292
EPILOGUE 298

CHAPTER ONE

I see his face all over the city, a voiceless ghost just out of reach. Like a stalker who's been spotted, he fades into the crowded streets the moment he realizes I've seen him. I push my way through the group of people flooding the crosswalk, my eyes locked on his back. He's wearing his Chicago Cubs ball cap that looks like it's seen better days, one I've threatened to throw away on numerous occasions. My feet move without my permission, and I close in on him. A lump forms in my throat as I reach my hand up to his shoulder just before he turns to face me.

But it's not his face I see. Instead, I stare at the face of a stranger, and my mind begins to panic. Of course it wasn't him—it's never him. Tears well in my eyes, and I take a step back before the stranger tries to engage me.

Too late.

"Are you okay?" The voice is so foreign, it startles me.

I don't answer right away, but as soon as I see the man reaching for me, I blurt out, "Sorry, I thought you were someone else," and quickly turn to walk as far away from him as possible.

The perk of living in a city as large as Chicago is there are enough people here to know I will likely never see this stranger again, leaving little to feel embarrassed about. From the distance I quickly put between us, I watch him as he puts an earbud in his ear, falling back into his lax cadence down the city block.

I call these occurrences hauntings. It's the only way to describe what happens to me. Not like I'm going around telling people—only the ones closest to me know about them. It's been the better part of a year since the last time one occurred, but no matter how much time has passed, I can always count on him making a ghostly appearance today, of all days.

When you hear someone say they're haunted, you're quick to assume it's the ghost of someone who has died. I no longer make that assumption—because for the past five years, it hasn't been the dead who have haunted me, it's the missing.

I shake the uncanny feeling and continue to my destination. When I walk up to the front door of Melrose, I'm greeted by a neon sign that informs the world of *Pancake Specialties*. Its fluorescent glow settles over my face, a familiar invitation beckoning me in. I swing the door open and make my way past the glass dessert display and settle into our usual booth. Melrose used to be a weekly occurrence for us, but now I only show my face here once a year.

I reach across the table to flip over the coffee cup before turning over the one in front of me, signaling to the waitress there will be two of us today. Right on cue, a young girl, not older than eighteen, shuffles up in front of me with two steaming hot pots of coffee.

"Morning. Decaf or regular?" she says between chews of her gum.

"Regular, please." I respond with less emotion than I intended.

Her tattooed arm reaches over to pour the coffee, and before she can leave, I motion to the empty cup across from me. He's always on time, so the worry of it getting cold is never an issue. The waitress looks at the empty space across from me and pauses for just a moment before complying. After she fills the second cup, she tells me she'll be back with some menus.

"Oh, no thanks. It'll just be coffee today."

Her deep sigh as she walks away tells me she's not thrilled to have one of her tables filled with a "just coffee" tab. The realization that her tip from my bill won't help her hit a minimum wage hour this morning. I know just as well as she does how much of a grind serving tables is—it's why as soon as I turned twenty-one, I started bartending. The tips are way better, which allows you to actually make a livable wage without having to work more than forty-five hours a week. Livable wage is a generous term for what a bartending job can afford you in this city, but so far, it's kept my bills paid with enough to spare for the occasional night out with Esther. Let's just say my savings account isn't anything to brag about, and any thoughts of a vacation to somewhere tropical are just fantasies.

Today won't be a quick visit. I plan to be in this booth for a few hours, but I'll make sure my tip makes up for it.

I pull out the *Chicago Tribune* and a pen from my bag and settle into the daily crossword while I sip my coffee. After every word I get, I make sure to look up at the door—as though he'll miss me if I'm not looking directly at him when he walks in.

Two cups of coffee and an hour or so later, I can tell my server is starting to wonder if my companion is ever going to join me. What was once an aura of annoyance that surrounded her has quickly morphed into pity that I've been stood up. She makes her way back over to the booth and asks if she can get a fresh cup for my friend.

"No, that's alright… No need to waste perfectly good coffee," I say with a smile that I know doesn't quite reach my eyes. "I'll take a warm-up, though."

As she walks away, I see a familiar face walk through the door. Not exactly the face I was hoping to see, but a welcome one all the same. Eddie, a server who might be older than this establishment, makes eye contact with me and immediately heads in my direction.

Eddie slides into the booth across from me, already wearing her apron with her serving book tucked inside and a faded name tag that reads *Edith*. She tilts her head as she looks at me, like the way one would look at a baby animal who's lost their mother.

"Hey, kiddo. Has it really been a year already?" she asks in disbelief.

"Mmmhmm," is all I manage to get out with a single nod of my head. I instantly break eye contact with her to avoid the look of concern I know lingers on her face. As I sip my coffee, I notice her grab the untouched cup across from me. Before I can swallow fast enough to warn her away from it, she takes a pull from the cup and then makes a bitter face once her senses register how cold it is.

Swallowing it down, she clears her throat before saying, "Looks like you've already been here for a while."

And there's that head tilt again. Jesus, I've got to redirect where this conversation is going.

"So…are you ever going to get that name tag changed to your actual name?" I say with a hint of humor in my voice.

She looks down and back up at me. With a scoff she says, "Edith is my name, Cosette," tapping her finger on the name tag.

"Oh, come on, when's the last time anyone called you Edith, Eddie?" I say with a playful tone on the only name I've ever known her by.

She raises an eyebrow and lets out a giggle.

"Well, you've got me there." She grabs the cold cup of coffee again. "Jesus, why do I keep drinking this?"

I laugh, and the sound of it shocks me. I think it's been a few weeks since I had a genuine laugh. At work I force them all the time, but that's purely to avoid scaring off the patrons and to avoid getting a bad tip. No one wants to tip a sad girl.

"Why the second cup anyway?" Eddie asks, causing the smile from my face to drop.

I pause, considering my answer. Do I tell her the truth? That the reason I come here once every year on the same day is that I have some unrealistic hope that he'll finally show up? Do I tell her that the second cup of coffee has become something of a superstition for me now, that I've convinced myself if I don't order him one, the probability of him walking through the door instantly drops to zero? No, telling her that would only paint me in a more pathetic light than she already sees me in. I keep my response short instead.

"Sentimental, I guess."

I drop my head back down to my crossword. It's nearly finished, with only one clue left to solve. I already know what the word is; a little irony to complement my morning. The delay in writing it down only serves as a purpose to stay a little longer. I always make a deal with myself that once I complete the puzzle, I leave. Otherwise, I would be here all day.

"Mind if I take a look?" Eddie says as she reaches a hand out, gliding it over the newspaper. I sit back, allowing her to rotate the paper toward her to make an assessment. As she reads the clue, I see her lips move silently, mouthing, "Beyond the realm of possibility" to herself as she ponders on what the word could be. I've already filled in a few of the letters, so I'm not surprised when she quickly figures it out.

"Implausible," she says, peering up at me with a glee of satisfaction plastered on her face.

"Oh yeah…" I laugh—this one fake. "Can't believe I got stuck on that one." I take the paper from her, mock-admiring the puzzle in its completion.

"I've got to get to work before the boss man starts docking my pay," Eddie says with sarcasm and an exaggerated eye roll. As she slides her way out of the booth, she reaches out to give my hand a little squeeze. "It's good to see you, Cosette. Take care of yourself, hon."

Her hand lingers on mine as she leaves the booth, and when she's finally gone, I wave over the young server that was taking care of me. It's gotten busy since I arrived, and I know she's happy to have me free up the booth for her. She quickly grabs her black leather booklet out of her apron, flipping through the checks until she finds mine and rips it out.

"Looks like your friend is a little late," she says playfully as she lays my bill down. She has no idea how late he is. I throw a twenty on the table and grab my things to exit the booth.

"Give me just a sec and I'll grab you some change."

I wave my hand. "Keep it."

I exit the diner without looking back to the booth. After a few hours of sitting alone, watching his coffee go cold, my mind can finally reckon with the reality that, for now, he'll remain a ghost.

CHAPTER TWO

The quickest way to get back to my apartment would be to walk nine minutes to the Belmont station and catch a transfer to the orange line, but today I'll take a detour through the financial district. The same detour I have taken for the past five years after I leave the diner.

It's the latter end of morning rush hour, so the red line isn't as busy as it could be, but there's still only standing room when I board the train. I reach up to grip a hanging loop above me and make a point to look at every face in my vicinity. I know none of them belong to him, but old habits die hard.

When I exit the train, it takes me only six minutes to walk to the building I took this detour for. I stand on the street opposite so I can take in the full view of its facade. Ryland Corp. Headquarters is located in a modern-style skyscraper made of dark glass and steel, absent of any true character, appearing like a bruise against the surrounding classical buildings made of limestone and marble that Chicago is known for. A chill travels down my neck, and I can't tell if the goosebumps traveling along my arms are from the morning wind rolling off the lake or the sterile frigidity this building emits.

It's strange to think that five years ago today, somewhere along the route I took to get here, my father seemingly vanished into thin air, never making it to his next destination.

A ping on my phone brings me back to reality. It's a text message from Esther. Before opening it, I'm distracted by what time it is.

"Shit," I say out loud. I'm going to be late to work…again. I'll be wasting a good amount of money on cabs today; relying on the CTA will be a dicey game to play if I want to keep my job.

When I finally reach my apartment building, I'm in such a hurry, I'm practically running up the stairs. So much for washing my hair today; guess I'll be looking as shitty as I feel. I get to my front door and start rummaging through my bag for my keys. After failing to find them in the twenty different pockets, I take a breath, blowing out my irritation. Today, I have very little patience, and I don't surprise myself when I crack.

"Who the fuck even has use for twenty different pockets on a backpack?" I yell out to no one in particular, considering the empty hallway.

Just as I hear the keys jingle in the bottom of my bag, the door swings open. My aunt stands in the doorway with a spatula in hand and a look of judgement on her face.

"Morning, Bill." I greet her with a half-smile.

"Well, hello there, sailor. What's all the cursing about this early in the day?" she says while walking back to the stovetop to continue cooking whatever is filling up my entire apartment with a mouthwatering aroma.

Unlike my dad, Billie is often offended by my colorful language. But he isn't here anymore, and even though it's been five years, I still have to actively remind myself that she's the new parental figure in my life.

I begrudgingly hold up my backpack to display the cause of my irritation.

"Twenty pockets, Bill, and I can never find anything in this damn bag."

"Oh no, that is soooo tragic, Cosette. Whatever shall you do?" She responds to me in a sing-song voice that she knows will irritate me. Pleased with herself, she gives me a crooked smirk while flipping over a piece of bacon in the pan.

My aunt's sarcasm is something I have come to cherish. It makes life feel less serious while also putting me in my place when it's due. I will always appreciate her healthy reality checks.

We don't live together anymore, but she does stay over at my apartment from time to time when she has a shift that ends late to avoid traveling home in the dark. She's usually gone long before this time of day, but I should have known she would linger today to see if I was okay upon my return from my annual trip to Melrose. Considering she's the only close family I have left—my mother passed away when I was thirteen and my father is missing—I've extended full access to my space by giving her a key.

She technically should be retired, but after my uncle passed away two years ago, leaving her with a whole lot of debt, my aunt started doing some temp jobs to make ends meet. She lives about an hour away from the city, so her crashing at my place sometimes is completely understandable.

"Sorry I won't be able to hang around and have breakfast with you," I say to her, hoping she doesn't make me feel bad about rushing out of here.

"That's alright. I figured you'd be working today. I suppose it's good to keep your mind busy."

She's trying to be understanding, but I can hear the disappointment in her tone. She points over to my pathetic excuse of a coffee maker. "I tried putting a pot on for you, but that thing is making some unsettling noises, and I won't have you blaming me when it finally kicks the bucket. Although, I'm sure you've already had more than enough caffeine this morning."

She's not facing me, but I know all too well she has a look of judgment on her face. I laugh and tell her there could never be enough caffeine to get me through a day like today, and I will in fact be stopping for more before I head into work. I really do need to get a new coffee maker—or at least take the time to figure out what's wrong with the one on my counter.

"If you say so. I don't know how you drink the stuff. Gives me the shakes." She shimmies her shoulders to give me a visual effect and I click my tongue.

"Don't be dramatic." Even though I know she's not being dramatic at all.

The last time I saw my aunt drink coffee was during all the press interviews about my father's disappearance. She had to practically sit on her hands due to how visible the shakes were. If you didn't know better, you would have thought she was using a much stronger substance than caffeine. Not that anyone would have blamed her, considering the circumstances. The poor woman was averaging less than two hours of sleep a night and managing a seventeen-year-old she inherited.

My uncle at the time was absent to the world, locked away in his office, lost in crazy theories about what happened to my dad. If my aunt didn't bring up all his meals and set them at the door, he probably would have withered away. Eventually, he did, but that was a few years later.

My aunt turns with a plate full of bacon, eggs, and a slice of toast perfectly cut into two triangles.

"Here! You better eat something before you go. You look like you've lost ten pounds since the last time I was here."

Shoving the plate into my hands, my aunt stares at me like she's not going to blink until she witnesses me take a bite. I grab the bacon and practically inhale it. Setting the plate down on the counter, I look at my aunt with a smile.

I'm not one for scales, but I have noticed my clothes feeling a little roomier lately. The weeks leading up to my father's anniversary are always daunting, and when I'm stressed, I don't have an appetite.

My mind gets caught on the idea of today being an anniversary. The word sounds too jubilant to be used to describe one of the worst things to happen to me. When I think of an anniversary, I think of moments in life that bring us so much joy that we must create a holiday and celebrate them year after year. Today's date brings me nothing close to joy, yet it is an anniversary all the same. Even though it's been five years and I'm no longer bombarded by phone calls from sleazy reporters trying to concoct some pity story about me, I still feel like the world is watching me mourn. And that's exactly what I've been doing the past few weeks.

"Don't be dramatic, Bill. You saw me four days ago. I'm pretty sure I haven't lost ten pounds since then."

My aunt switches on the parental role. Pointing her spatula at me, she scolds me like I'm seventeen all over again.

"Ah, ah, ah! Don't act like you don't know what I'm talking about, Cosette. Your clothes are hanging on you, and I can't remember the last time I saw you eat a proper meal."

I consciously pour all my effort into keeping my eyes from rolling into the back of my head and say as calmly as possible, "I eat, I promise."

We both pause, and she soaks in my lie.

"I appreciate you worrying about me, but it's just been a stressful few weeks with my training and today being…well, you know what today is. Anyway, I gotta run. Jeremy really hates when I'm late."

I turn and start flitting around my living room like a hummingbird, quickly grabbing the necessities needed for the day. *Where the hell is my phone?* I begrudgingly grab my backpack, the ire of my day, and start shoveling my hand through each of the twenty pockets I cursed earlier this morning. After more minutes pass than I have time for and no luck finding my phone, I drop the bag on the floor, my fist clenching.

"Gahhh, absolutely useless fucking pockets."

"Language!" Billie's eyes bore into me.

"I'm sorry, but I can't find my phone."

I drop my shoulders in defeat and walk over, grabbing another piece of bacon to keep her satisfied. I have no idea who all the bacon is for; she's always cooking in quantities that could feed a small army. Now that I'm actually taking the time to chew this piece, I can taste how amazing it is. My brain releases a little bit of dopamine as the greasy, crunchy, salty ensemble dances around my mouth.

"Well, maybe if you weren't rushing around the house like a chicken with its head cut off, you would've noticed it's right here on the counter." She lifts her hand with the spatula again and points it toward said phone.

Usually, I would be irritated with such a cliché remark from her, but as I chew and swallow, I realize I haven't eaten since yesterday's lunch. If you can call a protein bar and two cups of coffee lunch. My brain is so satisfied by the bacon that its euphoric state doesn't allow me to reply with a snide remark. I pick up my phone from the counter, give my aunt a kiss on the cheek, and hurry out of the apartment.

CHAPTER THREE

Thankfully it didn't take long for me to hail a cab, but the driver refuses to put the AC on, supplementing with the front windows down. It's a happy accident that I was forced to pull my hair back today. I sit directly behind the driver's seat and turn my head at a ninety-degree angle to look out the window. I love watching the city speed by through this view, watching all the buildings melt into a uniform image.

I live in a neighborhood that's a mixture of different levels of income. Although I know it won't stay that way forever, I like the idea of seeing wealthy people walk a block from their home and get slapped in the face with the reality of what poverty actually looks like. Some of the new residents are paying upwards of a million dollars to live a few blocks from what used to be the projects. It breaks my heart to know long-term residents of the community will eventually be forced to leave a place they call home due to the cost of living skyrocketing within the coming years . And even though I wouldn't consider myself a long-term resident, I will probably be one of the many who will leave the area if rent keeps increasing.

The air is stale and lacking any wind flow, the morning coolness fading upon a full sunrise. It's one of the hotter days of the summer, and the city trash and homeless urine smell extra ripe. I don't mind a hot day; in the Midwest, the summers are short, and the winters are long. So, I have come to appreciate even the most miserable of summer days.

I'm suddenly feeling thankful that I decided on a cab today. The train would have caused me to sweat right through this cheap polyester dress I threw on. The car ride allows my brain to decompress from the rushed morning, and I already feel my anxiety levels returning to normal. Now that I can see the sign to Pour Man's Coffee, I have a bit more faith that this day won't be a complete disaster.

I always get a kick out of the juxtaposition of the coffee shop's name. It was obviously a play on words, but the place calls its employees baristas. Baristas performing slow pours and serving French press is the opposite of what I imagine a poor man drinking in the morning.

My phone pings with a text. Looking down, I see it's from Esther. Shit. I've been meaning to call her back for the past few days, but my mind has been elsewhere. Esther is my oldest friend. We met when I was in second grade and have pretty much been inseparable since. She's the closest thing I'll ever have to a sister and probably the only person capable of forcing me out of my black hole of anxiety and back into society.

When my mom died, my dad ended up picking up extra hours at work to pay off my mom's hospital bills and make ends meet. Esther made my life not so lonely when he wasn't around. Their desire was always to have a big family, but the universe had other plans, and the cancer made sure siblings for me were not in our future. As sad as I felt for them, I was glad it didn't work out. I couldn't imagine my dad having to raise more than one kid on his own.

I order my usual Americano and an English breakfast tea for the boss man and run out the door. The Lonely Olive is only three blocks from the café, and I spend the entire five-minute walk thinking of excuses to tell Jeremy why I'm late. I walk in and immediately see him sitting behind the bar going through inventory sheets.

"You're late…again."

I look at him and try to plaster on an apologetic look.

"I know, I know. I'm so sorry, Jeremy. This morning was crazy, and I had to walk five blocks just to hail a cab."

He raises a brow at me. He absolutely does not believe me.

He sighs and says, "I'm calling your bullshit, Cosette. And do you want to know why I'm calling your bullshit?"

I entertain him. "Why?"

"Because you never take a car unless you are trying to make up time for being late. So, my guess is you slept through your alarm, called a car, stopped at the café because you can't function without caffeine, and then grabbed me a tea because you thought it would make up for you being late for the fourth time this week."

He says all this with a straight face, only raising his eyebrow at the end of the lecture. "Did I hit the nail on the head?"

Not exactly, but I won't be telling him the real reason is because I waited hours at a diner for my missing father to show up.

"Yeah…you're pretty close. Does me getting you a tea help my case?" I ask hopefully.

Shaking his head, he lets out an overly dramatic sigh.

"You're lucky I like you, Cosette, because I sure as hell don't like English Breakfast enough to deal with your punctuality issue."

I slowly walk over to him and hand him his tea. Pulling up a chair to sit across from him, I ask, "What am I learning today, Boss?"

I've come to learn that Jeremy enjoys being called boss, and you better believe I milk that word dry when he's pissed off at me.

"For starters, how to be on time. But today, I'm going to show you how I build out the employee schedule."

"Well, that sounds boring." The words leave my mouth before I know better to bite my tongue.

Jeremy's only response is another deep sigh and a shake of the head.

After Jeremy and I build out the schedule for the next three weeks, I work on opening up the bar to get ready for the afternoon rush of drunkards. The Lonely Olive is a pretty fun place to hang out at in the evening, but any time before five o'clock, we only get the weirdos with drinking problems that never tip well. It's my least favorite shift, but I've been working them after each of my training sessions so I can spend more time with Jeremy while he shows me the ropes on how to manage this place. Today, I'm not too bothered by working the afternoon shift. I'm not exactly feeling social, and working the evening shift always makes me feel like I have to put on a show.

While I polish glasses, I think about my aunt. I always wonder how the anniversary affects her. She never shows any type of emotion when it comes to my father or my uncle not being in our lives anymore. Sometimes I feel like there's only so much grief a person can allow themselves to feel before their mind goes into self-preservation mode. Some of us may have a larger threshold, continuing to feel the weight of it for years and years, while others purge it and get on with their lives much quicker. My threshold must be vast because I feel like I've been grieving most of my life, and no matter what I do, the hole my parents once filled somehow feels as if it's growing as time goes by.

If someone told me five years ago that I would miss my dad as much as I do now, I would have thought they were crazy. Don't get me wrong, I loved my father, but he was almost never around. Working seven tens to rake in the overtime pay left him literally just enough time to eat and sleep before waking up and starting all over again. It wasn't until a year and a half before he went missing that he was physically present.

He'd finally mustered up the courage to start looking for a job that had more sustainable hours. He heard about an opening for head of maintenance at Ryland Corp. and did everything he could to land the position. It was equivalent pay to what he was making and only required him to work a maximum of forty-five hours a week. When he got the job, we thought it was the best thing that happened to us. Little did we know that it would be the last place he would be seen before he disappeared.

After my shift passes by, I head to the register to tip out and go home. Before I can make it there, Jeremy cuts me off with a look on his face that says he's about to ask a favor he knows I won't say yes to.

"Want to know how you can make up for being late?"

"No, but I'm sure you're going to tell me."

"Chrissy called out for the evening shift, and I need you to cover it."

"Are you asking me or telling me?" I quip with a dead face because I already know it's a telling-me situation. When you're trying to get a promotion, there's no such thing as saying no to requests from your boss. And if I have any hopes of Jeremy making the temporary manager position a permanent one, I am stuck being a yes-woman for the foreseeable future.

"You know I wouldn't ask if I had anyone else to cover, but it's a Friday night and I will never be able to handle the bar by myself."

"Fine, but I'm inviting Esther to come hang out, and she's getting free drinks all night."

"Deal, but just her, Cosette. I swear to God if she shows up with the other two girls from last time, I will personally escort them out."

The "last time" he is referring to is three weeks ago when Esther met two already drunk girls and then allowed them to throw more drinks on the bar tab. Long story short, one of the girls ended up puking on the bar and the other broke two glasses. Jeremy knows that we had just met them that night and have no intentions of ever hanging out with them again, but he still loves to hold it over my head.

"Oh my God, Jeremy, when are you going to let that go? You know we don't talk to those girls. Esther just likes to make new friends after a few vodka sodas," I say as the corners of my mouth turn up.

"Yeah…well, no new friends tonight. And tell Esther she'll be cut off from vodka sodas if she dances on the bar again."

Now that was not something I could promise. Esther is probably the closest thing to my opposite as you can get. She loves to have a good time, and when you get a few drinks in her, she becomes the life of the party. Me, on the other hand, I have no problem sitting in the corner and observing all the shenanigans that my friend gets up to, quietly sipping my martini.

As if the devil heard us talking, Esther comes strolling through the front door, and damn does she look pissed. Probably because I still haven't texted her back. I'll be given a "get out of jail free" card only because of what today is, but I won't be spared the lecture on how worried she's been about me. Even though Esther's face looks like she could rip someone's head off, she still looks effortlessly beautiful. We are similar in stature, but Esther has a lither frame, and she moves like a ballerina through the bar. Her long blonde hair looks a little windblown but if anything, it only adds to her fae-like grace. She is the one person I have ever met that is equal in beauty on the inside as she exhibits on the outside. I know I'm about to get a lecture, but I can't help but smirk as my angry friend approaches me.

"What the fuck, Cosette? I have been trying to get a hold of you for days." Her voice drops an octave on the last word for added dramatics. "Before you say anything, I already know what today is and I already know why you haven't gotten back to me. Which is why I am taking you out tonight, and I will not accept no for an answer. You need to get your mind off all the negative shit and let loose. I am officially dragging your ass out of the introvert cave you have been hibernating in the past few weeks." She flips her long hair over her shoulder.

"As much as I would love to go out with you tonight, I have to work," I say, feigning disappointment. I don't know why I even try to pretend to be bummed out about it when I know Esther sees right through my façade.

"What do you mean you have to work tonight? Didn't you work the day shift?"

"I did, but there was a call out, so I am covering to help Jeremy out. BUT!" I manage to get the last word out before she cuts me off to lecture me on why I need to start telling Jeremy to go fuck himself. "Jeremy said you can hang, and all your drinks are on the house." I wiggle my eyebrows at her because I know she will never say no to free drinks.

She walks around one of the low-top tables and plops down on the stool across from me at the bar counter. Pulling out her phone, she begins typing something and glances up at me with a devious look.

"Fine, but I'm inviting some friends."

"What friends? I already told Jeremy we wouldn't have a repeat of the last time you gave friends free rein to the bar tab."

"Oh my God, is he ever going to get over that? And these friends are of the male variety. You need a distraction, if you know what I mean."

"Jesus, Esther. I'm not going to have a one-night stand to get over my dad's anniversary."

"You say that now, but wait until you see this guy that Mark is friends with. He's like a chiseled piece of marble. I swear he must be part god, and if it's any reflection of what he's got going on down—"

"All right!" I cut her off before she gets herself any more excited about what this guy has going on in his pants. "That's about all I need to hear about this friend. Whatever, invite them, but I'm not making any promises of entertaining this guy. I'm working, remember?"

Esther smiles and waves at me with rolling fingers, the way you would wave at a toddler, and practically dances out of the bar. I love Esther, and I honestly don't know what I would do without her, but this is one of those times that I wish she would be the let's-get-ice-cream-and-watch-a-cheesy-RomCom-on-the-couch kind of friend.

Now not only do I need to put on a face for the evening shift, but I also need to mentally prepare to be around Esther-level energy.

CHAPTER FOUR

It's eleven at night, and I have officially served Esther her last vodka soda. One more, and she will definitely be dancing on top of the bar, making me think of all the different ways to apologize to Jeremy before I close up for the night. She is currently hanging all over her "boyfriend of the month," Mark, while he is most likely whispering sweet nothings in her ear to get her to go home with him tonight. I can't deny I'm a little jealous she is going to be getting some tonight. I can't even remember the last time I had sex, let alone good sex.

Mark's friend lives up to Esther's description and might actually be half god, but he might also be the most uninteresting human being I have held a conversation with. If you can even call it a conversation. I don't think we've spoken more than ten sentences to each other all night. Thank God the music is loud in here, so I don't have to suffer through awkward silences with him. Even though we are clearly not hitting it off, it doesn't stop the predatory glare he's fixed me with like I am something to devour later. I wish I could be like Esther and take a guy home purely based on his looks. I have never been able to be intimate with someone that didn't entertain me intellectually or, at the very least, make me laugh in a genuine way. I've definitely laughed at Mr. Marble, but those laughs have been forced and very fake. I honestly can't believe he hasn't caught on yet. Maybe he has and just wants to get in my pants. I'm going to guess the latter.

After dishing out another ten drinks, I see Esther making her way over to the bar. She has a sultry look on her face that I can only assume was brought on by Mark. *Looks like you'll be getting lucky tonight after all, Marky Mark.* Mark is a nice guy. A little too into himself at times, but he seems to treat Esther well; at least from what I've seen. I give it another week before she realizes he's just like the million other men she's dated. Nice enough, but there's nothing about him that stands out enough to keep Esther's attention. He'll take her on a few shopping escapades down Michigan Ave. and then she'll be on to the next. Esther's family was always a bit more well-off than mine, but she wasn't wealthy by any means. Still, she tends to blend right in with the social elite and attracts wealthy men like moths to a flame

Esther finally makes it up to the bar to tell me she's going to head home with Mark.

"Don't forget to use protection," I say with a wink.

"You are so immature, Cosette," she replies with a grin worthy of the cheshire cat.

"Text me when you get home, so I know you made it safe," I say as she's walking out.

She gives me a wave, and then she's gone. I turn to look down the bar to see if any of my patrons are ready for another round, and I am met with Mr. Marble staring directly at me like I'm a meal.

"When do you get off tonight?" he yells over at me.

"I'm closing it down, so not for another two hours," I scream back at him. I'll most likely be done way before that, but he doesn't need any more incentive to hang around and wait for me. I honestly want him to leave; his ego and unwavering belief that he's going to get lucky tonight are really starting to annoy me. There are a million other girls in this bar; I have no idea why he is stuck on the idea of going home with the bartender.

"Cool, I'll hang out, and then I can make sure you get home okay."

To many, this statement might seem endearing: Aww, what a sweet guy to want to make sure I'm seen home safely. But I know what it really means—this guy could care less if I made it home or not. What he cares about is that I make it home with him in my bed. Well, not going to happen tonight, buddy.

"Oh, you don't have to do that. Two hours is a long time, and I can't have anyone in here once I lock the doors to clean up anyway."

He isn't ready to throw in the towel just yet and says, "That's okay, O'Malley's is open an hour later than you are, I can wait over there for you."

"You really don't have to do that. I'm going to call a cab anyway, so it's not like I need a companion for the train," I say with an awkward laugh, because now it's getting awkward. This guy really won't take a hint.

"What, you trying to get rid of me?" he says as a last-ditch effort to guilt me into agreeing to his take-me-home plan.

Before I can respond, I hear a loud metal scraping as a man pulls the stool out directly in front of me. He's looking at Mr. Marble while he orders a 42 neat. I have to use a step stool to grab the bottle off the top shelf and pour three fingers into a rocks glass for him. I slide it over and ask if he wants to open a tab. Without responding, he looks down at the glass and slides a one-hundred-dollar bill over to me. He still hasn't looked at me, which is making me feel super awkward. Does he know Mark's friend? He's looking at him like he wants to smash his face in. I grab the cash and quickly hand him back his change. I don't know every single soul that comes to The Lonely Olive, but I have definitely never seen this guy in here before. He looks out of place in a black suit and a watch on his wrist that probably cost more than my aunt's house. Also, what person under the age of fifty pays with cash anymore?

Finally, he looks up at me and asks, "Is this guy bothering you?"

I must be standing there looking like a deer in headlights

because I am so taken aback by how gorgeous this man is. He has piercing green eyes, jet-black hair, and a jawline sharp as a knife. What in the actual fuck? It doesn't make sense for someone to be that good looking. I instantly feel uncomfortable that this man's eyes are fixated on me in all my stained-apron-bartender glory. The Lonely Olive is not the kind of bar that worries about hiring hot girls and dressing them in booty shorts and fitted tank tops. This is the type of person you don't want to be caught standing next to in a photo because it will most likely shed a light on all the not-so-perfect features you have.

"Cosette, are you okay?" Mr. Marble says. He is now standing next to the dark-haired man with his elbow propped on the bar in front of him. Definitely an attempt at an intimidating power move.

"Uh, yeah. I'm sorry." I look at the man I just served our most expensive tequila to. "I didn't catch what you said."

"I asked if this man was bothering you." He's looking me straight in the eyes, and those emeralds feel like they are staring through my soul.

"What's your problem, bro? Of course I'm not bothering her, I'm with her."

Whoa. First of all, did he just call this masterpiece of a man *bro*? And second, did he just say he was with me? Hell. No.

"What? No, I am not with him. And really, he's fine; he is a friend of a friend," I say with a playful tone.

I'm super irritated by this show of peacocking right now, but the last thing I want is a bar fight while I'm on the clock. Finally, Mr. Marble seems to take the hint that he is not going to end up lucky tonight and throws his hands up in a show of surrender and walks away. I can't deny that I am relieved to be rid of him. Now I can finish my shift without feeling like I have someone undressing me with their eyes all night. I grab the disgusting bar towel and start wiping off the counter to give myself something to do that allows me to exit the very awkward situation I've found myself in with this stranger in a suit.

"You're welcome," he yells over to me.

He can't be talking to me. "You're welcome?" What in the hell am I welcome to? I look over and, sure enough, he is talking to me. His cocky demeanor has suddenly caused him to lose some of the appeal he came in with.

"And what, may I ask, do I have to thank you for?" I say, placing a hand on my hip as I stare down the bar at him. I shift my weight to one leg and raise an eyebrow, tapping the fingers of my opposite hand on the bar counter as I wait for his response.

If it wasn't for the slight upward curve in the corner of his mouth, I would think this guy was being dead serious, but now I can see he is flirting. Not sure why, with the way I look right now. There must be some kind of allure to hitting on a bartender, because never in my life before serving did I get hit on by so many men and women. Maybe it's the unattainable aspect. I'm on the other side, unreachable, and most likely going home alone.

He grabs his drink and moves three stools down so that he's sitting directly in front of me again.

"You're welcome for getting rid of that guy who looks like he eats steroids for breakfast."

I genuinely laugh. He *was* a little too muscular for my taste. Looked like at any moment, he might rip out of his T-shirt like the Incredible Hulk.

"Oh, I wasn't aware that I needed a knight in shining armor to rescue me."

"You did. That guy wasn't going to be giving up anytime soon, trust me. And as for shining armor, sorry to disappoint, but I hope the suit makes up for it." He winks.

He actually winked at me. Who does this guy think he is?

"Well then, I guess I will thank you for saving me from another hour of boring conversation. And speaking of the suit, what's with the get-up? You look like you came from a funeral."

"Maybe I did."

Shit. That was inconsiderate of me.

"Oh, shit. I'm so sorry."

To my relief, he starts laughing immediately. "I'm joking. I had a presentation for work today, which then led to celebratory drinks, so I didn't have a chance to change. Next time I come in, I'll make sure to wear some jeans for you."

Next time? He is definitely flirting with me. I'm now suddenly feeling exactly how long it has been since I've been with someone. I need to get ahold of myself. I can't and won't take this man home. He is a stranger and most likely a serial killer with how perfect he presents. When it's too good to be true, it usually is.

"You don't come here often. I'm usually working the evening shifts, and I don't think I've ever seen you before."

"First time here, actually. I just moved back to the city last week. But I think I may become a regular."

That explains why I don't recognize him. If he's going to become a regular, I better put the charm on. The man is drinking top shelf after all, and I could use a fat tip to end the night.

"Well in that case, your next round is on the house. Call it a housewarming gift."

I pour him another tequila and turn to walk away.

"What's your name?" I hear him ask.

I turn to see him standing, glass empty. Damn, he didn't waste time with drink number two.

"Cosette."

"Cosette…" The way he says my name makes me want to pull him into the back alley. *Jesus, Cosette, get ahold of yourself.*

"I'm Dylan. It's been nice chatting with you, Cosette."

He turns and walks out of the bar, leaving me standing there yet again like a deer in headlights. I snap out of the trance he left me in and look down at the counter to see a hundred-dollar bill sitting under his empty glass. A smile spreads across my face, and I can't remember the last time I felt this giddy. I grab the money off the bar counter and begin my closing duties.

After locking up the bar, I crawl into the back of a taxi to head home. I check my phone to see a text from Esther asking how things went with Mark's friend. I reply and tell her he's not my type, and I can perfectly imagine the sound of her scoff when she reads it.

It's well past midnight, and the anniversary of my father's disappearance is officially over. Yet, the melancholy that lingers in my soul will be ever-present. When I get to my apartment, I notice the corner of an envelope sticking out from under my door. My shoulders instantly drop in defeat. I'm too tired to ponder what bill I'm past due on. I open the door, pick it up off the floor, and go to sit on the couch. The outside of the envelope is blank, and when I flip it over, I notice it's also not sealed. Fuck, the only time I've received a letter like this was when I had an eviction notice for being two weeks late on rent. Opening it up, I slowly remove a piece of folded lined legal paper. Handwritten is a note addressed to me.

Cosette,

5 years is a long time to go without having answers. Without asking questions. Why was 7/16 the only day in the entire year that the cameras were down? You will never find answers to questions you never ask.

When you're tired of being complacent, speak to Remy.

Who the fuck left this here, and who the hell is Remy? I look down at my phone to call my aunt but it's almost two in the morning . I quickly dial Esther, and it goes to voicemail.

"Hey, I know you're probably sleeping or doing, umm, other things, but I need you to call me as soon as you get this."

I hang up and start to pace in my living room. I read the letter five more times before I place it on the counter. July 16th was the last day anyone saw my father. When my dad went missing, I was only seventeen. I never had the opportunity to look into anything or ask questions because that was what the police were for. My aunt and uncle did most of the legwork of staying up to date on the case, but they never seemed to have any leads. I instantly feel shameful for the fact that I know nothing about my father's case, nor have I ever inquired about it. If I'm being completely honest with myself, when my aunt told me they had officially marked him as a missing person, I shut down. All that mattered was that I had no parents left.

My aunt and uncle did their best to shelter me from the journalist, and the only time I had to participate was when the CEO of Ryland Corp. made a public plea for information. He praised my father and pointed at me for sympathy, but it felt performative. How well could a billionaire CEO really know his head of maintenance? My aunt agreed but said any exposure might bring answers.

At first, I asked her every day if the police had news, then weekly, then monthly. Until finally, I got sick of seeing the hope fade from Billie's eyes every time she had to tell me, "No news yet, love." I started to accept the idea that my father was never coming back.

I know most people would tell me to stay hopeful, that missing people can turn up after ten, fifteen, even twenty years of being gone. But I've already grieved the loss of my father. I know he's gone; I don't need a body to start that process. I just wish I knew why this happened.

When my mother died of cancer, I learned there isn't always an answer to why something terrible happens. No rhyme or reason that the universe decides to take away someone you love. Asking why when there isn't an answer only leads to feeling anger instead of sadness, and I spent my fair share of being angry when my mom died.

A year after my mom passed, I was suspended for breaking a cheerleader's nose after she said my clothes weren't "girly enough" because I didn't have a mom.

When my dad picked me up that day, he said something on the way home that stuck with me.

"You're allowed to be angry, Cosette. You can be angry as long as you want. But if you think that you can replace the sadness you have in your heart with anger, you're wrong."

He took a deep breath and ran a hand down his face. Staring at him, I could tell he was struggling to find the right words to convey his message to me. With his eyes on the road and his mouth turned down, he continued.

"Anger is just the beginning. You've got to let yourself feel the rest if you ever want to find peace. Eventually you'll find yourself thankful that you had any time with her at all. The only way to find that peace is through feeling it all, the sadness included."

I could see the contemplation on his face before he said, "Don't you think that your mother's memory deserves more than just rage, sweetheart?"

He was right. I was so angry that I started to lose sight of all the amazing times I had with my mother. That night, I finally allowed myself to feel something other than rage. I broke open, and every emotion I had been shoving down came flooding out. I must have sobbed for hours that night, and my dad held me through every minute of it.

It wasn't the first time I broke apart, and every time, he was there to see me through the ugliest of my feelings. My father may not have been physically present for most of my life, but he was there when it mattered most. Sure, there were times I resented him for working so much, but deep down, I knew he was doing it for us, to make sure I lived the most comfortable life he could provide.

When he went missing, I remembered what he once told me about anger—and skipped it entirely. I sank straight into sadness, and I don't think I've surfaced since.

You can't fully grieve someone you never got to say goodbye to. Most people take funerals for granted. I know I did. I would give anything to lay my father's body to rest—just to know it's truly over. But with him, there's always that sliver of hope, the cruel *what if* that never fully dies.

When my mom passed, it was final. My dad and I held her hands as she took her last breath. I said goodbye.

The last thing I said to my dad was, "I'll see you at Melrose for breakfast." He never showed, and I sat alone in the booth drinking way too many cups of coffee waiting for a man that would never show.

Looking at the note sitting on my counter, I'm beginning to think maybe being angry would have forced me to ask more questions about his disappearance. For starters, why the police had zero leads. A person must leave some kind of trail behind, right?

The first thing I'll do tomorrow is speak to my aunt. I need to understand what this letter means, who this Remy person is, and why, after five years, someone felt inclined to shine light on a cold case.

CHAPTER FIVE

I wake up to the light shining through my apartment blinds. As my eyes adjust, I notice little particles of dust dancing in the rays cutting through. Even though I know it's a sign that I need to do a better job of cleaning my place, I can't help but get transfixed by the snow globe-like movements as they settle onto my carpet.

I sit up, wipe a hand over my eyes, glance over to the opposite side of my bed, and reach for my cell phone. I notice I have two text messages and three missed calls from Esther. I almost forgot I left her a voicemail last night that was a little vague after reading the disturbing letter a few too many times.

I'm no longer in the mood to explain things to her, but I need to call her back or she's going to show up banging on my door or worse: call my aunt.

I reluctantly get out of bed and head to the kitchen to put on a pot of coffee. There is no way I'm going to get through this phone call with Esther without caffeine in my system. I need to mentally prepare myself for a million and one questions, knowing I will most likely have answers to none of them.

My sad little pot spits out a pathetic amount of coffee before making a noise that makes me fear it's on the verge of blowing up on my counter. I rush over to quickly tap the red power switch to the off position and expel a defeated breath.

"So, it's going to be one of those days, huh?" I mumble out to my empty kitchen, as if the universe cares what kind of day I'll be having.

After I've consumed the measly amount of coffee the universe deemed worthy of me having today, I pick up my phone and call my best friend. She must have been staring at her phone waiting for my call because she answers on the first ring. Before I can say hello, she immediately starts spiraling into the million and one questions I tried my best to prepare for.

"What is going on? Why did you call me at two in the morning? Did you go home with Mark's friend? Are you okay?"

"Jesus, Esther, take a breath! No, I did not go home with him, and yes, I am okay. You're supposed to let someone answer your first question before asking the next."

She heeds my advice, and I can hear her take a deep breath over the phone.

"Sorry, you're right. You just had me really freaked out. You never call me that late unless it's an emergency."

"I know. I didn't mean to worry you. I just had something really weird happen to me when I got home last night, and I didn't look at the time before I called you. It's really not a big deal; I'm going to try to get lunch with my aunt to figure it out."

Before I can change the subject, she continues scolding.

"Clearly it was a big enough deal that you called me at two in the morning. Don't try to brush this off, Cosette. Spill the fucking tea!"

I should have known better than to think she would let me off without telling her why I called. Running my fingers over the letter on my counter, I realize there is no way to tell her about it that would make it sound like a normal scenario. "I... I kind of got a letter."

"Cosette, what the hell are you talking about? A letter from who?"

"Well, that's why I called you. I have no idea who wrote it. I found it slipped under my door last night when I got home, and it's not signed by anyone. It's about my…" I pause, suddenly feeling sick as all the anxiety I thought I had purged last night hits me like a tidal wave.

"Cosette? Are you still there?"

"Yeah. Sorry, I'm still here. The letter—it's about my dad."

I say the words like I'm vomiting them. The reality of how creepy and strange this letter is finally sinks in, and I need to get off the phone with Esther so I can call the one and only person who might actually be able to shed some light on this.

"Oh my God. What did it say? Why would someone write you a letter about your dad?"

"One question at a time, Esther."

I wait to see if she has any more she would like to spew out before I read the letter to her. She stays silent, so I quickly go over the contents and wait for her response.

"That's fucked, Cosette. It's been five years. Who would want to dig this back up? Do you think it could be one of those journalists who were always trying to get you to do an interview with them?"

A journalist. That didn't cross my mind last night, but it's not too much of a stretch to assume they could be the anonymous author of this letter. I stay silent as I mull over Esther's very rational explanation.

"Oh my God. I didn't think about it being a journalist. See, it isn't a big deal after all."

I say the words, but I'm not believing them. This doesn't feel like a journalist. For starters, they usually leave a card or a phone number to get in contact with them. This felt a little too intimate to be a random journalist wanting to get an interview with me. I don't have time to go down this rabbit hole with Esther; if I'm going to find out who could have written this letter, I need to talk to Billie.

I end my call with Esther on a promise to get brunch with her tomorrow. As soon as I hang up, I text my aunt.

> **Me:** *Hey! Are you free for lunch?*
> *I need to talk to you about*
> *something Dad related.*

> **Aunt Billie:** *Hi, Cosette.*
> *Can you do 1 p.m. at Hollywood?*

> **Me:** *That works perfect.*
> *See you soon!*

Why do old people always text like they are writing an email? I look at the time, realizing I have just over an hour to meet her, and if I'm going to go out in public, I need to wash my hair. Lucky for me, my aunt must be working in Wicker Park today, and Hollywood Grill is just a few blocks away from my apartment.

I arrive at the diner ten minutes early, grab a booth, and order another coffee and a Diet Pepsi for Billie. Sometimes I surprise myself with how much caffeine my body can consume without going into cardiac arrest. It's my only addiction, so I give myself a pass for the bad habit.

Not long after the waitress sets down the drinks, my aunt strolls in wearing her Pepto-Bismol pink scrubs. I giggle to myself, thinking how I could probably spot her a mile away in a crowd full of people in that get-up.

She slides into the booth and takes a sip of pop and then clears her throat. "What about your dad did you want to talk about?"

She isn't wasting any time today. "Nice to see you too, Bill. My day has been slow. How about yours?"

She lifts an unimpressed brow at me in response.

"Fine. I got a strange letter shoved under my door last night about Dad and wanted to know if you could make sense of it."

I slide the letter across the table and tuck my hands back at my sides. Staring at the letter for what feels like forever, my aunt grabs it off the table and opens it up. She must be reading it over and over because she is staring at it way longer than it takes to read five sentences. Finally, she folds it up, placing it back into the envelope. Sliding it over to me, she says something I wasn't expecting.

"Throw it away and don't spend another minute thinking about it."

"What?" I almost yell.

"Shhhh. Don't get hysterical."

Lowering my voice, I say, "I'm not getting hysterical, but you can't possibly expect me to not be curious about what this means. Who is Remy? And what are they talking about with the cameras?"

She takes another sip of her Pepsi and places her hands on the table. She says her next sentence on an exhale. "Remy is the PI your uncle was working with on the case. He had some theories about the camera system at the Ryland Corp. building, but nothing came of them. Your uncle went down a rabbit hole because of the theories this investigator was feeding him and spent way more money on his services than he should have."

She looks up to keep the tears from spilling from her eyes. My aunt is not a woman who shows too many emotions, especially not in public, but every now and again, speaking about my uncle will get her welled up.

"I'm sorry, Bill. I didn't mean to make you upset. I just want to know why I got this letter after five years of Dad being gone. Who would write this…and what do they get out of it?"

"I know, and you have the right to ask questions. He was your father, after all."

It doesn't elude me that she refers to him in the past tense, like she has accepted the permanence of him being gone from our lives.

I'm not sure where to take the conversation from here, but before I can say anything, she adds, "I don't think the police did everything they could have when it came to finding out what happened to your dad, and I don't blame your uncle for wanting to seek outside help to get answers. Your dad was his best friend, his only friend. But then it turned into an unhealthy obsession, and I always worried about that obsession consuming you too."

She's now grabbed a napkin from the metal dispenser and is

dabbing her eyes.

"A year after your dad went missing, the communication between us and the police became almost nonexistent. I guess they felt like they didn't need to call us if they didn't have any news. But it drove your uncle crazy not having updates on the case. As soon as your questioning stopped, his kicked into full gear. I was equally worried for both of you. I wasn't sure if you not asking for updates anymore meant you were coming to accept what happened or if you were slipping into a dark place like your uncle. When your uncle passed away, I told myself that I would let go of the case, so you and I could move on and live some semblance of a normal life."

It breaks my heart hearing her tell her side of the story. I always assumed my aunt was more emotionally equipped compared to my uncle and me; that she was stronger than us. To find out all along it was because she had to be strong for us makes me feel guilty that she never had her opportunity to break down, that my uncle and I never got the opportunity to be strong for her.

"I'm so sorry, Billie. I had no idea how hard it was for you."

"No need to be sorry, hon. You were a child. You still are in my eyes, but you deserve to ask questions, and you deserve some answers." Her tone was gentler than her initial reaction to the letter.

She shakes her head like she's going to regret the next thing she's going to say. "I still have all the research your uncle and the PI did on the case. If you want, you can come over and take a look through it. I'll be honest: I never went through any of it myself, and I don't know if you'll find what you're looking for…but you are more than welcome to it."

Words couldn't begin to explain the gratitude I have toward my aunt. She's willing to let me dig through my uncle's stuff, rehashing some of the most awful memories for her, just so I can get my closure. The woman is the epitome of selflessness. In an instant, I decide that I won't force her to be involved in this. She's done her fair share of carrying the burden of my father's disappearance. It's my turn to try to find answers for us.

"Thanks, Bill. I really appreciate that."

Without skipping a beat, she picks up the menu the waitress placed on the table fifteen minutes ago and says, "You can come over tomorrow while I'm at work. You still have a key to the house?"

"Of course, I still have the key to your house." Again, she raises an eyebrow but is smiling this time.

"Can't be too sure. You'd lose your head if it wasn't attached, Cosette."

I click my tongue in protest even though I know she's right. The waitress must have sensed that the tension at the table died down because she suddenly popped up to take our order.

For the remainder of our lunch date, Billie does her best to change the subject by asking me about work and if I had anyone special in my life yet. I told her no exciting news on either but couldn't help thinking of the green-eyed man I met the night prior. With all the drama of the letter, I almost forgot how I felt coming home from the bar that night. He managed to force a smile from me and made me feel like a teenage girl. I felt content that I would most likely never see him again and that his purpose was served by ending a terrible day on a positive note.

Walking home from the diner, I feel my phone vibrate in my purse. Pulling it out, I see I have a message from Jeremy. *Please don't ask me to come in. Please don't ask me to come in.*

Jeremy: *Need to take my wife to the airport. Can you cover me for 2 hours tonight?*

Me: *You're just now realizing you have to take your wife to the airport?*

Jeremy: *Don't be a smart ass. Her ride fell through.*

Please… it'll only be for a few hours.

I promise you'll be out no
later than 10.

> **Me:** *Fine, but after I wrap up, I'm*
> *drinking top shelf tonight on*
> *your tab.*

> **Jeremy:** *Deal. You're a lightweight*
> *anyway. How much can you really*
> *cost me? Lol*

He's not wrong. I can barely make it past three drinks without feeling hungover the next day. I pull up Esther's name in my contact and shoot her a message.

> **Me:** *Olive's tonight at 9:30?*

> **Esther:** *Tell me you did not*
> *pick up another shift…*

> **Me:** *I'm covering for 2 hours.*
> *Technically not a shift.*

> *Just come… top shelf on*
> *Jeremy tonight.*

> **Esther:** *Why didn't you start*
> *with that?! See you tonight! ;)*

Smiling, I shove my phone in my pocket and head back to my apartment. The past few days have been a whirlwind, but I need to find joy in whatever place I can get it. Esther will always be that place for me. I slept like shit last night, and a nap sounds like the perfect remedy before embarking on a Saturday evening with Esther.

CHAPTER SIX

What I intended to be a quick nap turned into a multi-hour event. I wonder at what age it will become unacceptable to sleep away an entire afternoon. Spending about half a second on that thought, I pivot to something more important. Since I'm not working a real shift tonight and Jeremy doesn't uphold a specific dress code at the bar, I'm going to put some effort into my hair and what I'm going to wear. On my budget, my wardrobe isn't anything to brag about, but I've always been pretty savvy at a vintage shop. Last week, I found a vintage little D&G number; a black silky slip dress that I've been dying to wear that does wonders for my not-so-large breasts. I throw on a pair of my favorite boots. Typically, I would wear a pair of heels with a dress like this, but I'm not trying to break my neck behind the bar tonight.

As I walk off the train, I feel a strange sensation of vigor. I know that my nap probably made up for some of the lost sleep I had accumulated over the past few weeks, but there's something else that puts some extra pep in my step. It's this newfound feeling of determination to finally get answers about my father. I'm not naïve;

I know that whatever I find will most likely not lead to finding him, nor will it present me with any semblance of a happy ending. But if life has taught me anything, it's to be a realist, and the realist in me is feeling satisfied with finally finding some closure. Closure doesn't have to mean solving the mystery of my dad's sudden disappearance; it can simply be allowing myself to do my own digging. I'll be okay if I don't find any answers, but at least I can continue life knowing that I went in search of them. That I tried.

Maybe my lack of anger caused a lack of curiosity when it came to my dad. He told me years ago that grief comes in stages; maybe it wasn't wise to skip some of those stages. I was so worried about getting lost in anger like I did with my mother that I forgot to allow myself to feel that emotion at all. I've realized I've gone all these years believing that I had grieved my father. Grieved, as in past tense. But I'm far from being complete; I'm still currently grieving. And just like with my mother, I'm not going to find peace until I feel it all.

The question now is, am I angry? Yes, and in this moment, I can feel it simmering below my skin, waiting for the right moment to boil over. The scary thing about anger is it's an emotion that usually doesn't adhere to rational thought. It can be consuming, and most of the time it will be directed at the wrong person or situation. I should know; I spent a long time being angry at just about anything after my mother died. So, who am I angry with now? My dad for leaving me? My aunt for keeping me in the dark? The world for dealing me such a shit hand in this life? While I'm stopped at a crosswalk, I glance over and see my reflection, and reality crashes into me like a freight train.

Me. I'm angry with myself. How could I be so complacent all these years? I look down at myself and suddenly don't feel so pretty in my little black dress and curled hair. I suck in a sharp breath as my eyes start to sting with moisture. I dart my eyes up at the sky to keep any tears from gathering. *Don't you dare cry in public, Cosette.* I repeat the thought a few more times until the stinging in my eyes goes away. A shoulder knocks into me, and I notice I've stopped in the middle of the sidewalk. I must look a little crazy to all the passersby. A ping on my phone pulls me out of the darkness of my thoughts.

Esther: *What are you wearing tonight?*

Me: *LBD and my Doc's*

Esther: *Edgy, I like it! Getting ready now, see you soon!*

Thank God Esther is coming out tonight. If anyone could help me sort through these feelings, it would be her.

I walk into Olive's and head to the back to hang up my purse and throw on an apron. Before I can make it around the bar, I meet eyes with Jeremy, who's putting on his jacket and heading to the door.

"Thanks again for covering. My wife would have hated me if I made her take the blue line."

I shrug my shoulders and act like I'm not impressed with his graciousness. "I'm sure she would have forgiven you," I respond in a bored tone, even though I completely understand why he wouldn't want his wife riding the blue at night.

"Well, either way, I appreciate it. Just a heads up, you'll probably be able to pull some good tips tonight. Chrissy seems very distracted with some guy at the bar and will most likely not be serving anyone else until he leaves." He nods his head in the direction of where Chrissy is currently leaning over the bar, allowing her breasts to fall out of her two-sizes-too-small scoop neck tee. She's talking to a dark-haired man wearing a plaid button-down and grey denim. I can only see the back of his head, but if he's causing Chrissy to ignore the bar, he must be easy on the eyes.

Looking back at Jeremy, I snort a quick laugh. "Well, in that case, let's hope he stays the whole time."

"Be back by ten!" Jeremy yells as he walks out the door.

"You better be, or the bar will be at the mercy of a very distracted Chrissy tonight," I yell back. He's already gone by the time I look back and most likely didn't hear me.

As I make my way around the bar, Chrissy looks over at me. "Were you talking to me, Cosette? I thought I heard my name."

Looking down the fully seated bar with many empty-handed patrons, I say, "No, just saying how I'm excited to work with you tonight." It's a lie; I am not excited to work with Chrissy. She is the laziest bartender that we have on staff. Jeremy got so tired of people trying to switch shifts when they were scheduled with her that he made a rule that all shift switches had to be approved by him. I don't mind making extra money when she decides to cherry-pick who to serve, but I do not want to act like her barback every shift while she flirts it up and keeps all the tips.

I hear Chrissy make an obnoxious fake laugh and say something along the lines of, "I'm sure you'll have no problem fitting in." In my rush to start dishing out drinks, I didn't even look to see who Chrissy was obsessing over this time. When I turn, I'm taken aback by who I see smiling back at her. Dylan, the man who left me a very generous tip and sent me home thinking not-so-innocent thoughts.

I'm instantly annoyed with how attractive he still is. Not that I thought he would look different, but sometimes when you see someone again, the first impression allure wears off. Unfortunately, that is not the case with this one. His shoulders are still broad, adorned with a perfectly tailored shirt that cuts down his torso like it was made at an atelier. His dark hair is thick and styled with a product that makes the shine in my hair look like a dull penny, and those green eyes are still enough to make a girl forget the next thing she's about to say.

Unfortunately, those green eyes are currently staring down at Chrissy's cleavage. Good God, this man must have a thing for bartenders. I'm not sure if disappointment is the word I would use to describe my current feelings, but I would be lying to myself if I said I didn't feel a pinch of jealousy seeing his attention directed at her. The man was gorgeous after all, and he tipped very generously.

Swallowing down whatever annoyance the image of the two of them sparked in me, I look over and take the drink orders of three girls wearing pink boas and penis beads. We don't get bachelorette parties often, but when we do, they always entertain me.

I make my way down the bar and back and officially feel like I made it out of the weeds Chrissy created. I check my phone and see that Esther texted me.

Esther: *Running late,*
be there closer to 10.

Pocketing my phone, I look up and see that I'm standing right in front of Dylan, who just so happens to be staring directly at me.

"Not even going to say hello?" he asks with a sarcastic grin.

After watching him ogle Chrissy for God knows how long, I'm not as smitten with him as I was the night before.

"You seemed preoccupied. I didn't want to interrupt," I reply a little sharper than I meant to.

He stares down at his glass and lets out a short chuckle.

"Feel free to interrupt anytime."

"I'm not sure Chrissy would have appreciated that," I quip.

"Chrissy, was that her name?" he says, smirking as he lifts his drink to his mouth.

The nerve of this guy. I can't believe he just openly told me he didn't have the common courtesy to remember her name. I bet he also doesn't remember my name, just another bartender to flirt with.

"You know, us bartenders do have names, and if you cared to remember them, you might get faster service." This guy was getting a rise out of me, and I needed to disengage before I said something I would regret. "Now if you don't mind, there are some guys at the end of the bar who need drinks and just so happen to remember my name."

Before I make it two steps, he yells, "When you have a moment, Cosette, I'll take another tequila."

My cheeks instantly heat. I can only imagine the bright rosy hue they must be turning. I glance over my shoulder to see Dylan, back straight with a smirk that is way too attractive to be legal. I keep on toward the opposite side of the bar. I'm going to stay on this side until Jeremy comes back. Chrissy can grab Mr. Tall Dark and Handsome another tequila.

A few minutes later, Esther walks in. For claiming to have a fashion emergency, she looks like she walked straight off a Vogue cover. Dressed in a fitted red dress, black ankle booties, and a tweed blazer, she squeezes in between two drunk guys who could barely hold a conversation with each other, let alone notice someone was now standing between them.

"You look like you had quite the fashion emergency," I sarcastically tease her.

"Shut up. I went through four outfits before landing on this one. I started my period and everything I tried on made me feel like I was suffocating and ugly."

If my eyes rolled any further back, they would probably get stuck. "Esther, I'm convinced you could walk out of the house in a trash bag and still look phenomenal."

Esther scoffs. "Yeah, well…you're supposed to say that. You're my best friend."

"No, I'm not. I'm supposed to tell you the truth." Shaking my head, I grab a bottle of vodka to pour her a drink. "Jeremy should be back any minute now, and then we can head somewhere else, anywhere other than here."

"Wow, you seem a little irritated tonight. Everything okay?" Esther looks at me with a concerning stare, and I realize I left her hanging today with the letter situation.

"I'm fine, just feeling a little out of sorts after talking to my aunt today. I found out that Remy is the PI my uncle was working with on my dad's case after the police information dried up. I'm going over to her house tomorrow to take a look at some of the information he was able to dig up."

Taking a sip of her drink, she slowly lowers it to the bar without making eye contact with me. "So, you never found out who wrote the letter?"

"No." Who *did* write the letter? The thought left my mind when my aunt brought up that she knew who Remy was. I was so focused on that piece of the puzzle, the anonymous person who left me the letter was the least of my concerns. But now it's top of mind, and I'll have to add it to the long list of questions I have no answers to.

Seeming as unsatisfied with that response as I was, Esther finally looks up from her drink. "Well, I think the letter is creepy, and it seems whoever wrote it knows more about your dad's case than they cared to share. If I were you, I would put finding out who wrote it at the top of the to-do list."

She isn't wrong. Whoever wrote me the letter has to know something they're hoping I'll find out. Why else would they want me to get in touch with Remy after all these years? Looks like tomorrow, I'll not only be sorting through my uncle's files, but also trying to find a way to contact this Remy guy. Hopefully, he'll have an idea of who wrote this letter.

"I agree. Hopefully, I can find Remy's contact information at my aunt's tomorrow and ask him about it."

I pour myself a drink and see Jeremy walk through the door. Thank God he's back because I need to get out of here. I feel Dylan's eyes on me from across the bar, and the last thing I need is for Esther to take notice of a cute guy taking an interest in me.

Jeremy walks around the bar and puts on an apron. "Thanks for covering for me, Cosette. I owe you one."

I lift my glass to him. "I think you owe me more than just one." Winking, I down my drink and take off my apron. After Jeremy tips me out, I have to walk by Dylan to get my purse that I stowed away on the opposite side of the bar. I shove my tips into my bra and make a mental note to not work in a dress without pockets again. I walk past him without making eye contact, but before I can reach for my bag, I hear him say, "You never called."

This man has managed to catch me looking like a deer in headlights for a second time. Surely, he isn't talking to me. After all, I didn't even have the guy's number.

He must have been saying it to someone else, but it becomes apparent that's not the case.

"I'm sorry, what?"

"You never called me," he says again, with a completely straight face.

"Why would I call you?" I say, purely curious now.

"Ouch," he says with a snorted laugh.

"I'm sorry, I didn't mean that in an offensive way. I just meant I don't know you or your number."

Running a hand through his hair, he finishes his drink. "Well, this is embarrassing."

He's smiling at me now, and I'm officially confused. Lifting my brows, I look at him and wait for him to continue his explanation.

"I…uh, wrote my number on the tip I left you last night. Guess it wasn't as slick of a move as I thought."

My mouth is hanging open. Did he just tell me that he left his number on the hundred he left me? That is the most ridiculous thing I have ever had a guy do. Before I can stop myself, I'm laughing in his face. I know it probably isn't the nicest thing to do to someone who openly admitted to being embarrassed, but it's so obnoxious that he would do such a thing. And to be honest, his ego could probably stand to be knocked down a peg or two after that move.

Catching my breath, I notice Esther making her way over to us. Before I can break away, she slides up next to him and, in a voice that could only be described as sounding like a feline purr, she says, "Cosette, don't you know it's rude not to introduce me to your new and very cute friend?"

Oh my God. Now I'm the one feeling embarrassed. Before I can say anything, Dylan is reaching out his hand.

"I'm Dylan, and I don't have any intention of being friends with Cosette. I'm trying to take her out on a date, but she doesn't seem to want to entertain the idea."

"What? No. You never asked me out on a date." I quickly go from being embarrassed to irritated.

Esther's smile is all but touching her ears, and she's wiggling her brows at me . "Cosette, why won't you date this delicious-looking man?" She's turning on the charm, and I'm shocked that Dylan's attention hasn't shifted over to her.

"Let's get something clear. No one asked anyone on a date," I say to them both.

"You're right, I didn't ask you on a date. I did give you my number though, and you have yet to call me," he challenges.

Esther giggles. "Oh, trust me. You'll be waiting forever for that date if you rely on Cosette calling you. She barely calls me, and we've been friends since we were in grade school."

She grabs a napkin and jots something down on it.

"Here." Handing it over to Dylan, she winks and says, "Ball's in your court now."

Noticing the napkin has my phone number written on it, I tut in annoyance and grab my purse. Making my way around the bar, I grab Esther's arm.

Looking at Dylan, I say, "I hate to cut this short, but we have a girls' night planned, and considering I wasn't supposed to even be here tonight, I am more than ready to leave my place of employment."

Waving the napkin in the air, he yells, "It was nice to see you again, Cosette."

I don't look back as I drag Esther out of the Lonely Olive.

"Oh. My. God. Cosette!" Esther is practically skipping down the block. "That man is gorgeous! How could you not call him?"

Shushing her, I continue walking. I reach into my bag for my wallet and search for the hundred-dollar bill he gave me the night prior. Finding it, I unfold it. I'll be damned; there was a phone number written on it.

"This guy is way too into himself and a showoff if you ask me. Who tips someone a hundred on a two-drink tab and then writes their number on it?" Shoving the bill back into my bag, I let out an irritated sigh.

"A guy who is trying to impress you, that's who," Esther says matter-of-factly.

"Whatever. I didn't call him because I had more important things to worry about when I got home last night." My tone comes off snarkier than I meant it to, and I immediately feel bad for directing my stress toward Esther. "I'm sorry. I'm not trying to be a bitch. I'm just a little stressed out about tomorrow and what I may or may not find."

Esther grabs my arm and pulls me to a stop. "You don't have to apologize for anything. This whole letter thing has brought up a lot of emotions. I know you want to find closure in all this, Cosette, but don't let it consume your life. Your dad wouldn't have wanted that for you." She pulls me in for a hug.

Esther gives the best hugs. I raise my arms to wrap around her, and I instantly feel the sense of comfort I've been needing all day. I don't know what I would do without her. I don't plan on involving her in any of this PI stuff, but I'm glad to know that my friend will be there if I need her.

"Also, you should one hundred percent not call this guy now that he has your number. Let him come to you." She gives me a wink.

"Yeah, okay. I'm not making any promises to answer if he does. I need to get my life sorted out before I start welcoming new people into it."

Pulling open the door to the new bar she's been wanting to take me to, she says, "That might take longer than you want it to, Cosette. Some people live their whole lives without getting their shit together. Don't deprive yourself of having fun because life isn't perfect."

I don't plan on it. Fun is exactly what I plan on having tonight, and from the sound of the music that is traveling up the stairwell, I have a feeling we will be having plenty of it.

CHAPTER SEVEN

I wake up feeling like I passed out in the Sahara Desert, my mouth tasting like sandpaper and a headache that only severe dehydration can cause. I look down and see that I'm still in my black dress from last night and can feel I'm still wearing a gross amount of makeup . If I didn't wash my face, I sure as hell didn't brush my teeth. No wonder my mouth tastes like stale beer and bad decisions.

I take note that I didn't make it to my bedroom either. I must have crashed on the couch in my intoxicated state last night. I can't tell if my body needs to vomit or if the nausea could be cured with some French fries and Sprite. Probably best to start off with water. I stand up and make my way to the kitchen but stop short when I hear a toilet flushing. Oh my God…did I bring someone home last night? Closing my eyes and trying to rewind through my memories, I recall getting out of a taxi with Esther. Esther is here…I hope.

I hear the door opening and cautiously open one eye at a time. "Please don't be a stranger, please don't be a stranger."

"What the hell are you doing?" Esther's voice cuts through, instantly turning into nails on a chalkboard as my headache roars to life.

"I thought you might have been a guy I brought home last night."

"You wish," she replies flatly, clearly feeling the effects of our night out. I didn't go to college, but that hadn't stopped Esther from teaching me how to drink like a college student. I don't often drink to the point of blackout, but when I do, it invariably involves too many shots and too many Esthers staring at me at the end of the night .

"Jesus, what the hell did we drink last night? I haven't felt this hungover since your twenty-first birthday."

I slowly make my way to the kitchen to grab a water bottle from the fridge, grabbing an extra for Esther without asking. She looks to be in worse shape than I am. As I hand it to her, she shushes me like I'm a toddler in a library. "I think the question we should be asking ourselves is what did we not drink last night?"

Taking the bottle, she sits on the couch and pulls out her phone. From where I stand, I can see she's calling the cab service we use. "Avoiding a walk of shame this morning?" I tease.

She looks up with a deadpan expression. "It's only a walk of shame if it involves a one-night stand."

Chugging my water, I start to feel more alive. I wipe my mouth and chuckle at her logic. "Is that so? I always thought it was the act of walking home after a night of any type of drunken regret."

"I don't have any regrets from last night," she snaps.

"That tone and the green hue of your face beg to differ," I retort , as a childish grin spreads across my face.

She shoots me a devious glare and throws a bottle cap at me, missing by a foot. Laughing, I walk back to the kitchen to flip on the coffee maker, waiting for the aroma of life to fill my apartment. I'm immensely disappointed when I hear a gurgling hiss and then a popping noise, followed by a fizzle.

"For the love of God Cosette, that thing is a fire hazard. Please tell me you'll get a new one before I have to read about my best friend in the news." She lifts a hand in the air to present a headline, "Died by Coffee Pot."

Picking up the water bottle lid Esther tossed at me moments ago. "You are so dramatic when you are hungover," I tease.

I chuckle while I watch a theatrical Esther gather her things. She's missing a sock, which I wager won't turn up for at least a few weeks. Closing my eyes, I try to recall more of the previous evening—images of Esther and me dancing in a basement club, taking shots with cute guys. As crappy as I feel today, I have to admit, I enjoyed myself last night. I needed a distraction from what I have to do today.

A ping from Esther's phone interrupts my thoughts. She looks up at me with disgust. "My ride's here. I hope I can hold off on vomiting until I get back to my place."

"Maybe tell him you get carsick, so he doesn't drive like an asshole," I suggest .

Shrugging on her blazer and shoving her phone in her purse, she walks over to the door. "That's not a bad idea." She places a hand on it for balance while she shoves her shoes on, one still sockless. "Hey…I know you're going over to your aunt's today to go through your uncle's things, and on any other day I would offer to come with you, but…" She hesitates. "I really think I might be dying of alcohol poisoning. Can I be a support system remotely today?"

She looks like death warmed over, and as much as I want her company, I also want to go through my uncle's things alone today. I don't know what I'll find, and I'll likely need time to process it before discussing it with Esther. As crappy as she feels right now, I'm relieved I won't have to tell her I don't want her there.

"Of course," I say, trying to sound cheerful. "It's probably going to be super boring anyway. I can only imagine how much junk I'm going to have to dig through before I find the files I'm looking for. I might not even find anything today."

Nodding, she opens the door and heads into the hall. I follow to lock up, watching her head for the stairs. She waves goodbye, and as I close the door, I realize there is no way I'm going anywhere until I shower and get a few more hours of sleep.

Looking around, I spot my phone on the floor under the couch.

Picking it up, I notice a missed call and a text from my aunt.

> **Billie:** *Hey Cosette, I'm heading*
> *to work but feel free to come by*
> *whenever you want today. There's*
> *leftover pizza in the fridge, and the*
> *key to the office is in the drawer*
> *under the microwave.*

Pizza? Bless her; it's like she knew I would be hungover today. Leaning against the wall for support, I head to my bedroom, feeling all the little bumps from the textured paint. I really hate textured walls—when did that become a trend anyway? You can't go into any apartment these days without seeing textured paint jobs. It was like whoever remodeled was trying to hide something. What happened to flaws adding character to a place?

The house I had with my dad had flat walls painted a yellowed white that my mom had picked out during one of her painting kicks. Every year or so when I was growing up, my mom would get bored and drive to Home Depot, buy some paint, and start on a different room in the house. My dad would come home to furniture covered in plastic and she'd hand him a paint roller upon entering. At first, he would complain, but when the room was finished, the joy that radiated from her was contagious, and he would instantly forget his irritation over the impromptu painting session. He could never deny her something that brought her happiness.

A year after she passed, I came home from school to find him sitting in the living room with a roll of plastic and a few buckets of paint. I asked if he needed help, but he just shook his head and walked to his bedroom. He never used the paint, and the living room stayed that yellow-white color until the day he went missing. I was glad he didn't paint over it; that room was the last room we painted with her. Even though the color wasn't the most vibrant she had picked over the years, it held a memory we weren't ready to cover up.

I drop my hand from the wall. It's funny how something as simple and meaningless as a textured wall can bring back such a profound memory. These memories have visited me less and less over the years, and one of my biggest fears is that they will cease completely. A tear sneaks down my cheek; wiping it away, I notice the black smudge it leaves on my fingers. Last night's makeup begging to be washed off. Guess I'll be heading to the bathroom to clean my face before climbing back into bed.

After sleeping off my hangover and drinking my body weight in water, I leave for my aunt's house. It takes an hour and twenty minutes and three train transfers to finally arrive, reminding me why I don't visit her often. Thankfully, she works in the city, or I'd hardly see her. I make a mental note to put more effort into visiting more frequently and walk around the back of the house to enter through the back door. The spare key my aunt had given me only works on the back door and doesn't unlock the deadbolt, so I hope she hasn't forgotten to leave that unlocked for me.

Slipping the key in the door, I turn the knob and thank whatever higher power that she remembered. The last time I came over when she wasn't home, she hadn't left it unlocked, and I was stuck standing outside in the cold for almost two hours waiting for her to get home from work.

I walk in and instantly feel a wave of nostalgia. Even though my aunt has only been living in this house for a few years, she still has all the same furniture and décor from the old townhome.

The back door leads into the kitchen, where a round wooden dining table is filled with pastries and sweets, ranging from Hostess cupcakes to circus peanuts. A half-opened case of Diet Pepsi sits on the floor, and I click my tongue. I honestly don't know how my aunt manages to stay a size 4 with her sweet tooth. Unfortunately, I have not inherited those genes; a single Snickers bar seems to instantly add five pounds to my thighs. I cut out soda a few years ago and dropped two pant sizes after the first few months. Needless to say, sugar is not my friend.

I walk over to the microwave and open the drawer to grab the office key. My movements halt as I stare down at a stack of old photos. Lying on top is one of my uncle and dad on a fishing trip in Michigan. I pick up the stack and flick through them. Quickly sorting through pictures of me as a toddler, I land on one of Mom and Dad sitting at the dining table in my aunt and uncle's old townhome. Dad had a cigarette hanging out of his mouth, a Miller Light in hand, and sported the most '90s mustache imaginable. Mom's perm made her resemble a poodle you'd see at the Westminster dog show, yet she still looked beautiful. The photo must have been taken in summer; Mom's sun-kissed complexion made her smile gleam as white as snow. They look so happy here, and I understand why my aunt keeps these photos out of sight in a junk drawer. They likely stir up feelings of sadness and longing for her. I place them back in the drawer, more organized than I found them, and shove my hand to the back, feeling around for the key. Finding it, I shut the drawer of memories and step into the hall, my gaze settling on the office door. I find myself unexpectedly overcome with nervousness and anticipation of what I may or may not find inside, knowing both outcomes could leave me with more questions than I already have.

CHAPTER EIGHT

I unlock the door to a chaotic room that resembles more of a storage unit than an office. My eyes widen as I take in the cramped space filled with boxes, some labeled and some not. They're stacked on top of each other haphazardly, causing me to navigate carefully around them. I do my best to contort my body to avoid knocking into anything that would create a domino effect, trapping me until my aunt returns home. In the far corner, I spot a box dated the year after my father disappeared. Disbelieving my luck, I open it and find case information on my dad. What are the odds I find this in less than five minutes of being in the room? I had prepared myself to sift through junk for hours before finding anything useful.

I pull out a stack of files and begin reading. Some are police records, others are still photos pulled from camera footage at the Ryland Corp office building where my dad was last seen. Apparently, he was called in for an overnight shift due to a corporate party the owner was hosting, and there was an issue with the AC. Statements from attendees claimed they never saw him there, which didn't sound abnormal considering he probably focused on fixing the AC rather than socializing. The head of security mentioned the cameras went down shortly after my dad arrived, attributed to an electrical issue. AC and electrical issues on the same night? Either the building was a mess, or it was an unfortunate coincidence.

Setting the files down, I pick up a folder and a few photos slip out—black and white photos of various men, reminiscent of those in a true crime documentary. Flipping through, I find several of Mr. Ryland, the owner of Ryland Corp. A few include a younger male and a man who seems vaguely familiar, though I can't place him. I continue until I come across one with a face recognized city-wide: the mayor. Why would the PI my uncle was working with be investigating the mayor for my dad's case? The next photo shows the mayor having lunch with Mr. Ryland—perhaps not unusual, considering Ryland was a major donor for the mayor's last election. The final photo shows the mayor standing next to the head of the Chicago police department—the face I couldn't place earlier. I flip back to Mr. Ryland's photo and hold it up next to the others. The head of police appearing with the mayor wasn't surprising, but being photographed out of uniform with Mr. Ryland felt odd. Closing the folder, I dig through the rest of the box to see if I can find any information on this Remy person. At the bottom, buried under folders, I find a sealed manila envelope with a sticky note on top in my aunt's handwriting.

Some guy dropped this off this morning, said to have you give it to Remy.

See you tonight.
Love, B

B was obviously my aunt. Curious about its contents, I open it; if my aunt hadn't wanted me to see it, she wouldn't have given me free rein. Carefully peeling off the sticky note, I tear open the envelope and pour out its contents. A single item falls to the floor—a memory stick. I haven't seen one of these since high school. Wishing I brought my laptop with me, I eye my aunt's archaic desktop computer.

Jumping to my feet, I walk over to the desk covered in dust and boxes. Pressing the power button on the tower, I wait patiently for it to turn on. As I tap my fingers on the mouse, I examine the memory stick—a slim black rectangle with a silver USB jutting out. Flipping it around, I notice a raised logo on one side.

Carefully holding up on the light from the window, I recognize it as the Ryland Corp. logo—the same logo I remember being on Dad's work polo and coffee mug. Whoever left this must have been a Ryland Corp. employee. Esther has mentioned to me in the past how companies brand everything, treating employees like a sports team. I find it strange, leaning more toward cultish indoctrination than team spirit.

The note instructed that the envelope was to be given to Remy, but that leaves the question: why is it still here and not with him? Remy was also still a question floating through my mind. How was I going to get in contact with him? So far, I've had no luck finding a phone number, but a part of me has a feeling that Billie has the information I need. I didn't ask her for his information at the diner because she didn't seem too fond of him, and I didn't want to push my luck with getting her permission to go through my uncle's stuff. Considering I'm already here, knee-deep in dusty old files with a mysterious memory stick, I think it's safe to ask her for his number now. While the computer is still booting up, I pull out my phone and shoot her a text.

> **Me:** *Hey Bill, made it to the house. Call me when you have some free time today. Love you!*

Slipping the phone into the back pocket of my jeans, I kneel on the floor in front of the desk. The fact that there isn't a chair for this desk tells me just how little this computer gets used. It will be a miracle if it turns on. After waiting fifteen minutes, I decide the computer is shot, and I'll have better luck taking the memory stick home with me to use on my laptop. I look back down at the file box and consider how much of an inconvenience it will be to lug it home with me on the train. I should have brought my backpack with me, but I'm still holding a grudge against its excessive pocket situation. I can't find shit in that thing. Frowning, I decide having the files at my place will be worth it. I place the memory stick back in the envelope and set it on top of all the files in the box, then carry it out of the storage unit of a room.

Slipping the key back into the memory drawer, I smile when I remember my aunt said she had leftover pizza, which is perfect, since I'm starving. When I open the fridge, my eyebrows shoot up in surprise to find that it's nearly empty. There's a bowl of clementines, a carton of milk, and a few bags of uncooked vegetables. The pizza box sits on the lowest shelf, and I lift the lid to find there are two pieces left. There is no way she's going to stop for dinner on the way home; she won't risk getting stuck driving home in the dark. The empty fridge feels abnormal for her, but after speaking with her at the diner and seeing the look of emotional exhaustion on her face, I take note that the Aunt Billie I'm used to may be wearing a little thin.

I hear my stomach make a slight gurgling sound, but I refuse to eat the last two pieces of pizza, saving them instead for her when she gets home. I opt for the clementines, grab a few, and shut the door. Setting two of them down on the counter, I begin peeling while I stare at all the photos and magnets on the fridge.

My aunt started collecting magnets years ago from all the trips she and my uncle went on. She has them from all over the world, and I can't help but smirk at the Mona Lisa that's holding up a pizza menu to Aurilio's. My eyes wander over the surface of the fridge, taking a tour of the globe as I move from magnet to magnet.

Popping an orange slice in my mouth, I see that my aunt has some papers under a magnet on the far side of the fridge that's partially covered by the wall. I eat the rest of my cutie and stare at them, wondering why she would have them shoved somewhere she can hardly see them. The whole point of placing things on the fridge is to make sure they're in plain view to remind you of said item. Like coupons you don't want to forget when you go to the grocery store, a wedding invite you don't want to forget to RSVP to, or in my case, a utility bill you don't want to be late paying.

Wiping the remnants of fruit off my hands, I walk over to get a closer look. Slipping my hand between the wall and the fridge, I slide the papers toward me, dragging the magnet holding them up along with it. I must have pulled too fast because the magnet falls off and a few of the items scatter to the floor. The papers are invoices for services from Leroy and Associates. My eyes are glued to the numbers at the top of the bill. The service these Leroy and Associates guys are charging for is not cheap. No wonder my aunt has these shoved somewhere she can't see them every day. I wouldn't want to be reminded of that amount of money owed either.

My uncle left a lot of debt behind when he passed away, and I suddenly feel sick thinking about how hard my aunt works to make ends meet. I know when you're married you share everything, but I don't think it's right to make a sixty-seven-year-old woman pay for debt she didn't even know her husband had. I feel bad for snooping and place the invoices back where I found them, fastening the magnet in place to look like they were never moved. My mouth pulls down in irritation when I see a small card that must have also fallen from the pile stuck between the fridge and the wall.

I kneel again and stretch my arm, but the space is too tight; I can't reach it. I sigh and scan the room for something I can use to pull it out, spotting a container on the counter filled with an assortment of cooking utensils. Grabbing the one with the longest handle, I try again. The silicone spatula works like a charm, and I slowly finagle the card toward me. When I flip it over, my sense of accomplishment is replaced by shock. My mouth drops. I don't fucking believe it. The small card I hold in my hand is the business card of Remy Leroy, private investigator.

A flurry of emotions overwhelm me when I come to the

realization the invoices are from him. Excitement that I found Remy's information, curiosity as to why my aunt has this card on the fridge, and finally, anger that this piece of shit is billing my aunt for services performed years ago for her deceased husband. Who the hell does this guy think he is, shaking down an old widow? Pinching the bridge of my nose, I instantly feel bad for thinking of my aunt as an old widow, but technically, at her age, she's considered a senior and she is, in fact, a widow.

The fleeting guilt fades, and I go right back to being angry. I can't wait to call this asshole and give him a piece of my mind. There is no way in hell I will let my aunt pay those bills, and if he thinks he's going to get a dime out of me, he's got another thing coming. Skeptically, I wonder if he is the one who left the note at my door. It would make sense: leave a note telling the daughter of a missing man to contact a private investigator who can get her answers and also take her to the bank for everything she has.

My phone rings, and I drop the business card again. Thankfully, this time it fell to a place that does not require the assistance of a spatula. I pull the phone out of my pocket and lean against the counter, a picture of my aunt's face lights up the screen. Shit. I don't exactly need to ask her for Remy's information anymore, so I'll have to make up another excuse for why I called her. Taking a breath to collect myself before I pick up, I slip into a calm demeanor.

"Hey Bill!"

"Hey, hon. Is everything okay? I saw your text and called as soon as I had a second away from the chair."

Closing my eyes, I make another attempt to will myself to normalcy. My aunt can always sense when I'm stressed out about something, and I don't want to worry her.

"Oh, yeah, everything is fine. I left my laptop at my apartment and needed to use your computer…but seems like it's seen better days." The short laugh I let out isn't exactly fake. I find it hilarious that she is hanging on to that piece of junk that won't even turn on.

"Oh God, that thing probably hasn't been turned on since your uncle passed away. I use my iPad for everything these days. Sorry, sweetheart. I hope you didn't need it for anything urgent."

Not wanting to tell her that I found the hard drive, I do the next best thing: I lie.

"Oh, it's no big deal. I just wanted to check my work schedule that Jeremy emailed me. Nothing urgent." I cringe as the lie slips through my lips. I've never been good at it; the few times I have tried to lie my way out of a sticky situation, it has never worked out in my favor. My dad used to love telling me to never play poker, like it was some kind of life advice he was bestowing upon me.

My aunt is silent on the line, and I ask if she is still there.

"Yeah, I'm still here, Cosette… Are you sure everything is okay? You sound off."

Damn it, she knows.

"Yeah, I'm good, I promise. Esther and I went out last night, and I'm still a little hungover." That was not a lie, and the truth of it saves me from any further speculation from her. I hear her give a soft chuckle on the other end.

"You girls are something else. Did you find what you were looking for in your uncle's stuff?"

Half-truth time.

"Not a lot of anything new, but I'm going to bring the box back to my place and take my time with it this week."

"Alright, hon, don't get too lost in it. I have to get back to work. Call me if you need anything else."

"Okay, love you, Bill!"

"Love you too, hon."

I shove my phone into my pocket and look down at the file box sitting by the door. Fuck it, I'm calling a car. There is no way I'm lugging that thing back with me on a train.

My car arrives shortly, and I walk out the back door and lock up. As I make my way down to the cab, I notice a man across the street staring at me while he smokes a cigarette. Well, that's not creepy at all. He's wearing a zip-up grey hooded sweatshirt with the hood pulled up, so I can't make out his face. He's dressed fairly normally, but then I notice he's wearing dress slacks and dress shoes, which now makes the hoodie seem a bit incongruous. Maybe he's a new neighbor?

Before I get into the car, I look back at the stranger to politely wave, but he's already turned around. As he walks away, I can't help but notice that those nice dress shoes he's wearing have red bottoms, and it's not lost on me that people in this neighborhood don't spend money on Christian Louboutin. I duck my head and get myself seated in the back of the car, then practically break my neck turning to look out the back window to see what house the misplaced man goes into. He passes by two houses before he opens the door to a black car with a matching black grill. I'm not a car person, but this one, like the dress shoes, also looks to be a bit extravagant for the area.

"Cosette?"

I startle, whipping my head around to look at the cab driver. He's staring at me, waiting for a response, but I'm so engrossed with watching this man in the black car that I look at the person in the driver's seat like a lost toddler.

"What?" I manage to get the single word question out in a stupor.

"You're Cosette, right? Just need to confirm who I'm picking up." The driver eyes me up and down like he's concerned he might have picked up someone deranged.

"Oh, yeah, sorry. Yes, you have the right person."

I reach my hand up to rub my eyes and then turn again toward the hooded man. The car is still there, but I can't see him behind the tint of the windows. The taxi driver pulls out and drives by the parked car. As we pass, I stare at the emblem on the grill that appears to look like a trident. Yeah, I'm really not a car person. I couldn't tell you if that was a Lamborghini or a Porsche, but what I can say is that it does not fit the median income of this suburb. I settle back into the seat and talk myself off the paranoid ledge I'm on. The rational explanation is he's probably someone from the city who is visiting. He definitely doesn't live here, and if he does, he's living outside of his means with those shoes and that ride.

I have a forty-minute ride back to my apartment and I put

on a podcast to distract myself from the information overload I've had today. It doesn't work because I spend most of the ride home studying Remy's business card, strategizing when and how I'm going to approach him and what questions I'll be demanding answers to first.

CHAPTER NINE

Taking a sip of my coffee, I stare down at my hand, which is keeping itself busy this morning by flipping Remy's business card over and over, as if it will help my brain conjure some epiphany of how to approach this ridiculous situation I've found myself in. I had to splurge on Pour Man's today because my cheap Mr. Coffee is still broken and I have yet to take the time to buy a new one. After Esther's *died by coffee pot* comment the other morning, I've officially unplugged it from the wall in fear it might actually burn my place down. I guess you get what you pay for—it served me well the past three years. Silver lining, the new barista at Pour Man's can really make a mean Americano. Sticking the card back in my wallet, I grab my phone and keys off the table and head to the door. I look down at my phone to take note of how much time I have to speed walk to the bar in order to start my shift on time and run into a very large, very toned chest.

"Shit, I'm so sorry!" I really hate being the person who seems oblivious to the outside world because their eyes are too glued to their phone screen. I mean, I'm a millennial and love my screen time just as much as the next, but I'm no screen zombie. Just a few weeks ago, I read about a girl who got hit by a taxi because she stepped onto the crosswalk staring down at her phone and not at the oncoming traffic. Thankfully, she didn't die, but holy shit, what an embarrassingly tragic way to go out if she did.

"Cosette? Hey! Where are you running off to in such a hurry?" a deep, familiar voice says to me. I look up and see an equally familiar, chiseled jawline.

"Dylan… Hey! What are you doing here?" The words come out before I can register how awkward they sound.

One side of his mouth ticks up, and I instantly feel like a thirteen-year-old girl again.

"Well…I suppose I'm doing the same thing you are… Getting coffee."

Right. What an idiotic question to ask.

"Yes, that would be the most logical explanation." I let out an uncomfortable chuckle. "I guess I just didn't expect to see you in this area this time of day. Don't you have some fancy office job to be at?" I recover with my best asset, sarcasm.

"I do, but I have a flexible schedule." He winks. What is with this guy and winking? Who does he think he is, Joey Tribiani?

As I lift a skeptical brow at him, he continues. "I'm actually glad I ran into you here."

"You are?" I ask, my tone holding just as much skepticism as my lifted eyebrow.

"Uhh…yeah. I wanted to ask the other night when I saw you at the bar, but you seemed pretty eager to leave with your friend. If I'm being honest, I was only there in hopes I would see you again."

Oh jeez, here we go.

"Would you like to have dinner with me tonight?" He asks so confidently, I almost answer yes without giving my brain a moment to consider that I have other plans tonight. Plans that include tracking down Remy and solving my father's disappearance.

Okay, maybe the solving my father's disappearance part is a little hasty, but I don't want to put off speaking to Remy any longer than necessary.

"Oh… I uhh." I lift my hand to the back of my neck, rubbing while I search for the words to gracefully shoot this beautiful man down.

It's his turn to raise a brow at me as he slides his hand in his pocket. Smooth as a cucumber, this guy.

"I sort of already have plans tonight." It comes out more like word vomit and not at all graceful.

He smiles and says, "Okay, how about next week? Wednesday night?"

Damn, he is persistent. Although, with that face and those arms, I'm sure he isn't used to being told no too often.

"Wednesday night." I say it out loud as I dig into my brain for another reason why I can't go out to dinner with this man. I don't have any plans Wednesday night, which is rare, considering how many extra shifts I've been picking up at the bar. Well, shit. I guess I'm going to accept this invitation to dinner.

"I actually don't have any plans, so I suppose that would work. What time were you thinking?"

He smiles and looks me up and down like he's planning on having me for dinner. Slow down, buddy, before I change my mind.

"Does eight o'clock work?"

Looking down at my phone, I realize I'm officially late for my shift. God, Jeremy is going to fire me.

"Sure, eight works perfect."

"Great, I can pick you up around seven-thirty." He reaches for his phone, and I almost agree before all my senses kick in.

Oh, I don't think so. I never let guys know where I live on first dates. Never know which ones are going to turn out to be stage-five clingers. And this guy already knows where I work and where I get coffee. There aren't many places outside of those two that one might find me.

"Oh, that's okay. I can just meet you at the restaurant. Text me where and I'll see you there." I toss my hair over my shoulder as I rush out the door. Hopefully, he still has my number Esther gave him, or he'll have to make another trip to the bar today.

After practically sprinting the few blocks between the café and bar, I try my best to slither in unnoticed by Jeremy. I'm late again, and I'm really in no mood to hear the same lecture he likes to toss at me. If it wasn't for practically knocking myself on my ass by running into Dylan, I would have been on time. Maybe.

I couldn't tell you why I'm always tardy, but I am. Never in a dramatic sense. I've met people who are notoriously thirty to forty-five minutes late for everything. Me, I'm the five to ten minutes late kind of gal. Never late enough to piss someone off, but consistently late enough to be an annoyance. I don't know where I get it from. My dad was obsessively punctual, and my mom… Well, I don't remember much about my mother's punctuality, but if she was married to my father, I can imagine the woman knew when to leave the house.

I duck below the bar to stash my purse and grab the apron I left here during my last shift. I could use a clean one from the back, but maybe if I skip walking back there, Jeremy will assume I've been here for the past ten minutes.

"What's the excuse today, Cosette?" Jeremy towers over me while I'm hunched below the bar tying the back of the apron.

"I don't know what you're talking about." I stand up straight with a bottle of simple syrup in my hand and give him a toothy smile.

"You know exactly what I'm talking about, and you're lucky you're the best bartender we have here, or you would have been fired months ago." He looks at me with a curious gleam in his eye. "Did you really think you could trick me into thinking you have been here the whole time?"

"No, but I was hopeful that maybe just this once you would be too busy to notice me sneak in." I tease. I let my shoulders lower a little once I see Jeremy is in a good mood today. He's actually a really nice guy when he's not running the bar on a skeleton crew.

"Take your bag to the back. The last thing you need is some drunk reaching over the bar and taking your credit cards on a trip down Michigan Avenue." He says this in a parental tone that reminds me of my dad. If anyone tried to steal my credit cards, they wouldn't get far. Two of them are maxed out, and my checking account barely has enough to buy an outfit off the sale rack at Macy's.

However, I am glad Jeremy brought it up. There's something potentially way more priceless in my purse today than credit cards. I brought the memory stick I found at my aunt's house yesterday with me. I accessed the files on my laptop last night, but all it contained was camera footage of my father's old office building. Three different files showed the same door being recorded with hours of footage. I didn't get through all of it, but from what I did manage to keep my eyes open for, it left me with more questions than I had at the start of the day.

I plan on going straight to the address listed on Remy's card after my shift today in hopes he can shed some light on why the sticky note had instructions to give it to him. The last thing I did before I went to sleep last night was google the office he's located in to make sure he is still operating out of it. To my relief, he is, and operating hours were listed until seven. I have an intuitive feeling that something on that memory stick is important; I just don't know enough to spot what it is.

I finish up my shift at the Lonely Olive and head toward the train station to catch the blue line down to River North. Two delays and forty minutes later, I arrive at a building with large orange numbers on the front. Six-Two-Zero. The color looks hideous against the exterior brick of the building, and I can't help but question the thought process behind that decision. On a positive note, a cab driver would have no issues locating this address on a drop-off.

I walk in the front door and locate the directory on the wall next to the elevators. Remy's name is at the halfway mark, located on the fourth floor. When I step off the elevator, the floor looks empty. There are no chairs in the waiting area, and all the lights are off apart from one door to my left. I'm suddenly feeling nauseated and consider turning around and coming back another day. What if this guy is a scam like my aunt said? What if he's a crazy conspiracy theorist and tries looping me into a never-ending story like he did with my uncle?

Running my hand through my hair, I look up at the ceiling and take a slow breath. In and out. In and out. I can't come off as desperate for information, or he'll know that he can take advantage of me. But I can't seem apathetic, or he may see me as a waste of time. Gathering my nerves, I knock on the door once, twice, three times, and step back. I hear papers shuffling and drawers slamming before footsteps shuffle toward me. Pulling the door open so fast that a breeze pulls a few strands of my hair forward, a man who appears to be in his fifties stands in the doorway. He's fair-skinned with gray-blue eyes that pin me with an urgent glare. My eyes shift up to his hair, the epitome of salt and pepper, and then back down to meet his cold eyes once again. Silence seems to stretch for longer than necessary, and I finally break our staring contest.

"Hi, I… I'm looking for Mr. Remy LeRoy. Am I in the right place?"

The man's eyes give me a once-over. Tilting his head and pinching his chin between his index finger and thumb, he studies me. Without saying a word, he turns around and walks back into his office. The door swings open wider, and I get a better view of the interior. In the far-right corner, there's a wooden desk that looks a little worse for wear. The adjacent wall hosts an assortment of books shoved into a shelf that appears to be running out of space. To my left, there are metal filing cabinets stacked on top of each other at least five feet high. Once I finish scanning the room, my gaze returns to the man who now sits in a worn-out black leather Eames chair. I take one step forward so that I'm no longer standing in the doorway but now existing in the room with the man. If I didn't know any better, I would think this guy is a mute. He hasn't said one word since opening the door. I once again break the awkwardness.

"Are you Remy?"

Silence.

"I'm Cos—"

"I know who you are, Cosette Emery. What I don't know is why you're here." He cuts me off with a tone drenched in irritation before I can introduce myself and run through my spiel I prepared on the train ride here.

"Well, that's creepy." *Shit, did I just say that out loud?*

He barely breaks, but I see a slight twitch on the right side of his mouth that tells me he found that comment entertaining. So, I continue.

"You're Remy?" It comes out more like a statement than a question. "I received a letter telling me to talk to you, and I found your business card at my aunt's house."

He releases a deep sigh and brings his hand up to rub his face. His shoulders are slouched in a look of defeat.

"I can't help you, Cosette. You need to leave." He stands and moves toward his desk. Pulling open a drawer, he takes out a bottle of what appears to be dark liquor and a crystal glass and pours himself two fingers.

"What do you mean you can't help me?" I demand. "I haven't even told you what I need help with."

I reach into my purse and pull out the note and shove it in his direction.

"Do you know why someone would write this and leave it at my front door?"

He leans forward and grabs the paper from my hand. Keeping his eyes locked on mine, he slowly unfolds the note. Finally, he breaks eye contact and looks down, skimming over the contents of the letter. He carefully lays it flat on the desk, setting a hand on each side of it. He eases himself back into his chair and looks up at me.

"I don't know who wrote this, and I surely don't know *why* they would write it."

This is already not going well if he can't even tell me why someone would tell me to seek him out. My hands start sweating, and I'm suddenly feeling panicked that I'll have to resort to being completely oblivious of any and all details of my father's disappearance.

No! I refuse.

"Listen, *Remy*." It's my turn to start over-enunciating. "I know you worked with my uncle on my father's case, and I know that you have information that I am not privy to. If you can't tell me who wrote that letter, fine. But you *can* tell me everything you know about my father's disappearance." I straighten and force as much confidence in my delivery as possible. It's time for me to put my foot down. I deserve answers.

A gray eyebrow shoots up like he's shocked at my demand. "You're right, I can tell you everything I know. But I won't. I closed the door on this case years ago, and honestly, I should have done it sooner. Maybe your uncle would still be around."

Wait…my uncle? What is that supposed to mean?

I rub my sweaty hands down my pants. I can't leave here without getting something out of this guy. Fuck not coming off desperate. I am desperate, and he needs to know it.

"Please…" Oh God, have I really resorted to begging? "Please, Mr. Leroy. I need to know what happened to my father. Don't you think a daughter deserves to have some closure?"

I take a step forward, putting me only half a foot away from his desk. He's forced to tilt his head to look up at me, and I know he can see the pain in my eyes.

He grabs his drink and throws back what remains in the glass. Setting it gently back down, he looks up at me. The expression on his face can only be described as one of mourning. My God, the sorrow this man is emitting is palpable, and I have to fight my traitorous eyes from shedding tears in front of him.

"You do deserve closure," he says matter-of-factly. "Jesus, you deserve to still have your father around… But what you deserve more than the closure, Cosette, is to live a long and happy life. And to do so safely. It's what your father…and your uncle would have wanted for you." He stands and walks around his desk so that he's standing next to me. "How I can help you is by not going down this rabbit hole again. Investigating your father's case only led us in circles and put your uncle and myself in danger." He leaves my side to walk over to the doorway and gestures with his hand for me to leave.

I don't understand. Why is it dangerous for me to know information about the case? I didn't think it would be possible, but I now have more questions than I did before coming here.

My anger creeps to surface, and I whip around to fully face him. This guy has no idea what my father would want for me. What my father would want is for me to find him, to find answers.

"Fine, if you're not going to help me, I'll do my own digging. I have all the files from my uncle's house, so if you won't give me answers, I'll find them myself." I turn to storm out before I remember the memory stick. My last resort to entice this man into telling me what he knows.

Looking at him with a face of stone, I pull the memory stick out of my purse. "Here." I shove my hand out toward him. "I found this in my uncle's things. It had a note that it was to be given to you."

He looks down at me with disinterest. Shit, he's not going to take the bait.

"What is it?" he asks me with boredom.

"I actually have no idea. It's a bunch of security footage of a door at the building my dad worked at." I shrug and gesture the memory stick toward him so that he'll take it from me.

His eyes go wide, and his mouth drops open. Holy shit, he's actually interested in this thing. He takes the stick from me, staring at it like it's an artifact from the Stone Age.

"How did you get this?" he demands, not waiting for me to answer before he pivots back to his desk and opens a laptop. I watch him plug it in and scroll to pull up the footage. His eyes are like lasers on the screen, and he starts to shake his head.

"I can't fucking believe this," he whispers to himself.

Beyond intrigued by his reaction, I walk over to the chair in the corner and take a seat. I'm rooting my ass here until he tells me what the fuck is going on and why he is in such disbelief over security footage.

"What is it?" I ask calmly so as not to push my luck. The demanding tone didn't exactly win him over.

His head whips over to me as if he has forgotten I was still here. "Where did you find this?" he demands.

"I told you. I found it mixed in with my uncle's things." I feel like I'm in an interrogation room now.

"Does anyone know you have this? Did anyone follow you here?" He's standing and looking out the window now.

"What? No, I haven't told anyone about it. I didn't even know what it was." And now I feel like I'm standing trial, defending my actions for something I know nothing about. "Wait, why would someone be following me?"

He moves to the office door, shutting and locking it in one smooth motion. Can't say that makes me feel comfortable. My warning bells are going off, and suddenly my fight-or-flight response is kicking in. He's standing in front of the door, so I guess that takes flight off the table. Oh my God, I'm suddenly aware that I didn't tell anyone I was coming here. If this guy tries to kidnap me or lock me away, no one will know where to look. Holy fuck, I'm going to end up just like my father.

Glancing at me like he suddenly realizes my body language has shifted, he throws his hands up.

"You're safe with me, Cosette. I'm not the one you have to worry about."

What the hell is this guy talking about?

"Yeah, well, locking the door doesn't exactly make me feel safe," I say with confidence that shocks me.

He takes a step back, giving me some breathing room. Which is a smart move because I have my hand set to reach for my pepper spray if this guy makes a move. I watch him pace back and forth in front of me, tapping the memory stick against his thigh and then stopping in front of the window. He looks out again as if he's going to see someone appear out of thin air. He runs a hand through his salt and pepper hair before he finally turns to me.

"Cosette, I'm going to tell you some things, and I need you to pay very close attention."

"Oh, now you're ready to share?" My tone is dripping with

sarcasm. "By all means, Mr. Leroy, let story time begin."

"I'm serious, Cosette. This is not a joke. If the wrong people found out that you and I are in possession of this…" he cuts himself off and shakes his head. "We're as good as dead."

CHAPTER TEN

My head is spinning. Did this man just say dead? Hell no, this is not what I signed up for. I look beyond him to the locked door, feeling claustrophobic. I need to get out of here. Remy notices where my eyes have drifted to and again throws his hands up.

"I promise I will unlock that door and escort you home myself. I am not the bad guy here."

I don't think he's the bad guy, but I'm also not sure he's a good guy either. Before I pulled out that memory stick, he wanted nothing to do with me, all but kicking me out the door.

"But before I let you leave, I need you to understand the possible danger you are in and why I stopped looking into your father's disappearance."

The promise of answers makes the claustrophobic feeling subside. I look at him speechless, waiting for him to do the talking before I ask him any more questions.

"What do you know about the case?" he asks, and I immediately feel self-conscious because I know very little. I stay silent.

"Cosette, what do you know? I want to make sure I'm not

wasting time telling you information you already have."

I have no choice but to admit to my ignorance. "I know very few details." I pause to swipe a hand down my face. It feels hot, and I'm worried my cheeks are red with embarrassment. "I know about as much information as anyone who was watching the news that year."

He nods his head as if he is remembering all the details from the media. "Ok, anything that wasn't said on the news? Any information that your aunt or uncle shared with you?"

"No, my aunt stopped telling me things when I stopped asking, which was about a year after his disappearance. And as for my uncle, he practically became a recluse once he started working with you on things."

Remy looks away from me, but before he does, I catch a glimpse of the sadness returning to his eyes.

With a sigh, he tells me, "Your uncle was a good man."

I already know this. I don't hold any of his behavior after the disappearance against him. He was hurting and decided to turn that pain into something productive. Something I should have done but was too much of an emotional coward to consider.

I sit and listen as Remy goes through a quick review of the information I already know: that my father was on record of arriving at work, the camera system being down, and the lack of information the police were able to uncover. It's not lost on me that anytime the police are brought up, his tone becomes skeptical and irritated.

"Your uncle came to me when the police communication slowed down… He found it strange that they had no leads or persons of interest even though there were a ton of people present in the office the night your dad never resurfaced."

He walks to the desk and pours himself another glass of whatever alcohol he keeps hidden in the drawer. "Your uncle wasn't convinced that the Ryland family was as innocent as they were claiming to be. There were a lot of unanswered questions and vagueness around their whereabouts that night. Both of Ryland's sons worked for him but couldn't recall if they were in the building the night of your dad's shift.

"Our source said otherwise, but with no security footage and not being able to get our hands on the personnel logs, we had no way to prove it. Let's be realistic; an entire security system going down on the night one of your employees goes missing is a little too convenient. Your uncle didn't buy it, and neither did I."

I stare at him and then dart my eyes to the bottle of alcohol on his desk. As if he can read my mind, he slowly pulls open the drawer and reaches in to grab a second crystal glass out. He pours another two fingers and holds it out for me to take. I oblige, throw the entirety of the glass back, and set it down for a quick second. We repeat this two more times until my chest is warm and my nerves seem to ease.

"Where are his sons now?" I ask.

"As far as I know, the oldest one still works for him and has been practically running things since Mr. Ryland was checked into assisted living. The other one was sent off that same year to study at some fancy college overseas." He pauses, and I can see he's considering something. "He could be back by now, though. I haven't really been keeping tabs on them like I once did. But, needless to say, the whole family is shady."

Remy's face slowly morphs from contemplation to something more somber as he swirls his rocks glass. He looks up at me with a sliver of pain behind those aging eyes.

"I'm going to be straight with you, kid." Remy has moved away from the formalities of using my name and seems a little more relaxed with me. "I'm a realist. I'm not a man who will feign hopefulness to make you feel better about the situation. Hope is a dangerous and fickle emotion, and there's no room for it in my line of work. I stick to factual information and follow the trail it leads me down."

He takes a deep breath and looks back at his laptop screen that's paused on the image of the security footage.

I can respect a realist. Hell, I consider myself one. And as for hope, well, let's just say any sliver of it that lived in me died the day my mother's cancer came back, and we found out she had less than a year to live. I'm relieved to hear that hope is not the path Remy plans to take me on.

I continue to use his earlier move of silence and allow him to continue talking.

"With that being said…I know it's probably not the easiest thing to hear, but I believe your father is dead."

I break eye contact with him and stifle a gasp. Deep down I know it's the most rational explanation. If he was alive, he would have found a way back home. He would never leave me. I tamp down on my emotions before they spiral out of control and look back to Remy.

"Remy, please don't take offense to what I'm about to say. You are telling me things that I already know, that the whole world already knows. I need you to stop treating me like a child and start getting to the being in mortal danger part."

He nods his head in agreement. "Right, well, the only defense the Ryland family had that kept any further investigation into them and their company was the fact that there was no evidence that proved your father didn't leave his shift as normal and went missing on his own accord or had something happen to him after his shift."

He clicks out of something on his laptop and pulls out the memory stick, holding it up and giving it a little shake with his wrist. "This right here is the evidence no one seemed to be able to get their hands on, the evidence that, according to Ryland Corp., shouldn't exist if the camera system was truly down that night. It also answers my suspicions about your uncle's death."

It all finally dawns on me. The security footage on the memory stick is from the night and early morning my dad went missing. If there is footage, that means they lied to the police about the systems being down. Why lie if you're innocent?

"Wait… What does this memory stick have to do with my uncle?"

Remy stares at me with a worried look on his face. He spins the chair around and peeks out the blinds of his office window like one of those paranoid conspiracy theorists. Now I understand why my aunt was so skeptical about this guy.

"Are you going to enlighten me or are you going to keep staring out the window waiting for the boogeyman to appear?" I toss the remark at him, drenched in my bitchiest, sarcastic tone. I'm becoming impatient and tired of waiting for answers.

"You know your uncle didn't die from natural causes, right? Please tell me your aunt, at the very least, told you that much." His tone tells me he's becoming agitated with my ignorance-is-bliss lifestyle.

She didn't. From what I know, my uncle died of a heart attack, and my aunt blamed it on his obsession with the case.

"Please don't insult my intelligence, Mr. Leroy, and do not insult my aunt's integrity." He's pissing me off, and the last thing I need is his judgment of what my aunt did or did not decide to divulge to me about my uncle.

"I'm not insulting your intelligence, Cosette. I've already told you; I'm simply trying to gauge how much information you are privy to so I can save time by not telling you things you already know."

Okay, he's got me there.

"Your uncle and I were working with a lead that worked security at the Ryland building when your father was employed there. He was the first person to bring to our attention that the security cameras were working perfectly fine the night your father disappeared." He pauses, and I see something like regret in the look he's giving me now. This man is a rollercoaster of emotions determined to give me whiplash by the end of the night.

He continues to explain how they brought in one of the detectives from Chicago PD that wasn't working on the case, and my mind wanders back to the files I found at my aunt's house. My mind flashes to the photos of Mr. Ryland having lunch with the mayor, and then a different photo of him walking with the detective I saw so many times on the news discussing updates on the case. My thought is interrupted when I hear Remy say my name.

"Cosette…are you still listening?" He looks at me with a confused look like he's never seen someone drift off in thought before.

I look over to him and blurt out the first thing that comes to my mind.

"Mr. Ryland supported the mayor's campaign…and donated money to the police department."

Remy looks at me with a blank expression, then slowly nods. "I'm glad you're beginning to connect the dots."

There's melancholy in his voice, and I have a feeling he's about to tell me something that's going to break my heart. As if it could be any more shattered.

"We didn't know how many pockets the Ryland family was in… We thought by pulling in a detective that wasn't connected to the case, we would be safe."

He stands and walks over to the filing cabinets, pulling out a small silver key from his pocket. Unlocking one of the drawers, he reaches in and pulls out a cream-colored file that has my uncle's first initial and last name on the tab. Walking over to me, he holds the file out, gesturing for me to take it.

"What is that?" I ask with a shake in my voice, losing my grip on my confident demeanor.

He continues to hold the file up and raises a brow at me. "It's answers, Cosette. You either want them or you don't."

I do want answers; that is the sole reason why I came here tonight. I just didn't expect to get answers to questions I hadn't yet thought to ask. I grab the file and take a seat in the chair that has become my place of comfort in this god-awful room and slowly open the file. Remy tells me to turn to page seven, and I oblige him. Looking down, I try to wrap my head around what is in front of me.

After reading and re-reading the toxicology report, I look up at Remy, waiting for an explanation.

He looks at me and says, "Well, do you want to ask me anything?"

I want to ask him a million things, but I home in on the most important question first. "Why does this say that my uncle had a plethora of drugs in his system? My uncle didn't do drugs."

Remy is nodding now and grabs the file from me, turning to

quickly lock it back up in the file cabinet.

"No, he didn't." He sits back down at his desk and pours himself another drink. I have no idea how this man isn't falling over at the rate he's consuming, but that's beside the point. I wait for him to continue before I ask my follow-up question that's currently burning a hole in my brain.

"The day your uncle died was the day he was supposed to meet up with our source. The source had agreed to give us proof that the camera system was functioning properly that night in exchange for witness protection that would move him out of the state."

Remy is watching me to make sure I'm absorbing the information before he continues.

"Your uncle was found dead in his car with enough drugs in his system to kill a cow… And our source was found dead in his apartment with a gunshot wound to the head, ruled a suicide."

I can't believe what I'm hearing. How has none of this made the news? Why was my uncle's death not further investigated?

"This is crazy. Why didn't my aunt report this?" My mind is racing, and none of this makes sense.

"She didn't report it because I told her not to. Looking into your father's case was more dangerous than I anticipated, and I couldn't live with myself if something happened to her too."

He pinches the bridge of his nose. I can't imagine how much weight this man carries on his shoulders. Two people dead and a missing person case that he was never able to solve. As angry as I am that he gave up, I also empathize with him. He was between a rock and a hard place; I can't say I would have done any different.

"I told her to box up all the evidence your uncle had and move on. It wasn't worth putting you and her in danger. If I had known she had this memory stick the whole time…" He trails off, and it's painful to see the regret painted on his face.

"I'm going to fix this, Cosette, but I need you to promise me you won't keep digging into it. Stay away from Ryland Corp. and most importantly, stay away from anyone in the Ryland family. Do not go poking around in this shit. I need you to act like you still know nothing and let me handle things. I have a friend in the FBI that will help now that we have this." He holds up the memory stick like he's got the world's biggest diamond in his hand.

There is absolutely no way that I'm going to be able to feign ignorance after everything I've learned tonight, but I lie and tell him I will.

CHAPTER ELEVEN

I part ways with Remy at the end of my block. He insisted on accompanying me home to make sure nothing happened to me. I found it slightly obnoxious, considering I've been fine until now. The memory stick has been sitting at my aunt's for years. If no one has discovered it yet, I doubt anyone suspects anything different now.

As I walk up the last flight of stairs, everything hits me at once. I have to stop and sit down on the top step to steady my breathing. My chest feels like someone is sitting on it, and I realize I'm having a panic attack. Closing my eyes, I put my hands around my ears to block out any noise and focus on breathing in and out. After a few minutes, I find my breaths have slowed, and I can focus on my surroundings. Peeking around the corner, I see my apartment door and rise to my feet to get inside. The last thing I need right now is for one of my nosy neighbors to see me having a mental breakdown in the hall.

I'm a few feet from my door when the hairs on the back of my neck stand up. Something is off. I look down at the doorknob and see that my lock is busted. Scratch that—my door is busted. It looks like someone kicked it in. There are wood chips scattered on the floor, and it only takes a gentle tap of my fingers for the door to slowly creak open. The lights are off, but looking to the right, I can see that someone made a mess of the kitchen. It takes a few moments, but I finally register that someone has broken into my apartment. My body goes into fight-or-flight mode, and I rush back down the stairwell.

I knock into my neighbor, who is walking up with her dog.

"Cosette! Are you okay? You look like you've seen a ghost," she exclaims in a worried voice.

I look at her like I've suddenly lost my ability to speak English but then quickly turn my brain back on and explain to her that someone broke into my apartment. She asks if I've called the police, and it dawns on me that I haven't. After my conversation with Remy, I'm not so sure I should call them. Before I can respond, she has her phone out and is already speaking with the emergency operator. I guess that decision has been made for me.

Immediately, I remember that my aunt was supposed to be at my place tonight after her shift was over. Panic courses through me, and I run back up the stairs. Oh my God, what if she was here? I can't even fathom something happening to her—she's the only family I have left. I can hear my neighbor screaming at me not to go in, but I ignore her and shove the broken door open.

"Bill! Billie, are you in here?" I yell as I make my way through every inch of the apartment.

The place is turned upside down, but it's empty. No intruder and no Aunt Billie. I pick up my phone and call her. No answer on the first ring, but I immediately dial again. She answers on the second ring.

"Hey, hun…"

Before she can get out another word, I cut her off. "Oh my God, Billie, where are you?" I demand.

"I'm at the store grabbing some things for dinner. What's going on, Cosette? You sound out of breath."

I am out of breath. I feel like my chest might explode at any moment. The sound of her voice is the only thing keeping me from absolutely losing my shit.

"Holy fuck, I was so worried... I thought, I thought…" I choke out as many words as possible before the tears begin pouring from my eyes.

"Cosette, what is going on? Are you okay? Are you at home?" she asks, and I manage to squeak out a no and then quickly a yes, I'm at home.

"Stay there. I'm just around the corner," she says firmly.

She doesn't give me a chance to say anything else before she hangs up. If I know my aunt, she's probably dropped everything she had in her hands in whatever aisle she was in and is now running over here.

The police show up before my aunt does and do a sweep of my apartment. Once they announce it's clear, they come out to the hall and begin their round of questions. They ask if I know anyone who would do this. Was there anything of value in the apartment? Have I brought anyone I didn't know back to the apartment recently, like a date or someone I met on Tinder? I answer no to everything. I have no idea why someone would break into my place—I have nothing of value.

The officer questioning me asks if I need a copy of the report and suggests I don't stay here alone tonight. I ask if this type of break-in is common in the area, and he replies with a simple no. He explains it doesn't make sense for it to be a random break-in since I'm not on the ground floor and that it was most likely someone I know or someone looking for something they thought was here. Neither of those statements makes me feel any better about the situation. I assure him my aunt will be staying with me tonight and that I'll contact my landlord immediately to fix the lock.

Luckily, I didn't have the deadbolt locked, which saved it from any damage the break-in caused. I can still lock up for the evening and will avoid having to hike all the way out to my aunt's place tonight.

My aunt finally walks into my apartment as I'm finishing up with the detective. Clearly flustered and yelling at the other officer standing out in the hall about police not letting her in the building. How many officers do they have down there?

The detective gives me a number to call to get a copy of the report for insurance purposes and assures me they'll have someone patrol the block tonight but doesn't expect the intruder to return. I thank him and stand at the door while my aunt looks at me wide-eyed and slack-jawed. She immediately wraps her arms around me, telling me I'm okay over and over again. Although, it feels more like she's telling herself that than me.

We walk into the apartment together and assess the damage. My kitchen is completely trashed—dishes and glasses broken on the floor, with cabinets and drawers left wide open. I make my way to the bedroom, and it's no better. My mattress is flipped over, and papers are scattered around the floor. Looking down at the papers, I see some of the case files I found at my aunt's, and it dawns on me.

The memory stick.

This whole time, I've been naïve in thinking I didn't have anything of value in my apartment. I wasn't completely wrong—the memory stick, thankfully, is no longer here. It's with Remy. But how would anyone know I had it to begin with? No one knew I had it other than Remy, and the only person who knew I was going through my uncle's things was my aunt. I don't even think anyone saw me come home that night with the file box.

As I rack my brain, another realization hits me. I remember the strange man staring at me as I loaded the case files into the taxi outside my aunt's place.

Holy shit.

Remy's paranoia is rubbing off on me, and I'm starting to feel like it's justified. I peek out my window to see if there's anyone suspicious standing outside.

I look over, and my aunt is staring at me with an impatient glare.

"Do you want to explain why you have all these files here and why your eyes look like your mind is moving a million miles a minute?"

I'm stuck between a rock and a hard place, and I surrender my strategy of not including my aunt in any of this but remain as vague as possible.

"I found something in your office the other day, and I think whoever broke in here was looking for it. As for the files, I told you I was going to take the box home." I do my best to keep a straight face so that she doesn't sense my anxiety.

Remembering what Remy told me about my uncle, I decide now is as good a time as any to bring up what she's hidden from me for years.

"Why didn't you tell me about Uncle Ron's toxicology report?"

She takes a deep breath, tilts her head back, and keeps her arms at her side. I keep quiet and wait patiently for her response. I'm not mad at her, but I need her to know I'm not exactly thrilled she kept this from me.

Finally, after a deep breath and a few quick swipes of her fingers to clean off the tears staining her face, she looks at me, and I see nothing but pain and regret in her eyes.

"I just wanted it all to be over, Cosette. You had lost so much, and I couldn't fathom going after people who had way more power than I could ever imagine and ending up just like your uncle. I was scared… And I couldn't imagine leaving you alone." She walks over to my bed. Pulling the mattress off the ground, she slides it back into place on the bed frame and takes a seat.

"So, you also think Uncle Ron was murdered?" I ask, slight skepticism in my voice.

My aunt shakes her head, and just as I think she's about to dispute my claim, she says, "I don't think your uncle was murdered. I *know* he was."

My body goes stiff at her statement. There was no hesitation in her response, and I look at her with wide eyes, waiting for her to continue, because I can tell there's more she wants to say.

"I was with your uncle for twenty-six years, and not once have I ever known him to use drugs. Hell, he wouldn't even smoke pot, and we lived through the sixties and seventies." She finishes with a chuckle that lacks any humor. She stays seated on my bed, placing her hands in her lap. She won't make eye contact, and I know she feels guilty for keeping this from me.

"I'm not upset that you kept it from me. You were doing what you thought was best," I say without prompt. I don't think anything I've said has given her reason to think otherwise, but I figure it will still bring her comfort to hear me say it out loud.

She nods in acceptance of my statement and pats the bed next to her. I oblige, and for a few moments, we sit next to each other in silence.

"Do you think they got what they came for?" she asks as she looks around my room.

I follow her line of sight and fully take in the wreckage. My dresser drawer has been pulled out and thrown across the room. I can see the contents scattered across the floor—pens, hair clips, and some old photos of me and Esther create a chaotic collage near my feet. My closet door is open, and clothes hang halfway off hangers that have been pushed to one side.

I shake my head. "No. What they were looking for wasn't here."

She nods and accepts my vague answer. I don't want to tell her about the memory stick. I can't imagine how terrible she will feel if she knows she's been sitting on the only evidence that could bring us justice. But I need to know if she remembers getting the package from someone.

"Do you remember getting a manila envelope from someone around the time Uncle Ron died?" I ask calmly.

She looks up at me with a confused expression. I toss her another clue to jog her memory. Standing, I walk over to my purse and pull out the empty envelope with the sticky note so clearly written in her handwriting. I hand it to her. Her hand reaches out, trembling, and she looks up at me with wide eyes, as if she just remembered something.

"Some guy came by the house on one of the rare nights your uncle left to meet with Remy. I remember him asking for Ron, and when I told him he wasn't at the house, he shoved this in my hand and told me to give it to Remy. I asked him why he couldn't just wait to give it to him himself, but he kept mumbling that he could no longer meet up with him, and then he left without another word. I wrote the note and put it on the kitchen counter. I honestly haven't thought about it since." She looks down at the envelope with an expression of wonder, then returns her eyes to me.

"What was it?" she asks.

I don't want to lie to her, but I also don't want to make her feel bad for never giving it to my uncle.

I sigh and say, "Another piece of evidence, but not enough to solve anything. Remy has it now."

"You went to see him?" she asks, though it comes out more like a statement. I nod in confirmation.

"Do you remember how many days later Ron passed away?" As soon as the question leaves my mouth, I instantly regret saying *passed away* instead of calling it what it was. He was murdered.

Billie looks up at me and shakes her head. "I'm not sure. I believe it was shortly after. Maybe a day or two."

I nod, recalling what Remy told me about their source, who was found dead days after my uncle. The guy who gave my aunt the memory stick had to have been him. He must have known they had been found out.

If only he could have warned my uncle and Remy.

CHAPTER TWELVE

It's been almost a week since the break-in, and I still haven't been able to get a good night's sleep. My door has been replaced, and my aunt helped me clean up the apartment, which took less time than I thought it would. Most of my dishes and glassware couldn't be salvaged, so I ordered a new set from Amazon that set me back two hundred dollars.

I filled Remy in on the break-in, and his suspicions aligned with my own; someone must have seen me leave my aunt's with the box of evidence and wanted to see exactly what I had. He's not convinced anyone knows about the memory stick; if they did, my aunt's house would have been broken into years ago. He assured me that he has it somewhere safe and has already sent a copy of the footage to his FBI friend. He also tried convincing me to move in with my aunt, but I told him I wouldn't risk putting her in danger if I'm being watched now. I want to keep her as far away from this as I possibly can. He wasn't happy that I refused to find a new place to live, but I assured him that I would have Esther stay with me most nights.

After telling Esther about it, she's called me every night she hasn't physically stayed over, and I've been grateful for her company. I haven't told her everything about what I learned at Remy's last week, but I did tell her there has been a development in the case. I'll let her make what she will of that information. I don't want to clue her in too much because she'll get too hopeful for me, and that's the last thing I want. Who knows if this FBI friend of Remy's will be able to do anything with the footage.

I sit at my kitchen counter, hunched over a cup of coffee I grabbed from the café down the road. It's no Pour Man's but it get's the job done. I really need to get a new coffee pot. It's almost ten in the morning, and I don't have anywhere to be today. I texted Jeremy to see if I could pick up an extra shift, but he shockingly said he was staffed and couldn't afford the payroll hours to have me sitting behind the bar.

Sipping from my cup, I notice my phone screen light up with a text message from an unknown number. It has a 312 area code, so it's someone local. Maybe it's one of the new bartenders looking for someone to cover their shift.

I pick up my phone and open the message.

> *Still up for dinner tonight? I got us*
> *a reservation at Boka.*

Shit. I completely forgot about my date with Dylan. With everything that's happened, I didn't even tell Esther about it. She's going to kill me when she finds out I kept this from her. I smile to myself at the thought of her lecturing me about something so trivial. I contemplate canceling so I can be a hermit and not leave my apartment today, but if I'm being honest with myself, I could use the distraction and a good meal. I save his number and reply that Boka sounds great. I quickly dial Esther, fill her in on my evening plans, and ask if I can raid her closet for something to wear. I don't *need* to raid her closet, but I know she'll appreciate being included in the first real date I've been on in over a year. I tell her I'll be over within the hour before

I hang up and gather everything I need to get ready for the evening.

On my way to Esther's, I stop to grab coffee and sandwiches. We sit in her kitchen eating while she fills me in on her new male interest. She dumped Mike and has moved on to a guy who started working at her company a few weeks ago. Apparently, he's not her type but gives off Robert Pattinson vibes she can't resist. I try to keep up with the conversation as I quickly google who Robert Pattinson is. She's right—he is not at all her type, but if the guy from her office looks anything like him, I can see why she's smitten.

Lifting her brow as I set my phone down, she asks, "Did you really just have to Google who Robert Pattinson is?" Her tone drips with amused judgment.

"So what?" I quip in defense.

"I swear, Cosette, sometimes I feel like you live under a rock." She laughs.

Esther and I spend the next few hours hanging out in her apartment, watching *Bravo* and picking out the perfect first-date outfit for me. We settle on a red silk dress with ruffles on the shoulders and sleeves, paired with strappy black leather heels to edge it up. I have to admit, the outfit is better than anything I could have thrown together with what's in my closet.

I arrive at Boka thirty minutes early so I can grab a drink and relax my nerves before Dylan gets there. Walking up to the bar, I see he must have had the same idea—he's seated on a leather stool, sipping what looks like a tequila neat. I pull out the stool next to him and tell the bartender to give me whatever he's having. Dylan looks over at me and laughs.

"Oh man, you caught me pre-gaming before our date," he says with a shit-eating grin.

I shrug my shoulders and feign disinterest. "Great minds think alike."

We finish our drinks and catch up on how each other's days went. I learn that Dylan is filling some big shoes at his company after the CEO retired and hopes to land a promotion. I'm not sure I fully understand how corporate senior leadership works, but he seems a little young to be in the running for the C-suite. Then again, I can never tell how old men really are—they age so differently from women. He sounds extremely driven in his career, which I find attractive. He also knows when to toe the line on work talk, seamlessly shifting to topics about family and friends.

We finally make it to our dinner table thirty minutes after the reservation, second drinks in hand. Dylan continues to ask me about my future plans and if I plan to stay in Chicago long-term. I find it hard to answer because I haven't given much thought to the future beyond getting promoted at The Olive and making sure my rent is paid every month. I've always dreamed of opening my own spot one day, maybe a place that serves coffee in the morning and offers a killer wine and beer list in the evening. The reality of it feels so impossible right now that I push the thought back down and focus on the "moving away" part of his question.

"I'm the only family my aunt has, so I can't imagine moving away and leaving her here alone," I say, my voice laced with unintended sadness.

Dylan gives me a look of pity, and I hate it. He takes a drink and says, "I get it. The reason I came back to Chicago is because my dad is sick. Sometimes family keeps us grounded in places we didn't plan on being rooted to."

After hearing his response, I realize the look on his face wasn't pity—it was empathy and understanding. Immediately feeling uncomfortable talking about family, I change the subject to his time away from Chicago.

"So, when did you move away from Chicago?" I ask.

He looks equally relieved to shift topics. "A few years ago. I moved abroad. My dad wanted me to experience living in other countries, but I think it was just his way of getting rid of me. My mom didn't oppose me leaving either, so off I went."

There's an even tone in his voice, as if it was no big deal. But I can see sadness in his eyes.

"I never wanted to leave. I love Chicago. I had a tight friend circle, and my career path was looking promising." Dylan takes a deep breath and looks down at his drink. "But if you knew my dad, you'd understand he's not a man to negotiate with. I guess it worked out. I had a great time traveling Europe, experiencing new cultures."

He quickly takes a drink, and suddenly, I feel lost for words. This conversation took a really sad turn—I need to pivot back to something positive.

"Well, I'm sure your friends and family are really happy to have you back," I say with the sincerest smile I can muster.

He shrugs. "I suppose so. But it's weird, you know?"

I don't know. I've never left the area. Also, I've really only had one friend I actually cared about. I raise an eyebrow, urging him to continue.

"Weird how?"

He raises his empty glass to the server walking by, a silent order that would normally annoy me. "Weird because life doesn't stop. I left and lived my life, and my friends stayed and lived theirs. Some are married with kids, some are not married but still have kids, and some are divorced and remarried. Just feels like, even though I was traveling and seeing the world, my life didn't seem to move as fast as theirs. Now they're in a completely different stage of life, and I can't find anything to connect with them on anymore. I find myself missing them even when I'm in the same room with them."

The server interrupts with a fresh drink. Dylan grabs it and nearly finishes it off.

"Anyway, I don't mean to sound like a pity party."

I look at him, and the last thing I see is a pity party. What I see is someone who is lonely and feels like a tourist in a place he used to call home. I'd be lying if I said I hadn't felt that way a time or two after my dad disappeared.

"I understand. And you're far from a pity party," I say, raising my glass to him. "Here's to new beginnings."

He echoes my cheers, and we both down what's left of our drinks.

I'm curious to ask more about his family, but I think better of it, assuming any topic involving his sick father might not be the best first-date conversation. Instead, I ask him about his travels abroad.

Dylan's stories of living all over Europe are fascinating. It's a lifestyle I can only dream of experiencing. The places he's been to are places I've only ever seen in picture books, and I find myself hungry to hear more. We finish eating and continue talking for another hour, barely touching our drinks. Eventually, we get the hint that the restaurant is closing and the server is trying to wrap up for the evening.

I'm having such a great time that I don't want the night to end. I suggest we go to a bar that Esther and I like to visit every now and then when we're feeling up for a late night. They usually have live music on Wednesdays, and it'll give me a chance to see Dylan in an atmosphere that doesn't involve sitting down and throwing back expensive tequila. Let's see if this man can dance.

CHAPTER THIRTEEN

Dylan was more than happy to entertain my suggestion of extending the evening, and we catch a cab over to the club that already has a line to get in. We make our way to the front, hand the bouncer our IDs, and head down the stairs to a dark room with red and purple lighting. There's an R&B singer performing tonight, and couples are paired off on the dance floor, arms above their heads and hips rolling to the beat.

We make our way to the bar and I order two shots of tequila and two house lagers. This spot is known to have a rotating tap of local breweries, but the house option has yet to fail me. After ordering, I turn to see Dylan giving me a look that could probably get a girl pregnant. Jesus, does he need to look at me like that?

"What?" I ask, because if I didn't say something, I probably would have done something stupid like kiss him or take my dress off in public.

He smiles and shakes his head. "Nothing, you just look… You're beautiful, Cosette," he says while placing a hand on my arm. He takes a step closer, and I have to tilt my head up to maintain eye contact. "And with that drink order, I'm inclined to think you're trying to get me drunk."

He's close enough to me now that I can smell the tequila on his breath. The bartender comes back with our drinks and thankfully interrupts our intimate conversation. I immediately throw my shot back and say, "I don't need to get you drunk, Dylan. You seem to be able to handle that all on your own."

Grabbing my beer, I head out to the dance floor and leave him standing at the bar with a shot in hand. I look over my shoulder to see him laugh before throwing it back.

I work my way through the crowd and let myself get lost in the music. I find an opening and start to roll my hips to the beat of the music. The alcohol is finally kicking in, and my body feels like it's floating around the room. Within a few minutes, I feel a very large, very solid body slide up against me. He places his hands on my hips and aligns my back to him to match my movements.

My body is suddenly aware of how long it has been since I've been intimate with someone and responds in such a way that has me sweating under my silk dress. I didn't wear a bra, and the feeling of the fabric on my nipples is enough to make my body combust.

I feel hot breath against my neck and then hear Dylan whisper in my ear.

"If you keep moving your hips like that, I don't know if I'll be able to let you go home alone tonight."

I roll my hips in response and can feel his arousal behind me.

"What makes you think I want to go home alone tonight?" I ask in a sensual voice that only comes out when I've had too much tequila.

His only response is a low groan that's nothing short of primal. He spins me around, grabbing my waist to pull me against him, and the way we are dancing now has his thigh between my legs while I grind on him. Keeping his hand on my waist, he slips his other up my back and into my hair. He slightly tugs, just enough to force my head back to look at him, right before he seizes my mouth with his. He kisses me like a man starved, and there's nothing I can do other than part my lips for him. He rolls his tongue over mine and nibbles on my bottom lip, making me release a soft moan. He pulls back and looks me in the eyes, but as quickly as I blink, his attention is directed at something behind me. Our dancing has stopped, and if he weren't so beautiful, I might feel a little awkward standing completely still in the middle of the dance floor. I want to keep kissing him, but before I can lean in to capture his mouth again, he grabs my hand, leading me out of the crowd toward the front door.

He positions me against the wall and digs his hand in his pocket, pulling out his phone.

"I'm going to call a car to take you home," he says as he navigates a taxi site on his phone.

The fact that he said he's calling *me* a car and not *us* a car doesn't go unnoticed, and I'm instantly disappointed. Maybe the date wasn't going as well as I thought it was. Why would he kiss me and then send me home alone?

"Okay, are you…" I start to say but then can't seem to finish the sentence.

Not looking up from his phone, he says, "Don't worry, I'm not going to send you alone. I'll drop you on my way back to my place."

Jesus, this guy really has no idea what kind of mixed messages he's putting off tonight. Crossing my arms across my chest, I nod and turn to walk out the door.

The car pulls up within minutes, and I open the door and slide in. Dylan closes my door and walks around to get in on the other side. I don't remember if he mentioned what neighborhood he lives in , but I know my apartment is at least a fifteen-minute drive from here. This is going to be an extremely awkward ride home if Dylan stays silent because I sure as hell won't be initiating conversation.

I stare out the window and replay the evening, trying to decipher where things went wrong. It must have been the kiss. Maybe it wasn't good for him, or maybe I have bad breath. Oh my God, what a nightmare. The first date I've been on in over a year, and it's ending with an extremely tense ride home with a gorgeous man who might think I have bad breath. I squeeze my eyes shut to fend off the headache that's beginning to form from my hyper-functioning thought process.

"You're upset." Dylan finally breaks the silence. He says it more like a statement than a question.

"I'm less upset and more confused," I say without looking away from the window.

"What are you confused about?" he asks as if he has no idea what just happened within the last thirty minutes.

I let out a cynical laugh. Okay, now I'm upset.

"Well, let's see. We have a lovely dinner, even better conversation, you kiss me like I'm the last woman on Earth, and then, all of a sudden, you are hands-off and calling me a car to go home. I mean, what? Am I a bad kisser or something?"

I throw my hands up in defeat. He attempts to say something, but I cut him off.

"I'm sorry, I haven't been on a date in a while, so maybe this is the new normal, or maybe this is the European way of dating." I tilt my head to the side to accentuate my sarcasm. "I'll have to make a mental note not to be confused the next time a man abruptly ends an evening after being physically intimate with me. I mean, Jesus, you could have at least told me you were tired or something." Shaking my head, I look over at him, and the man is actually smiling. Does he have a death wish?

He slides his hand across the seat until our pinky fingers are gently touching.

"I'm not taking you home because I didn't enjoy the way you kissed me, Cosette…" He looks over at me, his smile slowly fading back to reveal a face void of the playfulness he had only moments ago.

Leaning back, he lets out a sigh of frustration, and I'm back to feeling like I'm missing something. Does this man want me or not?

Looking over at me, he says, "Please believe me when I say tonight has been the most fun I've had in the past year. But…" He pauses like he's deciding whether he wants to be this honest with me.

"But…what? You have a girlfriend or something?" I say, only half-joking. When he doesn't answer, I panic. "Oh my God… You have a fucking girlfriend!"

"What? No…no, I don't have a girlfriend. It's not like that. I just…" He searches for the words, and suddenly, the back seat of this car feels extremely small.

"I saw someone that I wasn't expecting to see, and it's not someone I particularly wanted to run into while I was with you," he says cryptically, and now I'm really lost.

"Ok… So, like, an ex-girlfriend?" I ask, still as confused as I was ten minutes ago. Before he can answer, I cut him off to save myself from sounding desperate.

"Look, we don't have to do this…" Shaking my head, I accept defeat. I'm not going to understand this situation, and the more I think about it, the less I think I want to. My life has been stressful enough the past few weeks. The last thing I need is some guy with baggage he isn't ready to talk about.

I pull my hand away from his, and in the blink of an eye, the warm and fuzzy feelings I had fade away. The realization of how badly I needed this night to be an escape from reality hits me. In minutes, I will be walking up to my apartment, only to enter a space void of everything but my haunting loneliness.

I quickly blink away the tears forming in my traitorous eyes and look out the window. I refuse to let Dylan see me cry.

I feel a shift of weight on the seat, and when I turn to look back at him, his face is so close to mine I can count every beautiful lash that adorns his green eyes. He's pinning me with his stare like he's committing my face to memory.

"What are you doing?" I ask, without so much as blinking.

He answers me with silence and slowly lifts his hand to the nape of my neck, grasping gently while he works his fingers through the base of my hair. Another arm wraps around my waist, and before I can take another breath, his mouth is on mine, kissing me deeply. This kiss is different from the one in the club; this time, he's gentle and patient. Slowly, he explores my mouth with his tongue, and I melt into him.

After what feels like the slowing of not nearly enough time, Dylan pulls away just enough to look down between us, where his hand has now moved from my waist to the bare skin of my upper thigh.

And oh my God, I don't know if I have ever been this turned on. I need to get inside my apartment immediately before I mount this man right here in the back of the car.

My eyes are wide, and I squeeze my thighs together to give myself some relief from the heat that has manifested between them. My back is now pinned straight against the seat, and I try to steady my breathing. I barely register that the car has stopped moving. Dylan looks over at me and says, "This is you."

What I am about to do is completely out of character for me, but my body is on fire, and my brain has officially surrendered to it. I grab his face with both hands and kiss him so intensely I don't think I'm even breathing. Pulling back, I look him straight in the eyes and say, "Come up to my apartment."

If he denies me, I'm going to be mortified and will probably hide under a rock for the next week. But if he comes up, I have a feeling it will be the best sex I've ever had.

"Fuck," Dylan growls out and looks me in the eyes, almost as if he is waiting for me to rescind my offer. "Yeah, okay."

In one swift movement, he has the door open, telling the driver, "This will be the last stop."

CHAPTER FOURTEEN

We barely make it up the stairs to my apartment with all our clothes on. I'm currently fighting with my keys to try to get my door unlocked while Dylan is behind me, placing soft kisses down the back of my neck.

Damn this new lock.

I hear a click, and finally, I manage to get the door open and walk into my apartment. Dylan follows in after me, throwing the door shut behind him. I barely notice that he has managed to get my dress unzipped until I feel a slight chill down my back. Turning around, I see him slowly walking toward me. I slide out of my heels and kick them to the side of the couch. Now that I'm on flat feet, I can fully appreciate the size of him. This man must be well over six feet tall, and the width of his shoulders makes me feel that much more petite.

He grabs me and pulls my body against his. With my hands on his chest, I slowly trail them down until I reach his belt buckle. Pinching the leather, I pull it back and quickly move to the button of his pants. I look up to find Dylan staring down at me.

"Are you sure you want to do this?" he asks.

Is he really giving me an out right now?

"We've both had a lot to drink, and I don't want you waking up with any regrets tomorrow morning."

He is totally giving me an out right now.

Keeping my eyes on his, I slowly trail my hands up his shirt, unbuttoning one button at a time.

He reaches up, grabbing my hands in his.

"Cosette."

My name comes out of him in a warning, and I realize he's looking for verbal consent.

"I'm sure," I say, and before I can take another breath, he's pulling my dress down my body, letting it pool on the ground around my feet. I'm standing in front of him completely nude except for a pair of tiny black lace panties.

He steps back and drinks in the view of me. I see the corner of his lip twitch up in a predatory smirk.

"My God, you are gorgeous," he states in a low, almost whispered voice. And before I can issue a response, his lips are on mine again.

His hands roam from my breasts, down my waist, and land on my ass. I return to my previous task of unbuttoning his shirt, each one revealing a toned chest with a light brushing of hair spread across it. After I fully remove his shirt, I let my hands explore the firm ripples of his abdomen. While being lost in his mouth and the task of getting him naked, Dylan has walked us into the hall and now has me pressed against the wall. He breaks away from my mouth and slowly kisses down my neck to my breast, causing my head to toss back as I release a moan.

He lowers to his knees and sprinkles kisses across my stomach. Fully focused on my body, he moves his hands up to my hips, hooking two fingers under the sides of my panties and pulling them down to my ankles. While keeping one hand on my hip, he uses the other to lift my foot, helping me step out of them.

This feels like a fever dream. I've had my fair share of casual sex, but not with anyone who has been this attentive to my pleasure.

He tosses them to the side and returns to trailing kisses up my thigh, inching his way closer to the most sensitive part of me. He takes his hand and places it behind my knee, pulling my leg up and around his shoulder. I'm now fully exposed to him and breathing so hard, I'm bordering on panting. Looking up at me, he repeats his earlier sentiment.

"Fucking beautiful."

He dips his head, and I am overcome with waves of pleasure. Time is nonexistent; the only thing my mind can process is the feeling of release my body is slowly building to. Eyes fluttering, I brace one hand on his head and the other on the wall supporting me. My breath hitches as my euphoria comes to a crescendo. My body and mind are completely lost as I cry out my climax.

He slowly pulls back and lowers my leg to the ground. I feel him stand, and my blurred vision slowly gains clarity again. He leans in and lazily kisses me, then lowers his hands to my ass and lifts me so that my legs are wrapped around his hips.

"Which way is your bedroom?" he asks.

I point to the door on the right, and we stride down the hall, staying completely consumed in one another. One of his hands leaves me to open the door, and he walks us into my bedroom. He lays me down on the bed and removes his pants and then his briefs. My eyes widen as I finally get to see the entirety of him.

Good God, he is a masterpiece of a man.

He bends over to pick up his pants and reaches into a pocket to pull out a condom. In a few smooth motions, he has it open and sliding down his length. His body returns to mine and positions himself between my legs. He kisses me again, and suddenly, a panicked thought pops into my head.

I don't know his last name.

I have never in my life slept with someone and not known their full name. I actually like this guy, and I haven't once asked him his last name. What the fuck is wrong with me? His mouth moves to my neck, and I feel him reach down to position himself at my entrance, and I shout out without thinking.

"Wait."

I hear him take in a sharp breath, and his body goes stiff. He lifts his head and looks at me with a worried crease between his brows.

"What's wrong? Are you okay?" he asks.

Oh God, I freaked him out, and I hurry to recover before he thinks he did something wrong.

"Yes, I'm okay… Better than okay." It comes out like a purr, and I lift my head to kiss him. I let out a small giggle.

"This is embarrassing…but I don't know your last name."

He smiles a predatory smile again.

"That's okay, I don't know yours either." And before I can respond, he thrusts into me, making me cry out. Pulling out slowly and pushing back in, he continues with an agonizing pace. I lift my hips to take more of him as we continue to get lost in each other, him going deeper with each stroke. I run my hands through his hair and pull while he continues to hammer into me. He lifts up and changes his angle, and I cry out as he hits a new spot that shoots heat up my core. I cover my mouth in fear I'm becoming too loud, but he quickly reaches up and pulls my hand away.

"Don't you dare. I want to hear the noises you make when I make you come, Cosette," he groans out.

He flips us over so that I'm straddling him. With his hands on my hips, he guides me, moving me back and forth. The movements are slow, and my eyes close as my body starts to tense up. I place my hands on his chest, lifting myself to gain more control of my movements. Looking down at him, I take in just how beautiful he truly is. His lips are parted, and there's a crease between his brows.

Tossing my head back, I fuck him until I see stars in the backs of my eyes.

"That's it. Come again for me," Dylan commands. And I do.

My body begins to tremble on top of him, and I lose all cognition of the sounds coming out of me. His grip tightens on my hips, and his thrusts become manic as he chases his own release. Slowly, we come back to reality and lay exhausted and sated in my bed.

We lay there in silence for some time, and I finally slide off him.

I let out a playful giggle and say, "And to think, I almost didn't ask you to come up."

He looks over at me with a raised eyebrow. "That would have been a tragedy."

"Only because you would have let me," I reply, and it comes out more aggressive than sarcastic.

I look up at him and catch a small twitch of his mouth that signals he's still entertained. I want him to stay the night. Is he already planning to? Before I give myself time to answer my own question, I see him sit up and grab his briefs, then his jeans. Guess I found my answer to that question. The words are coming out of my mouth before my brain can comprehend what I'm saying.

"You can stay…if you'd like."

I can't remember the last time I gave a man permission to sleep over, and there's always the possibility I'll get buyer's remorse. But right now, I feel utterly blissful, such a drastic change from the melancholic state I've been in for the past few weeks. If there's one thing I've learned over the years, is that opportunities to feel joy, to feel pleasure, don't often present themselves to me. And when they do, the moments are fleeting. So tonight, I'm going to draw out this feeling for as long as I can.

"You sure?" he asks, looking over his shoulder at me with that damned raised eyebrow again.

Smiling, I say, "Under one condition."

"Oh, there are conditions now?" He's already put his briefs on, and I'm instantly disappointed that this beautiful man is no longer fully naked in my bed.

"Well, actually, there are two conditions now." I can't help but let out a soft giggle. "The first being, you need to remove those briefs again…"

He looks at me with a feral grin. "If I sleep next to you fully nude tonight, I can't make any promises that there won't be a second act."

I release a shuddered breath and reply in my sexiest voice possible, "One can only hope."

He slowly removes his briefs, and I'll be damned, this man is already rock hard again. My body is all but singing for him.

"And what is the second condition?" he asks, and his voice brings me back from the very dirty, yet very pleasurable thought I was having.

"That you tell me your last name. Can't have a stranger staying at my apartment overnight," I say a little awkwardly.

"Ahh, but you'll let one eat your…"

"Hey!" I shove him before he can finish that sentence. "Who knew you had such a dirty mouth?"

He's laughing, and that smile is enough to melt me where I sit. He leans back against the headboard and rubs the back of his neck, and the next words out of his mouth leave me speechless.

"My last name is Ryland."

CHAPTER FIFTEEN

I feel like someone just shoved my head underwater, and there's no air left in my lungs. Eyes wide, I slowly move away from this beautifully dangerous man. I'm suddenly assessing my surroundings and how I can physically escape this room—escape this man who is the last human on this planet that I should be alone with. Does he know who I am? Was this all a ploy to get me alone?

Things instantly start adding up. He moved away to study abroad. He's back because his dad is sick. How did I not put two and two together? Remy warned me that this family is dangerous, and here I am, lying naked in bed with one of them.

I look over at him, and our eyes meet. His brows are furrowed, and he's watching me with pure confusion.

"Cosette, are you okay? You look like you've seen a ghost."

I finally snap myself back into reality. I've not only moved away from him, but I'm also holding up a sheet to cover my body—like he didn't just lick almost every inch of it.

"Umm, yeah, I'm fine… Ryland as in Ryland Corp.?" I ask, unable to hide the shakiness in my tone.

He looks at me and shakes his head.

"Please don't tell me you're freaked out by that?"

Freaked out is an understatement, and I realize he doesn't know who I am. He has no idea why I am acting the way I am right now. This might be my saving grace. I just need to play it cool long enough to get this guy out of my place.

"What, you don't think being the heir to a billion-dollar company is enough to justify my reaction?" And being the son of my father's possible murderer… But I don't dare say that part out loud.

"Jesus, you can't be serious." He looks at me with pure annoyance on his face now. This is good. Maybe I can offend him enough to make him want to leave without me asking him to.

"What?" I ask in defiance.

"Nothing. I just didn't take you to be a person who cares about how much money I'm worth. Guess I was wrong," he says as he stands and starts to get dressed.

"I'm not that kind of person," I spit back at him.

Shit. Why am I defending myself? I'm supposed to be trying to offend him to get his ass out of here. But I can't help but feel bad about making someone think I'm judging them based on something so superficial.

"Yeah, well, you could have fooled me," he says as he slides his jeans back on. He's looking around my bedroom for his final piece of clothing before he realizes I took it off him in my living room.

I stand and grab my robe off the back of my bedroom door. I open it and storm out into my hallway, flipping the lights on. My dress and his shirt are lying on the floor just a few feet from the front door. I walk over, grab it, and turn on my feet, walking back toward my bedroom. He walks out shirtless, hair disheveled.

Shoving his shirt into his hands, I say, "Here. Clearly, this was a very big mistake."

He looks down at the shirt and slowly grabs it from my hand. I don't know why I don't immediately let go, but when I look up, our eyes meet, and I'm not sure what it is that I'm seeing in his. Sadness? Regret? Pity? They burn into me, and I quickly turn to walk away when I can't take it anymore. But before I can take a step, he grabs my wrist and flings me back toward him.

Eyes burning like fire, he asks me, "Was it, Cosette?"

I don't immediately answer him because I'm too distracted by the way his eyes drill into me to fully comprehend what he's asking. As if he reads my mind, he asks again, "Was it a mistake?"

Pulling my wrist from his grip, I break eye contact, and in a voice that's almost a whisper, I respond to him, "I don't know."

I turn again to head to the door out of my apartment, and when I place my hand on the handle to open it, I hear his footsteps coming toward me.

"I think it's best if you don't stay tonight," I say, turning and expecting him to make his way out. But when I look, he's not walking toward my door—he's walking toward a framed photo that I have sitting on an end table.

No. No. No.

He picks up the frame and studies the picture of my father and me. It's a picture taken a few months before he went missing. We took a weekend trip up to Michigan with my aunt and uncle. It was one of my favorite trips with them and one of the few full weekends my dad had off work. He was so excited to get out on the lake and fish for two days straight. And that's exactly what we did. We fished, they drank beer, and we stayed up late swapping old stories by a campfire. It was the last time the four of us were all together. The last time I felt truly happy.

Rage rips through me when I realize who is now holding that precious memory in his hands. A man whose family is responsible for brushing my father's disappearance under the rug. Who may be responsible for his murder. For my uncle's murder. And the poor security guard who tried to help.

I stomp over to him and grab the photo from his hands, pulling it in and holding it to my chest. Dylan is now studying me like I'm a wild animal. Closing my eyes, I tip my head back to keep the tears from falling.

"You're the Emory girl."

And though his voice is soft and quiet, the pity in his statement is loud and clear.

Yes, I am the Emory girl. The seventeen-year-old orphan who lost her mother to cancer and her father to a mystery. The girl who was exploited by the media for years, who just wanted to lock herself in her room and never return to the world. The girl who lost hope and stopped looking for it.

Dylan reaches up for me, but I quickly pivot my shoulder away before he can make contact.

"I'm so sorry, Cosette. I didn't know…"

He trails off into silence.

"You need to leave," I state blandly, keeping my face void of emotion.

He clears his throat and throws his shirt over his head. I turn my body so that I can lean my back against the wall, still clutching the frame to my chest. It gives him room to walk by me toward the door.

Without looking back at me, he pauses at the doorway. "This wasn't a mistake for me."

Before I can blink, I hear the door shut, and he's gone.

My legs officially give out on me, and I crumple to the floor. I can no longer keep the emotions bottled inside of me, and I break. I cry like I cried the day my father brought me home from school and told me I was allowed to feel sadness. The day he held me while I fell apart.

Only now, there is no one to hold me. No one to help put me back together.

CHAPTER SIXTEEN

I stay lying on the floor of my hallway, clutching the photo of my father for a few hours before finally pulling myself together enough to make it back to my bed. My body is wrecked with emotions, and sleep is not going to come to me anytime soon.

It has been hours since Dylan left, but I can still smell him on my sheets—on me. Honestly, the whole room still reeks of sex. What are the odds the first guy I take home in what feels like ages ends up being a Ryland? Slim. The odds are fucking slim. Not to mention, the sex was some of the best I've ever had. Oh my God, I'm going to puke.

I remove myself from my bed and head to the bathroom. I need to wash this night off me. I need to tell someone about this, but it can't be my aunt or Esther. I don't want to involve either of them in this nightmare. I pick up my phone and text the only person who will understand exactly how fucked this situation is.

Me: *Hey, Remy… I may have*
broken one of the rules you gave me.

I set my phone down on the sink, not expecting a response. After all, it's not quite six in the morning yet. I turn the water on for the shower and wait until the bathroom steams up—an extremely hot shower is a necessity today. As I remove my robe, I hear my phone vibrate.

> **Remy:** *Why am I not surprised?*
> *Meet me at Hollywood Grill in an*
> *hour.*

So demanding. I set my phone back down without responding. A part of me has a feeling Remy will be at the diner whether I plan on going or not. I step into the scalding shower and let it wash away whatever lingers from the night.

I quickly throw on a pair of leggings and an old Columbia sweatshirt Esther left here ages ago and head to the door. I'm hoping that Hollywood serves a good cup of coffee because I am not going to make it through the day with no sleep. And as sobering of an experience as finding out who Dylan was, I fear I might still be a little drunk. Yes, lots of coffee will be needed today.

As I make my way down to the street, anxiety sits heavy on my shoulders and in my mind. How the hell am I going to tell Remy about what happened last night?

Walking into the diner, I immediately spot Remy sitting in a booth in the back corner. In front of him is a steaming cup of coffee and a folded-up newspaper. He's staring at his phone as I walk up and doesn't make eye contact with me until I've sat down and stolen his cup of coffee.

"You know…I could have had one waiting for you if you had confirmed you were coming," he says in an unamused tone.

"Yes, but then I wouldn't have had the pleasure of seeing that annoyed look on your face," I spit back sarcastically, raising the coffee cup in a one-way cheers before bringing the magic liquid of life to my mouth.

He shakes his head and raises a hand to the waitress, clearly flagging her down for another cup. I casually pick up the newspaper and see a front-page article about the mayor no longer running for re-election. However, his son will be. There's a picture of the two of them at what appears to be some political soirée, standing next to the police chief. I toss the paper down on the table with annoyance.

"Nepotism at its finest."

Remy nods his head and gives a grunt of agreement.

"All people do in this city is complain about how the mayor doesn't make good on any of his campaign promises, yet they keep re-electing him. They'll probably elect his son in a landslide and go right back to complaining about the same bullshit," I add, crossing my arms and leaning back in the booth.

I've already downed the cup of coffee by the time the waitress comes over with a second cup and a fresh pot for Remy. Perfect timing. I'll have to make sure he leaves a good tip. After she fills our cups, he raises his cup like I did a moment ago in a mock cheer and says, "And the cycle continues."

We sit in silence for a few minutes, and I'm grateful. The empty air allows my coffee to kick in and my brain to gather my thoughts. Once my cup is empty again, I set it down and begin.

"So…about that recommendation you made in regard to steering clear of the Ryland family—"

"It wasn't a recommendation, Cosette. You can't go near any of the Ryland family members. It's too dangerous for you until we know exactly who is involved," he cuts in with an irritated tone, but then I instantly see empathy fill his face. He takes a drink of his coffee and then lifts a hand to pinch the bridge of his nose before he continues with his lecture.

"Look, I know you want answers, and I wish it was as simple as going straight to the source…but the second you start poking your nose around, they're going to know we have something worth looking into. These people are powerful and have enough money to pay off God himself for their sins. Right now, whoever it was that did something to your dad, to your uncle—they think they got away with it. And I'm inclined to continue to let them think that until we have enough to bring them down."

I start to second-guess telling him about Dylan. I nervously rip apart a napkin that was sitting in front of me.

"So, you're looking for more evidence?" I ask.

"Yes, I told you I would. I've already started working with my friend at the FBI. He sent me all the old case records turned over to them by the Chicago Police Department," he says.

I scrunch my brows in confusion "Old case records? I didn't realize the FBI was involved back then."

Remy shakes his head. "Ryland Corp. was being investigated for more than just your father's disappearance. But the media became feral when they caught wind of a billionaire company being involved in a missing person case that the rest of their bad deeds were overlooked. And my god were the Rylands good at manipulating the narrative."

The memory of flashing camera lights and Mr. Ryland pleading to the media for anyone with information to come forward while I stand silent and terrified next to him comes rushing back. I break eye contact with Remy to take a sip of my coffee, hoping to hide my nerves from him.

"How is it, that not even the FBI could figure out what happened to my dad?" the question dripping with equal parts anger and hopelessness.

Remy's face softens "I wish I had all the answers for ya kid, nothing keeps secrets better than money."

"And what about now? Have you found anything new? Anything that was missed?" I ask eagerly.

"Not a ton, but there are a few leads I want to follow up on. And I was able to run through a few of the witness reports from the people who attended that company party the night your dad went missing." He says "company party" while giving air quotes.

I can't help but quirk a brow and mock his gesture, asking, "What do you mean by company party?"

Remy continues to tell me about a gathering that took place at the building the night my dad disappeared and how there weren't enough people there to justify calling it a company party, considering the number of people they employ. Apparently, it was just a few of the younger executives and some of the female interns. The part that catches my attention the most is that both Ryland brothers were in attendance. Dylan was in the building during my father's last shift.

What the actual fuck?

My brain starts racing—he must know something. I cut Remy off in the middle of him talking about one of the interns and ask, "Was Mr. Ryland there that night?"

Remy throws his hands up and leans back in the booth. "That's the thing: he was there, and we know that both of his sons were there. But we have no physical evidence to show that they were. Anytime they were questioned, they all answered the same. They remember celebrating but don't recall if they were there at the same time as your father."

I take a second to absorb this new information. All three Ryland men were in the building at some point that night, but we have no proof that it overlapped with my father's shift. Sounds to me like the company party was just an excuse to have a regular party at Daddy's billion-dollar tech company building.

"What were they celebrating?"

Remy shakes his head. "I don't have the exact details, but all the employees in attendance mentioned celebrating an acquisition."

Okay, so maybe it was a company party. An acquisition does add up—Ryland Corp. is notorious for buying any tech company that they see as a possible competitor, absorbing their intellectual assets for themselves to eventually sell to consumers. It's honestly kind of gross the way they operate, but that's good ole capitalist America for you. I draw a deep breath before I ask the next question.

"What do you know about Dylan Ryland?"

Remy raises a brow. "Not much. The year your dad went missing was his first year officially working for his father. He was fresh out of college and seemed to be quite the overachiever. From what I gather, he was the golden child from his third wife, set to take over once Daddy was ready to retire or simply too old to keep working.

Most likely the latter."

"Fresh out of college?" I say with some skepticism. "I thought he'd been studying abroad for the past few years."

"Someone's been doing some research..." Remy replies with a look on his face that screams, *Why the hell do you know anything about Dylan Ryland?* "That same year he started working for his father, he moved overseas for his postgraduate studies. From what I've gathered, he stayed after completing his schooling and has only been back in the States a few times in the past five years."

Guess I'll have to be the one to break the news to him. "Well, he's back in Chicago, and he's working for Ryland Corp. again."

"How the hell do you know that, Cosette?" Remy leans in, realizing he said that a little too loudly in this nearly empty diner.

I swallow the lump that's forming in my throat and tell him everything. Well, not everything. Remy doesn't need to know about the mind-blowing sex. I explain to him that I had no idea who Dylan was at first and that my intentions were not to go poking my nose around. Just when Remy's face begins to relax, I tell him my intentions of poking my nose around *have* changed. If Dylan was there the night of my dad's last shift, then he might know something. I have to find out if he saw him or saw anything for that matter. Any information is better than what we currently have.

"Absolutely not." Remy's face is so stern, he reminds me of when my dad told me no the first time I asked to stay the night at my high school boyfriend's house.

"Look, I don't even know if he will want to see me again. But I have to try. For fuck's sake, Remy, he was there!" I bring my hands down to my sides to refrain from pounding on the table. It's probably a combination of no sleep and the hangover slowly creeping up that's got me so worked up.

Remy is still shaking his head like that will get his point across. "I can't let you do this, Cosette. I won't be able to handle it if something happens to you. I've lived with your uncle's death on my conscience every day. I should never have let him get as involved as he was in the investigation. I won't make the same mistake twice."

I can see the pain in his eyes, the guilt that I know is eating away at him. But what happened to my uncle isn't his fault.

"My uncle would have gotten involved whether you asked him to or not. My dad was his best friend, and I'm going to get involved whether you ask me to or not." I blink a few times, keeping the tears at bay, the regret of doing nothing all these years weighing on my every word. "I sat around being complacent for five years. I understand guilt, Remy. I've been feeling it ever since that note showed up on my doorstep. I'll never forgive myself if I don't try to find answers. So…you can either help me find them or not, but I'm going to go looking either way."

Peering at me like I'm crazy, he runs a hand down his face and sighs. "Fine. But I'm not letting you do this without a well-thought-out plan."

"Guess we better order some food then. This might take a while."

After two hours of discussing the parameters of how I will go about interacting with Dylan, I ask Remy something that has been weighing on me since I left my aunt's house with a box of evidence.

"Why are you still billing my aunt for this case?"

Remy looks up at me from his newspaper with a look of confusion. "What do you mean?"

"When I was at her house, I saw an invoice for your business on her fridge. I get that it's your job and that my uncle hired you on his own volition, but my aunt had nothing to do with those decisions. I just feel like it's kind of unfair to expect her to pay the bill that her dead husband left behind." I say all this with my arms crossed, hoping he gets the message of my displeasure with the situation. He shakes his head and begins to say something, but I cut him off. "I mean, fuck, what are you going to charge me for all this?"

His brows soften and he looks at me with sad eyes. "I'm not billing your aunt for anything. And if you must know, I stopped accepting your uncle's money months before he passed away." I look at him, my face painted with confusion, waiting for him to continue his explanation that makes no sense.

"Your uncle became a friend, and I became as invested in the case as he was. I make enough money with other jobs—I don't need money from your aunt." He says this so smoothly it's hard not to believe him. But that invoice was there.

"Okay…so, explain why my aunt still has an invoice on her refrigerator?" I challenge.

"I don't know, maybe it's something she holds onto to make herself feel better about hating me. It's probably a super old one. Did you look at the date?"

I didn't look at the date.

"Trust me, I haven't sent a bill out on this case in years, and I won't be starting now. Consider the work pro bono." He waves his hand in front of me, a sign the conversation is over. We finish our coffee, and Remy pays the waitress. As we're walking out, he looks at me and says, "Please tread lightly, Cosette. This shit has layers we aren't privy to."

CHAPTER SEVENTEEN

My meeting with Remy at the diner was almost a week ago, and I still haven't heard a word from Dylan. I'm starting to regret the agreement between Remy and me that involves waiting for Dylan to come to me. At the time, I pictured the sadness and longing in his tone as he walked out of my apartment, telling me the night wasn't a mistake, and assumed it would be only days before I heard from him again. Clearly, I was being too presumptuous. I filled Esther in on what was going on. I needed someone to confide in, and Remy wasn't exactly the perfect person to give dating advice.

Esther and I sit at Pour Man's and watch out the window as the rain assaults the city streets. Sipping from her latte, she looks back over at me. "He's going to call you, Cosette. He's probably just freaked out by the whole thing. I mean…" She lowers her voice before adding, "He should be freaked out—you're planning on fake dating him to get information."

I snort offensively.

"Yeah, but he doesn't know that. And stop saying things like that out loud in public," I say in a low tone as I look around the coffee shop. "Did you already forget that I ran into him less than a month ago here?"

Esther holds both her hands up in apology. "Fine, fine. But I still don't understand why he must be the one to initiate contact with you. Doesn't Remy get that we live in the modern world where it's perfectly acceptable for women to make the first move?"

I roll my eyes at her and explain that me reaching out to him could look suspicious after how I treated him at my apartment. She only shrugs—a sign of submission on the matter—and holds up a key fob, jingling it around with a feline grin plastered across her face.

"What is that?" I ask.

She giggles. "This is the key to Harold's penthouse that overlooks Millennium Park."

Harold is some wealthy financier that lives in New York but comes to Chicago for business every few weeks. He's way too old for Esther to be dating, but she's taking full advantage of the fancy dinners and shopping sprees he takes her on every time he's in town.

"What kind of name is Harold? Please tell me this guy is younger than fifty."

She waves a hand at me. "Listen, I don't care how old he is. His body doesn't look older than forty, and he's got that George Clooney salt-and-pepper vibe going for him."

I laugh and snatch the key fob out of her hand. "And tell me why you have a key to his penthouse?"

I practically choke on the word—*penthouse* sounds so ridiculous to say out loud. I know Esther came from a background that had a bit more money than my family, but she by no means had *that* level of wealth. The way she feels so comfortable with the social elite will forever be a mystery to me.

Esther plucks the key fob out of my hand and explains how Mr. Big Shot is throwing a party this weekend, and she offered to help him with some of the preparations while he's in New York.

"Literally all I have to do is be there when his cases of champagne show up and organize the catering company schedule," she says with pure aloofness, flipping her hair over her shoulder.

"And fuck him when he gets into town?" I say with a little bit of venom in my voice. A part of me feels like this guy is taking advantage of Esther, and it really creeps me out that he is old enough to be her dad.

"Yes, I will be fucking him when he gets into town—more than once. But trust me when I say he wouldn't have to bribe me with a penthouse for that to happen. The man is phenomenal in the bedroom." She's practically purring.

I roll my eyes again, glad to know one of us is having good sex. My thoughts instantly shoot to my night with Dylan.

"All right, change of subject," I say as I squeeze my thighs together.

Esther is instantly laughing—she loves making me uncomfortable with talk of her sexual escapades. I stand and head to the counter to set my empty coffee mug down. Turning back toward Esther, I say a quick goodbye before heading out the door for work.

"You're coming, you know?" she says before I make it more than a few feet.

"Huh?"

"To the party this weekend. You need to get your mind off all this Dylan stuff. You're going to drive yourself crazy sitting around waiting for him to text you."

She's right. I haven't gone out since my date with him. I nod my head and tell her okay as I make my way out of the coffee shop and into the rainy city streets.

I finish my shift at the Lonely Olive and head back to my apartment. Remy sent me a few text messages with some updates on the case. Apparently, he found out there was a second guy named Connor Wilder who was working in cybersecurity for Ryland Corp. and quit shortly after my dad went missing. Conveniently enough, he was never interviewed as part of the investigation . If he was, it never went on record. He now works freelance, and according to Remy's FBI friend, he's been suspected of getting mixed up with some shady people and has hacked some pretty wealthy individuals all over the country. He worked as an inside man for the FBI on one of the big sex trafficking busts a few years ago. Remy seems to think it wasn't out of the goodness of his heart; the perpetrators just decided not to pay his blackmail, ignorantly assuming he was bluffing about the dirt he claimed to have on them. When I asked Remy why this guy hasn't been arrested for said blackmail, I was given an answer I already assumed—he's more valuable out of jail than in.

There's also a woman who was never interviewed but attended the company party that night. Apparently, she was here on a school visa from Ecuador and worked as an intern at Ryland Corp. Remy said he's going to try to locate her to see if she's still in the States. If she is, she would be here illegally, as her visa was never renewed after that year. I'm not going to hold my breath on him finding her—I would bet she's long since returned to her home country.

All my money is on Dylan. He must know something. The way he apologized to me that night in the hallway felt too personal. I've made up my mind that if I don't hear from him in the next week, I'm going to call him. Wouldn't be the first Remy rule I've broken.

I'm sitting in my apartment eating my favorite takeout from a Nepalese spot around the corner. Popping a plump little chicken momo into my mouth, I patiently listen to Esther go on and on over the phone about the hot guys who'll be attending the party this weekend. I'm starting to look forward to the event, even though I still feel awkward about how old Harold is.

"Are there going to be people our age at this party?" I ask skeptically.

"There will be people of all ages there. Don't be such an ageist, Cosette," she quips back.

I *am* being ageist, only because I don't see why anyone would want to hang out with people twenty years younger than them. I mean, the generational gap makes a huge difference in what you can even discuss when it comes to life experiences. If Harold is as old as I think he is, he was probably a full-blown adult when the first Mac came out—when Esther and I were getting keyboarding classes in elementary school.

Something outside my window catches my eye when I go to place my leftovers in the fridge. I walk up to the window, pull back the curtain, and see someone standing on the sidewalk across the street from my apartment. It's a male with a zip-up hoodie pulled over his head, smoking a cigarette. Normally, something like this wouldn't raise any red flags to me, but this guy is staring directly up at my window. He's near a light post, but the shadows and hood he's wearing block his features just enough that I can't make out what his face looks like. The hairs on the back of my neck stand at attention when I feel like I'm experiencing déjà vu.

"Hello? Cosette? Are you still there?"

Esther's voice on the other line pulls me back to reality, and I tell her about the strange man. She giggles, telling me I'm being paranoid and jokes that Remy has gotten into my head. I'm almost inclined to agree with her—until the guy begins walking down the street toward a black parked car. He walks directly under the light post, and that's when I see what my intuition was trying to tell me. His shoes.

I've seen those shoes before—outside my aunt's place the day I found the memory stick and took home all the case files.

Holy fuck.

It dawns on me that this guy was watching me and probably followed me home that night. I bet he was the one to break into my apartment. I quickly pivot to the front door and make sure it's locked. Then, I run back over to the window and shut the blinds.

"Esther, I need to go," I say, urgency in every word.

She senses it too because she's instantly drilling me with questions.

"Cosette? What's going on? Don't hang up on me. Do I need to come over there?"

She's barely taking a breath between questions, and I know I'm going to have to convince her I'm fine before hanging up on her— lest she show up here in the next thirty minutes. And with this creep outside of my apartment, that's the last thing I want her to do if this is the guy who broke into my place. Even though I would much rather not be alone right now, the reality is we are both safer if we each stay where we are.

"Listen, Esther, I'm fine. There's a strange man outside the apartment, and it's probably nothing. But…I'm going to give Remy a call just in case. Don't panic. I promise I'll call you first thing tomorrow morning."

With an overdramatic sigh on the other end of the line, she says, "Fine. But text me as soon as you talk to Remy about it."

"I will, I promise." And with that, I'm off the phone with Esther and dialing Remy as fast as I can.

He answers with a groggy voice—I must have woken him. I quickly apologize and then tell him about the man outside my window and how the man I saw outside my aunt's place looked suspiciously similar. It doesn't take much convincing—Remy is the overly skeptical one—and he tells me he's sending a friend to come sit outside my building until tomorrow morning. I'm informed his friend will drive a green minivan and that I need to text him as soon as I see him outside my window.

Within fifteen minutes, I see a green minivan with tinted windows pull up and park on the curb outside my place. I'm not sure what good it will do when the mystery man left before I could even explain to Remy what was going on. But I'm happy to know there's someone out there keeping an eye on things with the off chance he comes back.

After I finish getting ready for bed, I crawl under the covers and lie down with my eyes wide open. My brain is spinning with thoughts of who the man outside could have been. When I saw him outside my aunt's place, he definitely knew I had seen him because my dumb ass waved at him, thinking he was a new neighbor. And tonight, although it was dark, I had the creepiest feeling that he also knew I saw him.

Who would dare to stalk someone so boldly?

Unless.

Unless they're trying to intimidate me.

Does this man know that Remy and I are researching my father's case again? If this guy is trying to scare me, it's working.

But I refuse to give up on this. I *will* find my answers.

CHAPTER EIGHTEEN

The weekend arrived in the blink of an eye, and I can't believe it's already Saturday. Since receiving the anonymous note under my door, the days seem to blend into each other, with no fine lines to define the start and end. I feel like I'm suspended in this gray space of never-ending anxiety where my past and present are colliding and the crash never presents me with the answers I so desperately need. I'm lost, and the feeling of having no control over my life has recently left me moving through the hours of each day like a zombie.

Today is the day of the penthouse party that Esther has been so diligently preparing for, and if it wasn't for her texting me every waking moment about it this week, I probably would've forgotten about it. It turns out the few things Harold asked her to do turned into a whole party-planning job. Esther has been on the phone with vendors all week, organizing everything from service staff and catering to picking out what bottles of champagne will be served. Apparently, the DJ who's supposed to play tonight canceled last minute, and she's been having a full-blown panic attack about replacing him. Thankfully, Jeremy knows a guy who works at a few nightclubs in Boystown. Esther had to offer a stupid amount of money to get him to cancel his current gig and agree to work the party. But hey, it's not her money.

Unfortunately, I couldn't get out of working tonight but was able to bribe Chrissy into switching shifts so that I don't have to close. If I'm lucky, I should be able to get out of here by ten.

"Heard you went out with that tall, dark, and handsome guy," Chrissy croons.

She says it like a statement, but I know it's meant to be a question. Chrissy is the type of person who wants to know everyone's business so that she has something to talk about with the rest of the staff. I never tell her anything I don't want the whole world finding out, and that includes my dating life. I toss my hand up and feign ignorance.

"I don't know what you're talking about."

She sets a drink down in front of one of the drunk patrons who has been here pounding whiskey on the rocks for the past hour and a half. His name is Frankie, and he comes in once every two weeks, gets piss drunk, and then tries to leave without paying his tab. Jeremy warned him that the next time it happened, he would call the cops and refuse to serve him. Chrissy and I have a bet on whether or not he tries it again.

"Oh please, I have it on good authority that you know exactly what I'm talking about." She's turned to face me now, a feline smile plastered across her face. "You know, the new guy who was in here a few weeks ago. He was, like, obsessed with you."

"Oh yeah, Dylan. We went out to dinner a few weeks ago, and I haven't heard from him since," I say, crossing my fingers that she drops the topic. I still haven't heard from him, and my ego is officially bruised.

She lets out an annoyed breath of air. "Ugh, you're so boring."

If she only knew that my life has been the complete opposite of boring.

"You know me, good ole boring Cosette," I say, flashing her a sarcastic grin. "Hey, it's pretty slow. Do you care if I cut out early?"

Chrissy looks around the nearly empty bar, which has only a

handful of people, half of whom have already cashed out. She waves me off. "Yeah, yeah, get out of here and go to your fancy party."

I finish up my end-of-shift duties and take my apron off. After cashing out, I head to the back to grab my purse. Thankfully, the bar was slow tonight because I still need to head home and change for the party. I never would have made it there if I had to work the full shift. I pull my phone out to call a cab and notice I have five missed calls from Esther and a text message.

Esther: *Call me when you get this!*

I try calling her back on my way home, but she doesn't answer. If I know Esther, she's treating this party like it's her own and playing hostess.

I make it to my apartment and get changed in record time. Thankfully, I was able to do my hair and makeup before my shift, and by some grace of God, it's still holding up. Esther said the party was going to be cocktail attire, so I borrowed one of the dresses Harold bought for her the last time he was in the city. It's a blush pink mini dress with a built-in corset that fits my waist like a glove and makes my breasts look devastatingly full. The silky fabric drapes gorgeously and has an asymmetrical hem that cuts a little too high on one side. Paired with a pair of nude strappy stilettos that practically blend in with my skin, I feel like sex walking down the street. When I questioned the risqué hemline, Esther simply laughed and said, *How else are you going to find a hot guy to take home?*

Touché.

The taxi drops me off in front of a gorgeous building that looks like it was built in the early 1900s. I walk up and am greeted by a doorman, who quietly opens the door for me. I nod and thank him politely before heading to the concierge.

"Hello, my name is Cosette Emery. I'm here for Esther and Harold," I say a bit uncomfortably. The man behind the desk keeps an apathetic expression and looks down at what must be a list of names. I can hear the pages as he flips through them before setting the clipboard down and walking from behind the desk. He doesn't say a word to me as he starts toward the elevator. I assume I am to follow him, and by the time I catch up, he already has the elevator door held with the button to the 46th floor pressed.

He releases the door after I enter and is gone before I can turn around and thank him. As I ride the elevator up, I pull out my phone to text Esther.

> **Me:** *Tried calling you back.*
> *Riding the elevator up now.*

I place my phone back in my clutch as my nerves catch up to me. I've always found it hard to fit in with the wealthy. Hopefully, I can locate Esther sooner rather than later, so I'm not stuck having awkward conversations with wannabe sugar daddies.

The elevator dings, and the doors slowly open to a scene similar to a party from *The Great Gatsby*. People are everywhere—women in gorgeous dresses, men in fine tailored suits. Some are dancing, some are standing in close groups laughing and throwing back drinks. I make my way through the crowd, appearing to be invisible.

Good. The less I get noticed, the quicker I can find my friend.

The penthouse is nothing short of gorgeous. I'm pretty sure I've seen it featured in *Architectural Digest*, if not something very similar. Floor-to-ceiling windows, marble floors, marble archways. The furniture is a mix of mid-century modern and contemporary. No wonder rich people love to throw parties. I bet when this place is void of people, it feels cold, but right now, it's warm and inviting.

I make my way over to the open bar and order a glass of tequila on the rocks. I'm late, so there's no need to take it slow tonight. To the right of the bar, there's an open terrace where people are dancing and lounging on plush linen sofas. It's also where the DJ is set up, and I would put money on it that Esther is out there dancing the night away.

I gracefully move through the crowd and notice a few people flicking their eyes toward me like I'm out of place.

I *am* out of place.

I know absolutely no one.

I make a round of the terrace and still don't spot Esther, so I post up by the railing and admire the view of the park.

I can't believe people live like this. My whole apartment could fit inside half of this terrace. Enjoying the slight breeze on my bare shoulders, I feel a presence before I even have a chance to look over.

"Haven't seen you at any of Harold's parties before."

I look up to find a tall, lanky man with blonde hair shamelessly assessing me like I'm a product to be purchased. I'm wearing a dress that screams sex, and *this* is the first guy I attract?

I smile shyly at him and confirm his statement. "No, you haven't." I turn to face him so that I don't seem rude. Just because I'm not interested in this man doesn't mean I have to piss off the first person I come into contact with. "I don't actually know Harold, but my girlfriend does. She invited me tonight. How do you know Harold?"

The man throws himself into a long-winded story about how he met Harold, dropping names that are lost on me. I politely nod and casually take sips of my drink. I scan the party behind him, looking for Esther, and my eyes stop on another familiar face. I choke on my tequila and instantly start coughing.

Sitting on one of the linen sofas is Dylan, and he's staring directly at me. He's got his arm around a woman, who in return has a hand on his thigh . I quickly turn and cover my mouth to stifle my cough, unable to stop the pang of jealousy that briefly hits me at seeing him here with another woman . It's a completely irrational thought, but a thought, nonetheless. The blonde man who's been talking at me puts a hand on my arm and asks if I'm okay. I lift a finger up to him and manage to get out, "I'm going to find some water," before hurrying in the direction of the bar.

I grab a water and finally pull myself together, scanning the room again. I need to find Esther. A part of me is screaming to leave, but I know I need to stay. I need to try to make amends with Dylan so I can maintain some sort of relationship with him. I turn back toward the bar and ask for another tequila. As I lean over, I feel a hand grab my waist, a large body press up behind me, and hot breath against my ear.

"I was hoping you would show up," he says in a low, deep voice that makes the hair on the back of my neck stand up and my thighs tighten.

I grab my drink and slowly turn around to meet Dylan's eyes. His hand is still on my waist, and the other is positioned on the bar top, encasing me.

"I find that hard to believe," I say, breaking eye contact to take a drink. How was he hoping I would show when the man hasn't so much as sent me a text after our date? Not that I blame him.

He finally straightens and drops his hand from my waist. I let out a breath of relief. I was starting to feel like a trapped mouse, and he's the cat. He runs a hand through his hair and has a look on his face that tells me he's disappointed in my response.

"And why is that so hard to believe?" he asks.

I let out a snarky laugh. "Well, for starters, you're here with someone else."

Now he takes a step back, like the roles have reversed and I'm the prowling feline.

"And," I say, taking another sip of my drink for courage, "I haven't heard a peep from you since…that night."

My confidence wavers, and he can sense it. He's staring at me, his eyes burning through my soul. After seconds that feel like forever, I can't take the awkward silence. "That's what I thought. I need to find Esther."

I turn to walk away, but he grabs my arm before I can take more than one step. He pulls me close to him. "If I had known you would be here, I wouldn't have brought a date. I didn't begin hoping to see you until I arrived and saw Esther here." He grabs my drink and downs it, still clutching my arm. Setting the empty glass down rather aggressively, he turns his head back toward me. "And I haven't called you because you fucking kicked me out of your apartment that night after finding out who I was."

He says the last part like he's angry at me for doing it, and God help me, all my emotions from the past few weeks finally boil over. Ripping my arm from his hand, I say, "Can you fucking blame me?"

He gives me the same look he gave me in my apartment hallway when he realized who I was, and then it quickly turns into something more agonizing, like I've wounded him.

I can't do this right now. This is not how I was expecting my next interaction with him to be. I see a server walking by with a tray of champagne, and I reach for two, tossing one back and discarding the glass on the bar.

"I really need to find Esther," I say and turn to walk away.

"Cosette, wait. Please."

He's begging, and it sends a ripple of guilt through me.

"You don't want to keep your date waiting," I say and turn before I can see his reaction. Leaving him, I disappear into the crowd.

I venture deeper into the place; it truly goes on forever. There are a million different rooms, all filled with people. The concept is open, making navigation much harder because everything seems interconnected. I can't tell which rooms I've already been in and which ones I haven't.

Finally, I see Esther. She's sitting on a leather couch with a glass of champagne in her hand. The man sitting next to her has salt-and-pepper hair and a tan complexion. He's definitely giving George Clooney vibes. He must be Harold. I make my way toward them, and Esther spots me. She shoots up and waves me over.

"Hey! Oh my God, I tried to call you!" she says in a voice one decibel too high.

I can tell she's had one too many drinks, and pretty soon, she'll either be dancing on a table or pulling dear old Harold into the bedroom for some pillow talk. I take a seat next to her and give her a hug. She introduces me to Harold, who couldn't seem less interested, then leans over to whisper in my ear, "You'll never guess who is here."

I give her a look that tells her I already know, and before I can tell her to be discreet, she says, "Oh my God, you already saw him."

I down the rest of my champagne. "Yep."

Esther quickly starts apologizing that she didn't warn me, and I wave it off, telling her not to worry about it. She *did* try to warn me, after all—five times, to be exact. It was just an unfortunate situation that I missed her calls.

"I can't tell if you're mad at me or just mad at the situation. I thought you wanted to talk to him," Esther says, concern written on her face.

I can tell my mood is killing the vibe. She's not wrong in her assessment. I might not be mad at her, but I *am* angry. Angry about my dad. Angry that I'm having to scheme my way back into Dylan's life. Angry that the first guy to give me butterflies in years is wrapped up in this shit show. And angry that he's here with someone else. The last one is probably the most troublesome emotion I'm feeling right now.

I need to get my mind straight, be rational, and not let my feelings get in the way. I mean…it was just a one-night stand. Why do I feel like I have some claim on him?

And then there's the fact that he might be involved somehow in my father's disappearance—or, at the very least, related to someone who is.

There are a million reasons I should be putting my feelings aside, but a part of me has found this sliver of hope that he doesn't have a clue about any of it.

Even if using him for information turns out to be a dead end.

I look at Esther and put a hand on hers. Looking her in the eyes, I tell her, "I promise I'm not mad at you. I just really hate this entire situation. And you're right—I do want to talk to him. I just wasn't prepared for it to be tonight."

Esther looks at me and nods in understanding. "Then let's pretend he isn't here and embrace the open bar and great music."

She quickly turns and kisses Harold on the cheek—who is currently having a way-too-serious conversation with the man sitting across from him—then grabs my hand, leading me off the couch and onto the terrace where everyone is dancing.

Once we're out on the dance floor, Esther makes a hand motion to one of the servers, and he quickly shows up with a bottle of tequila and shot glasses. We throw back one, two, three shots before she sends him away. I'll be lucky if I remember the night.

We start to dance, and before I know it, we have company. Two men dressed in way-too-similar navy suits join us. The one behind Esther looks oddly familiar, but alcohol has officially kicked in, and in my haze, my brain can't place where I've seen him. He has sandy blonde hair swept back in feathery layers, creating a middle part that would make a teenage girl swoon in the nineties. Though he's dancing with Esther, his blue eyes pivot between watching her and looking over at me. His lips are full and have a slightly feminine shape to them. He's attractive but in a pretty-boy kind of way.

I spin around to get a better look at who's dancing behind me. If Esther's dance partner is pretty, mine is devastatingly handsome. He has dark brown hair that almost appears black and his eyes are a chocolate brown that look like they fade into his pupils. He's scruffy but not in an unkempt way—his facial hair is maintained and cut short to his face, framing his high cheekbones and chiseled jaw. He doesn't look like a man who wears a suit often, but my God, he's pulling it off spectacularly. I make eye contact with him briefly before I have to look away—this man is *uncomfortably* attractive and looks like he could wreck my life in a mere evening. This is someone who knows exactly what he's working with in the looks department and takes full advantage of the privileges it affords him.

He spins me so that my back is to him and places his hands on my hips to pull me back against him. His grip is firm, and I can't say I'm upset about it. He leans over and asks me what my name is. I don't tell him; instead, I turn my head and ask for his.

"Ladies first," he says again, in a voice made for sex.

I respond with a giggle and roll my hips a bit more dramatically to the music.

"This dress looks like it was made for you," he says.

Okay, now he's breaching a point of trying too hard.

"Thanks. It's a bit constricting, in my opinion," I say with a bit of venom in my response. I love a compliment as much as the next person, but can a girl at least get one that isn't textbook?

He laughs, a deep and delicious sound.

"Well, I'm sure we can find a room where you can relieve yourself of it."

Okay, I'm officially blushing. Thank God my face is turned away from him.

My eyes roam about the room and catch on Dylan. He's no longer with the woman he was with earlier. He leans against the terrace, white-knuckling his drink. If I didn't know any better, I'd say he's furious that I'm dancing with the mysterious dreamboat, and I'm too drunk to care.

I toss my head back and close my eyes as I let the music and alcohol take over. I will deal with the Dylan situation on a different day.

When I open my eyes again, Dylan is cutting through the crowd of people, making his way toward us. I keep dancing like I don't notice him.

"Mind if I cut in?" Dylan's voice cuts through the music. It's less of a question than a demand, and I hear my dance partner laugh again.

"No, baby brother , I think I'll hang on to her for a little while longer," the voice from behind me says in a domineering tone.

My eyes shoot open, and my movements become staggered. Did he just say *baby brother*?

Oh my God.

Did I happen to attract the *other* Ryland brother? The odds of that seem a little too slim. Suspiciously slim.

Holy fuck, I am way too drunk for this.

Quickly, I decide I'm not going to deal with it. Not tonight.

This can be tomorrow's problem, when sober me can break down this clusterfuck of an evening.

I push away from the older Ryland brother and walk off toward the bar. More like stumble off—it turns out I *am*, in fact, too drunk. The room begins to spin, and I make my way to the hallway, hoping one of these doors leads to a bathroom.

Passing three doors, all of which are locked, I'm relieved when the fourth opens, and thank the gods above—it's a bathroom.

I shut the door, locking it behind me, and head for the sink. I turn on the cold water and splash some on my face and neck. I've never been a puker, but with the way the room is spinning right now, I wouldn't put it past me. I sit on the edge of a giant bathtub that looks more like a jacuzzi and drop my head between my knees.

My dress is suffocating, and I have an urgent need to get it off. Reaching my hands behind me, I grab hold of the zipper and pull. The corseted bodice opens, and I can finally get a decent breath.

A knock at the door pulls me out of my drunken stupor, and I instantly panic.

There's no way I can get up right now.

I need to sit this out until I can get the room to stand still.

"Occupied!" I yell out.

Another knock.

"Cosette, it's me! Open up."

The voice is muffled through the door, but I know it's Dylan standing on the other side.

Maybe if I just stay quiet, he'll leave.

"Cosette, are you okay?"

His voice sounds pleading now.

No. Absolutely not.

I am *not* letting him see me like this right now.

I slide down from the edge of the tub to the floor so I can lean back against it.

I'm just going to wait this out.

I let my eyes drift shut for a moment.

I'm jolted awake by a loud *crack* and the bathroom door swinging open.

Dylan is standing in the doorway, looking a little out of breath.

"What the hell are you doing in here?" I ask, my speech stringing words together in a slur.

"Why the fuck didn't you answer me?" he yells—or at least I

think he's yelling. "We need to get you home."

Home. Yes. I want to go home.

I look up at him, still confused as to how he got in here.

"I locked that door," I inform him.

"Yes, and I broke it down. Can you walk?" he asks as he bends down to stand me up.

I *think* I can walk.

I stand up with his assistance, and my dress starts sliding down, revealing my breast.

Oh my god.

I forgot that I unzipped it.

Dylan stares down at me, and I think I hear him mutter some profanities under his breath. He pulls my dress back up to cover me while reaching around to pull the zipper up just enough to hold it in place.

He grabs my face and says something about leaving, then wraps his arm around my waist, holding me upright as we walk out of the bathroom.

We make it to the elevator, and the ride down feels like it takes a decade.

Once we're in the lobby, Dylan sits me on a leather sofa near the entrance. He leans down to ask me again if I'm okay, and I answer him with a nod.

He tells me he'll be right back, and I settle into the sofa, perfectly content to sleep here for the night.

I come to in the back of a car, Dylan sitting next to me.

Slowly sitting up, I quickly become aware I'm still very drunk.

"Where are you taking me?" I demand.

With a shake of his head. "I'm taking you home, Cosette."

I accept this answer and lay my head against the door of the car.

The next time I'm awake, we're at the door of my apartment.

"Cosette, I need you to open the door."

I look at Dylan in a daze and stare down at my purse, digging my keys out.

Within moments, we're inside, and he walks me to my room and lays me down on the bed.

He makes to stand, but I grab his arm and pull him toward me. It's dark in my room, and I can't place his face well, but I can feel him staring at me.

"I'm sorry," I say softly.

"It's okay… Everyone, at some point, has consumed too much alcohol."

I move my hand from his arm up to his face and place it on his cheek.

Shaking my head. "No, not for that."

I feel a pair of lips softly press against my forehead.

And then I'm sleeping.

CHAPTER NINETEEN

My eyes slowly adjust to the sun shining through my blinds, warming my face. I look around my bedroom and try to recall how I got home last night. I bring my hand up to my head—it's pounding—and my stomach is in knots. Rolling over, I see a bottle of water and some ibuprofen sitting on my nightstand. That's strange. I've never once drunkenly prepped for my hangover the next day.

Sitting up, I grab the water and down the meds. Placing my hands on either side of me to hold myself up, I close my eyes and try to recall the night prior. I remember showing up at the penthouse and seeing Dylan, drinking a lot of tequila, champagne, and then more tequila. I cringe at the thought of alcohol.

Oh my God. I remember dancing with Dylan's older brother. What did Remy say his name was? That's not relevant right now—I need to remember how I got home.

I search my memory for any clues, and then it hits me like a crashing wave. Dylan breaking into the bathroom, us in a car together, him walking me to my bedroom.

Fuck.

If I hadn't scared him off the first time he was here, I definitely did last night. I look down at myself and notice that I am not in the dress I wore last night. Reality hits me that he probably changed me into the oversized band tee I'm currently wearing. Before my brain can process another memory, I hear a clanging noise in the kitchen. Panicked, I shoot out of bed and fling my door open, praying that it's my Aunt Billie. I walk down the hallway and see Dylan standing in my kitchen, leaned over my coffee maker with an overly focused look on his face.

Clearing my throat to make my presence known, he stands and turns toward me with an empathetic look.

"I, uh…wanted to have coffee ready for you when you woke up, but I can't get your machine to work." He lifts a hand to rub the back of his neck.

"It's okay. It's been broken for the past few weeks. Haven't gotten around to ordering a new one," I say, walking to the fridge to pull out another bottle of water. "Want one?" I offer to Dylan, and he nods, grabbing it from my hand.

I head to the couch and plop into it.

"Listen, about last night—"

"It's okay," Dylan says. "This whole situation has been weird. Can we just start over?" he asks, a corner of his mouth pulling up in an attempted smile.

I meet it with a half-smile of my own. "I'd like that."

He walks over to join me on the couch, and I notice he's wearing sweatpants and a T-shirt—not the fancy designer suit he was wearing at the party. Looking over at the door, I see a duffel bag sitting on the ground and glance back at him with confusion on my face.

"I was supposed to stay at my brother's last night. I grabbed my bag out of his car before I brought you home," he answers as if he read my mind.

"Oh my God, your brother. I was dancing with your brother." I hide the embarrassment on my face with my hands.

"Yeah, that's an image I would like to block from my memory indefinitely," he says with a hint of bitterness in his tone.

"I didn't know he was your brother," I say in defense.

"I know. At that point, I don't think you would have known who Brad Pitt was if he walked up to you," Dylan teases.

I'm beyond mortified, recollecting the events of the evening, but at least Dylan is being nonchalant about it.

"You broke the bathroom door." I throw the accusation in his face before I can stop myself.

"Yeah… I've already sent a contractor over to Harold's to fix it." Now it's his turn to look embarrassed.

I nod my head. I guess having unlimited amounts of money at your disposal has its perks. Remembering the awkwardness of dancing with his brother, the idea of Dylan staying with him feels off.

"You were going to stay at your brother's last night?" I ask, my tone laced with skepticism.

"Yeah, why?" He arches a brow at me.

"Well, maybe it's just my drunk brain not remembering the situation correctly…but it didn't seem like you two were super thrilled to be around each other," I say.

Super thrilled was a light way of putting it. If my memory serves me—which it might not—Dylan had a look of hate in his eyes when he was talking to his brother. And now that I'm running through the scene in my mind, his older brother calling him *baby brother* sounded more condescending than endearing. Definitely some disdain there.

Dylan turns and starts tinkering with the coffee maker again, clearly uncomfortable with my assessment. I stay silent and wait for him to respond. He lets out a contemplative "Hmm" and then quips, "Our relationship is complicated."

He pops the plastic backing back onto the Mr. Coffee, then flips the switch, and I'll be damned—it starts brewing coffee. My fucking hero.

He turns back to me, and his eyes are like lasers cutting through me.

"You know, for how drunk you were last night, you sure did

pick up on a lot. Maybe you weren't as drunk as you appeared to be, and it was all a ploy to get me back to your apartment," he says with a sensual tone.

I scoff and immediately wave off his theory. The last thing I was trying to do was have him back in my apartment again. Remy would be losing his shit right now.

"I'm a bartender, Dylan. It's my job to sense when two men are about to throw down."

Now it's his turn to scoff. "We were not about to throw down," he replies defensively.

"Could have fooled me."

I stand and walk over to the kitchen to pour myself a cup of liquid gold from my repaired coffee maker. As I place the pot down, I feel two hands land on either side of me, caging me against the counter. This guy really likes to pull this oddly sexy male dominance move. He presses his body against my back, giving me no room to turn around and face him.

Leaning down toward my ear, close enough that I can feel the heat of his breath, he says, "I'm not going to lie to you, Cosette. Watching another man touch you—brother or no brother—made me feel like I could rip someone apart."

My heart is pounding, and my hand is visibly shaking, so I set my coffee cup down on the counter. This is the side of Dylan Remy warned me about. As sweet as he has been with me, he feels violent right now. I push my body back, taking him off guard just long enough for me to turn around and face him.

"You know, after only sleeping with me once, one could claim you're acting a bit possessive."

This situation feels like I should be more mindful of how I speak to him, but a piece of me wants to see how far I can push him. I want to prove he isn't the bad guy, because if he is, then I'm in way over my head with the way my body is responding to him right now. He doesn't say anything, just stares directly into my eyes and then slowly drags his gaze to my lips.

Damn it. If he tries to kiss me right now, I know I won't stop him. But before I can say anything else, his mouth is on mine, kissing me slowly, his tongue tracing my lips and exploring my mouth like a choreographed dance. His hand comes up to cup my face, and he finishes his torturous movements with a bite to my bottom lip that has me letting out a soft moan. He pulls away just enough to look at me again before he rests his forehead against mine.

On an exhale, he says, "I haven't been able to stop thinking about you. Ever since you kicked me out, I have been going out of my fucking mind thinking about you, Cosette."

His earlier dominant tone is gone, replaced by one that borders on pleading. I place my hands on his chest and apply the slightest amount of pressure, creating the smallest pocket of space between us.

"This is really confusing for me," I say, and it's not a lie. I have no idea what the fuck it is that I am feeling right now. "And…to be honest, it's kind of fucked up, considering the whole *my dad went missing from your dad's headquarters* thing."

There.

I said it.

The elephant in the room has officially been addressed. He steps back from me and nods, keeping his gaze on the floor.

"Do you think my family was involved?"

What the hell? Did he really just ask me that?

I don't know what to say because *of course* I think his family was involved. But if I admit that to him, he's never going to tell me anything about that night. I shake my head and almost whisper my response.

"I don't know what I think."

I don't realize I'm crying until Dylan raises a hand to wipe a tear that has fallen down my cheek. I look up at him and say, with a little more confidence, "I don't know what to think because there isn't enough evidence to even form a theory on what happened to him."

I push away from him and start walking toward my bedroom, needing to put some space between the two of us before my anger gets the better of me. I can't believe he had the nerve to ask me if

I thought his family was involved. I collect some fresh clothes and a towel to take a shower. When I turn to walk back out toward the bathroom, Dylan is standing in the doorway.

"What are you doing?" he asks.

"What does it look like I'm doing?" I respond, holding up a towel. "Do you mind?" gesturing for him to get out of the way.

He pivots his body, allowing me barely enough space to squeeze by him. Quickly, I walk to the bathroom and set my things on the sink counter so I can turn the shower on.

I shut the door to give myself some privacy, but Dylan is *again* standing in the doorway.

My eyes widen. What the fuck is he doing following me around like a lost puppy? Before I can throw a bitchy comment about him acting like a stalker, he steps into the bathroom and asks if he can join me. I look at him in disbelief shake my head.

"I'm not having sex with you right now, Dylan," I say a little aggressively and reach for my hairbrush, gently combing the snarls out of my bedhead.

I see him in the mirror take a step closer to me. He reaches up and, to my surprise, he takes my brush and starts brushing my hair for me. My mouth hangs open, empty of words. I don't think I've ever had a man, other than my father when I was a little girl, brush my hair for me. It feels extremely intimate and nurturing.

We both stand there in silence while he meticulously brushes away all the frizziness the drunken night left. When he's done, he sets the hairbrush down on the sink and looks at me. I watch him stare down at me through the mirror, and I finally muster up the courage to turn toward him. He gently lifts his hand and tucks some of my loose hair behind my ear.

"I'm not trying to have sex with you. I'm simply asking if I can join you in the shower," he says, finally breaking the silence.

"That sounds a whole lot like trying to have sex with me," I reply.

He smiles the most gorgeous smile I've ever seen and holds his hands up.

"I promise to behave. Plus, it's not like I haven't already seen every inch of your naked body." He finishes the statement with a wink.

Asshole.

I wave my hand dismissively. "As you wish," I say, turning to check the temperature of the water.

It's steaming hot, just how I like it. Esther is always lecturing me about how super-hot showers are actually terrible for your skin, but I absolutely love them. I lift the oversized tee over my head and pull down my white panties. Not exactly the sexiest pair I own, but in this moment, I'm not too concerned about being sexy. I step into the shower without giving Dylan another glance and let the hot water wash away the previous night.

I hear the curtain pull back and Dylan steps in behind me while I lather my body with my favorite soap that I buy at one of the markets in Wicker Park. I hand it over to him, and he starts to lather himself.

I glance down and take in his gorgeous body, my mouth slightly parting as the soap suds roll down his muscular abdomen. *Jesus, Cosette, pull yourself together*. I bring my eyes back up to his face, and he's smiling like the Cheshire Cat.

"See something you like?" he drawls in a low voice laced with desire.

I turn my head around so fast I practically give myself whiplash. "Nope."

I grab my shampoo to lather my hair, but I'm stopped by Dylan when he pulls my hands down.

"Here, let me."

I look at him with an eyebrow raised. "You want to wash my hair?"

He steps closer, his body a hair's breadth away from mine.

"Yes, I want to wash your hair. Does that make you uncomfortable?"

One hundred percent it makes me uncomfortable—but not for the reasons it should. My mouth responds before my brain has a moment to rationalize my answer.

"No, I just… I've never had a man ask to wash my hair before."

"Well, maybe you aren't dating the right men," he says while he lifts his hands and begins massaging the shampoo into my hair.

My eyes practically roll to the back of my head, and my body languidly relaxes back into his. I can feel the length of him, hard against me, and it almost distracts me from what he just said.

"Dating?" I manage to hum out.

"Mmhmm," is his only reply.

He continues to work the lather and then pivots me so that my head is under the water. I let him finish washing my hair, and as a thank you, I wash his. I'm glad to have his eyes closed and covered in suds so I can unabashedly stare at all the features of his face. He is quite beautiful, with his angled cheekbones and almond-shaped eyes, perfectly framed by thick, well-manicured eyebrows. He clearly shaves daily, but a slight shadow of facial hair peppers his jawline and neck.

Pivoting him under the water, I tilt his head back so he can rinse off. My hands have a mind of their own and trail down his chest, landing on his abdomen as I take in the rest of his physique. He clears his throat, and it rips me out of the trance I'm in. I drop my hands and reach for a towel as I step out of the shower. Dylan follows me out, and we both dry off and get dressed.

I exit the bathroom and head back into the living room to sit on the couch, where I will probably stay for the rest of the day. My hangover is starting to kick in full force, and the only thing I can imagine doing right now is binging *New Girl* and shoveling down take away stir-fry noodles.

Grabbing my phone from the couch cushion next to me, I notice that Dylan's is sticking halfway out from the couch. It must have slid down there when he was sleeping last night. I look around the corner to see if Dylan is still in the bathroom finishing up. Noting the light on and the door closed, I take my chances and grab it.

It's obviously locked, but he has several notifications that have collected on the screen, and it doesn't look like Dylan has them set to private. I hold down on the messages and watch as all the notifications expand to show me exactly who has been texting him. There are a few names I don't recognize, one of which is a female name.

Summer Rhodes. What a ridiculous name.

I swallow my irrational jealousy and move on to reading the rest of the names. I hear a toilet flush and panic. Quickly, I pull up the camera app on my phone and snap a picture of his screen so I can look them up later. I press the lock button to make the phone go dark and quickly shove it back between the couch cushions.

A few moments later, Dylan walks out, and I lazily scroll on my phone, trying my best to look as innocent as I can.

"I have to run to my dad's to check in with his nurse," he says, like he feels guilty about leaving.

I honestly didn't expect him to stay as long as he has, but I look up at him with doe eyes anyway.

"Ok… Umm, thanks for taking care of me last night," I say and quickly look back down at my phone.

I hear his steps making their way closer to the couch, and when I look up, he's looming over me. He bends over, placing a hand on the couch arm, making our faces almost level.

"I'd like to see you again." His tone is demanding but doesn't hold as much confidence as he usually exudes.

"Okay. I, uh… I'm sure we'll see each other around."

I try to act as aloof as possible without coming off as rude. I mean, we did just bathe each other, for Christ's sake.

"Planning on getting shitfaced at more penthouse parties?" he asks with a smirk.

"Don't you know? It's my favorite pastime."

I return his sarcasm and giggle.

"Seriously, Cosette. I want to see you again, and I don't mean just running into you."

He waits for me to answer his request, and I oblige.

"Fine. When would you like to see me?"

"Every day if I could, but I'll settle for tomorrow night as a start."

His smile couldn't be more charming. I tell him that I work tomorrow, but he's persistent and convinces me to come over to his apartment after my shift.

He gives me a long, sensual kiss that leaves me breathless.

After he pulls away, I see him start to pat down his pockets and I already know what he's missing. Reaching for his phone, still shoved into the cushions, I hold it up and ask, "Looking for this?"

Grabbing it, he serves me another delicious smile and leaves my apartment. As soon as he's gone, I call Esther and tell her everything. She's practically screaming with excitement over the phone. I'm not sure exactly what she's so excited about. I'm pretty much fake dating someone to get information on his family, and even worse—I think I might actually have feelings for this guy.

After I finish telling Esther about my intense morning, I ask her how her evening played out. She gets giddy and asks if I remember the guy she was dancing with before I stormed off. I gasp in offence at her *stormed off* comment but then try to remember.

"Umm… I vaguely remember an attractive blonde man," I say, quickly running through the memory in my head. I remember thinking he looked familiar but couldn't place him.

"Does Landon Wexford ring a bell?" she asks in a giddy, schoolgirl voice.

Landon Wexford. *Holy shit, that was him.*

No wonder he looked familiar—I was just reading the article about him in the newspaper. He's even more attractive in person. Leave it to Esther to start dating the mayor's son.

"As in, future mayoral candidate Landon Wexford?" I ask as a laugh breaks out of my mouth.

She continues to swoon over the guy and tells me how Harold passed out drunk, and Landon asked her to go home with him. And of course, she slept with him. And of course, she has a date with him next weekend.

I lean back, kick my feet up, and settle in for all the details. This is my favorite thing about being Esther's best friend—I get all the tea on her romantic interests. The mayor's son might be the most high-profile person she has dated, and I can't wait to hear all the juicy details Esther is going to spill.

After my phone call with Esther, I remember the photo I took of Dylan's notifications and instantly open the picture to look at the names.

Four messages from Clive Ryland—Dylan's older brother.

A single message from Summer Rhodes. *What a ridiculous name.*

Another message from Landon. No last name, but considering my conversation with Esther, I think it's fair to assume Dylan knows Landon Wexford.

And three messages from a *C. Wilder.* I pause, my focus narrowing on that name. Could this be Connor Wilder, the ex-cybersecurity guy that Remy mentioned to me? Considering he used to work for Ryland Corp., I don't think it's too far off to assume it is. After all, *Wilder* isn't exactly a super common name. I set a reminder in my phone to call Remy about it tomorrow. I also need to get an update on the leads he said he was looking into. If Dylan has a connection to this hacker, I'm going to find out why.

CHAPTER TWENTY

After a much-needed early night to bed, I actually feel sort of refreshed, considering how miserable I felt less than twenty-four hours ago. I don't have to be at The Olive until later this afternoon for my shift, so I take my time meandering around my apartment, slowly getting ready for the day. Sipping my coffee from my newly repaired machine—*thank you, Dylan*—I text Remy and let him know that I have some things to discuss with him and ask if he has some free time today to chat. Setting my phone down, I open my laptop and do some digging on the people Dylan communicates with.

I start with Summer Rhodes, hoping that with a name like that, it won't take long to find a social media profile. The first thing that pops up is a local real estate site. Summer has a headshot and a cheesy bio about how passionate she is about luxury real estate. As I expected, she's the woman Dylan was with at the party. She's absolutely gorgeous, a walking Barbie doll. In her photo, she has beautiful long blonde locks that look like she just left the salon with a fresh blowout. Striking blue eyes, high cheekbones, and lips that even I wouldn't turn down. There's a tinge of resentment, but I remind myself I don't know this woman, and she may be a really nice person. Also, who am I to get jealous of who Dylan dates? It's not like I have any intention of a relationship with him beyond getting information on my dad's whereabouts. A flash of him washing my hair while our naked bodies were pressed against each other inconveniently enters my mind, and I squeeze my eyes shut to force it away. Maybe I do feel something for him, but realistically, I could never see it through. The irrational side of my brain is screaming at me, but I need to stay focused, and I can't do that if I allow my feelings to run astray.

I exit the real estate page and start a new search for Connor Wilder. I get absolutely nothing other than an obituary for an eighty-seven-year-old man in California and a LinkedIn account for a CPA in Virginia. Just as I'm about to click on another search result, my phone pings with a text from Remy saying he's free to chat now. I pick up the phone and immediately call him.

"Hey, kiddo, whatcha got for me?" he says as a greeting. The "Hey, kiddo" catches me off guard. It's what my dad used to say to me when he answered the phone. It's endearing hearing it from Remy, and I get a slight ache in my heart because I would do anything to hear my dad's voice again.

I tell him about my evening at Harold's party and my morning with Dylan, obviously leaving out the shower part. I tell him about the notifications I found on his phone and explain how I can't seem to find any information on Connor. Remy tells me he's not surprised and that people like Connor usually keep a low profile on the internet due to how many shady people he works with.

"Hang on a sec, I have a picture of him from my guy at the FBI. I'll email it over to you," he says and then goes silent. I hear him typing over the phone, and then he's back.

"I'm going to Dylan's apartment tonight for a hangout…or a date…or something," I tell Remy awkwardly. I hear him take a deep breath before he very seriously tells me not to get attached.

"I'm not going to get attached, Remy. I need to get close with him, so he trusts me enough to talk about stuff." What that stuff entails, I'm not sure, but I've made up my mind that any information is better than no information. "Plus, if I'm at his house, maybe I can do some snooping when he isn't paying attention. I already found those notifications on his phone; maybe I can get it unlocked and see what kind of relationship he has with Connor." As soon as I say his name, the email Remy sent me pings my inbox. I open it up and see a photo of a very familiar face.

"Holy shit," I say under my breath.

"What? Cosette, what's going on?" Remy asks from the other line. I push back from my laptop, placing my hand over my face. Esther has no idea how big of a payoff Harold's party was for me. I'll have to remind myself to thank her later.

"Cosette, do I need to come over there?" Remy demands through the phone, and I'm snapped back to our conversation.

"Sorry, I'm fine. It's just… I met this guy," I say with a calm tone. I don't want to freak him out. He already doesn't like that I am interacting with the younger Ryland son, let alone a shady hacker.

"What? When?" he demands.

I explain to him how Connor came up to me when I was at Harold's party. The conversation was superficial, but it was definitely him. Harold seems to be quite connected; I guess that's a result of being ridiculously wealthy. Damn, I wish I would have known it was him. I would have spent way more time chatting him up. I have a feeling if I keep attending these over-the-top events, I'll run into him again. Hopefully, with Esther dating Landon, there will be plenty more parties in the future.

"You need to be extremely careful around him, Cosette. Connor Wilder only looks out for himself. He's no stranger to switching sides and working with the bad guys if it suits his pockets."

Remy, as always, sounds way too serious, but I'll heed his warning. I change the topic to the other leads Remy was following up on. I learn that his friend at the FBI is sending over all the surveillance footage from the surrounding businesses and buildings of Ryland headquarters.

"It's all been looked at before by the police department, but you know how I feel about their investigation. I wasn't able to get my hands on it before. There's most likely nothing there, but it doesn't hurt to check it out." He pauses, and I can sense there's more to this than he's sharing.

"And…?" I ask.

"And this is why you need to be careful who you speak to. He had to request the footage from Chicago PD, which means they'll know the case is being looked at again," he says, exasperated.

"And you're worried there are still some shady people working in the department?" I follow up.

"Yes. My guess is that by next week, if not sooner, the Ryland family will be notified and will continue their efforts to keep this case under the rug."

I hum in agreement. Not ideal, but not the end of the world. I've done a pretty good job of being ignorant to everything the past five years. Why would anyone think that I would act differently now? I end our call with a promise to keep him updated if I find anything else out, and he does the same for me.

My day flashes by, and I'm now standing in the back of The Lonely Olive, listening to Chrissy talk to the barback about how one of the new bartenders made out with a patron in the alley last weekend. I'm not annoyed with the gossiping—it comes with the territory of the service industry. What annoys me is hearing her tell the story in a judgmental tone, like she's never done the same and then some. I grab a stack of clean glassware and head out to the front. I'm really hoping for a steady night because I need the tips. Since Jeremy started training me to manage the bar, my shifts have gotten longer, but I spend less time actually serving the bar. I need to muster up the courage to ask for a raise in my hourly wage. It's either that or I give up on getting promoted to manager. At this rate, I won't be able to afford rent next month.

Thankfully for my landlord, the bar is packed. The Bears are playing Monday night football, and even though we aren't technically considered a sports bar, we have three TVs that Jeremy puts the game on. I'm not a sports person, but like any true Chicagoan, I'll watch pretty much any Chicago sporting event. Unless it's the White Sox—the only time you'll catch me watching a White Sox game is if they're playing the Cubs. My dad was a huge Cubs fan and would always treat us to bleacher seats a few times a year. They almost never win, but there's something magical about Wrigley Field, a cold beer, and scarfing down a Chicago dog. My father never let me drink alcohol, but when we would go to a game, he would allow me to have half of one beer. "Just to wash down the dog," he would say with a wink. I haven't been back to Wrigley Field since before he went missing, and I can't bring myself to drink an Old Style without him. My father worked so hard to make sure I got to do "fun things," as he called them, and wanted for nothing. Being a teenager wanting for nothing is impossible no matter how much money you have, but he did his best to make sure I felt content with our middle-class life. I was more than content. My biggest regret now is never telling him that.

I finish out my shift as the bar starts to clear out. The Bears lost again, which can sometimes mean people hang around to drink beer and console each other while repeating, "Next year, next year." Or, if the team really had their asses handed to them, everyone goes home to sulk. Tonight was the latter. I cash out and check in with Chrissy, who is working the closing shift again. No complaints here. I make sure there isn't anything she needs help with and grab my stuff to head over to Dylan's.

Dylan texted me his address earlier today while also trying to convince me to let him pick me up from work. I refused, explaining to him that serving shifts don't work like a nine-to-five and there's no way of knowing if I get off at ten or one in the morning.

The taxi drops me off in front of a gorgeous building in the Gold Coast. I forgot to text Dylan I was on my way, but I'm already here and it might be fun to surprise him. I step into the lobby with the assistance of a silent doorman. This place looks like it should be on the front of a West Elm catalog—all the furniture gives off a mid-century modern vibe with a contemporary twist. I scan the room, and my eyes land on the front desk. I casually walk up and greet another silent and stoic-looking man.

"Hi, I'm here to see Dylan Ryland. He's expecting me," I say with a smile.

"Ahh, yes. Mr. Ryland did say he was expecting someone. Do you mind if I see your ID?" The man behind the desk reaches a hand toward me.

Well, I wasn't expecting to be carded upon entry, but I suppose that's what security is supposed to do. I dig around in my purse and find my beat-up old Fossil wallet that Billie gave me my senior year of high school. I hand the pleasant man my ID, and it's returned with a silent nod of the head.

"Thank you, Ms. Emory. Please follow me." He leads me to an elevator with giant gold doors that look a little obnoxious. He presses the button to the eighteenth floor and waves me in with his hand.

"Have a wonderful evening, Ms. Emory." I hear him say as the giant doors close. The elevator is oddly silent—no music, not even a ding when the doors open. I step out and glance back down at my phone to check his unit number again. I start to round the corner before I hear what seems to be an argument. Pausing to be nosy, I zero in on what sounds like three men having a debate.

"Listen, I don't know what the fuck Dad was instructing you to do, but I'm not depositing any more money into that account."

My eyes widen when I realize the voice belongs to Dylan. I press my back against the wall but lean my ear closer to the corner.

"You don't get to just show up here and act like you know what the hell is going on. I've been practically running this shit for the past four years," another voice says. This one has a deeper tone, but I don't recognize who it is.

"Actually, I have legal documents that say otherwise. And you! I don't know how the fuck you play into all this, but anything your dumb ass is involved in can't be good," Dylan retorts to someone else.

"I'm involved because my dad is the motherfucking mayor."

Holy shit. That's Landon Wexford.

"Yeah, still don't see how that has anything to do with my father's finances. Just because my father bankrolled your dad's campaign doesn't mean the same will be done for yours."

Damn, Dylan is a hard-ass when he wants to be.

"All accounts payable, with the exception of anything that keeps our lights on and the business running, will be on pause until I have a moment to figure out the shit show you've been running for the past few years. Trust me, I would love to have Dad give me all the rational explanations for why each person gets their piece of the Ryland pie, but he's not lucid enough to do that right now."

Dylan's last sentence must have held some weight because the other two voices are silent.

"You're right, Dad isn't lucid and once I convince the board he also wasn't lucid when he appointed you to be CEO you won't have to be bothered by this *shit show* any longer. You have no idea what you're fucking with, baby brother."

Okay, so the deep voice is Clive Ryland.

"Enlighten me, Clive," Dylan spits.

Silence sits stagnant in the air, and then Dylan breaks it. "And tell Connor to stop fucking calling me—it's not helping his cause."

"You need to answer those calls Dylan, and if you don't want to deal with him then—" Clive is cut off before he can get another word out.

"I don't *need* to do shit, and I swear to fucking God Clive, if I see that asshole out following me again while I'm on a date, I *will* deal with him…and not in the way he's used to." Dylan's voice is raised just enough to show he's serious, but level enough to be terrifying.

What does he mean by deal with him? That sounds ominous as fuck. Was Connor the person Dylan saw when we were out? I think back to what he said to me when we were in the car, something about seeing someone he didn't want to see. No wonder he laughed at me when I jumped to conclusions about it being an ex-girlfriend.

Distracted by my own thoughts, I don't hear the last part of their conversation before I hear footsteps moving closer to me. Shit. If they see me, they'll know I was eavesdropping. I take a few steps back, turning to look where the other hallway leads. I silently make my way toward the stairwell and quietly inch the door open. Realizing I'm a little out of breath from my nerves, I slide my back down the door until my ass hits the floor.

I'm starting to second-guess myself and this whole thing. Who do I think I am, Nancy fucking Drew? I close my eyes and try to remember why I'm doing this. My father's face pops into my mind along with the guilt of living an ignorantly blissful life for the last five years. I guess it wasn't exactly blissful, but that doesn't excuse the ignorant part. Once I've collected my thoughts, I stand and walk into the hall to make my way back to Dylan's apartment.

I knock and anxiously wait for him to answer. What feels like an eternity passes, and no one comes to the door. I pull out my phone and shoot him a text letting him know I'm here. A minute later, he's swinging the door open with a perturbed look on his face.

"Hey," I say while awkwardly lifting a hand to wave.

"Hey… Hi, come in," he replies without looking me in the eye. He turns and gives me his back while walking into the apartment. I follow him in and scope out my surroundings. His apartment entrance leads to a long hallway with a few doors on each side. The walls are an off-white with a contrasting white molding near the ceiling. At the end of the hallway, the place opens to a giant open-concept living room and kitchen. The place is enormous, with floor-to-ceiling windows that overlook Lake Michigan on one side and downtown on the other. The furniture resembles the design down in the lobby; everything is very minimalist. There's an L-shaped couch that fills the room but has a low-profile back that somehow seems to make the room look even more sprawling. There isn't a lot of personality in here, and it feels more like a property staged for an open house. I turn to look at the kitchen and see Dylan walking around the giant waterfall island made of beautiful black marble.

He's on his phone and has his lips closed so tight his mouth looks like a straight line. I'm suddenly feeling like I shouldn't be here—maybe he changed his mind about wanting to see me tonight.

"Everything okay?" I ask.

Dylan snaps his head up to look at me, and his mouth is open like he's surprised to see me in the room.

"I can go if it's not a good night to hang," I offer.

Dylan's eyes go wide, and he instantly gets defensive. "What? No, no. Please stay." He sets his phone down and throws his hands up like he's surrendering a fight.

"I'm so sorry, how fucking rude of me. I've just had a really crazy day; this work stuff never really stops." He runs a hand through his hair, bringing it to rest on the back of his neck. "Do you want something to drink?" He motions to the counter where a little wine fridge sits. "I have wine, or if you're not into drinking, I also have sparkling water."

I smile and tell him wine is fine. My eyes dart to the fridge; I haven't had anything to eat since this morning. As if reading my mind, Dylan says he ordered in some Indian food and that he hopes I like Chicken Korma. I almost choke because I don't just like Chicken Korma—I love it, and it's kind of eerie that he ordered it.

Dylan hands me a glass of wine, and I settle in on the enormous couch. For as stiff as it looks, it's really quite comfortable. He takes a drink of wine, and I mirror him. For a moment, we just stare at each other in silence before I break away and look down at my phone. I've made the decision that I will not be sleeping with him again. I need to keep myself focused, and I can't do that if my emotions are involved.

"Are you okay?" he asks, placing a hand on my leg, his touch practically searing through my leggings. I move to reposition myself in a way that pulls my leg out from under his touch.

"I'm fine. Are you okay?" I ask, and before he can answer, I add, "You're the one that welcomed me in with a sour mood… You've barely made eye contact with me since I walked in."

He looks like I made him uncomfortable with my comment. Rubbing the back of his neck, he lets out a low and drawn-out moan that is drenched in irritation. "I know… I'm sorry." He finally gives in and shares, "I had some unwanted visitors before you showed up, and they left me in a shit mood…but I promise I'm over it. I'm better now that you're here."

Unwanted visitors? That's a strange way of describing his brother. He sets his wine glass down to refill it but doesn't pick it up. I turn my body completely toward him and take my turn at putting a hand on his leg. His line of vision goes straight to it and then back to my face.

"Do you want to talk about it?" I ask, hoping I can get him to admit who was here.

"No, I don't, actually. It would be a complete waste of energy," he says, giving me a smirk that doesn't match his tone.

Well, it was worth a shot. He tops off my glass, and I turn away from him. This is starting to feel awkward. I don't know what to talk to him about. I should leave, but I've convinced myself that any time spent with Dylan needs to result in some kind of progress on information. Going home now would be a complete waste of time. Looking back over, I notice that Dylan is eyeing me with a look of contemplation . Before I can get a word out, he dives forward and kisses me.

The kiss takes me off guard, and I awkwardly move away, spilling my wine on the couch.

"Oh my God," I shriek, setting my glass down on the coffee table. "Oh my God, I am so sorry," I say again and shoot up toward the kitchen. I can hear Dylan saying something, but my mind is drowning him out with the thought of how the couch I just spilled red wine on must have cost a fortune. I instantly start opening drawers, looking for paper towels or something to clean up the mess I made. I'm halted by Dylan's hands on my waist.

"Hey, hey. It's okay," he says, pulling me in toward his body. "Don't worry about it; it was my fault anyway."

What the fuck is he talking about? Don't worry about it? There is red wine all over his beautiful white couch. He presses into the crook of my neck and inhales, leaving a kiss before he pulls away. He stays silent as he walks to a cabinet and pulls out a bottle of cleaning solution and paper towels. I watch him as he meticulously cleans up the stain over the course of ten minutes. I have to admit, I'm impressed. I thought he was going to pull some rich-guy move and say he would just order a new one.

After he finishes, he invites me back over to sit next to him on the other end of the couch. I oblige him and take a seat, sitting up with my back pin straight. I know my unease is rolling off me because he looks at me with an empathetic look.

"Listen, I had a really long and stressful day. Why don't we put on a movie and relax until the food gets here?" he says while pulling me into him.

I'm folded under his arm while he scrolls through the list of movies on HBO. I hate how comfortable I feel curled up next to him. My body is molded to his side so perfectly, as if we are two puzzle pieces fitting just right. He's warm and smells of something earthy. Without thinking, I take a deep breath in, inhaling his intoxicating scent. He notices right away and looks down at me with a lifted eyebrow.

"You smell…nice," I say awkwardly before tucking my head back down on his shoulder. I feel his body jerk as he chuckles to himself, which then makes me laugh.

"I'm sorry, that was super creepy of me," I say as I continue to laugh, placing a hand to my face to cover the pink hue I know is settling into my cheeks.

"Don't be embarrassed, Cosette. I'm quite pleased that you like the way I smell."

The evening ends up being a pleasant one. The takeout Indian food was delicious, and to my delight, Dylan is a Star Wars fan. We had a moment of nerding out over it and debated with each other over movie rankings. When the movie ended, we had a Star Wars marathon and continued with another. Halfway into the second movie, I look over to see Dylan sleeping, his phone conveniently sitting on the coffee table, begging for me to look through it.

I pick it up and see that Dylan has two missed calls from Connor and multiple text messages. I instantly think back to his comment from earlier when he mentioned not wanting to hear from him anymore. I swipe up and, to no surprise, find the phone is locked with a passcode. I set it back down on the coffee table and look back over at Dylan, who is still sleeping like a baby. I need to make a quick exit before I find myself snuggled up next to him and staying the night, I slowly ease myself out from under the blanket we share and head to the door.

Placing my shoes on one at a time, I realize I had one too many glasses of wine and lose my balance. I catch myself on an entryway table, knocking over a key bowl to the floor. Wincing, I pause to hear if I woke Dylan. Not hearing anything, I continue toward the door.

"Are you seriously going to leave without saying goodbye?" Dylan says in a low voice laced with the remnants of sleep. Before I can turn around, I feel his warm hands sliding around my waist and pulling my back against his chest. He dips his head to the crook of my neck and inhales, causing my skin to prickle. His massive body envelops me, and for a moment, I forget that I was leaving.

"I didn't want to wake you," I say on a soft exhale. He slowly turns me around and tilts my chin up so that I'm looking into eyes that are either hooded with sleep or something else entirely that sends heat down to my core. In response, he slowly leans down and seizes my mouth with his.

He kisses me languidly, with his hands slowly roaming up the curves of my body until one hand is on my face and the other is in my hair. I'm completely pliant, my body clay for him to mold into whatever position he desires. Coming to my senses, I place my hands on his chest, giving a slight shove to break the kiss.

"Stay," he says, commanding me with his lustful gaze to agree.

I shake my head and fully remove myself from his hold. "I can't. I need to get home." I'm playing a dangerous game with my emotions right now, and if I stay the night, I know exactly what is going to happen. I came here with the intention of getting information and ended up thoroughly enjoying myself. Dylan might be the first person that I have laughed with outside of Esther in a very long time.

"Can't or won't?" Dylan asks.

His question takes me off guard and feels a bit pushy, snapping me back to reality. The answer is both—I can't stay here, and I won't stay here. I don't answer, but the look I shoot him hopefully speaks for itself.

He grabs my arm and pulls me back into an embrace. "I'm sorry, I didn't mean for that to sound like I'm pressuring you. I just…" He pauses and steps back, putting space between us. "I had a really good time tonight. Your presence is quite addicting, Cosette." He finishes with a smirk that sends that heat rushing back through me again.

He lets his eyes linger on me suggestively, and if I didn't know better, I'd think he was trying to seduce me into staying.

With a smirk of my own, I say, "I think you're addicted to something other than just my presence." And with that, I lean in to kiss him on the cheek and walk out the door.

I'm halfway to the elevator when I hear Dylan yell down the hallway, "Wait!"

I turn around to see him jogging toward me. Jesus, this guy doesn't know when to quit.

"Dylan, I'm not staying the night. Please don't make me say it again."

"No, no, I know. What are you doing tomorrow night?" he asks.

"Tomorrow night?" I'm confused by the urgency—it's almost one in the morning, and he's asking me about my plans tomorrow night?

"Yeah, there's this political fundraiser tomorrow that I have to attend, and I thought…"

Before he finishes, I'm already shaking my head. There is a multitude of reasons why I will be declining this invitation. The first being, these events are usually very formal, and there is no way I'll have time to find something in less than twenty-four hours. And secondly, I can't spend three nights in a row with this man. My head is already a mess of emotions that are diverting me from what I should be focusing on right now.

"Please, Cosette, I really hate these things and having you there will really turn the evening around."

I look at him with wide eyes, finding it really hard to say no to him. As if he's sensing my discomfort, he says, "Just think about it and let me know tomorrow."

And with that, he kisses me on the cheek and walks back toward his apartment.

CHAPTER TWENTY-ONE

"Cosette, you have to go."

I'm sitting in my kitchen, simultaneously sipping my coffee as I shoot a glare toward Esther while she pleads for me to attend this event tonight.

Turns out it's a gala being hosted on some enormous boat to raise funds for Landon's campaign. Esther has been invited but not as Landon's date. Apparently, he isn't trying to make any relationships public prior to being elected. Being a single man in politics isn't ideal. Most people love to elect a family man. But apparently, being a playboy doesn't reflect well in the polls either.

"Come on, it'll be so much fun. Free drinks, pretty dresses, and a lot of wealthy men to fawn over," she says with a sly smile.

Of course, Esther is excited about this; she thrives at these sorts of events.

"Plus, it's going to pretty much be all the same people that were at Harold's. So, it's not like you haven't already molded into that crowd before."

I scoff at her choice of words, if molded means letting my

anxiety get the best of me while I consumed copious amounts of alcohol and locking myself in a bathroom. Sure, I *molded* into the crowd.

The thought alone of that night has my face heating with embarrassment. I'm still suffering from hangover anxiety from the drunken mess Dylan and I made of Harold's bathroom. Esther told me that Harold doesn't know anything about it, as the door was repaired before he could notice, but I'm still internally mortified. What a wild reality to live in a home so large that you don't notice a whole broken bathroom door. I'm about to tell Esther that I'm not going to this stupid, showy political event when a thought pops into my head.

Connor was at Harold's. Maybe he'll be at this event. I mean, he seemed pretty connected at the party the other night. I even saw him conversing with Landon a few times. Fuck. I have to go to this event.

Placing a hand on my face to hide my embarrassment, I say, "Esther, I know you love these over-the-top events but they really aren't my scene. I'll probably just end up making an ass of myself again." In my head I've already conceded to going, but she doesn't need to know that yet.

"That is such a pathetic excuse not to attend this, and you know it. You have to stop being so in your head about what scene you fit into. You're a gorgeous, intelligent woman. Every scene is your scene." She shoves my shoulder playfully like she's gently trying to knock some sense into me. "Plus, you're the one who has been saying you want to get information. How exactly do you plan to do that if you refuse to spend time with these people?"

Esther shoots me a look with her eyebrow raised, patiently waiting for me to tell her she's right. She has a point, and we both know it.

Before I can concede, we both turn our heads toward a knock at my door. Confusion lining my face, I toss my hands up to show Esther I have no idea who it could be.

Casually padding over to the door, I open it to a man holding a black box with a white ribbon tied around it.

"I have a delivery for a Ms. Cosette Emory," he says with a friendly smile.

"Umm…that would be me."

He hands me the box and then untucks a clipboard from under his arm.

"Sign here, please."

Setting the box down on my kitchen counter, I return to the man and jot down a quick signature.

Closing the door, I look over to Esther, who is all but glowing with excitement.

"Oh my god, Cosette, who is sending you gifts from Saks?" she squeals.

Shaking my head, I grab the card that's tucked under the perfectly tied white ribbon and open it.

I hope this helps in convincing
you
to join me this evening.

- D.R.

I slowly hand the card off to Esther before she pounces on me for it and proceed to open the box.

My jaw goes slack upon opening it. I hold up the most gorgeous dress I've ever seen. It's a navy silk gown with a cowl neck connected to two thin diamond straps that form one long diamond strand that cuts straight down the back of the dress, connecting to another cowl that dips low enough to make undergarments near impossible to wear. It's scandalous, and I love it. I turn, holding it up for Esther to behold with a grin on my face that probably makes me look a little insane.

"Well, that settles it. It would be an absolute crime to let a dress like that go to waste. You, dear friend, are definitely going to the party." she says, clapping her hands in celebration.

I quickly pull out my phone to send a text to Dylan.

> **Me:** *The dress was very convincing… see you tonight.*

> **Dylan:** *I'll pick you up at 7. ;)*

Esther and I spend the rest of the day on Michigan Avenue picking out a new dress for her to wear tonight. We've decided to get ready together at her house since I will be borrowing some accessories from her to pair with the dress Dylan sent. She also has the bigger bathroom. I haven't told Remy about tonight's event, but I figured I would fill him in if anything newsworthy came out of it. The last thing I want to do is make him more worried than he needs to be. I don't doubt any of the things or evidence Remy has shown me about my dad and my uncle, but the more time I spend with Dylan, the harder it is to believe he had any involvement. I have mixed feelings about the whole thing for two reasons. One, if Dylan has zero involvement, then my feelings for him could possibly go somewhere. Two, if he has zero involvement, then he will have zero information for me to extract. I want my cake and to eat it too.

I'm currently sitting on Esther's bed, drinking a glass of champagne while she does my hair. Esther has always been amazing at updos; she did both of our hair for every high school dance we attended. My dad was always thrilled because it saved him a ton of money by not having to take me to a salon.

"All done!" Esther says with a tone of pure satisfaction in her work.

"Now go put that dress on. I'm dying to see how it fits you." I slip into the closet, take the gown off the hanger, and step into it. Due to the thin silk fabric, I opted to forego any undergarments tonight. The cool silk feels sensual on my skin, and instantly, I'm thinking about Dylan. Pushing the thought of him out of my mind, I slip on the black strappy Louboutin heels that Esther loaned me and walk out to show her the finished product.

"Oh my God, Cosette. You are pure sex in that thing," she says with lifted brows.

Blushing, I turn to face Esther and find myself stunned by the sight of her. The teal dress she picked out earlier today makes her look ethereal. It has a high neckline that cuts in toward her neck to show off her beautiful clavicle that leads to her dainty, sharp-cut shoulders. Like mine, her dress also dips low in the back, but unlike my flowy silk that drapes my curves, her dress hugs her all the way down to mid-thigh, showing off just how spritely a figure she has.

"Oh, Esther. You look beautiful," I say as I walk up to stand beside her.

After we ogle ourselves in the mirror and Esther gets her one hundred selfies, we head to her living area to finish off the bottle of champagne and wait for our rides.

"Are you sure you don't want to ride with Dylan and me?" I ask.

Esther got weird when I offered for her to come with us, claiming she didn't want to crash our date as a third wheel. We argued back and forth over it until I finally gave up. If she wants to take a cab, that's her prerogative. We are literally going to the same place, so if she wants to show up alone, fine by me.

A part of me feels self-conscious that maybe it's because she doesn't agree with my scheming with Dylan, but I quickly shove that thought aside. I know Esther would never judge my actions when it comes to my dad.

While we were out shopping today, I admitted to Esther that I was mainly going to this fundraiser in hopes of bumping into Connor. She knows about all the missed calls and messages from him to Dylan and also thinks there's more to that story. If there is, I'm determined to find out. Something inside me is buzzing, like I'm close to unlocking something.

Call it intuition or whatever weird sixth-sense nonsense people like to claim they have. I don't think it's a sixth sense, but more like an awakening from ignorance.

I look down at my phone to see it's seven o'clock on the dot as Esther's door buzzer sounds. It's Dylan, and he's right on time.

Stepping off the elevator, I see Dylan standing in the lobby. He's wearing a black suit cut perfectly to his body with a matching black shirt underneath. He looks sinful, and as I trail my gaze up his body, our eyes meet. He's gazing at me like I'm something to worship, and my knees go weak. I gracefully waltz over to him and lean in to place a kiss on his cheek.

"Hi," I say.

His lids are lowered, and his lips are slightly parted as if he is in awe of me. He takes a deep breath, closes his mouth, and finally says hello in a gravelly tone more suited for the bedroom than the lobby of this apartment building.

He raises a hand and points toward the exit. "After you," he directs.

I turn and walk out the door to where a black Rolls Royce is waiting outside. The driver opens the back door for me to climb in, and I can't believe I'm actually riding in a car that costs more than my aunt's house. I settle into the butter-soft leather material and lift my chin to watch as Dylan slides in on the other side of me.

"A Rolls Royce, Dylan? You really pulled out all the stops tonight," I say sarcastically.

I can see the expression on his face change, and I sense that maybe I hit a nerve with that comment. I forgot how upset he was with our first encounter when I led him to believe I was uncomfortable with how wealthy he was.

I laugh and quickly try to recover.

"I'm just joking, Dylan. This is very nice. Actually, I've always wanted to ride in one," I say, and give him a half-smile.

"It's my father's car. He insisted I take it tonight for the gala. I personally think it's a little over the top, but that's the type of show he likes to put on for these types of things," he says.

There's a melancholic undertone to his statement, and I remember Remy telling me his father was ill, which is why Dylan is now acting CEO of Ryland Corp. Dylan also mentioned on our first date that his father was sick, and it was what brought him back to the States.

I start to wonder what kind of illness his father has, and then I panic at the thought of him possibly attending this gala tonight. I'm not sure I'm ready to meet the Devil himself.

"Umm…will your father be attending tonight?" I say, trying to hide the nerves I know are shaking my voice.

Dylan snaps his gaze over to me and looks confused by my question. "No, my father will not be attending tonight," he says, his tone sharp.

He notices my discomfort in the way he responded and reaches for my hand.

"Sorry. I don't usually talk about it… My father has dementia. He has good days and bad days. When he insisted on the car, he was completely lucid. But tomorrow, he won't even remember there was a gala to fuss over."

My heart breaks for him. My grandmother had dementia in her later years before she passed. I don't remember because I was so young, but my dad always told me it was like losing someone over and over again. That every time they forget you, your heart breaks all over again. When they finally pass is when you find peace, and then you feel guilty for feeling relief instead of grief.

"I'm really sorry, Dylan," I say as I place my other hand atop his and give a little squeeze.

He looks at me, his piercing green eyes silently deciding if my empathy is genuine. He doesn't respond to my apology, but the corners of his mouth tip up in a slight smile, and that's enough to know he's not upset about what he revealed to me.

He trails his eyes down my body, and I can tell his mood has instantly changed. I clear my throat, bringing his eyes back up to mine.

"Thank you for the dress. It fits perfectly," I say, still wondering how he knew what size to buy.

"It does. Maybe too perfectly," he agrees with a wink, his voice sounding predatory.

I finally give in to my curiosity and ask how he knew my size.

He smiles a wicked grin that tells me he's very satisfied with himself before he leans in so close I can feel the heat of his breath on my ear. "The image of your body is seared into my mind, Cosette. It wasn't hard to find something that would fit it perfectly."

His words burn through me, and I know my face is flushed. My God, how long is it going to take to get to this damn gala?

Dylan notices he's riled me and sits back with a satisfied look on his face. I cross my legs to give myself some relief from the pressure that's building in my core. And as if the higher powers heard my desperation, the car comes to a stop. I look out the window to see a large boat decked with beautiful string lights twinkling against the dark backdrop of Lake Michigan. Esther is walking up the ramp to enter the event and I wonder how she got here before us.

Dylan must read my expression because he quickly says, "I had Roy take the long route. You'll be able to catch up with Esther soon enough."

My eyebrows draw down in confusion. "Why the long route?" I ask before my brain has time to decide whether the question even matters.

"Because once we get in there, no one is going to be able to keep away from you, and I selfishly wanted a few extra minutes of you to myself."

I blush at his response, and even though it sounds a little possessive, it's also kind of sweet.

"Well, we can sit in the car for a few extra minutes if you'd like," I offer.

That earns me a chuckle from him, and he quickly informs me the cars waiting behind us would not be pleased.

We exit the car and make our way up the ramp to board the boat. There are more people on this boat than I expected. I quickly survey the crowd and notice a few familiar faces from Harold's party. We walk below deck and enter an area that resembles a nightclub. There's a DJ in the corner and lounge-style tables with low seating. I quickly spot two bars and remind myself I will not be drinking to the excess of Harold's gathering.

As we make our way to the front of the boat where most of the attendees are, I take in the view of people mingling around white table-clothed high-tops while servers dance around with trays of bubbling champagne. Toward the front of the boat, I see a table of hors d'oeuvres and an ice sculpture that looks like some kind of bird. I take a sip of the champagne Dylan handed me to mask the laugh that escapes at the sight of it.

"Care to share what you find so amusing?" Dylan whispers in my ear.

"I didn't know ice sculptures were still a thing," I say innocently.

"Only for the most obnoxious," he replies, and we both laugh as we approach a group of people near the bar.

Dylan is pure elegance when he mingles with the group. You can tell he grew up in this world with the way he confidently molds into the circle like he was already leading the conversation. I notice he has a slight mask when conversing, one that comes off when it's just the two of us. I smile and nod at the comments directed toward me and only chime in occasionally when I feel confident that I actually know what the conversation is about.

Swiveling my head, I spot Esther perusing the food table. Looking back at Dylan, I nod my head toward her and politely excuse myself to join my friend in finding a snack.

"Anything good?" I ask as I sneak up on her.

"Oh my God, Cosette. You scared me," she says, gently slapping my shoulder with her free hand.

We laugh, and I ask her how the evening has been for her. It's hard to believe we've already been here for an hour, and I'm just now getting a chance to catch up with her. Being fake nice with strangers sure does make the time go by.

Esther seems a little agitated and explains to me that Landon has a few other women here who were invited by him. She's not one to get jealous, but I think she's realizing just how sleazy politicians can be. After venting to me, I can tell she's already over it and eyeing up her next fish in the sea. Esther is absolutely gorgeous and has a catch of a personality. If Landon doesn't want to entertain her tonight, another man will. And she knows it.

While Esther and I stuff our faces with teeny tiny bites of food, I hear my phone go off. Setting my glass of champagne down on the table, I grab it out of the small black beaded minaudière Esther loaned me for the evening and see I have a missed call and text from Remy. My heart drops into my stomach. I never told him I would be coming here tonight. I quickly swipe up on my screen to read his message.

> **Remy:** *They know… The Rylands know your father's case is being looked at again.*
>
> *Be careful, Cosette. Call me when you can so I know you're okay.*

"Fuck," I say under my breath but not quietly enough that Esther doesn't hear me. I quickly shove my phone back in my purse.

"What's going on?" she asks, her voice laced with worry.

I quickly explain to her what I just learned and decide I'm due for another drink. I ask Esther if she needs anything from the bar, and she shakes her full glass of wine in a no-thank-you gesture.

I leave Esther at the table talking to a very attractive, middle-aged gentleman in a finely tailored suit, and head toward the bar. I weave my way through the crowds of people, and my eyes land on Dylan's. He's now locked in a conversation with what looks to be the real estate agent he was with at Harold's. Her hand rests on his chest as she throws her head back to laugh at something he must have said. Seeing my eyes dart to her hand and then back to him, he instantly takes a step back out of her touch.

He has guilt written all over his face, but I'm too concerned with what Remy just told me to care. We aren't exclusive. He can entertain whoever the hell he wants.

Okay, maybe I care a little. But right now, it's the least of my worries.

Finally making my way up to the bar, I order a glass of red wine and contemplate whether I should call Remy or simply send him a text message. While I'm waiting for my drink, I feel a warm hand graze my arm to gently turn me around. It's Dylan, and before I can say anything, he's already word-vomiting all over the situation.

"Cosette, I'm sorry. It's not like that. She's my real estate agent. It's not…"

I raise a finger to his lips to put a stop to the overly defensive response he's giving me and marvel at how soft they feel against it.

"Dylan, it's fine," I say softly. There's more disappointment in my tone than I intended. The way he's going into defense mode tells me that she's not just his real estate agent, and the guilt on his face says that it is like that. Maybe not tonight—tonight, he's here with me. But there is no doubt in my mind he's been intimate with this woman at some point. A part of me is relieved to be disappointed in him; it makes this situation so much easier.

"Really, it's fine," I say again as I grab my glass of wine off the table. "This is your world, and I know you need to show face at these events. Why don't you make your rounds, and we can catch up later?"

I don't need to hang on his arm all night, marking my territory. Dylan's brows pull tight, and he looks visibly flustered, like he doesn't understand my rational tone. He looks out into the crowd of people, and I notice something on his cheek. A faint outline of pink lipstick remains from when I kissed him in greeting earlier. I raise my hand to wipe it off but then pull it back, deciding to leave the whisper of myself on him.

"Seriously, go enjoy yourself. I need to find the ladies' room anyway. I'll catch up with you in a little while," I say.

He looks back at me and nods his head, his mouth turned down, and I know he's battling inside himself on whether walking away from me is the right choice to make, wondering if I'm testing him. I'm not—I actually want to be distanced from him right now. I can work out the Barbie realtor situation later if I decide I care enough. I make the decision for him and walk toward the lower deck of the boat, where I know the bathrooms are located.

I walk around the boat instead of through it to avoid the crowd of people that have now made their way to the lounge area of the party. Noticing I'm finally alone, I place my hand on the railing and look out into the dark lake waters. I can only see a few feet ahead of me, but I know across the lake on a clear day, you can see straight over to a beach my parents used to take me to when I was a young girl. The beach was in Indiana, with sand dunes that seemed as big as mountains to a little girl. I remember climbing to the top with my parents and then sliding down the sand like you would on a snowbank. I would sit in the sand at the bottom of the dune and run my hands through the sun-warmed grains.

Sometimes, on *really* clear days, we would stand on the edge of the shore, and my father would point out the Chicago skyline across the lake. He would always mumble, "So close, yet so far." We would spend the entire day there, eating nachos and ice cream from the concession stand before we loaded up in the car, taking a little bit of the sand dunes back with us. The journey home would feel like forever, probably because of how tired my little body was from the long day. But I would always wonder why it took so long to get home when we could see the city from the beach. So close, yet so far.

I blink back a tear before it can escape and lean my body back against the side of the giant vessel. Just like looking out toward the city skyline with my sandy toes in the water, these memories of my dad make me feel so close to him, yet so far away. God, I miss him.

I drag my phone out again and call Remy. It rings once, and he answers with urgency, worry oozing through the phone.

"Cosette, did you get my text?" he asks quickly.

I tell him I did and also fess up about where I am. When I ask him about the likelihood of Dylan knowing, he starts to ramble about how the family lawyer knows, which means the family knows. He continues to lecture me for a few minutes and then begs me to stop seeing Dylan and to let him and his FBI friend deal with figuring this whole thing out.

I don't agree to any of the requests he is asking and lie about losing service so I can get off the phone.

I spent years letting the system try to figure this out, and it failed. The police, the FBI—the system failed. It failed me, my father, my uncle, and it failed my aunt. I'm tired of standing on the sidelines. I have my in with Dylan, and damn it, I'm going to use it.

Tucking my phone away, I turn to head back toward the party. I stop before I can take another step and see a dark figure standing a few feet in front of me, smoking a cigarette.

His presence feels ominous, and I start to panic as I wonder how long he's been standing there and what he may or may not have heard me say to Remy. I straighten, smooth out my dress, and consider if I turn around and walk the other way, it'll look super suspicious.

I start to walk forward and plan to just ignore the man, but before I get close enough to see his darkened face, he speaks.

"Cosette Emory, right?" he asks.

Okay, could this guy be any creepier?

"Umm…yes?"

"Bored of my brother already?" he says, finally turning to face me as he tosses his cigarette overboard.

Holy shit. Alarm bells are blaring. Clive fucking Ryland. What did he hear?

He walks over to me so smoothly I swear it looks like he floated over. He places himself between me and the railing, our bodies practically touching. I look up at his face, and he really is quite beautiful. What is with this family and their ridiculous good genes? He looks so different from Dylan, and I remember Remy telling me they are half-brothers—Clive being much older than Dylan, from Mr. Ryland's first marriage.

I lift my chin and look directly into his eyes in defiance. I'm not going to let him intimidate me.

I don't answer his offensive question about being bored of his brother. Clearly, there is some sibling rivalry between the two of them. With Clive being the eldest son, I'm sure he wasn't thrilled with Dylan waltzing in this year and taking over the company.

"You really are exquisite. I can see why he's so enamored with you."

Before I can say anything, he continues to talk.

"Why he can't stay away from you, even though it would be in his best interest." He lifts a hand off the railing and places it a mere inch away from my head. Leaning in close to my face, I see his eyes dart to my lips.

I finally find my voice. "What are you talking about—his best interest?"

He smiles, and my God, this man is alarmingly beautiful. He smells of tobacco and mint as he begins to speak again.

"I can't blame him, though. I'd be lying if I told you I haven't been thinking about that body ever since I got my hands on it the other night."

Oh God. He's talking about when we were dancing. I was pretty drunk, but I remember those roaming hands. The fire in Dylan's eyes when he saw me dancing with his brother. I swallow down a whimper.

"And then you show up tonight in this dress. You must be trying to torture me. Or…" He runs a hand down my side, pinching the fabric of my dress and rubbing it between his fingers. "Maybe it's my brother who's trying to torture me. He is the one who bought it for you, after all."

I shift my body, making the fabric fall from his fingers. "This is highly inappropriate," I manage to say on a gasp. This man has me so rattled, and my brain is screaming at me to get out of this situation as quickly as possible.

He laughs and steps to the side, allowing me to shift past him. "Yes, I agree, Cosette. This whole situation is inappropriate." At that, he turns and walks in the opposite direction.

I let out an exasperated breath and clutch my hand to my chest. What the hell was that all about? I can't tell if he was threatening me or coming on to me. Maybe both.

I need to get the hell off this boat.

CHAPTER TWENTY-TWO

I make my way back to the front of the boat, where I see Esther chatting it up with a few people I recognize from Harold's party. I instantly regret walking over when I see Summer standing in the group. God, she's even more gorgeous in person, with her perfect hair, perfect complexion, and perfect tits. She's wearing a plunging neckline that shows them off, and even I can't stop staring at them.

"Cosette, where have you been? I was beginning to think you went overboard," Esther says jokingly.

Before I can laugh at my friend, I hear a woman say sarcastically, "What a shame that would be."

I turn my head, and to no surprise, realize it was Summer. Here we go—let the pettiness begin. I've had about enough of people attempting to intimidate me for one night, so I turn to face her, extending a hand.

"I'm sorry, I don't think we've met. I'm Cosette," I say to the gorgeous blonde.

She looks down at my hand and back at my face with the most fake smile plastered on.

"Oh yeah… You must be Dylan's new flavor of the week," she says in a melodic voice. She chuckles while flipping her hair over her shoulder, exposing even more of her cleavage. "Heard he found you in some dive bar out in the west side. Let me guess, he left you a nice tip? That's something I've always admired about him; he always takes care of the help."

The help? Alright, now she's just being plain nasty.

In the corner of my eye, I see Dylan approach the circle, curious to know what the two of us are talking about. Esther steps up beside me, and I can tell she's a little concerned with the tension between me and Barbie. But I'm not going to let this woman bait me into making a scene.

If she wants to be funny, let's be funny.

I laugh—a little too maniacally. Stepping up to her, I say, "Flavor of the week? No, no, no." I laugh a little more, stepping even closer. Let her think I'm a little crazy. People don't like to fuck with crazy people. "Dylan isn't lucky enough to get me for a whole week. Actually…" I pause, looking over my shoulder directly into Dylan's eyes before I turn back to Barbie. "I think he's gotten enough of a taste of me tonight."

I take a sip of my wine without breaking eye contact.

"But maybe tonight's your lucky night. I think Dylan might be willing to settle for something a little more *vanilla*."

Stepping back, I lean an elbow on the high-top table everyone is congregating around and drain the last dregs of my wine. Setting the glass down on the table, I turn to Esther.

And as if on cue, she says, "Refill time."

We link arms and walk toward one of the servers carrying a tray of champagne, both lifting a glass off and setting the man's balance off just slightly. I throw him an apologetic look and turn back toward Esther.

Esther is dying laughing—literally bent over, cackling. When she finally rights herself, she's singing my praises.

"Oh my god, Cosette. That might have been single-handedly the most entertaining thing I have ever watched you do." She starts to laugh again. "I mean, what the hell is that woman's deal, calling you a flavor of the week in front of all those people?"

"Forget flavor of the week, she called me *the help*. What's wrong with being a bartender?" The comment got under my skin more than I would care to admit.

I shake my head. "Women can be so petty when it comes to men."

Esther laughs some more while nodding her head in agreement. Her laugh is contagious, and I can't help but let out a giggle myself.

"Oh, I almost forgot to tell you!" she exclaims.

She pulls a napkin out of her purse and shoves it at me. I look down at it and see a name, phone number, and address written on it.

"Esther, what is this?"

"What does it look like? It's that Connor guy's number and the address of an after-party tonight. He invited us to come once the boat docks."

I could fucking kiss Esther.

Just when I thought this night was going to turn out to be another road to nowhere, my gorgeous, charming, genius friend comes in with the win I so desperately need.

"You're fucking amazing, you know that?" I pull her in to kiss her on the cheek. "The pull you have over men, I'll never understand, but I will also never complain about it." I finish on a chuckle as I look down at the napkin.

"I actually didn't have to use too much charm. I think this guy has eyes on you, Miss Sexy Dress. The second I told him I was here with you, he couldn't pull the pen out fast enough."

I raise an eyebrow. "Oh, nowwww you're here with me?" I'm going to be giving her a hard time about not riding with me for the rest of the week.

"Shut up. You know I don't like being a third wheel." She gives my shoulder a shove.

"When does the boat dock?" I ask impatiently.

She looks down at her phone. "In forty minutes."

We continue to entertain ourselves for the next thirty minutes before Esther stops our conversation to give me a warning.

"Incoming," Esther says, and I look up to see Dylan making his way toward us. "I'll leave you to it. Find me when the boat docks, and we'll catch a car to the after-party."

I nod and watch my friend leave me to deal with the awkward aftermath of Barbie and Dylan.

I'm truly over it…I think.

What happened with Dylan was fun, but I need to be realistic. I'm not shocked to find out he's a fuckboy who has a "new flavor" every week. He's gorgeous and extremely wealthy. I would be shocked if he wasn't sleeping with beautiful women regularly. How can I be upset? I'm using him to get info on my dad. I need to keep emotions out of this.

"There you are," he says as he strolls up to me with the most casual air about him.

"Here I am," I reply, a little less casually.

"I'm sorry about Summer. That was insanely inappropriate for her to say to you." He places a hand on my arm, and I swear I feel a shock of something.

"Hmm," I hum. "But she's just your realtor. Tell me, Dylan, did you sleep with her before or after she sold you your million-dollar apartment?"

Oh shit. Guess I'm not over it.

Flustered, he looks up at the sky and lets out a deep breath.

"Listen, I'm not going to lie to you. Summer and I have been intimate before, but it's not like that now."

I shake my head. I don't have the emotional capacity for this interaction, so I do what I do best—I shut down.

"It's fine, Dylan. I really don't care," I say in a tone laced with defeat.

"Don't say that, Cosette. Don't say you don't care." His voice is pleading, and it tugs on my heart just slightly.

I turn my body looking for the exit. The boat should be docking any minute, and I can't get off this vessel quickly enough. But my line is blocked by Clive.

My god, does this guy have a knack for showing up at the most inopportune times.

"My, my, my, is the happy couple already fighting?" he says, setting a hand on my shoulder and swinging me back around to face Dylan.

"What did you do, baby brother? She catch you with your pants down?"

"Shut the fuck up, Clive." Dylan's voice is laced with poison.

"I tried to warn you, Bro. Juggling two women at the same time is not as easy as you think," Clive says with a shit-eating grin on his face.

The vessel gives a slight shake, indicating that the boat has docked.

Thank God, because I can't handle any more of this bullshit.

Dylan explodes and shoves Clive, and that is my cue to leave. While the two brothers are tossing insults at one another, I turn and head toward the exit.

Before I get out of earshot, I hear Dylan yell, "What is your problem? You know I came here with Cosette! You're the one who invited Summer!"

I pause and look back. I want to see Clive's face to know if that last statement is true. I see the smile of a madman spread across Clive's face right before he says, "Chill, she knows I was just joking about the juggling thing."

I shake my head and proceed to walk off the boat.

Time to get some fucking answers.

I catch Esther up on the Ryland brother shit show, and as our taxi pulls up, I hear my name being called. I know exactly who that voice belongs to, but I refuse to turn around. I'm so over this gala, and I need to put some space between myself and Dylan so I can get my feelings in order. I don't like the way he makes me feel like I have some sort of attachment to him. I barely know this guy, and tonight proved that.

"Cosette, please wait!" I hear Dylan say again. He's close now, and it's obvious he knows I heard him. I look at Esther, who is already sitting in the back seat of the taxi. She raises a brow at me and tells me to make it quick.

I turn to see a disheveled Dylan. Did he have a physical altercation with his brother?

"Where are you going?" he asks.

Like it's any of his business.

"An after-party," I answer vaguely.

"What? No, please just come home with me, and we can talk about what happened."

I look at his pleading face and almost feel sorry for him—until Remy's words come back to me.

All three Ryland men were there that night.

And just like that, the pity is washed away.

"There's nothing to talk about, Dylan."

"Cosette, please," he begs, and a small crack forms in my hard exterior.

"I can't," I whisper, and lean in to kiss him on the cheek. "Thank you for the dress, Dylan. It really is lovely."

I duck into the back of the car and close the door. I don't look at him as we drive off, but when I glance over at Esther, she's staring at me with something akin to pity.

"That was brutal, babe."

"Yeah, I know. But it was necessary," I say, laying my head back on the headrest.

"Let's go get you some answers, and then let's get fucking drunk," she says, slapping a hand on my leg.

Sounds like a plan to me.

CHAPTER TWENTY-THREE

Esther and I arrive at an address in the West Loop. It's a lounge that I've never been to before but have heard is pretty exclusive to get access to. I look over to see the giddy expression on Esther's face—she loves this kind of invite-only shit. I pull the napkin with the address out of my bag one more time to check that we're at the right place, and something snags my attention. There's an odd familiarity that I'm sensing, but I can't place my finger on what it is. God, my head is a mess of emotions tonight.

We make our way to the entrance and get stopped by a large bald man working the door with an earpiece in. Without intending to, I let out a snort, amused by the absurdity of it all. Rich people and their love of a show.

Esther is flirting with said doorman, and he quickly scans a list and waves us in. We walk into a dark ambiance with red lights and carpeted floors. It's a long hall that leads straight to a set of stairs. Walking along the hall, I notice a lot of provocative art on the walls—women and men performing sexual acts mixed with some paintings that look to be from the Renaissance period. There's something about this place that screams bad news, and I can't put my finger on it.

When we make it to the top of the stairs, the room opens into a warehouse-type club with high ceilings and an additional level that looks to be a wrap-around balcony. There's fabric hanging from the ceilings where silk dancers are performing very impressive, acrobatic, sensual dances. At first glance, it looks like your typical nightclub, but as we make our way to the bar, I notice a lot of super young-looking girls entertaining not-so-young men. I look over at Esther, and she just gives me a raised eyebrow while lifting her shoulders, a silent *I don't fucking know.*

"This place is giving me roofie vibes, Esther," I lean over and say in her ear.

She rolls her eyes at me and orders us two tequila sodas. I've decided that this will be my only drink here—I want to keep my wits about me tonight. An hour goes by that we fill with dancing, and I switch to soda waters while I scan the room for any sign of Connor.

All of a sudden, I feel hands on my waist, and they're moving me to the beat of the music.

I feel hot breath on my ear before I hear him say, "I was hoping you would come."

I turn around, and Connor is standing right in front of me with a smile on his face. He grabs Esther's hand and says, "Come on, I have a table upstairs."

He leads us upstairs to a roped-off area that has four other men sitting around a table with multiple bottles of extremely expensive spirits. I notice each man has a girl entertaining him, and I can't help but notice how young they all look. These girls don't look older than eighteen, if that. And worse, they all look fucked out of their minds. I look over at Esther, and she notices too. Finally, we are on the same page.

Connor sits down and pours both of us a drink. I take it out of politeness, but I have no intention of drinking it. This Connor is a completely different version of the man who was awkwardly chatting me up at Harold's the other night. No, this Connor looks like he's sitting on a throne and owns the room.

"Come, sit, stay awhile," he says with a wild look in his eye and a fake smile plastered across his face.

I oblige him only because I need to get him talking to me about anything he might know about the Ryland family. If this guy is anything like Remy described him, then I know he has damning information on them.

Connor leans over and tells me how lovely I look tonight. I give him a half-smile and a quick thanks.

"You said you were hoping I came tonight?" I lean over and say, loud enough to cut over the music.

He nods. "Yeah, really happy to have you here."

"Why?" I ask pointedly. I might as well get straight to the point. From what I know about Connor, this man doesn't make any moves that aren't to his benefit. And Remy's comment about him being willing to switch sides as long as it benefits him comes back to me.

Connor laughs at my question and leans in too close for my comfort. "Because, Cosette, someone I know needs a little motivation, and you are very motivating."

If this guy is going to speak in code all night, I'm not going to entertain him any longer.

"Well, your motivation is tired. I think it's time for me to go home," I shoot back at him.

"That's all right. You've already done what I needed you to do," he says with a wink.

"And what was that exactly?"

"To be seen with me," he says quickly before downing his drink.

To be seen with me? I don't understand what he's talking about until I look over and lock eyes with Dylan. He's standing on the lower level with Landon and his brother Clive. As soon as he notices that I've spotted him, he moves toward the stairs.

It all clicks into place for me now. Connor wanted the Rylands to see me here with him. But why?

I rack my brain, and the conversation I eavesdropped on the other night surfaces—something about Dylan not making payments.

Tell Connor to stop calling me, is what Dylan yelled at his brother.

Connor is blackmailing the Rylands. *Holy shit.* He knows something—something damning enough for the Rylands to be paying him to stay quiet about it.

"You wanted Dylan to see me with you?" I ask. It's more of a statement in my mind, but I need him to give me some confirmation before I jump to the next thing I want to ask.

"Yes, sweetheart. I wanted your little boyfriend to see that I know other ways to motivate him." He leans over to pour himself another drink and turns to look at me.

"You see, the Ryland family is past due on some payments, and your little know-it-all boy toy needs some help understanding that when you take over a business, you also take over its debts."

Connor's tone is way too smug, and I can see on his face that he's extremely satisfied with how this evening turned out.

"What does any of this have to do with me?" I blurt out.

Connor laughs. He actually laughs in my face before he says, "Oh, sweetheart, you're a smart girl. I'm sure you can figure that out. People with money always have secrets, and the Rylands have ungodly amounts of money, so the secrets are plentiful—your father being one of them."

My heart stops. Hearing this man mention my father so casually has my stomach turning and my hands sweating.

"You know what happened to my father?" I say, my voice shaky and barely loud enough to hear over the bass of the club music. But Connor hears me. He smiles and leans in close enough for me to feel his breath on my ear.

"I know enough. And the Rylands have more than enough money to make sure the secret stays safe with me."

Before I can get another word out, Connor stands and grabs one of the girls who has somehow found herself dancing on the table.

I stare at him in shock, and that's when everything starts to snap into place.

I pull out the napkin that Connor wrote the address of this place on and recognize where the familiarity came from. It's the same handwriting from the note left at my door—the note that sparked my desire to find information.

He wanted the Rylands to feel the pressure again so he could continue to blackmail them for whatever information he has about my father's disappearance.

I'm instantly sick once I realize I was just a pawn.

I'll never find out what happened to my father because people like me—people of lesser means—have no control in this life.

We are just pawns for the wealthy elite to move around when the game gets a little boring.

I look around to find Esther and tell her we need to get the fuck out of this place before one of us ends up getting drugged, but she's gone. A knot starts to form in my stomach. I'm sure Esther is fine, but there are alarm bells going off in my head.

I make my way toward the stairs and notice Dylan is standing at the bottom with his brother, both men being blocked from coming up by a man bigger than both of them combined. I casually walk down the stairs and try to make my way past them in hopes that they won't notice me. As soon as I see Dylan set his eyes on me, I make my way through the crowd as quickly as my heels will allow. It's gotten really packed in the lower part of the club—hopefully, that helps slow Dylan down long enough for me to get outside and call Esther.

Gracefully, I weave around undulating bodies while every so often feeling a hand graze a part of mine. I finally make it to the exit and tuck into a dark corner I find right next to the stairs that lead into the long hallway we entered through. I quickly pull out my phone to call Esther. It rings and then goes to voicemail. I shoot her a text letting her know I want to leave with a photo of the stairs, so she knows where to find me.

Placing my phone back in my bag, I throw my head back and take a deep breath. I feel like this night has lasted an eternity. I hear my phone ping from my bag and pray it's Esther telling me she's heading my way.

"There you are," a deep male voice says. I don't need to turn to know it's Dylan.

"I'm leaving, so don't get too excited," I say to him without looking up from my phone.

Esther texted me back, telling me that she met a guy and she wants to hang back to see where the night goes. I love my friend, but right now, I really wish she wasn't so boy-crazy all the time. Horny bitch is always trying to find her next dick appointment.

I turn to walk toward the exit, but a hand on my arm pulls me toward a warm body.

"Cosette, please."

"Please what, Dylan?" I make sure to place an unpleasant tone on his name. I try to pull my arm away, but his grip tightens.

"Listen, you shouldn't be here. That guy you were talking to—he isn't a good guy."

Yeah, the guy your family has been paying blackmail money to.

"Let me fucking go," I say as I attempt to unsuccessfully pry my arm from him. He's starting to freak me out with how tight he's holding on to me.

"No, not until you talk to me. I don't want to end the night like this," he says with that pleading tone again.

And at that, I snap. "Okay, you want to talk, Dylan? Then let's talk. Why the hell does your family pay Connor?" I'm practically screaming at him.

His eyes flare just slightly to let me know I've hit a nerve, but he doesn't respond. So, I continue.

"And why did you stop paying him?"

Again, no response.

"And why the *fuck* did he think I would be good motivation to remedy that?" I'm fuming, my body practically shaking at how much anger is radiating off me. And yet Dylan still says nothing.

"Come on, Dylan, I thought you wanted to talk, or did you suddenly change your mind?" I yank again on my arm, but his grip holds strong.

"I don't know," he says finally.

"What the hell do you mean you don't know?" I demand.

"I mean I don't know why he was getting money from us. My brother was handling…" He pauses, and his hand drops from my arm. "It was happening before I took over, and he refuses to tell me what it was for. Only that it's in our best interest to maintain payments." He runs a hand through his hair and takes a step toward me.

"Bullshit," I spit out at him.

I seize my newfound freedom from his vice-like grip and start toward the exit. But Dylan is quicker and places his body between me and the stairs.

"Please, Cosette, you have to believe me."

"I don't have to believe shit. Now leave me alone."

He goes to reach for me again, and panic floods my system. I'm about to start running in a different direction when a second voice sounds behind me.

"What's going on over here?"

I turn and see that Landon is walking toward me. He looks down at where I'm holding my arm, now a little sore from Dylan gripping me so fiercely. He shoots Dylan a menacing look and says, "What the fuck did you do?"

"I didn't do anything! I was just trying to make sure she got home okay," Dylan says defensively.

"Well, I think she has that covered," Landon retorts.

He puts a gentle hand on my shoulder while leaning in to whisper, "Want me to walk you out?"

I nod, and just like that, Dylan steps aside and watches me leave.

Once we make it out to the sidewalk, I pull my phone out to call a car.

"It's okay, let me get you one," Landon says while pushing my phone down.

I could stand to save a few dollars on a ride home, so I don't argue with him.

"Thank you," I say quietly. Suddenly feeling exhausted, I can't wait to get home so I can trade this barely-there dress for a pair of sweatpants and an oversized T-shirt.

"What the hell happened back there?" Landon asks.

"I don't know… I guess I didn't know him as well as I thought I did," I reply, trying to stray from the truth of the situation.

"I mean no offense, but I'm kind of shocked he's so set on you."

Ouch. That was a little harsh.

I know Dylan is all tall, dark, and handsome with, like, a ton of money, but I didn't think I was all that bad of a catch.

Landon must see me furrow my brows because he quickly adds, "Not like that. I'm sure you have no problem attracting men. I just meant with everything that happened with your dad and Ryland Corp. It was a shit show for the family. Their dad being under the spotlight like that, being investigated."

Well, I guess that's one way to address the elephant.

"Hmm," is all I say as a response.

"Look, I can't imagine how hard it must be to not know what happened to him. I'm not here to compare experiences," he says.

"It's really fucking hard," I almost whisper, looking up at the sky to keep the water in my eyes from turning into tears.

"Is that why you're here? Why you're spending time with Dylan?" he asks.

Shocked at his bluntness, I look up at him with my mouth slightly parted.

I don't know how to respond, so I say just that.

"I don't know why I'm here."

He nods his head. "Well, if I were the two of you, I would drop whatever this thing is you guys have going on. There's no need to hash up the past. It's not like Dylan would know anything about your dad anyway."

The last sentence of that statement has the hairs on the back of my neck standing up.

"What are you talking about?" I say, my voice sharp enough to draw blood.

Landon puts his hands up in surrender.

"Whoa, whoa, relax. I'm not accusing you of anything. But it does seem a little odd that the moment you show up, the feds start looking into the Rylands all over again."

I know he says he isn't accusing me, but that sure sounds like an accusation.

I mean, I *am* the reason why they're looking at the case again, but I sure as hell won't be admitting that to anyone, let alone Landon. I'm going to play dumb and deny, deny, deny.

"What do you mean the feds are looking into the Rylands again?" I ask. Time to flip the script on Mr. Wannabe Mayor. "And how the hell would you even have that kind of information?"

"The Rylands aren't stupid, Cosette. They know you've been in contact with the PI your uncle was working with. And I'm privy to the information because Clive is my friend. Friends tell each other if they are being investigated by the FBI. Besides, I have to know that kind of shit—I'm running for mayor, for Christ's sake."

I guess that makes sense. It probably wouldn't look good for his campaign if his best friend turned out to be involved in a missing persons case. I'm still uneasy about them knowing about Remy, so I stick to the script.

"I've only met with Remy twice, and it was to tell him to leave me and my aunt alone. I got an anonymous letter that told me to speak with him about my father. I assumed it was his way of trying to get more money from my aunt and me," I say in my most convincing voice possible. I'm not sure if Landon is buying my lies, so why not add in a half-truth about the letter?

"You got a letter? What did it say?"

I wasn't expecting him to get hung up on that part, but at least he's not calling me on my bullshit.

"Yeah, a few weeks ago I came home to a letter telling me there was more to my dad's disappearance than what was reported and I should seek out this Remy guy for answers." I roll my eyes for added effect. "I mean, how fucking desperate do you have to be to leave an anonymous letter at my apartment?"

Landon looks away from me and nods his head again, but this time he seems to be agreeing with himself more than with me.

"Yeah, pretty desperate," he says under his breath, so low I almost didn't hear it.

"Anyway, Remy denied up and down that he wrote it. And as for Dylan, I didn't even know he was a Ryland until after we... Just trust me when I tell you it was a very inconvenient coincidence." Another half-truth.

Landon's phone lights up—probably the taxi company notifying him of their arrival. He looks me up and down with a straight mouth—he seems perplexed, not nearly as confident as when we stepped outside.

"Well, someone is definitely trying to rehash this whole situation, and I'm not sure if you would be able to convince Clive as well as you did me that it's not you. He's pretty dead set on making sure you and Dylan stop speaking."

That was obvious by his behavior on the boat. I need to be careful now that I'm on Clive's radar. Since Landon seems comfortable talking about all this with me, I try my luck at getting him to tell me some more useful information.

"Wait, why would I need to convince Clive?" I say, a bit of concern laced in my voice.

I can see him start to recognize that he's said too much before he looks at me and says, "You don't. It's just that if I were you, I would be trying to move on. The police and the FBI weren't able to find any evidence of the Rylands being involved in your dad's disappearance five years ago, and they aren't going to find any now. I would just hate to see your family and theirs go through this again."

He says this while staring at me with so much pity in his eyes that I actually believe he feels bad for me just as much as he feels bad for his friend. I reach over and place my hand over his, giving a little squeeze.

"I appreciate your empathy, but I don't think I'll ever be able to move on."

He gives me a nod of understanding, and the car he called pulls up. Opening the door for me, he takes my hand and helps me get into the back seat before handing some cash to the driver.

"Thank you for rescuing me from that situation with Dylan and for the ride home," I say awkwardly.

"Anytime."

And with a gentle smile, he closes the door.

CHAPTER TWENTY-FOUR

I cried the entire ride back to my apartment last night, and after I washed the night off my face and got into bed, I cried myself to sleep. The feeling of hopelessness is a heavy weight today, and all I want to do is stay in bed with the blinds drawn. As I gaze into my cup of coffee, I feel emotionally drained.

I called out for my shift at the Lonely Olive today. Considering it's not a common occurrence for me, Jeremy didn't ask any questions.

My phone rings, and I see it's Esther. I pick it up only to silence it and send her to my voicemail. I don't feel like talking to her right now. I'm actually feeling a little hurt that she was so quick to leave me last night when she knew what I was dealing with. I needed her, and she was more concerned with finding a guy to entertain her ego. I know I'll forgive her, but I just don't have it in me today to do it.

I pull the blankets over my head to block out the light, and before I can fall back asleep, I hear my phone ping with a series of text messages. Annoyed, I look down and see they are from Remy, telling me to call him immediately. Before I can pull up his number,

I get a call from a local number not saved in my phone.

"Hello?"

"Hi, is this Cosette Emory?"

"Yes, this is her."

"Your aunt is Billie Emory?" the voice on the other end asks.

My heart stops intuitively. Why would someone be calling about my aunt? "Yes… Who is this?" I demand.

I hear silence on the line and then finally—

"This is Holy Cross Hospital. Your aunt is here. You were listed as her emergency contact."

Before she can get anything else out, I urgently blurt out, "Oh my God, I'm on my way," and hang up the phone.

I fly out of bed like a madwoman, grabbing any clothing I can get my hands on. Just as I reach for my shoes, my phone rings again, and it's Remy. I don't have time to answer right now. My only priority is getting to the hospital.

I rush out the door of my apartment building, looking for a cab to hail. The street is practically void of vehicles, but I see a familiar car pull up in front of me. Remy rolls down the window with worry written all over his face.

"Get in the car. Something happened to your aunt."

My mouth drops open, but I don't hesitate. I run around the side of his vehicle and get in.

We drive in silence for the first few minutes, and I notice Remy periodically looking over, waiting for me to say something. So, I do.

"What the fuck happened?"

Remy shakes his head. "Someone broke into your aunt's house early this morning. They beat her and took a bunch of things from your uncle's office."

I just stare at him and let him continue.

"Your aunt gained consciousness long enough to call 911, but when they got there, she was in bad shape."

A small whimper escapes me as I silently cry into my hands.

This isn't happening. This is not fucking happening.

I feel a warm hand on my back, but it does nothing to calm me.

"How is she doing? How do you know all this?" I'm yelling now, but I don't care how crazy I sound.

"She had to be rushed into emergency surgery. Something about internal bleeding. I was called an hour ago by an officer I know from working your dad's case."

"Oh my God."

It's the only thing I can get out before another choked sob escapes me. This can't be my reality right now. Not Billie—she's all I have left.

Remy's hand returns to my back as I hunch over in his passenger seat, my head in my hands, trying to compose myself. He rubs consoling circles as he keeps repeating how sorry he is and it's going to be okay.

I shake my head and say, "How can any of this ever be okay?"

I know his lack of response is because he doesn't have an answer. We sit in silence for the rest of the drive to the hospital.

As soon as we arrive, Remy drops me off at the front doors before going to find a parking spot. When I reach the front desk, I'm told Billie is still in surgery and that someone will be able to give me an update shortly. The woman behind the desk directs me to the waiting area, and I cringe at the familiar, dated leather chairs and year-old magazines spread haphazardly on beat-up-looking side tables.

A few other people are sitting in here, and when I walk in, they all look up at me, anxiously hoping I'm a doctor here to give them news of their loved ones. When they see I'm just another nervous face, they quickly look away and continue their seemingly endless wait.

I take a seat, and I'm instantly brought back to the final days of my mother's life. There were so many hospital visits, so many surgeries before we finally let her live out her remaining days in the comfort of our home.

There's no comfort here. The air is sterile, and the room is set to a balmy temperature that eats into your soul. I pull down the sleeves of my sweatshirt and drop my elbows to my knees so I can cradle my head in my hands once more. I don't even have the energy to pull out my phone to scroll social media. I just stare out into the room, counting the scratched floor tiles until they meet the 1980s-style carpet.

A large figure sits in the chair beside me and holds a steaming cup of coffee out to me. I look up at Remy and then back at the coffee before graciously taking it. He takes a swig of his own and, without looking at me, says, "I found a nurse, and she said if all goes well, your aunt should be out of surgery in an hour or so."

I nod as I take a sip and let the warmth spread through my body.

After a while of sitting in silence, I pull out my phone and see I have multiple missed calls from Esther and one from Dylan. There are also multiple texts from both of them, but I open Esther's first.

Esther: *Hey girl! Been trying to call you.*

Hey, please call me back.

I'm getting worried, please call me when you see this.

Are you upset with me? I'm sorry I dipped out on you last night.

Please call me. I know you are mad, but I just need to know you're okay.

I put my phone down for a few minutes but then decide it's cruel not to tell her what's going on. Billie is like family to her, and she deserves to know.

Me: *Hey, sorry for not answering. It's been a rough morning. My aunt is in the hospital. I'm here now, waiting for her to get out of surgery.*

I hit send, and within seconds, I see a little typing bubble pop up.

> **Esther:** *OMG, what?! Tell me what hospital—I'm on my way!*

I quickly share my location with her and switch over to read Dylan's messages.

> **Dylan:** *Cosette, I am so sorry about last night. I should never have put my hands on you. I don't know what came over me.*
>
> *Please, Cosette, please let me explain everything to you.*

Before I can type anything back, Remy's large hand comes down over my phone and snatches it out of my hand.

"What the hell does he mean, never should have put his hands on you?"

Startled, I look up at him and try to grab my phone back, spilling his coffee in the attempt.

"Give me my phone back!" I yell, and everyone in the room looks up at us. I don't care if I'm making a scene. I don't give a shit about anything right now except my aunt.

"I will give it back once you explain what the hell happened last night."

I'm taken aback by his stern voice, and it reminds me of my father.

"It's a long story."

"We have time."

I click my tongue in annoyance. "You shouldn't be snooping over my shoulder, reading my shit."

"Clearly, I should." He's not going to budge until I tell him.

So, over the next forty-five minutes, I tell him everything—

from my interaction with Dylan's older brother to Connor being the one who wrote the letter, to Landon rescuing me from a semi-scary interaction with Dylan.

He stays silent and absorbs every little detail I share with him. When I'm done, he sighs loudly and curses under his breath.

"Cosette, you don't need to do this anymore. Some new evidence has surfaced, and I think we're finally going to get some answers. You don't need to be snooping around the Ryland brothers anymore."

"What do you mean, new evidence? Why the hell haven't you told me about this new evidence?" I throw air quotes up when I say *new evidence*.

"I'm serious, Cosette. The FBI is going to be making some moves, and the more pressure the Rylands feel, the more dangerous they are going to be. I need you to stay away from them."

"I'm not going to do shit until you tell me what moves are going to be made. I don't trust the police or the FBI to do anything, Remy. I'm sorry, but the first go-round of investigating didn't really get us anywhere."

"God dammit, Cosette!" Remy yells, and once again, we are the center of attention in the waiting room. He takes instant notice, grabs me by the arm, and pulls me out into the hall.

"Look at what just happened to your aunt." He's whisper-shouting now. "Do you think that was a fucking coincidence? These are dangerous people who have a lot of power, who do not want to lose that power, and will stop at nothing to keep their secrets under wraps. What part of your life being in danger don't you fucking get?"

I stare at him, my eyes wide, searching for words so I can continue to fight on this hill, but I'm at a loss.

"I know this isn't easy, but you have to trust me."

"Trust you like my uncle trusted you?" I snap at him, and my words hit their mark.

Remy leans back, looking as if I just slapped him across the face. I instantly regret saying them.

"I'm sorry," I say quickly. "This is just all so messed up."

"I know it is…" He pauses and runs a hand down his face, looking truly exhausted. "Your uncle and I didn't know what we were dealing with at the time, and it put him in danger. This time, I know what I'm dealing with, and I'm not willing to risk your safety. All I want is to protect you and your aunt, Cosette. Please believe that."

And I do believe that. I just don't know if he has the power to protect us.

"Fine. I will agree to stay away from the Rylands under one condition."

I pause to give him a moment to protest, but he just looks at me, waiting for my demand.

"I want to know every new piece of evidence you are told about. I want to know what moves are going to be made. Because I can't just sit around and wait for this to be swept under the rug again, Remy. I can't fucking do it. Not now, not after all this." I extend my hand in the direction of the soulless waiting room.

Remy looks at me and then up at the ceiling. "Okay," he says without looking down.

"Okay?" I ask, needing confirmation because I'm not convinced.

"Yes, okay. I will tell you."

He finally looks at me, and his eyes are so serious it kind of scares me. I'm about to demand he tell me now, but before the words come out of my mouth, he puts a hand up, halting me from speaking.

"If you repeat anything that I tell you, Cosette… it will jeopardize the entire case. The things I will tell you, this information—it's information I should not be privy to. Please do not make me regret this."

I lean forward, anxious to hear what he knows. "I understand. I won't repeat any of it."

He nods. "I'm not going to get into too many details, but I will tell you a few things that should hopefully give you some confidence in where the investigation is going. Is that sufficient for our little deal?"

He raises an eyebrow like I'm about to find some loophole and go back on my word.

"Yes, that is sufficient." This all feels so transactional now.

He nods again, then gives one more look around the hospital hallway. Once he sees we're still alone, he starts to speak.

"Because of the camera footage you found in your uncle's office and some additional evidence the FBI already had, they were able to get a few warrants approved."

I nod along, even though I don't really understand how warrants work, allowing him to continue.

"They were able to pull bank records and tap phone lines. A recent phone call was with Connor, and let's just say the man's position is thoroughly fucked."

I smirk at this because after last night, I got to see firsthand what kind of monster Connor was.

"There's going to be a raid on two of his downtown properties. I don't know when, so don't ask."

I was one hundred percent going to ask.

"Once that happens, things are going to get real. Hopefully, new evidence will be uncovered, but even if there isn't, Connor will most likely not be safe, given what kind of information he has on the Rylands and whoever else he's been blackmailing all these years. The hope is to flip him by offering witness protection. Given what he said to you last night, I think it's fair to assume he will have more than enough information to share in exchange for his safety."

My eyes are wide. This is insane information to take in.

"That's not all," he continues and finishes off his coffee.

"We also were able to pull surveillance footage from some surrounding offices that was just sitting in the Chicago PD evidence room. It was supposedly already reviewed, but we know there were people compromised on the local level. One of the businesses had a camera that overlooked a garage used for employee parking at the Ryland Corp. building. I'm still waiting to hear back on whether that gives us any additional insight into who was coming and going that night."

"Okay… So, we have Connor and old surveillance footage. What if the camera footage shows us nothing, and Connor lawyers up and somehow manages to weasel his way out of his sticky situation? Then we're back to square one."

I know I'm being a pessimist, but after last night's encounter and now standing in a hospital waiting to hear if my aunt is going to survive a home invasion, I'm drowning in hopelessness.

Remy sighs. "That's not all… I found one of the interns—the one who was here from Ecuador on a student visa."

I feel my breath whoosh out of me. This is huge. We know there were two interns there the night my father went missing. She could be a witness.

"It's complicated, though."

"What is complicated about it? If she was there, the FBI needs to speak with her. Find out what she knows."

"Well, for starters, she's not in the U.S. legally anymore. Her student visa expired years ago."

Well, that does complicate things. I can't imagine an illegal immigrant being willing to speak to the very people who could get her deported.

"And she's currently living in a house owned by the eldest Ryland brother."

"What the fuck?" Well, that's not suspicious whatsoever.

"I know. There's a possibility that she's dating him, but I don't think that's the case, considering how public the eldest son's dating life is. He's not shy about flaunting different women on his arm every weekend. My gut is telling me she knows something, and the Rylands are keeping her quiet by financially supporting her."

That makes the most sense in my head, too.

"Where is she? Does she live in the city? Can't your FBI friend just go speak to her? It's not like she has to be a witness, but if she knows something that could help…" My brain is moving a million miles a minute.

"She's in Evanston, and no, it's not that simple. If she's approached and the Rylands find out, we could be putting her in danger. She's here illegally—we can't guarantee protection for her even if she wanted to help us."

Fuck. She is right there. Evanston is just a short drive away, and we can't do anything about it.

I shake my head in frustration.

"I know it's frustrating, Cosette, but with the FBI involved, we've gotten a lot farther than five years ago. Just trust the process. We will figure this out."

A question pops into my head that I feel like I should have asked already. "How come the FBI is so involved now? Why not five years ago when all of this was fresh?"

Remy lifts a shoulder. "I don't know. Like I said earlier, bank records were pulled. I think the Rylands have more to hide than just what happened with your father. The FBI loves nailing white-collar criminals."

I shouldn't be surprised that a missing blue-collar worker wasn't enough to garner the full attention of the FBI, but I'll take their help where I can get it.

We're interrupted by a short man wearing a white lab coat. "Excuse me, are you Cosette Emory?"

"Yes, that's me," I say with rushed enthusiasm.

I'm staring at this man with all the hope I have left in the world. *Please tell me she's alive. Please tell me she's going to be okay.* I mentally project my pleas toward him. His mouth is pressed into a straight line, and his round glasses only magnify the exhaustion in his eyes.

"I'm Dr. Blinken. I'm your aunt's surgeon."

"Is she going to be okay?" Desperation leaks from my words.

"We've done everything we can for her. She had multiple broken ribs, a punctured lung, and her hip was shattered. We were worried about the injuries to her head but thankfully, her CT and MRI show no internal bleeding."

I slap a hand over my mouth as a sob escapes me. I can't imagine the pain she must have been in. How could someone do this to a poor old woman?

The doctor continues. "She's currently in an induced coma so her body can heal. Due to her punctured lung, she can't breathe on her own, so don't be alarmed when you see a tube in her mouth. If she makes it through this, she will need a few more surgeries to repair her hip, and there will be a lot of physical therapy to get her back on her feet."

I nod, soaking all the information in. This is bad, but I remind myself she is alive, and that is better than the alternative.

"Can I see her?"

The doctor nods his head. "Of course. She's in room 202. You can go in whenever you're ready. Visiting hours are until five, and please, only two visitors in the room at a time."

I shake the doctor's hand and thank him multiple times. I don't know how people do his job—delivering bad news to people all day long. Even if your patient is alive, they're still in the ICU. How does a man like that keep hope alive?

Remy and I walk toward the double doors that will lead us into the ICU rooms, but before we go through, I hear someone call my name. Esther rushes up to us, and she pulls me into a tight embrace.

"Oh my god, Cosette, what's going on?" she says into my hair, and I slowly let go of her so I can tell her. But before I can form the words to explain this insane situation, my eyes start to tear up.

Remy puts a hand on my shoulder, steadying me.

"Why don't you go in to see Billie, and I'll get Esther caught up on everything."

I sniffle out an "Okay," and turn toward the double doors.

Before I go through, I hear Esther say, "Who are you?" and I know I'll have at least a good twenty minutes alone with my aunt while Esther is filled in on everything.

Expecting 202 to be one of the first rooms, I'm disappointed to find the numbers start high and count down as I descend the hall. I slowly walk past so many rooms with families gathered around hospital beds—some saying their goodbyes, some just sitting to keep the injured company. I begin to feel the anxiety of everything crushing me with each step, with each room I pass. All these people doing the hardest thing they will ever have to do in their lives—watching a loved one survive an unimaginable injury or watching them die. I can't imagine the survival rate at an ICU being very high.

I heard a song once that said *love is watching someone die.* At the time, I found it a bit morbid, but after my mother passed, I thought about that song and the meaning behind those melancholic lyrics and realized that choosing to stay and watch over a loved one when they pass is the most selfless thing you can do. It's when you are losing someone that you truly realize how much you love them—the reality sinking in that this will be the last time you hold them or speak to them. I know we will all go through it at some point in our lives, but I don't think anyone truly understands what it is to love someone until you lose them, until you watch them die. In hindsight, I now understand what the songwriter meant, and I am not ready to do it again.

I finally make it to my aunt's room and peer in to see her frail body lying in the hospital bed. A breathing machine keeps her chest rising, and a ton of other monitors are ready to alert a nurse if her heart stops. She almost looks unrecognizable like this, but my heart knows it's her. I slowly make my way to the side of her bed as tears glide down my cheeks, dropping onto the cold tile floor. Pulling up a chair, I sit down, take her hand in mine, and gently rest my cheek on it.

"You can't leave me. You have to make it through this," I whisper.

I kiss her hand. "I'm not ready to be alone. I need you," I quietly admit to her and myself.

I lay my cheek back down on her hand and let my tears collect on her pale skin as I repeat, "I'm not ready to be alone. Please don't leave me."

I don't know how long I sit like this before Esther comes in. I'm in the only chair, so she kneels next to me, putting her hand over mine. She doesn't say anything, but she doesn't need to—her presence is enough.

"I can't do this again," I say to her.

She squeezes my hand and says, "I know."

We stay like this until a nurse comes in to inform us that visiting hours are over. Remy left after Esther arrived, and she told him that she would drive both of us back to her place. On the drive back, Esther tells me that she informed Jeremy about what was going on and that my shifts are covered for the rest of the week. I really can't afford to not work all week, but I thank her anyway because I also can't imagine working right now. I'll sort the shifts out when I'm in a more stable mental state.

When we get to Esther's, I crawl into her bed and cry until my eyelids grow heavy. My body is exhausted but my mind refuses to turn off. Panicked thoughts play on repeat in my head and bare down on my chest, making me feel like I'm suffocating.

Who did this to my aunt and who will they come for next?

CHAPTER TWENTY-FIVE

The days have gone by like I'm walking through fog. I did take Esther's advice and had two of my shifts covered at The Olive, but I'm not made of money, so I've been here every day since. Jeremy has given me some grace and made sure I didn't get placed on a busy shift. I think everyone knows I don't have the mental capacity to deal with the drunkards that show up in the evening. He also switched me over to a manager's salary, which has been a blessing because my tips have been absolute shit lately, but that's to be expected when you work the afternoon shifts.

My daily routine has kept me sane. I wake up and go straight to the hospital to sit with my aunt, who is still in a coma. Then I head over to The Olive to work my shift. When I'm done with work, I head to Jewel-Osco, pick up a pre-made meal, and go straight to Esther's. Esther and I don't speak much—I think she can tell I'm not up for socializing. She does ask the occasional question about my father's case and how my aunt is doing, but other than that, she has Netflix ready for me so I can sit on the couch and mentally check out.

Two weeks have passed like this, and I'm starting to feel like Billie will never wake up. The doctors took her off the sedatives that were inducing her coma, but she still isn't waking on her own. They say that the body is on its own timeline when it comes to healing and that she could open her eyes any day now. Their optimism is the only thing keeping my hope alive for her.

I'm in Esther's kitchen washing dishes. It's Sunday, and it's my first day off in ten days. I have no idea what I'm going to do with the free time, but I'll probably spend most of it at the hospital. Esther is still sleeping—she went out last night with a guy she met at the gym a few days ago.

I sit down with a cup of coffee and scroll through my phone. I pull up my text messages from Dylan and swipe through them. They have slowed down over the past few days, but he still sends me one text every morning asking me to call him—something I have zero intention of doing, especially not after the promise I made to Remy at the hospital.

I place my phone on the table and let myself get lost in my cup of coffee and thoughts about my aunt's recovery. At some point, I'm going to have to accept this scenario as my new normal. I can't stay with Esther forever, and I know I'll have to eventually go back to my apartment.

I'm pulled from my thoughts when my phone rings. It's the hospital's number, and I frantically grab it to answer.

"Hello?"

"Hi, Ms. Emory, this is Dr. Blinken. I'm calling with good news this time—your aunt is awake. She is talking but very confused about where she is and what happened to her. She's asking for you. Is there any way you can make it to the hospital today?"

"Oh my god, that's amazing news. Yes, I'm on my way now. Thank you, Doctor!"

I shove my phone into the pocket of my hoodie and scream for Esther. I quickly turn off the coffee pot and race around the apartment to grab my purse and shoes.

"Esther!" I yell again.

I wouldn't usually wake her up like this, but I need to get to the hospital *asap*, and I need Esther to take me there.

I see her slowly saunter out of the room with a hand on her head, definitely hungover.

"Oh my god, Cosette, what is with all the screaming?" she groans.

"Esther, she's awake! Billie is awake!"

She looks at me like a deer in headlights. "What?" She's completely disoriented, so I run over to her and shake her by the shoulders.

"Esther, get dressed! The doctor called, and Billie woke up! We have to get there now!"

The shaking works like a charm, and she snaps out of her sleepy stupor.

"Oh my God, oh my God, okay, give me five minutes."

She runs back into her room, and I can hear her frantically getting ready. I'm impressed when she comes back out—she really only took five minutes. She looks more put together than me, and I've been up for two hours already.

We arrive at the hospital in record time. Esther drove like a bat out of hell on the way, and at one point, I had to tell her that getting here alive was the priority. We walk past the nurses' station and into my aunt's room. When Billie sees me, she instantly starts crying, and I run to her side and gently hug her around the shoulders, careful not to touch anywhere she may still be feeling pain.

"Cosette, I don't know what happened," she cries into my chest.

"Shhh, it's okay. You're okay; that's all that matters. I'll explain everything later."

I hold her for a few more minutes until her crying subsides, then I let Esther have her turn embracing her. Esther isn't one to cry, but she's sobbing, and now my aunt is the one doing the consoling. We sit in silence for a while until I feel Billie has calmed down. The doctor told me not to overwhelm her with too much information, so I ask her what she remembers.

"I don't know. All I remember is hearing a loud knock on my

front door. I can't recall what time it was, only that it was still dark. Must have been really early in the morning."

She shakes her head, and I can tell she's getting flustered that she can't remember.

"That's okay. The doctor said it's normal not to have all your memories right away. I'm sure they'll come back."

As much as I would love to know who did this to her, I feel like it's a small blessing she doesn't remember. I can't imagine the trauma she'll have if she remembers being beaten nearly to death.

She nods her head and lays it back on the pillow.

"Is there anything I can have the nurses get for you, Billie?" Esther asks.

"Some water would be nice. Thank you, hon," Billie says through closed eyes.

Esther quietly excuses herself to track down a nurse. I look back over at my aunt—she looks so frail, so tired, lying in this hospital bed. Tears start to prickle my eyes, and I mentally thank the universe for not taking her away from me yet. I give her hand a little squeeze, and I see a small smirk appear on her face.

"You're going to be okay, you know?" she says to me without opening her eyes.

"Me? I'm not the one lying in a hospital bed. I'm not worried about me, Aunt Bill."

"I know; you're never worried about you. I just wanted to tell you that you're going to be okay. Just in case you doubted it."

She turns her head and opens her eyes to look at me now, and I'm so happy to be able to see those brown eyes staring at me. The last two weeks, I started to question if I ever would again.

"My little lilac," she whispers while her finger strokes over my hand.

"What?" I look up at her, confused.

"When your mother died, your father was so scared for you—how you would react. You were young, in the throes of becoming a woman. It's a time when a girl needs her mother most. I told him not to worry, that you were strong like a lilac. Sometimes the harshest of winters create the most beautiful blooms. And lord knows you have been through some harsh winters."

I look at her through my welled-up eyes. We haven't really talked much about my mother's death. It was a trauma none of us wanted to revisit.

"But look at you. You have bloomed into a wonderful woman. Every day, I'm in awe of what you have been able to overcome—how you still enjoy life even after all the loss you have had to endure."

She closes her eyes again and turns her head to settle back into her pillow.

I'm speechless, and afraid that if I speak now, I'll just end up breaking into a sob fit. So, I stay quiet and just sit with her, thankful to still be able to do so.

By the time Esther comes back, my aunt is sleeping. I shush her as she walks in with two large cups of water, and she sets them down on the table across from my aunt's bed.

"I think we should let her rest a while. Let's go grab a bite to eat somewhere," Esther suggests.

We leave to go to a nearby café to grab coffee and sandwiches. I had asked the nurse to call me if Billie wakes up while we're gone—I don't want to miss spending time with her on her first day of consciousness.

"What are you going to do now that she's awake?" Esther asks over a steaming cup of coffee. It's hot out today, but she and I both agree that iced coffee is just not the same.

"Well, she's going to need a few more surgeries, and when she's able to leave the hospital, she won't be able to live on her own for a while." I blow out a breath, dreading what I'm about to say. "I guess I'll have to get rid of my apartment and go live with her."

"I'm sorry, Cosette. I know you love that apartment…and the location is fucking great."

I throw my hands over my face. "Okay, okay, push the knife in a little more, why don't you?"

"Sorry, I'm just sad you won't be as close to me."

I'm also sad about that, and my commute to work is going to be a major pain in the ass.

"It's temporary, Esther. Once she's back on her feet, I'll be able to come back to the city."

She nods, accepting the situation. It's not perfect, but I won't complain because it could be so much worse—Billie could not be with us right now.

"Are you ever going to respond to Dylan?" Esther takes me off guard with her blunt question.

"What do you mean, respond to Dylan?" I feign ignorance.

"Oh, come off it, Cosette. You think I haven't seen all the missed text notifications on your phone? The man is practically stalking you."

"He's not stalking me." I don't know why I'm defending him. "I honestly don't know why he hasn't given up already."

"No kidding. Must have been some pretty mind-blowing sex. Are you sure you only did it once?" Esther jokes.

I almost spit out my coffee. "Oh my god, Esther, what the hell is wrong with you?" I say, trying to fight back a laugh.

"So many things are wrong with me, Cosette. You know this already." She gives me a feline smile, and we both break out in laughter.

It feels good to laugh like this. It's been so long; I miss the normalcy of it. When we finally catch our breath, I tell her how I promised Remy I wouldn't go around either of the Ryland brothers anymore and that I couldn't tell her exactly what I knew, but soon, shit is going to go down. Not soon enough, in my opinion. I wonder when the FBI is going to do the raid on Connor's apartments. I have no idea how long those types of things take to get approved and planned.

"It's a shame. Dylan is so hot…and so fucking rich," she says.

"Yes, and may have had a hand in my dad's disappearance." I retort.

"Well…nobody is perfect, Cosette." She's smiling at me again with that shit-eating grin.

"You are thoroughly fucked up, you know that?" I say, shaking my head. "Whatever happened with you and Landon?"

She lets out a dry laugh. "He's a fuckboy."

And we both burst into laughter all over again.

"You know…he kind of came to my rescue at the afterparty a few weeks ago."

"Oh yeah? Well, maybe you should date him," she challenges.

"Shut up. I'm just saying he's not a complete asshole."

Esther shrugs her shoulders with indifference, and we easily move on to other topics like what we'll watch on Netflix tonight.

CHAPTER TWENTY-SIX

Esther and I ended up spending a few hours at the café since the nurse never called, but we headed back, since there were only a few hours left before visiting hours ended. I still wanted to talk to the doctor one more time before heading home and give Billie a kiss goodbye, even if she wasn't awake.

Billie did end up waking up about an hour before we had to leave, and we spent it lightly chatting about all the mischief Esther and I used to get up to when we were younger. My aunt and uncle never had kids, but I think we were more than enough entertainment to fill that hole for them growing up.

Esther and I made our way back toward the waiting room, and I was instantly stopped in my tracks by the person I saw standing at the exit.

"Oh my god, he is stalking you," Esther says under her breath. "Do you want me to call the cops?"

I wave her off. "No, not yet, at least."

Dylan looks like a mess; nothing like the guy I first met at the bar. His dark hair is disheveled and well overdue for a wash, he has dark circles under his eyes, and the man is wearing sweatpants outside the house. I think I've only ever seen him in suits in public. It's quite the sight to see.

In any other situation, I might feel some sort of empathy for him based on how he looks, but I'm too consumed with anger.

I slowly walk up to him while he looks at me like he's about to jump out of his skin. It's clear he's been surviving on coffee.

"What the fuck are you doing here?" I ask in a low voice that only he can hear.

He puts his hand out, but I jerk back. "Don't!"

He immediately pulls it back and sticks it in his pocket.

"Please, I need to talk to you," he begs. "I need to explain. You don't understand, and I need you to understand."

"Understand what, Dylan? My aunt is lying in a hospital bed. She was fucking attacked in her home. Did you know that?" I turn away from him. Just looking at him makes me want to scream.

"I know, this is all so fucked, but I need to talk to you. I found something. Fuck." He runs a hand through his already disheveled hair. "I can't talk about this here, Cosette."

"Then why the hell did you come here in the first place?" I demand.

The woman at the front desk looks up with a raised eyebrow. I'm getting loud, and if I don't diffuse this situation soon, I'm going to make a scene.

"I came here because I need to explain things to you—what happened with Connor, whatever he said to you. I just need you to understand the situation."

He's offering me what I've been wanting—answers. But it feels too good to be true, like I'm being baited.

Esther has finally lost her patience and walks up beside me.

"Let's go, Cosette. This is not the time or place to do this," she seethes, pinning Dylan with a stare that could probably drop someone dead.

I put my hand on her arm. "Why don't you pull the car around, and I'll meet you out there?"

She looks at me with concern but nods and walks toward the exit.

"If you can't explain to me here, then where?" I ask him. I don't know if I'll regret this, but my curiosity and desperation are getting the better of my rational judgment.

"Come over to my apartment, and I'll tell you everything I know." He says it with a light in his eyes, relief washing over his face as if he didn't think I'd give in.

"I don't think I should be alone with you."

I see his face flinch at that, but I'm not above hurting his feelings. "Why not?"

He really doesn't get it. "Because…I. Don't. Fucking. Trust. You."

He shakes his head in disappointment. "Please, Cosette."

I hesitate but come to terms that he's not going to do this any other way. "Fine, but Esther will know I'm with you…and Remy."

He nods in agreement.

"I'll be there at seven. Now go home and shower, for the love of God. You look homeless."

Without letting him get a word in, I walk past him into the parking lot to meet Esther.

I get in the car calmly, but her eyes drill into me, waiting for me to spill the tea.

"Well?" she asks impatiently. "What was that about?"

"He wants to explain things, make me understand."

"What does that even mean?" she demands.

"I don't know… I'm going to go to his apartment tonight." I admit in a voice so low I'm hoping she doesn't hear that part.

"Oh my god, Cosette, are you fucking crazy? What about your deal with Remy?"

Her reaction is completely valid, but I have this feeling in my gut that I need to go—I need to hear what he has to say.

"I know. I'm going to tell him…but I have to go, Esther. If there is any information I can share with Remy that could help figure out this whole mess, that could put an end to it, I have to see it through. You saw what happened to my aunt. I don't think that was a coincidence. The longer the FBI is looking into my dad's case, the more danger we're in."

She takes a deep breath and blows it out, finally turning away from me. As she puts the car in drive, she says, "Fine. But I'm taking you, and I'm waiting outside his building. You have two hours with him. If you don't come down, I'm calling the fucking cops."

I nod in agreement as she drives out of the hospital parking lot.

Since Esther and I ran out of her apartment today with very little time to get ready, we both unwind with a hot shower and a glass of wine to calm our nerves. Because I was wearing a sweatshirt and jean shorts, I was sweating my ass off in them all day. I opted for a cool sundress, so I could be comfortable while I juggle the theatrics of Dylan Ryland. Esther being the same size as me has been very convenient while I've been staying with her.

It's getting close to the time I told Dylan I would meet him and the nerves are setting in. Esther must sense it because she throws back the rest of her wine and says, "You know you don't have to go over there."

"I know, but I want to. I want to hear what he has to say."

"Where does he live again? I'll look up how the traffic is looking. Wouldn't want you to be late to your date with the crazy billionaire stalker."

"It's not a date," I defend as I text her his address.

"Ugh, of course he owns a place in this building. It's fucking gorgeous. I swear this guy is like one of those creepy anglerfish."

I literally look at my best friend sideways. "An angler-what?"

"What?" she asks in a defensive tone.

"Why are you talking about fish? You're starting to freak me out."

She waves her hand at me like everyone should know what an anglerfish is. "You know, it's one of those fish that have that little glowy tentacle thing that's all flashy and pretty. It attracts all these smaller fish, and then once they're close enough, it eats them whole." She claps her hands together like a mouth snapping shut.

"I don't know why I'm friends with you."

"You're friends with me because I have a phenomenal wardrobe of clothing all in your size and because I'm funny as hell." Smirking, she looks back down at her phone, mapping out the best route to Dylan's place.

I laugh at her because she *is* funny as hell. I'm so thankful for Esther—she always manages to get me to giggle, even in the most unfortunate circumstances.

"Alright, weirdo, let's go. I'm probably going to need a few minutes in the car to mentally prepare myself before going in."

CHAPTER TWENTY-SEVEN

Esther and I pull up to Dylan's building ten minutes before I'm supposed to meet with him, and it feels like just yesterday I was here for a date night with him. I close my eyes and lean my head back while I count to ten; an attempt to calm my nerves. If I'm being honest with myself, I don't really think Dylan will hurt me physically. But there is something about him that makes me feel vulnerable, like he can hurt me in other ways. I take a deep breath and blow it out, grab my bag, and open the door. Looking over to Esther, I say, "Here goes nothing."

"Be back out here at nine or I'm calling…"

"Calling the cops… Yeah, yeah." I tease her.

She tilts her head, giving me a look that says she's not entertained by my jokes. "Just be careful, ok? Landon isn't going to be there to intervene this time."

I promise her I'll be careful and head into the building. The man at the front desk notices me right away and quickly greets me.

"Ms. Emory, so nice to see you this evening. Please, let me get the elevator for you."

His pleasantness takes me off guard—guess he won't be requiring my ID this visit. He leads me to the elevator and presses the button for Dylan's floor. The ride up feels like an eternity as my nerves get the better of me. The doors open, and suddenly eternity seems like not nearly enough time. I slowly make my way to Dylan's door, remembering the first time I was here, eavesdropping on the conversation he was having with his brother and Landon.

I can't bring myself to knock. I stare down the hall, toward the way I came. I don't have to do this. I can turn around and leave just the way I came. I can trust Remy and the FBI to finally figure out what happened to my dad. I close my eyes and picture my Aunt Blilie lying in the hospital bed. I know the police are still investigating, but in my gut, I know she was attacked because someone thinks they can intimidate us, and the longer this is drawn out, the more likely something like that happens again. I don't know what Dylan wants to talk to me about, but if this visit results in the smallest bit of information that can help, it will be worth it.

So, I lift my hand and knock.

I wait a minute or so and no one answers. I pull out my phone to check the time. I'm two minutes early. Not early enough to warrant him being busy with something else. I knock again, and on the third swing of my fist, Dylan answers. He peers at me wide-eyed, still looking exhausted. I take in the entirety of him in a vertical gaze. He's still wearing sweatpants and a T-shirt, but at least they look cleaner than what he had on earlier, with his hair damp from being freshly washed.

"Hi," I say quietly, diverting my eyes away from his glare.

"Hi, come in." He opens the door wide, inviting me in. When I walk into the familiar open-concept apartment, I notice it's a mess. There are papers strewn about the kitchen island and file boxes sitting on his couch and coffee table. On his dining table, I see boxes of Chinese food I'm not sure are old or fresh, and a half-consumed bottle of wine sitting next to them.

"I'm sorry for the mess. I… Once I explain, you'll understand why all this is here."

I slowly make my way around the mess of the dining table, pulling out a chair to take a seat in. Unfortunately, I select one that also has a stack of papers that topples over to the floor.

"Shit, I'm sorry," I mumble as I bend down to scoop up the pages unceremoniously and set them back atop the chair.

Dylan rushes over to my side but didn't make it quickly enough to assist. "No, no, it's ok. I'm so sorry for all the chaos in here."

When he speaks, there's a hint of nerves in his voice.

"You're very unsettling to be around when you don't have your overly confident demeanor," I say without meeting his eyes.

I instantly regret the words when they leave my mouth because they sound extremely rude, and I don't want to be hostile with him—not yet at least.

"Umm…ok. Not sure what to say to that."

"I'm sorry. That was kinda harsh." I force a slight smirk to ease some of the tension in the room. "Why don't you start doing some of that explaining you said you wanted to do?"

"Right. Uhh, why don't you take a seat on the couch." He shuffles over to said couch and moves some of the file boxes to the floor. I notice one has a pale-yellow sticky note on the side that reads "Properties" written in messy handwriting. I navigate my way around the obstacle course made of files and papers to take a seat in the section he cleared off for me.

I look up, and Dylan is staring at me like I'm some sort of ghost sitting in his apartment, not sure if he is scared or intrigued by me. He's still standing, and I'm wondering if he's going to sit down or continue to awkwardly loom over me. Without saying another word, I raise my eyebrows at him, hoping he takes the hint that I'm becoming impatient.

"Right. So, umm…" He's starting to pace around the coffee table now. "Fuck… I don't even know where to start," he says, putting both of his hands on his face.

"Why don't you start by telling me what happened the night my dad went missing? I know you were in the building, and I know you attended that little party your brother was having. Celebrating some acquisition, I believe." I can't believe I just said that, but fuck, I'm so tired of beating around the bush.

"What the hell, how do you know all that?"

"That doesn't matter. I didn't come here to tell you what I know, Dylan. I came here for you to explain to me what the fuck is going on. Well…" I raise my hands and rotate them around the room. "Here I am. Start fucking explaining."

"Right… Ok. Yes, I was there that night, but I was black-out drunk."

I throw my gaze to the ceiling because I'm beginning to think this is going to be a complete waste of time.

"I swear to God, I don't know what the fuck happened past ten. I was super young, fresh out of school, and just excited to be hanging out with my brother—who, by the way, never invited me around to do fuck all." Dylan is no longer pacing, and he's looking me directly in the eyes now.

"I took some pills one of the intern girls gave me and was blacked out and puking by ten. I woke up in my father's office the next day with no pants on. Within days, my father had me flying out to Europe to do some so-called growing up since I didn't do enough of it in college. His words, not mine."

He continues with his story, telling me that by the time the news broke about my dad being missing, he was already halfway across the world and checked out from his family's lives. How he felt embarrassed and that the whole reason he was sent away was because of his behavior at the office gathering. He's never seen the intern girls again and only came back to the States a few times over the past five years, mainly to see his mom around the holidays.

"So, everything about your dad's case was completely foreign to me, and I know that sounds super insensitive because it's an awful thing that happened, but I was completely removed from it. I didn't know the full details until after I met you and started asking my brother about it. I mean, my God, I didn't even know it was the same night as me getting shit-faced at the office until he confirmed it."

I nod, encouraging him to continue. I'm not sure if I believe everything he is saying at this point, but I can't deny how convincing he is…and his story isn't unrealistic.

He's now telling me how his brother has been very secretive about financial dealings since he took over the company, and that getting any sort of records on anything has been like pulling teeth.

"But aren't you like, the new CEO? Can't you access whatever records you want?" I challenge.

On a sigh, he pivots from his story to explain. "I'm only acting CEO; technically, nothing is official until the board votes on it."

Considering I know absolutely nothing when it comes to corporate America, I give a nod of acceptance, prompting him to continue where I cut him off.

"And then the calls from Connor started."

I look at him with wide eyes, waiting to see where this is going.

"I know what he said to you at the after-party, and you have to believe me when I tell you I had no idea the reason my brother was wiring him money. To be honest, I thought it was for drugs or hookers or something else fucked up like that. God knows my brother's no saint, and he's had a coke problem since his freshman year of college."

"I don't *have* to believe anything you say," I snap.

He throws his hands up. "You're right, you don't…and I don't blame you if you decide not to."

He starts to pace again, making his way over to the table and grabbing his glass of wine, taking a long swig as if it was water instead of alcohol.

"So, did you find out exactly what Connor has that is cause for your brother to be paying him off?" I ask bluntly.

He shakes his head. "Not yet."

"But you're still paying him off?"

Dylan's head snaps up at this. "Fuck no, I haven't paid him shit, and I'm assuming that's why he put on his little show of power at the after-party with you."

An ounce of hope stirs in me that Connor will put his blackmail to use since he isn't getting money from the Rylands anymore.

Maybe whatever he knows about my father will finally come to light.

"But then I found this."

Dylan sets a stack of papers in front of me, and I slowly pick up the top sheet. It looks like banking statements but with more numbers than the average person would be used to seeing. I flip through a few more pages that all look like the same thing.

"Dylan, I'm not even going to try to pretend like I know what this is," I say, slowly pushing the stack of papers to the center of the table.

"It's a statement of bank transfers." He points to a line on the page. "And this right here..." He points to another line. "...And here, and here..." He continues to point while flipping through numerous pages. "These are all transfers to a shell account owned by Connor."

Slowly starting to understand what he's trying to show me, I grab the top page again and notice the most recent payment was a week ago. I have to blink through how many zeros because I'm realizing how delusional Dylan has to be if he thinks this kind of money is for personal drug use.

Before I can make a comment about what I'm looking at, Dylan shoves more documents in front of me.

"And there's more!" he says energetically. "There are other accounts that payments have regularly been made to. I mean, this shit goes back years. I still can't sort out who these belong to, but I will," he says with conviction.

"Wait." I put a hand on his arm to stop him from grabbing more documents to show me. "If you don't know who these accounts belong to..." I grab the original pages he set in front of me and point. "Then how do you know this account is Connor's?"

He looks at me wide-eyed with a dazed look on his face. I'm assuming he didn't expect me to ask this question.

"Well?" I raise an eyebrow at him, and once again he's pacing. To say I'm unsettled by how nervous Dylan is acting right now would be an understatement.

"Look…" He runs a hand through his hair, and I'm starting to notice that this is his tell when he's about to share information he doesn't want to. "You may not trust me, but I'm going to make a decision right now to trust you…and I really hope you don't make me regret it." He walks over to a cabinet and pulls out a second wine glass. Walking back to the dining table, he pours the remaining wine from the bottle and hands me the glass. I reluctantly take it because I'm practically falling off the edge of my seat waiting to hear what he's about to say.

"Not long ago, I was notified the company was being investigated by the FBI. I assumed it had something to do with your dad—and it did—but that's not all. They're also looking into the company's finances. They had a warrant, and there was really no way around providing them with any documentation they asked for. When I saw there was weird activity our accountants didn't even know about, I decided I would help ."

"Help? What do you mean, help?" I ask, still not following where he's going with this.

"Help the FBI. I'm working with them to figure out what the hell is going on. I have nothing to hide, Cosette, and I want to make sure they know that—and you know that. They are the ones who told me the account belonged to Connor."

I lean back in my chair, not sure I believe what I'm hearing. Dylan is working with the FBI. I have so many questions, I don't even know where to start. I wonder if Remy knows. If he did, it seems that would be information he should have told me. Everything that Remy told me at the hospital is clicking into place. This is the evidence the FBI needed to get the approval to raid Connor's apartments—a raid that, hopefully, will happen very soon. Taking a drink of my wine, I look up at Dylan, who is staring at me, waiting for my reaction. The realization of him not knowing what happened to my dad hits me like a freight train.

"You don't know anything," I whisper, almost to myself, but Dylan hears me. "Oh my God, you don't know anything," I say again with a shaky voice. I'm starting to feel my eyes well up, and before he can see, I throw my hands over my face and shake my head.

I cry silently into my hands, and I feel Dylan crouch in front of me, placing a hand on my shoulder. I look up at him, a tear rolling down my cheek. He places his hand on the side of my face and gently swipes it away with his thumb. Lifting my hand to cover his, I close my eyes.

"But someone has to know," I say, trying to keep the hope that swells to the forefront of my heart at bay. "You know who was there that night—someone has to know!" I say louder, refusing to give up the last shred of hope that still lives within me.

Eyes open and staring directly into Dylan's, I see the light leave his eyes. He breaks our eye contact and shakes his head.

"No one willing to talk, Cosette. Anyone that knows anything about that night hasn't talked in five years, and that's not going to change now."

No. No, I refuse to accept that. Someone has to know something. People don't just disappear into thin air. Someone knows; I just need to find them.

I spend the next few minutes sitting in silence, drinking the wine Dylan poured me. I look around the room, taking in the chaos of file boxes and documents haphazardly strewn across every surface of his apartment.

Looking over at Dylan, I can see now how physically exhausted he looks, and my heart breaks for him. I can't imagine what it must be like for him—taking over his father's company less than a year ago, only to be at the center of an FBI investigation and to find that your family is being blackmailed. I stand and walk over to him. Placing a hand on his chin, I tilt his face up to me and lean forward, pressing my lips against his. The kiss is chaste, not one of indulgent intimacy, but enough to hopefully bring him an ounce of comfort.

"I have to meet Esther downstairs in thirty minutes, but I'd like to help you clean up all of…" I wave my hand around the room. "This?"

Dylan nods his head in understanding. "Thank you."

We slowly work our way around different parts of the room, organizing papers and placing them back in their respective boxes. I pull out my phone and shoot Esther a text message.

> **Me:** *I'm going to be ten minutes late, don't call the cops.*

> **Esther:** *I'm not making any promises.*

My eyes find the ceiling, and I shove the phone back into my purse. I look around the room and notice Dylan stepped out onto the balcony and is on the phone talking with someone. His back is toward me, so I can't tell if the phone call is a pleasant one or if he's dealing with more drama.

Walking around the couch, I notice the box labeled *Properties* again and get an urge to open it. Pulling the top off, I notice there aren't that many documents in here. I pull out the slender stack of papers to look through them. They appear to be documents listing different properties—some in the local area and some in other states.

"What are you looking at?" Dylan says behind me, and I almost jump out of my skin.

"Jesus, you scared me!" I gasp, dropping the papers on the ground. They scatter, and I quickly scoop them up.

"This box seemed kind of empty, so I thought some of these documents should go in there, but these don't look like bank statements."

He looks over my shoulder at the mess of papers I created from the jump scare.

"Oh yeah, no, those are just lists of different properties the family owns," he says, shrugging a shoulder.

"Why do you guys own so many?" I ask but then feel stupid because I already know the answer. They own them because they can. Rich people love to collect real estate.

"I don't know. Most of them are properties my dad invested

in before he got sick. Some are under my name, and some are my brother's. A lot of them are rented out right now—just another little family side business, I guess."

"Hmm," is all I manage to say as I file the pages back into the box.

"I'm going to go put a pair of shoes on so I can walk you down. I'll be right back," Dylan says before walking out of the living room.

As I continue to clean up the papers, one catches my attention. It's a property listing in Evanston, and my memory shoots back to my conversation with Remy.

The intern—the one who is living in the States illegally. Remy said she was living in a house in Evanston that was owned by Dylan's brother. My hands go clammy when I hear Dylan's footsteps heading back into the living room, and, making a fast decision, I fold the paper and shove it down my top. Not the most graceful of movements, but it's the only thing I can manage before Dylan steps back into the room. I immediately place the top back onto the box and stand up. Making my way over to my handbag, I throw it over my shoulder and ask if I can use his bathroom before leaving.

Once in the bathroom, I remove the document from under my shirt and give it another glance. There's little information on it that would give any indication that it's the property Remy was talking about, but how many properties can they have in Evanston? I fold the paper small enough to fit into my bag and head out to meet Dylan in the main room.

"Ready?" he asks, and I nod.

The elevator ride down was awkwardly silent, with neither of us knowing what to say to each other. I guess at this point there really isn't much to say. I feel guilty for stealing the document, and I'm not sure if I'm going to follow through with what I'm thinking about doing. I want to think Dylan is nothing like the family Remy described to me, and I'm relieved that he is working with the FBI, but I question if he's truly working with them or just cooperating. Will he continue to do so when he realizes his family could face serious consequences?

I know with his father's illness, it might be easy to justify him taking the fall when there's not much life left to live—but what if his brother is involved? Would his moral compass still work then? People do horrible things for their family. God knows I would. Even I can't stand here and say that if the tables were turned, I wouldn't try to cover something up if it meant keeping my family with me. The Rylands have so much to lose—a billion-dollar company's worth of things to lose. I don't think I can trust Dylan to get me answers, because who's to say his views will stay the same once he has them? No, I need to find the answers before he has a chance to bury them like his father did.

The elevator bell dings, pulling me out of my thoughts and back into reality. Dylan is staring at me like a sad puppy. It is a surreal experience to see a man as privileged as him looking at me like he's the victim. I search deep inside myself to empathize with him, but with the amount of loss I have experienced, it's hard to feel sad for a man who will ride his golden elevator back up to his penthouse in the sky . I break eye contact with him and step out and into the lobby. Through the glass doors, I can see Esther's car parked in front of the building.

"Well, that's my ride," I say casually, tilting my head in the direction of my best friend, who I know is watching through the windows, waiting for Dylan to give her any reason to call the cops.

"I'm really sorry, Cosette. For all of it," Dylan says, and pulls me in for a hug. I lean my weight into him as he holds me, and I'm ashamed of how good it feels to have his arms around me. There's something about this man that draws me in. I pull back to put some distance between us, but before I can remove myself from his magnetic field, warm hands are cradling my face and soft lips are on my own. Dylan kisses me with a fervent need I've never experienced, and before I can think better of it, I'm returning the kiss with a need of my own.

When our lips part, I don't notice I'm crying until he swipes a thumb over my cheek, once again wiping my tears away.

"Why don't you stay?" he asks me, but it sounds more like a

plea.

I stare into his eyes as he searches my face for an answer he knows he won't receive. I shake my head, and he answers for me.

"You can't," he says simply as he exhales a breath.

"I wish things were different," I say, and he nods in agreement. It's not a lie—I do wish things were different. Maybe in another life, Dylan and I could have been something. In a life where we weren't sitting on opposite sides of the social spectrum. But even without everything with my father, it still never would have worked. He lives in a world that will never be for me—the bougie parties, the opportunistic relationships, the emotionally empty lives. No, I could never live that way. I may not have monetary wealth, but I'm wealthy in all the ways that matter to me.

I walk out without another word. The goodbye is implied, because we both know we won't be seeing each other again. I know I have barely known Dylan, but I feel like I'm losing something today. Losing all the possibilities of what could have been. I'm not sure what I have done in this life to deserve so much loss. A laugh escapes me, thinking about the irony of finally finding a man I actually want to be around, only for him to be involved in the mystery of my father's disappearance.

I walk out and get bombarded by the overwhelming smell of a cigarette. I glance over and see the eldest Ryland brother leaning up against the building, taking a drag. I immediately want to tell him he legally has to be fifteen feet from an entrance to do that but quickly remember what an entitled prick he is and think better of it.

A sick feeling forms in my stomach. Dylan probably doesn't know that he's here. To offer an olive branch, I quickly pull out my phone and shoot him a text to let him know. I'm sure he wouldn't want his brother seeing all the documents he's auditing upstairs.

When I climb into the passenger seat of Esther's car, her wide-eyed gaze lands on me.

"What in the world was that?" she demands, and I know she's referring to seeing Dylan and me kissing.

I lean my head on the headrest and let out a heavy breath. "That was a goodbye."

CHAPTER TWENTY-EIGHT

The past twenty-four hours have gone by mind-numbingly slow. I've been to see Billie in the hospital, who still has little to no recollection of her attacker, and I've worked an insanely slow shift at The Olive where I made a whopping twenty-three dollars in tips. Thank God I'm on a manager's salary now, or I'd be living on the streets in no time. I'm feeling a bit dramatic today because every time I try to accomplish something, I find myself staring at the address of the Evanston property owned by the Rylands. Remy has been quiet about any recent developments—or lack thereof. Not a word about the raid on Connor, not a word on the camera footage obtained from the nearby businesses, and nothing on the investigation into my aunt's attacker. I know Remy asked me to be patient, but how patient can he expect me to be? I was patient for five years. Well, maybe patient isn't the right word to describe my position over the last few years—more like shamefully complacent.

I swallow that feeling of shame down and look at my phone for the hundredth time today. The last text I got from Remy was him informing me the FBI would like to speak with me. Remy has been very paranoid about putting me in direct contact with anyone from law enforcement to maintain my image of not being involved with the reopening of my father's case. With what happened to my uncle, I understand why. But that doesn't keep me from feeling a little excited to tell the FBI everything that I know. I want to tell them personally what Connor said to me at the nightclub. I'd also like to confirm what Dylan told me about working with them is true. I'm not stupid—I know they probably can't and won't confirm something like that. But hey, a girl can hope.

Hope. What a strange feeling to have again. I've learned it's an emotion that never truly dies. It's something that, on your darkest days, can be your only salvation or your biggest disappointment. For me, hope has been a source of continual disappointment, and so I allowed it to be stifled. Little by little, I would chip away at it until my lack of hope saved me from the disappointment of the inevitable unfortunate outcomes that have made up my life. This process doesn't happen overnight. No, it happens over a period of time, slowly and mostly unnoticed. Until one day, you're told by your aunt that your missing father's case is no longer active, and there's no shock, just numb acceptance. Numb acceptance of a traumatic outcome is a sure way to know hope is a long way from home.

But just like the spark of hope dims within a person, it can be reignited. It too happens over a period of time, until one day, it's the only reason you get out of bed in the morning.

People often think that you can't survive without hope, but they're wrong. I survived without it for years. Surviving isn't the hard part; people survive terrible things every day. No, the hard part is surviving while keeping that sliver of hope alive. Because waking up with hope oftentimes means going to bed with phenomenal disappointment . And that is exactly what I have been doing every day since getting that letter Connor wrote me. Even though his intentions were for his own gain, I'm thankful he did it.

I pull out my phone and tap on Remy's contact.

"Hello?"

"Hey! Are we still on for today?" I say quickly into the phone, my voice giving away more excitement than I want it to.

"Yeah…" He takes a deep breath. In my imagination, I can see him running a hand down his face. "Yeah, we're still on."

"Ok great, I'll see you in an hour." I quickly hang up and run through the questions I have for the FBI agent.

Walking into the diner, I make my way back to the usual booth Remy and I occupy when we meet for coffee. For once in my life, I'm early, but I couldn't bear sitting around my apartment for a minute longer.

A middle-aged woman with mousy brown hair pulled back in a giant claw clip, exposing her overgrown gray roots, flips over one of the four coffee cups on the table and pours until it's full of steaming liquid.

"Thanks, Donna," I say as I pucker my lips and blow on the rim of my cup.

She stares at me for a moment while I take a sip. She's got one hand on her jutted-out hip while the other holds up the pot of coffee. With her stained pink apron, she looks like such a cliché diner waitress, and if you didn't know better, you'd think you were watching a theatre production. Donna has served me almost every time I've been here. She's wearing very minimal makeup that doesn't hide her crow's feet or lip lines from smoking too many cigarettes during her lifetime. Still, she's pretty if not a little plain, and I bet she was gorgeous in her twenties.

"Where's your friend?" she asks bluntly.

"He'll be here any minute." I flip over the cup across from me and she pours some coffee for Remy. She knows we both take our coffee black, and she reaches over to remove the saucer holding the mini cups of cream, dewy from condensation.

"Actually, you can leave it. We have one more joining."

She lifts a skeptical eyebrow at me and slowly sets the saucer back down on the table, pours a third cup, and saunters away.

Within a few moments, I hear the jingle of the door opening and in walks Remy and a shorter man with dark brown hair trailing behind him. Remy is mostly blocking him as they walk toward me, but I can make out that he's wearing an unremarkable suit, and he looks to be about in his forties.

They slide into the booth across from me, and Remy wastes no time drinking his coffee.

"Cosette, this is Agent Byrne." Remy tilts his head slightly toward the agent sitting next to him.

"It's a pleasure to meet you, Cosette. Remy has told me a lot about you, and I have to say I commend your resilience in finding answers about your father."

I smile forcefully. "It's a pleasure to meet you as well, Agent Byrne."

"Please, call me Roger," he says, holding up both hands as if he's surrendering his title to me.

I look over to Remy and see his brows are pinched together and his mouth is slightly turned down. He's not comfortable with this meeting. Roger instantly takes note of where my eyes have landed and glances in that direction.

"Look, Remy has expressed his concerns with you being seen speaking to law enforcement of any kind due to the suspicious nature of your uncle's death. And I have to say, I think his concerns are justified."

Well, that's not very comforting to hear.

"With that in mind, I'm going to make this visit short and concise. I want to start off with a few questions I have for you regarding your aunt."

I look over to Remy, and he reassuringly nods at me to oblige Roger.

"Ok, what would you like to know?"

"Does your aunt smoke cigarettes?"

I almost choke on my coffee. The thought of my aunt smoking cigarettes is laughable, and I let out a chuckle before saying a firm, "No."

"Why is that question funny?"

I grab a napkin and wipe off the little dribble of coffee that made its way out of my mouth.

"I'm sorry. My aunt is a dental hygienist. She's obsessed with healthy gums and teeth. Smoking is the last thing you will ever catch her doing."

Roger takes out a little notepad and jots down a quick scribble of words.

"Do you or anyone who visits your aunt smoke?"

"No, not that I know of. My aunt doesn't get many visitors. Maybe the occasional old co-worker, but I don't think any of them smoke, considering their field of work. Why so many questions about smoking?"

He scribbles a few more things on his pad of paper and looks up at me. "Because we found multiple cigarette butts near your aunt's front door. We don't know for sure, but they may have been left behind by your aunt's attacker. We are going to run them through the lab to see if we get any leads."

No one that would be at my aunt's house would be smoking cigarettes. The fact that there were butts on her property gives me the creeps, and all of a sudden, a memory hits me.

"Oh my God..." I say, while Roger seems to be teetering on the edge of his booth seat.

"There was a man one night watching me as I left my aunt's place. I remember him looking like he didn't belong in the neighborhood." I pause, trying to flip through my memories of that night. "He was smoking."

After I say it, I realize that tons of people smoke, and I probably now sound paranoid.

"Why do you say he looked like he didn't belong?" Roger asks pragmatically.

"Well, the neighborhood isn't exactly what you would call affluent, and I remember he was wearing those overly priced shoes with the red bottoms."

"Louboutins?"

I'm shocked this man knows what those are but then remind myself he's FBI and probably deals with people from all different kinds of tax brackets.

"Yes, those…and the car he walked back to was a really expensive-looking sports car. Not the typical car you would see from someone who lives in the area."

Roger nods, takes notes, and continues to ask some follow-up questions about the strange man.

As I walk through the events of the past few months with the agent, I start to piece together things that no longer seem so coincidental. Like the break-in at my apartment right after leaving my aunt's with the box of documents and the now-notorious hard drive. And the strange man I saw standing outside of my apartment building one night, who I now believe to be the same guy that watched me leave my aunt's. Deep down I knew all these things were connected, I just didn't see the dots to link them all together. I feel quite stupid, if I'm being honest with myself.

For the next hour, the three of us drink enough coffee to power a small village, and I tell Roger all about my run-in with Connor. I also bring up what Dylan told me. He doesn't seem thrilled I'm privy to the other ongoing investigations, and it's very clear he will not be disclosing anything to me about that.

"Dylan shouldn't have spoken to you about that. It could jeopardize the entire case. I hope you understand that information should not be shared with anyone."

I want to scream "obviously" in his face but just nod instead. I'm not stupid—I wouldn't discuss this with anyone outside of this circle, including my aunt and Esther. She wanted to know so badly what Dylan had to say, but I just brushed her off and told her it wasn't anything significant. She let the topic go in the car, but I know Esther—it will get brought up again.

When we finish, Roger asks me if I'm willing to sign a witness statement on what I told him about my conversation with Connor. I hesitate before answering because I know the position it puts me in. So far, the odds for witnesses in my father's case have not fared too well. From the look on Remy's face, he isn't thrilled about the idea either.

"Don't you have enough evidence on him? Why would you

need me?"

"We do have evidence, and hopefully more soon." He takes a drink of his coffee. The man has loaded it with a million little cups of creamer, and it looks more like a glass of milk now.

"But we don't have anyone with a firsthand account of him bragging about his blackmail schemes. That could go a long way in court, Cosette."

I open my mouth to protest about testifying in court. I'm not sure how we went from me signing a witness statement to me testifying in court. But before I can get a word out, Roger cuts me off.

"Look, I completely understand your hesitation. No one is going to force you to do anything you don't want to do. But it will be helpful and could be the nail in the coffin on getting a jury to convict him. Connor is not a good man, and he's been skirting the law for a long time."

An image of Connor's smug face from the club pops into my head, and against my better judgment, I say, "I'll do it."

CHAPTER TWENTY-NINE

Remy and Roger leave while I hang back to finish my cup of coffee. I really need a moment to process everything in silence. Last night I saved the address to the Evanston house as a pin in my maps app, and I pull my phone out to look at it. It would only take me thirty minutes by car to get there. Unfortunately, I don't have a car, and I refuse to pull Esther into this. If I take the red line and transfer to the purple, I can get there in just under an hour and a half.

I set my phone down on the table and stare at it. What I want to do is absolutely insane and completely against everything I've promised Remy I wouldn't do, but something about agreeing to be a witness has made me realize I'm not really safe anymore, no matter what I do. If I'm going to be a witness, I want to make sure I have as much information to share as possible. Maybe this woman can't testify, but I can, and I can relay anything she's told me while keeping her anonymity. I think. I'm not sure how all of that works, but I can sort that out later.

I exit the diner staring down at my phone with the map up and smack into a man on the street. I look up with embarrassment, gearing up for an apology but pause when I recognize him.

"Landon? Oh my God, I'm so sorry!"

Landon smiles casually. "Well, well, well. Aren't I lucky?"

I tilt my head and give him a skeptical glare. He's flirting with me, and I'm not crazy about the prospect of a man that blew off my best friend hitting on me. He has been nothing but nice to me, though, so I soften my scowl.

"What are you doing in these parts of the city?" I ask.

Landon doesn't strike me as a guy to hang out in Wicker Park. He's a River North, Fulton Market kind of guy.

"Oh yeah, I don't usually find myself over this way, but with my campaign kicking off, my dad and my campaign manager thought it would be good to get out into different neighborhoods to talk to some of the local business owners. You know, see what changes the city wants to see from a new mayor."

That makes complete sense, and I actually find it really admirable that Landon is making himself a boots-on-the-ground kind of politician. Very grassroots of him—not that he needs to do it. With his father being the incumbent and extremely popular in the city, Landon is practically a shoo-in as long as he touts all the same talking points as his father.

"Are you heading to Evanston?" Landon asks, looking down at my phone screen.

"Oh, yeah, I am."

"Need a ride? I was just heading to my car."

It's really nice of him to offer, but it's the middle of the day, and if I'm going to catch someone at home, my odds will probably be better around dinner hours.

"Umm, I actually have to run home first. Thanks for the offer though!" I smile, and I genuinely think it was a nice offer.

He shoots me a politician's smile with a mouth full of pearly white teeth I'm sure he paid a pretty penny for.

"Anytime, Cosette. It was great to see you!" He waves and walks in the opposite direction of my route.

Back at my apartment, I occupy myself with cleaning out a few closets. I don't usually wish to be working, but it's too bad I don't have a shift at The Olive today. I could use the distraction.

As I make my way to the back of my closet, my hand lands on a small cardboard box. My breath hitches, recognizing instantly what it is. I slowly pull it out and walk over to my couch, setting it on the coffee table.

After staring at it for the last fifteen minutes, I open it. It's a box of memories I've hidden away because they're too painful to remember. I sift through the many photos of my mother—some of her by herself, some of her holding me as a baby and then a toddler, and some of the whole family. I pause on one of my mother and father sitting on the old family couch that was a hand-me-down from my grandmother. I can hear my father's voice perfectly in my mind as he joked with my mother about his in-laws.

"Thank God your mother was crazy and kept plastic on all her furniture. This is practically brand new. I truly don't know how your father managed to enjoy a single football game with all that rustling."

Just as perfectly as hearing my father in my memory, I can also see my mother's face blush as she giggled and then playfully swatted at his arm for teasing. She was a breathtakingly beautiful woman, but what outshone her exterior beauty was how kind her soul was. She would have volunteered every last hour of her life if it meant helping someone in need.

I stare at the picture for a moment and appreciate the way my father is looking at my mother. The admiration is palpable, even through the old photo. Although I no longer have either of my parents in my life, I will never stop being thankful they showed me what true love looked like. It's something I don't take for granted because I believe most don't ever get to see it, let alone experience it.

I set the photo aside and continue to pull out the rest of the contents of the box. Trinkets my mother collected—little angel figurines, a miniature glass bottle with sand from a beach in Florida, and an old watch from my great-grandmother that stopped working years before she passed. With each item I pull out, I take a moment to hold it because it's the closest I'll come to holding her now.

At the bottom of the box is a Polaroid picture facing down. I pick it up, turning it over, already aware of what I'll see. It's a photo of my mother and me.

My mother is standing on a little step stool with pruning shears in front of a massive lilac bush. I'm on the ground next to her with a handful of lilacs smashed into my little face, very clearly breathing in their elegant floral fragrance. On the bottom, *Michigan '97* is written, and even though I was only seven years old, I can remember that trip to the Michigan cabin. I remember how excited my mother was that the lilacs were still blooming when we got there. My mother loved going up to that cabin, and a part of me was convinced it was only to see the lilacs every year. As a child, I never understood all the excitement—didn't fully appreciate how special the perennial bush was. But as I got older and my mother taught me all the wonderful things to know about the plant, I grew to appreciate it just as much as she did.

One of the final requests my mother had before she died was to go up to the cabin to see her lilacs. My father promised her we would go for Mother's Day weekend, but she ended up being too sick from treatment and we had to postpone the trip. By the time we were able to load up in the car and make our way there, we all knew the lilacs wouldn't still be blooming.

When we pulled up, my father gently helped her out of the car, and we all walked together to the backyard. We smelled them before we saw them, and the gasp my mother made was one of pure joy. There was a historically cold spring that year, and it forced the lilacs to bloom later. I remember this because my mother talked about it like it was a tiny miracle that they were still blooming by the time we got there. I'm not sure I believe in miracles, but it was definitely something to marvel at.

If I close my eyes, I can picture my mother next to that lilac bush clear as day—the smile on her face showcasing her contentedness as she leaned in to smell one of the fragrant blooms.

"You know what's so special about these plants, Cosette?" she asks.

"That they only bloom for a few weeks a year," I reply confidently.

"Yes, that's right…but also, despite how delicate these beautiful blooms are, this plant has incredible resilience. No matter how brutal the winter is, this plant will persevere and keep blooming every year. In fact, this very plant has been here for the past twenty-three years and will most likely outlive us."

I furrow my brows at this, thinking she's making a statement about her dying again. I don't like to hear her talk like that—like she's lost hope. Before I can protest what she's saying, she asks me another question.

"Did you know that lilacs can live for centuries once establishing roots?"

My eyes widen. She *literally* meant this plant will outlive us all. I chuckle at this little factoid, and I file it away in the section of my brain reserved for all things my mother teaches me about plants.

"Just when I thought I knew all there was to know about lilacs."

When I open my eyes, I feel a warm tear fall down my cheek. It's amazing how much the mind can suppress when the memories hurt too much. I used to love the smell of lilacs—now it just reminds me of what I've lost. My mother didn't make it to see another bloom, so in a way, I suppose that year's late bloom was a sort of miracle crafted just for her.

I carefully place all the trinkets and photos back into my little box and walk past the closet to my bedroom. I set the box down on my nightstand, propping up the little Polaroid against it.

CHAPTER THIRTY

It's almost four in the afternoon, and it's time to head to the Evanston house. I don't know what I'll arrive to, and I know that I could be showing up to a house that doesn't have the person I'm looking for inside it. But I need to try. I need to do everything I possibly can to put all this to rest. Now that I've allowed myself a sliver of hope in finding out what happened to my father, I know I have to make choices that keep that hope alive within me.

The weather has become windy, and the summer nights are on the cusp of fall. I throw on a hoodie and grab my denim jacket before heading out the door. I take the stairs, squeezing by my neighbor carrying up groceries. Usually, I would offer to help, but I'm anxious to get this over with, so I avoid eye contact with Mrs. Wilkins.

When I step outside, I'm shocked by how much the temperature has dropped. The wind is fierce, and I'm debating on running back to my apartment to put on something warmer than a denim jacket. Looking down at my phone, I see that it's going to take me closer to two hours now due to a delay on the red line. Fucking awesome.

Throwing my hoodie up, I weave through a few people as I

make my way up the sidewalk toward the train station.

"Cosette!"

Someone calls my name, and I turn to see which one of the people I breezed by knows me.

"Cosette! Hey!" a now familiar voice yells out my name playfully. My face softens when I see it's Landon.

"Wow, twice in one day. What are the odds of that?" Landon says through a chuckle.

Those are very slim odds, especially in a city this big. Before I get a word in, he's talking again.

"Wow, can you believe how cold it got? What are you doing over here?"

"Umm, I live here," I say, pointing toward my apartment building. "What are you doing over here?" I ask skeptically.

He points to the door of the business we are standing in front of. It's a small used bookshop that's been in this neighborhood way before the gentrification started.

"Campaign stuff, remember?" he says with that smile of his.

"Oh, that's right. Sorry, it's been a long day." I pull out my phone to check when the next train is leaving. I need to cut this little run-in with Landon short.

"Well, it was nice to see you again, Landon, but I've got a train to catch."

I'm about to turn around when he says, "Still heading up to Evanston?"

"Umm, yeah, actually I am."

"Want a ride? I'm done making my rounds for the day. This wind has me wanting to curl up on my couch with a warm blanket."

"Umm, I don't know. I'm sure Evanston is out of the way for you," I say, even though a ride up there would save me so much time and get me out of this freezing wind.

"Nonsense. I have zero plans tonight. What kind of friend would I be letting you trek up there in the cold?"

Friend. We're friends now? I guess we qualify as friends—maybe more like acquaintances if you ask me—but as a politician, I assume Landon considers everyone a friend.

I hesitate to answer him. After all, Landon is friends with the Rylands, and particularly close with the eldest. Maybe he'll catch on to what I'm doing if he sees the address I'm going to.

"Ok, that would actually be such a time saver." I reply before I can dwell too much on the what-ifs. I don't have to give him the actual address; I can just have him drop me off at a café close by and walk the rest of the way.

"Great! I'm parked just a block this way." He points behind him in the opposite direction of the train station.

"Thanks," I say, and he gives me a smirk, waving his hand in show of the gesture being no big deal.

It takes just a few minutes to get to Landon's car, which is parked in an open car park. When we walk up, I take in the black sports car with amazement. I know that Landon's family has money, but I didn't know politicians had this kind of money. My eyes are wide when he opens the door for me. It swings open wide and reveals a deep, two-toned leather seat with exaggerated sides that look like it's going to hug my body from every angle.

I step in with a hand on the roof of the car to balance myself as I lower down into the seat. I feel like I'm sitting on the floor with how low-profile this car is. Landon shuts the door, and I look around the car, taking in all the fancy details. The leather dash is in a butter-soft cream-colored leather that has raised letters reading *Gran Turismo*, and just above that is an Italian flag logo. My eyes continue to rove around until they get caught on a familiar logo. Sitting just above the display screen in the center is a logo that looks like a trident. I scrunch my brows, trying to flip through my memories to pinpoint where I've seen it before. But before I can place it, Landon is opening the driver's side door and lowering himself in.

He looks over at me, looking smug, clearly noticing my wide eyes as I look around the car. He probably thinks I'm impressed, but I'm far from it. No politician should make enough money to buy a car like this. There are people in this city that are struggling to put food on the table, and their future mayor is driving around in a car that probably costs more than what they could make in five years combined.

"Nice car," I say with a mocking tone.

"What, you don't like it?" he jokes.

"Not exactly a car I pictured the future mayor driving around," I say, lifting a brow in judgment.

He laughs. "Future mayor, huh? Does that mean I can count on your vote?"

"Not while you're driving this car around."

He laughs again, even harder this time. I'm starting to feel awkward.

"Don't worry, it's not mine. I'm just borrowing it."

Now I'm laughing. Who in the hell would loan a car like this to a friend to just casually use? And then the realization hits me.

A ridiculously rich person that probably has loads of these types of cars—someone like Clive Ryland.

"Hmm, that's a really generous friend," I say, unimpressed.

"Yeah, Clive has quite a few cars at his disposal, so I'm sure he barely notices this one missing."

I'm instantly regretting letting Landon drive me. He's so charming and nice—such a polar opposite of Clive—that I forgot they are such good friends.

"So, where am I taking you?" Landon asks.

"Umm, The Drip coffee shop. Here, this is the address." I hold up my phone to show him a coffee shop I found that was just a few blocks away from my actual destination.

"You're going all the way up to Evanston just for a coffee shop? You know there are a ton of those within walking distance of here," he says with a playful tone.

I squint my eyes and shoot him a sarcastic gaze. "Yes, Landon, I know. I'm meeting a friend there."

"Ohhh, like a date." Now he's really smiling.

"Yes, a date," I lie quickly. Maybe that will get him to stop pushing me on the topic.

He chuckles. "I take it you and Dylan are officially over."

"We can't be over when we were never a thing. We went on a few dates, that's it," I snap.

"Ouch. I'll make sure not to tell Dylan you said that."

I let out an exhausted, "For the love of god," and sit back in the seat. Landon chuckles again and presses a button that makes the engine roar to life.

The car is a smooth ride, and I find the purring of the engine to be relaxing. My eyes roam around the car again, taking in the few belongings Landon has in here. My eyes stop on the center console where the cup holder is. In it is a pack of cigarettes, and I'm surprised that Landon is a smoker. He looks over, catching me staring at them, and says, "They're not mine."

"Good. Those things are terrible for you."

We chat briefly for the duration of the ride up to Evanston. There's more traffic than I anticipated, so Landon takes an alternate route. It honestly feels like we are driving to the middle of nowhere, but he swears this will be faster than sitting in all the rush hour traffic. My phone rings, and I look down to see that Remy is calling me. I quickly silence the call—Remy is the last person I want Landon to hear me talking to.

He's been friendly with me, but I don't doubt he would report back to Clive immediately if he heard any mention of a PI. A few minutes pass, and my phone rings again. I look down to see it's Remy for a second time. My god, could his timing be any worse? Quickly, I silence it again.

"Is everything okay?" Landon asks, looking over at my phone.

"Yeah, it's just someone I don't feel like talking to right now." Not completely untrue.

"Oh, okay. Well, you can answer it if you need to," he says, like he's giving me permission to talk on the phone. He must think I'm not answering to avoid being rude.

"No, it's okay. I'll just text them I'll call them later."

I pull my text message app up and send a quick text to Remy.

Me: *Hey! With Landon Wexford,*

> *can't talk right now. It's a long
> story, I'll call you later.*

I place my phone back in my pocket, hoping that will silence the phone calls for now.

Within seconds, my phone vibrates. Annoyed, I pull it out for the third time and see a text from Remy.

> **Remy:** *Cosette, why are you with
> him? You need to call me now.*

"Umm, I'm sorry, I need to make a phone call really quick," I say to Landon.

I click on Remy's name and hold the phone up to my ear. I press on the volume button to turn it down a few clicks to make sure Landon doesn't hear what Remy so urgently needs to talk to me about.

"Cosette?" Remy says with a hint of panic in his tone.

"Yeah, who else would it be?"

"Right, okay, I need you to listen very carefully. You need to get away from him. It was Landon. Landon was there that night, and he's also on record lying to the police about not being there."

My heart drops to my stomach and it takes everything in me to not show a physical reaction Landon will pick up on.

"Are you sure? How…how do you know for sure?" I ask, my mind having a hard time processing what I just heard.

Remy's cadence starts to pick up "Remember the camera footage we were reviewing from the building across from the Ryland office?"

"Yes."

"Well, we found something. There's footage of someone leaving the building that night from one of the parking garages. A person that was not accounted for."

My pulse is racing. This can't be real.

The hand holding my phone begins to tremble, and I can hear Remy take a deep breath on the other side of the line.

"Is there any way he knows who you're speaking to right now?"

I glance over at Landon, who's driving while also texting on his phone. Too distracted trying to juggle both tasks to be listening to me.

"No, I don't think so" I tell Remy.

"I had to convince Roger to let me tell you, but considering your current situation, I was completely right to warn you."

I hear him take another deep breath over the phone. My mind tries to convince itself I'm not in as much danger as Remy is alluding to. Just because he was there doesn't mean he's dangerous. Maybe it was a situation like Dylan, maybe he has no idea what happened. But the panic in Remy's voice is palpable and it wars with my internal dialogue.

"You need to do whatever you can to get away from him, I don't trust him Cosette. You need to get the fuck out of that car."

CHAPTER THIRTY-ONE

My mouth goes dry and that's when I realize it's probably been hanging open this entire time. I try my hardest not to look over at Landon, to give anything away.

"Ok, I understand. I'll be getting dropped off soon. I'll call you later and we can talk more about this."

I hang up the phone and slide it into my pocket. My hands are still shaking, so I clasp them together. We should be in Evanston soon, and to calm myself, I let my mind return to its earlier thoughts that I'm not in danger.

Why didn't Dylan tell me that Landon was there? I think back to our conversation when I asked him.

"No one that's going to talk," is what he said to me.

My thought is interrupted by Landon. "You okay? You look like you just saw a ghost."

"Yeah, I'm just cold," I say with a smile I'm sure is unconvincing.

"Yeah, this weather really dropped. I'll turn the heat up." He reaches for the large touch screen in the center of the console and taps a few buttons.

Then he reaches behind my seat and pulls out a black hoodie and hands it to me. "Here, you can drape this over your legs."

I take it, but something doesn't sit well with me about it. I look down at the hoodie on my lap, and then my eyes move to the pack of cigarettes, then to the trident logo I couldn't place before, and back down to the hoodie.

I swallow down my panic as my memories flood back into me, slowly putting the puzzle pieces together. The stranger outside of my aunt's house the night I searched my uncle's office was wearing a hoodie just like this one and got into a car with this same logo. The stranger watching me outside of my apartment window, wearing a hoodie and smoking a cigarette.

My mind struggles to make sense of it. Could it have been Landon? Or could it have been the owner of this car—Clive? Oh my God, I need to get the fuck out of this car. I turn my head to look out the window. I don't recognize where we are, and we've been driving for well over thirty minutes. I feel like we should have arrived in Evanston by now.

"Umm, Landon, where are we?" I ask hesitantly.

"We're taking a route to go around the traffic. I told you that already." His usual charismatic tone has left.

My hands start to sweat while my brain repeatedly tells me I need to get out of this car. I pull out my phone to see where we are on my maps application, but before I can tap on it, I feel the car slow down. I look up suddenly at Landon, who has pulled the car over into a dark, empty lot with one streetlight in the far corner. Looking around, I can only see a large warehouse-like building in the distance.

"Why are we stopped?" My voice is so shaky I almost don't recognize it as my own.

Landon takes a deep breath and throws his head back. His eyes are closed and he's shaking his head.

"Ooohhh, Cosette, what am I going to do with you?" he says in a sing-song voice that sounds nothing like the Landon from a few moments ago.

I slowly pull my phone up and tap on my location to share with Esther. We always share locations with each other in case we end up on a date with a serial killer. Right as I tap *share*, Landon rips the phone from my hands.

"Share location? Can't have you doing that." He exits out of my messages with Esther with a tap of his finger, then turns his body entirely so he's facing me. He reaches down and grabs the pack of cigarettes from the cup holder and smacks it on his palm.

Whack, whack, whack. Three times before he opens it up and meticulously selects a cigarette to gently rest between his lips.

"I thought you said those weren't yours?" I say, trying to distract him as my hand searches the door for the handle.

I'm going to run for it—straight back to the warehouse. There must be someone in there who will help me.

"I did say that…" he says with a smirk. "And I lied."

He's laughing now, and I can see that he's digging in his pocket for something as he pulls out a lighter and lights his cigarette. He inhales and releases a cloud of smoke into my face, causing me to cough.

"Oh, Cosette, I really wish you would have just listened to me when I told you to let this all go." He takes another drag of his cigarette. "But no, you had to dig up all this bullshit about your father again. Getting the FBI involved. Making me do things I don't enjoy doing."

"What… What do you mean?" I stumble on my words. My hand is now sitting on the handle. I need to wait for the right moment— for him to look away for just one second and give me an edge.

"You think I like beating up old women?" He looks at me with an eyebrow raised, like he doesn't believe my shock.

My heart stops and my eyes go wide. "You," is all I manage to get out.

"Yes, me." He takes another slow drag of his cigarette. "I knew it was either you or your aunt who dug this shit back up. I had to send a message somehow. She just happened to be the easier one to get to, with you always being with Esther or Dylan lately." Another drag of the cigarette and some ash drops on his shirt. He looks down to brush it off, and I see my window. I pull the handle and the door flies open. My feet are moving before I even realize they've hit the gravel outside. I run as fast as my legs can move, but I hear Landon behind me, and he sounds close. He's cursing, but my mind can't focus on the exact words when something heavy knocks me to the ground.

My hands catch me, but my chin still hits the gravel. I try to wriggle my way forward, to pull myself up, but a sharp pain radiates from the back of my head. It's a hand in my hair, ripping my head back to look into a face that is filled with malice and rage.

"You fucking bitch, you really think you can get away?" Landon bites out and then laughs—the kind of laugh you would hear from someone mentally unwell. I reach up and try to awkwardly fight back, grabbing at his face, but it's the wrong move because he slams my face hard against the ground, and I hear something crack. Sharp pain shoots into my eye, and before I can ready myself for the next blow, he slams my face down again, and this time I feel a definitive crunch.

I'm breathing heavily, my chest rising and falling. I'm crying, but I don't have enough breath in me to make audible noises, so the tears streak silently down my face.

I fight to lift myself off the ground, to escape, but the best I can do is rise on shaky arms. When I feel something cold and metal pressed to the side of my head, time stands still.

The realization that I'm going to die smacks me in the face harder than the gravel did. I'm going to go missing just like my father, and no one will ever find me.

"Please," is the only word I can get out before Landon raises his hand with the gun and slams it back down.

My vision goes before my mind does. I feel pain on the side of my head as I fall back to the ground . I reach out my hand into the dark abyss, feeling the cold gravel scrape under my palm. Another hit lands on my body, this time to my stomach, and it completely knocks the wind from my lungs. I'm fading. I can feel my mind slipping away from me. Another hit to my head, and my body finally gives in to the darkness my eyes have already succumbed to.

CHAPTER THIRTY-TWO

A light shines in my eyes and then pulls away, leaving me blind again, my eyes adjusting to the sudden loss of brightness. My vision is still blurry, but one eye is starting to gain clarity as I take in my surroundings. I'm cold, and an earthy scent penetrates my senses as my body lies prostrate on the ground.

I slowly rove my hand above the ground and no longer feel the gravel I lost consciousness on. Now I only feel cold, moist dirt as I put pressure on my hand. I don't know how long I've been knocked out for, but it must have been long enough for my body to be moved. I allow myself a few moments to blink away the throbbing pain behind my eyes and realize only one eye is able to open and close. I slowly push myself up so that I'm sitting partially propped up on my arm. A rush of dizziness hits me, and I press my other hand to the side of my head. There's something wet and sticky in my hairline, and when I pull my hand back to inspect the substance, I see that it's blood. *My* blood.

There's so much pain radiating through different parts of me that I can't focus on where it's all coming from. I take a breath, and a sharp pain jolts me, forcing memories of what happened prior to passing out to come back to me.

Landon. Running. Being beaten.

Questions start popping up in my head as I take in my surroundings. Where am I? Where is my phone? Where is Landon?

Looking around, all I can see are trees. I'm in a wooded area, and it's extremely dark, with the moon being the only thing that sheds any light on my surroundings. A bright light woke me, but where did it come from?

God, my head hurts.

I roll over and force myself to stand. Bad idea. I'm instantly dizzy.

I hear the silence of the woods being disturbed by footsteps. I turn to run but I'm blinded again by a bright light in my face, causing me to fall to my knees. The dizziness intensifies, and I fall, barely catching my face from hitting the ground with my bloodied hand. Before I can get a whole breath in, I'm heaving, vomit spewing all over the ground below me.

"You're awake… Wonderful. Now we can get to work," a familiar voice says behind the blinding light.

My vision starts to adjust to the light he's shining on me, and I can see him standing in front of me wearing a hoodie. I'm still on the ground when I hear something large thump beside me. A shovel. My stomach drops with the awareness of why a shovel would be next to me. I am going to die. This fucking psychopath is going to make me dig my own grave and then kill me.

"Pick it up." Landon shines the flashlight on the shovel, gesturing for me to grab it.

"Please, Landon, don't do this," I beg, but I know it's no use. Landon pulls out a gun from under his shirt and shoves the barrel to my head. The cold metal presses in on my injury and pain shoots behind my eyes. Tears roll down my face as I do my best to lean over to grab the shovel.

We walk for what feels like days, even though I know it's probably only been an hour. The dizziness hasn't left me, and I'm finding it hard to breathe. Carrying the shovel is another struggle—my right arm is almost useless due to the sharp pain I feel in my side every time I lift it.

It's a strange feeling, knowing you are going to die. I don't know if it's better to have more or less time to dwell on it. My mother had months to make her peace, and in the end, I do believe she found it before she left us. I won't have the luxury of months to make peace, and with every step I take, the more nauseous I become. The knowing of your inevitable end is torture. My body is not only shivering from the cold but shakes from fear of how Landon is going to do it. Does he even know how to use a gun? What if it's not quick? What if it takes me hours to die?

"Here." Landon says and puts a hand on my shoulder to stop me from taking another step forward. "Dig." He points to an area of the ground and holds the gun pointed at me.

"Why are you doing this?" I ask, still not understanding his connection in all this.

He looks at me and tilts his head, a corner of his mouth lifting in an entertained smirk.

"You mean, you and your detective friend didn't figure it out yet?" he remarks sarcastically.

"You killed my father." I state matter-of-factly, even though I have no evidence to back that statement up.

"Wrong!" he yells, stepping closer to me with the gun still pointing at my face. "Care to take another guess?"

I stare at him with my one eye , scared to say something else that will make him angry. I'm not ready to die yet. I shake my head.

"Ok, ok. I guess I can give you this one small mercy. I am a man of the people, after all." He stretches out his arms as if a crowd of people surrounds him, giving me my first moment of relief that the gun is no longer pointed at me.

"Clive Ryland killed your father." He says it so casually it almost doesn't register with me that this is the first time someone has confirmed my father is dead.

My hands shoot to my mouth. I feel like I'm going to be sick again. There is no air in my lungs to catch my breath, and all I can do is let out a whimper.

Landon predatorily circles me.

"It really was a tragic misunderstanding. I mean, it's not like Clive meant to kill him—his anger just got the best of him." He turns to walk in the opposite direction. "But he killed him all the same, and now, once again, I'm here to clean up the mess."

"I don't understand," I say to him, a plea for him to make sense of what he just told me.

"You see, Cosette, unlike the Rylands, I don't have the means to hire someone to take care of things. I told them from the very beginning that Connor needed to be dealt with." He pauses and turns to face me, taking a few steps forward until he's so close I can feel his warm breath on my face. He raises the gun and presses it into my temple again.

"I thought I told you to fucking dig." He demands.

I raise the shovel and release a guttural moan as the pain in my side becomes so overwhelming I think I might pass out. I drop my arms and try to catch my breath the best I can.

I can still feel the gun against my head, and through pure adrenaline, I raise the shovel again and start to dig while Landon continues with his story.

"I told them they needed to take care of all the loose ends. When that fucking piece of shit hacker Connor weaseled his way into the security system, I told them to get rid of him. But Mr. Ryland insisted that money could keep him quiet." He laughs and shakes his head like he just told the funniest joke. "You know what the problem with rich people is? They think money fixes everything. I knew Connor would get greedy. He was holding everyone's lives in his hands, and he knew exactly what it was worth."

I keep digging, and Landon keeps talking. He tells me how Connor will be dealt with, how Clive didn't bank on his father appointing Dylan to be CEO when he became too ill to run the company, and how Dylan was kept in the dark on everything.

Turns out no one knew Landon was there that night, and his

father, the current mayor, used that to his advantage. Landon kept quiet as long as the Rylands bankrolled his father's campaign. And as a cherry on top, he made sure the police department overlooked certain pieces of evidence, clearing a way for my father's case to remain cold. Police officers were paid off—the chief included. Everyone who knew anything is now dead, except for Connor. It's amazing how much Landon is divulging to me, but I suppose after all these years, it's probably cathartic for him to air out all his secrets. In any other situation, I would be asking myself why Landon trusts me enough to tell me all this, but the reality is, you don't need to trust someone if they're dead.

I dig my own grave with building rage and radiating pain. I'm so angry that for five years, money did fix everything for the Rylands. The son of a tech billionaire killed my working-class father and then paid all the right people to look the other way. If the tables were turned, the working-class man would have been behind bars before they even had enough evidence to convict him. The justice system is serving one purpose here—to deliver the illusion of safety. A sad reality that it's just all smoke and mirrors for the majority of us.

I'm knee-deep now, and Landon is looming above me. He's tucked the gun back into his waistband while he smokes another cigarette. I need to keep him talking. The longer he talks, the longer I can stay alive.

I imagine it takes quite a while for a human mind to come to terms with death when faced with the reality that there's no longer the option to survive. As humans, it's in our nature to survive. It's the most important goal—a goal that motivates every single choice we make in our lives. Even though I'm literally digging my own grave, there's a part of my mind that's still telling me there's a way to survive this. I just need a little more time to sort out how.

"Where is he?" The question comes out far quieter than I intend.

"Where is who?"

"My father. Where is he?"

Landon lets out a clipped laugh. "Fuck if I know. The only person who knows is Mr. Ryland, and with the state he's in, I would venture to guess even he doesn't know anymore."

I think back to my conversations with Dylan about his father. The only person in the world who could have told me where to find him doesn't even recognize his own sons anymore.

Time. I need more time.

"Why did Clive do it?" I ask when Landon's silence lingers too long.

I ask the question to keep him distracted from the purposeful slowing of my digging, but also because I want to know. If I am to die out here, I want to die knowing the truth.

I don't need to be looking at Landon to know that he just lit another cigarette. I can hear the flick of the lighter, the soft crackle of the tobacco as he inhales.

On an exhale, he says, "He did it because I told him to."

At his answer, I turn and face him. There's not an ounce of emotion I can find in his face. No remorse, no empathy, no excitement. Just utter indifference.

"Why?" I ask, but it sounds more like a plea.

Why, why, why? The question is screaming in my head.

"Because it was him or me," he says.

"What do you mean? That doesn't make any sense." I shake my head at his non-answer.

He flicks his cigarette into my partially dug grave.

"It doesn't need to make sense," he says, and I hear him step closer to the edge of the grave. "Keep fucking digging."

I grip the shovel a little tighter and reluctantly obey.

CHAPTER THIRTY-THREE

When I was eleven, my mom insisted I play softball. I was never a kid that liked to play sports—more the creative type than competitive. My mother played sports all through high school and was convinced it would be a great way for me to improve my social skills and to get me out of the house.

Of course, I put up a fight, but I eventually lost that battle and was signed up for a little league softball team. I didn't hate it, but I wasn't great and had played over half the season without hitting a single ball when it was my turn up to bat.

After every game, my mom would see how disappointed I was. She always attempted to console me, telling me I would improve and eventually get on base. What she failed to understand was the true reason I was upset. It wasn't because I couldn't hit the ball—it was because my entire team knew I was the weak link, and that doesn't bode well for making new friends.

The other girls on the team didn't make fun of me, but they did ignore me. And to this day, I'm not sure which one is worse.

My father, always the observant one, recognized this

immediately. One day, after a particularly painful loss, my father walked me to the concession stand to buy me an ice cream sandwich to cheer me up. When we got in line, he turned to kneel in front of me.

"I'm going to make you a deal," he said as he placed a hand on each one of my shoulders. "If you hit one ball this season, I'll convince your mother not to sign you up next year." I looked at him, almost heartbroken. I had never been able to hit the ball—in my mind, it was impossible. This deal my father was making had to be some sort of cruel joke. But I knew better. My father was anything but cruel, and if he was making this deal with me, it was because he believed I could do it.

I practiced my swing in the backyard multiple nights leading up to the next game. I knew I wouldn't survive socially through another season of playing on this team. Most of the girls I played with also went to school with me, and even though they rarely talked to me to begin with, I was sure that rare occurrence would quickly disappear.

The next game arrived, and my mother couldn't make it. It was just me and my dad, and he made sure to give me a nice pep talk on the way to the fields.

"Remember what I told you—you only have to hit it once. You don't even need to get on base, just hit the ball one time and you'll never have to play softball again." He smiled at me and drew a cross over his heart with his index finger.

When it was my turn to bat, I stepped up to the plate with the most determination I'd ever felt in my eleven young years.

One. Two. Three. The strikes were fast and painful. The pitcher didn't throw a single ball, almost like she was determined to remove any hope I had left in me. I walked to the dugout, dragging my bat behind me. When I sat down on the bench, my father was standing outside the chain-link fence.

"You looked good out there, kid!" he said with excitement. I didn't respond, just gave him a dramatic preteen eye roll. "Listen, the pitcher is throwing them low. You're going to have to swing up, kid. Don't lose hope yet—I know you can do this." He winked at me before returning to the bleachers. A few more innings went by before I was back up to the plate. I looked over my shoulder and my father was standing right next to the dugout.

"Don't overthink it, Cosette—just swing!" he yelled, and I gave him a confident nod.

Strike one. I heard the ball hit the catcher's mitt before I heard the umpire yell. I took a deep breath and readjusted my hands a little lower on the bat. I saw the ball leave the pitcher's hands and I didn't think—I just swung.

The crack of the bat rattled my hands, causing me to drop it on the ground. Time slowed as I watched the ball fly through the air over second base.

I could hear voices behind me yelling, "Run! Run!" mixed with cheers, but I couldn't take my eyes off the ball. It soared farther and farther until it finally dropped beyond the fence line. I turned to look over my shoulder, and my father was smiling from ear to ear, waving his hand to direct me to run the bases. I turned and did exactly that. I ran, my feet hitting first base, then second, then third, and right over home plate. But I didn't stop there—I ran right off the field and into my father's arms, and he swung me around in a celebratory circle.

When he set me back down, I looked him in the eye and proudly announced, "I did it. I never have to play softball again."

With a shocked face, he put a hand on his hips and asked, "You mean after all that excitement, you still don't want to play?"

I shrugged my shoulders. "Better to go out on a high note."

My father told that story for years. Most people thought it was a story to make them laugh, but every time I listened to him tell it, I didn't hear a story being told by a comedian. Instead, I heard a story being told by a proud father.

I stare down at the freshly dug earth that's being illuminated by the soft blue hue of Landon's phone. He's been quiet since he stopped sharing his secrets with me. I look over my shoulder, and he's face down, distracted by whatever is on his screen. One hand scrolling, and the other holding a cigarette. No gun in sight, and I assume it's tucked snugly into his waistband.

When I look back at the shovel in my hand, the puzzle pieces fall into place, and I understand what my way out is. I take a breath as I slowly toss a shovel full of dirt over my shoulder, angled toward Landon. I know I hit my target when I hear Landon curse.

"What the fuck," he yells, and I hear a thump on the ground next to him.

"Sorry," I say in a soft tone, and I angle my chin just enough to see him wiping the dirt from his arm. His illuminated phone is now lying on the ground.

I slide my hands down the shovel and grip the handle. My hands are already blistering, and my body is throbbing, but the pain only gives me clarity. Out of the corner of my eye, I see Landon bend down to grab his phone.

I close my working eye for a split second and hear my father's voice.

"Don't overthink it, Cosette—just swing."

I take a deep breath and do exactly that.

With the strength of my good arm, the shovel strikes true, and I watch Landon's body topple over into the shallow grave. He moans, and I see his hand move. My body doesn't give my mind time to register before I'm lifting the shovel and bringing it down on Landon's head. Once. Crunch. Twice, and a scream is ripped from my mouth.

I stumble back from his unmoving body, my grip finally releasing my weapon. The shock of what I did sends my body into tremors, and I double over to vomit the nearly empty contents of my stomach.

Landon lies lifeless in the grave meant for me, with a soft illumination coming from his phone next to him. Slowly, I crawl over to his body and pull the phone toward me. Placing it in my pocket, I pull myself out of the shallow hole, and without looking back, I run.

My lungs burn as I pump my legs as fast as I can, barreling my way through the woods while my mind works in overdrive to remember the way we came. Even though it was just a few hours ago, my brain can't seem to recall much of anything. The woods are dark, and the temperature is dropping, but my body welcomes the cold air as sweat pours down my head.

I slow when I remember what I have in my pocket. Now that my body is no longer running, I can truly feel how much my lungs are burning. Gasping for air, I navigate myself to a tree and drop down to the ground while shakily pulling the cell phone from my pocket. There are missed call notifications on the screen, as well as text message notifications, but the phone's privacy settings don't let me see who they're from. It's locked, of course, so I tap the emergency button to initiate a 911 call.

I put the phone up to my ear, and without a ring, I hear a woman's voice on the other end that causes me to release a sob.

"911 operator. What is your emergency?"

"Please…I need help," I cry into the phone. "Please… My name is Cosette Emory. I was taken by Landon Wexford." I suck in a breath of air before continuing. "He tried to kill me."

"Okay, Cosette, can you tell me where you are?"

"I…I don't know. I'm in the woods, but…" I start to cry, so I cover my mouth, hoping that I can keep all the emotions in long enough to tell this woman where I am.

"That's okay. We are going to look up your location. Just stay on the phone with me."

"Okay."

"Are you injured, Cosette?"

Breathing into the phone, I look down at my dirt-covered body to evaluate myself. Lifting my free hand to my face, I wince at the immediate pain I feel when I touch my cheek. As my adrenaline evens out, I notice my face is so swollen it no longer feels like my own under my touch, and there's a sharp pain on the right side of my ribs.

"Cosette? Are you still with me?" The operator brings me back to reality.

"Yes, I'm here. Umm…. Everything hurts, but my face—I think

my face is the worst."

"Okay, stay on the line, Cosette. Help is on the way. Where is the man that took you?"

"I… I don't know. I ran. He's in the woods somewhere. I think. I had to hit him to get away."

I start to shake, remembering the violence that took over me in my pursuit of survival.

"He…he has a gun."

My mind starts to fade, and a wave of dizziness hits me. If it wasn't for the tree behind my back, I don't think I would be able to hold myself up, even in a sitting position. I suddenly drop the phone as a wave of nausea overcomes me, and I wretch into the wet ground next to me. A sharp ringing fills my ears, and I scramble my hands across the floor of the woods to find the phone.

I'm fading quickly, and my vision is blurred enough that I can no longer see anything in front of me.

"Please…please send help," I beg, hoping the operator can still hear me. It's my last plea before darkness consumes me.

CHAPTER THIRTY-FOUR

I wake to a bright light and sterile smell. Slowly, I blink until the room comes into semi-focus. I'm in a hospital bed. There's an IV in my arm and a strange clip on my index finger and… Oh my God, my face hurts. I let out an involuntary moan that seems to make the pain in my face feel worse. There's a soreness on my side near my ribs, but it's nothing compared to the shooting pain behind my eye. Wires also come out of the neck of the horridly patterned hospital gown I'm wearing, and panic overwhelms me as memories flood my brain.

A machine I'm hooked up to starts to beep, and I'm sure it's saying that my heart is racing.

"Fuck," I moan again, and a woman wearing wine-colored scrubs walks quietly into my room. She moves around the room like a hummingbird, practically floating to the beeping machine. She hits a button and turns to me.

"Welcome back." Her voice is melodic, a soft contrast to the cold, sterile room.

"You gave us quite a scare there for a minute," she says to me as she jots down notes on a clipboard. "Your injuries were pretty severe, so you might be in some pain for a little while."

She hugs the clipboard to her chest with one hand and with the other pulls a tiny remote connected to a wire from the side of my bed. Placing it in my hand, she says, "Here. If you ever feel like the pain is too much, you can click this button. It will administer some medication to help."

I instantly click it and pray that it works quickly.

"Do you know what your name is?"

The question is gentle, but it still causes me to wince. I nod and attempt to swallow, but my mouth is as dry as the Sahara Desert.

"My name is Cosette." The words come out so strained, they sound like I'm whispering. My hand shoots to my throat as I become aware of another part of my body that hurts.

"Drink some water. We had to intubate you, so you may be a little irritated for the next day or so." She hands me a cup with a straw, and I gulp down. The fluid feels like silk caressing my throat, and I let out another moan, although this one is not of pain.

"I know you're probably very confused and would like to know what happened to you. I'm going to get the doctor so she can take a look at you and give you some answers."

I nod again, saving my voice for when the doctor arrives.

I finish my water but don't dare chew on the ice chips. Although the pain medicine is kicking in, my face still feels like I could fracture something from a mere smile, let alone biting down.

I lay my head back on the pillow, trying to fight myself from nodding off before the doctor comes in. A few moments later, another woman wearing a white coat with pens sticking out of a pocket on her chest walks into my room, along with the nurse who gave me the water.

"Hello, Cosette. I'm Doctor Sheila. How are you feeling?" She tilts her head as she silently assesses me.

"I've been better," I rasp out with a half-smile.

She smiles back with a nod. "I suppose you have. I'd like to take a look at your injuries. Would that be all right?"

I nod, and she continues over to the side of my hospital bed while pulling on a pair of gloves.

"You arrived here in pretty bad shape. You're a very lucky woman—a very brave woman—for what you had to survive."

She lifts my gown and gently palpates an area around my ribs. I wince slightly, but the pain medication has helped tremendously, and I don't feel too much discomfort.

"You had a broken rib that caused a small puncture in your right lung. It wasn't serious enough to need surgery, but we did have to operate on your face. You came in with a fractured orbital bone."

My face? Oh my God. That would explain the pain I woke up with. Doctor Sheila must see the panic spread across my swollen face.

"Don't worry, we have a phenomenal in-house plastic surgeon. Once you're healed, the scar should be hidden in your hairline." She pokes and prods around my head and face. "Stitches look good. She'll need her dressing changed. Let's also get her some ice packs to help with the swelling of her face," Doctor Sheila says to the gentle-voiced nurse, who nods and flutters out of the room.

The doctor glances back at me with a look I can't place as pity or concern. I'm hoping it's pity—the last person I want a concerning look from is a doctor.

"The fractured rib and orbital bone probably seem scary right now, but they will heal. You also have a brain contusion. It's small enough to heal on its own, but we will need to monitor you for a little while before you can go home."

She pauses to allow me to take in everything she is saying before she continues.

"Due to the severity of your injuries, we had to put you in a medically induced coma."

My non-swollen eye widens.

"How long?" I ask, fearing the answer. Immediately, my mind panics and thinks of my aunt. The last time I saw her, she was lying in a hospital bed. I need to see her. I need to know that she's all right.

Doctor Sheila looks at me like I'm the eighth world wonder.

"You've been out for six days. In all honesty, it's a miracle that you managed to fend off your attacker, let alone navigate your way toward the road in the condition you were in. Your body must have been operating on pure adrenaline and the will to survive…and that is exactly what you are, Cosette—a survivor."

She pauses to allow me to absorb the information. Six days. I lost six days. It's a creepy feeling to know that while I was unconscious in a hospital bed for almost a week, the world continued to revolve without me.

"Do you remember what happened to you?"

The question hangs suspended in the air while I gulp down my rising panic, and my brain starts to replay the events a normal person would only ever experience in a horror movie. Nodding my head, I tell her, "Yes. I remember everything." It comes out as nearly a whisper over the lump in my throat.

Doctor Sheila finishes her exam and leaves me with the nurse in wine-colored scrubs, who I now know is named Teresa. She makes small talk with me about all the things that have happened in the world over the past week.

Greece is apparently broke, Prince Harry was partying naked in Vegas, and there's a new movie being filmed in River North that's causing traffic to become horrendous. I ask her if anyone had come to see me while I was unconscious, and she nods, telling me that a young woman was here, an older gentleman with gray hair, and someone else who wasn't permitted to come into my room but sat in the waiting room for an entire day before being asked to leave.

I already know that the young woman was Esther, and the older man was most likely Remy. At least they know that I'm alive and have hopefully informed my aunt of where I am.

"I've been informed that a detective will be arriving today to speak with you. If you'd like, I can have Doctor Sheila tell him to come tomorrow instead."

I shake my head and tell her it's fine. As much as I would love to put off reliving what Landon did to me, I know that it's something I need to do sooner rather than later.

CHAPTER THIRTY-FIVE

I must have dozed off because I'm startled awake by Nurse Teresa coming to check my vitals. She refills my water cup like the saint she is and informs me that now that I'm awake, the detective is here to see me.

A few moments later, a familiar man in a suit walks into my room, and to my immense relief, Remy follows him in.

Remy takes two large steps to eliminate the space between us. He looks awful, like he hasn't slept in weeks. He grabs my hand, enveloping it in both of his.

"Oh my God, Cosette. I'm—" the words get choked off in the back of his throat, and I think he may be crying.

"It's okay," I tell him. "I'm alright."

He lifts his head to look at me, and I can see the moisture of a tear gather just below his lower lashes.

"No, you're not alright. You've been in a coma for the last week, for the love of God." His voice sounds infuriated, but I know the anger isn't directed at me. "But you're alive, and that's the only thing that matters right now."

He lets go of my hand and pulls over a chair to sit next to my bed.

"Cosette, you remember Agent Byrne?" He lifts a hand to gesture toward the FBI agent, and I nod.

"Good. I need you to recount everything that happened the night Landon attacked you. You can take your time—try to include every detail, even if you think it's not important."

I do exactly that.

I tell them everything, even the parts I didn't initially share with Remy, and I can see his eyes go wide when I mention my plan to go to Evanston. I pause to gain my composure when I get to the part where Landon told me my father was dead, allowing myself to shed some of the grief before continuing to the part where I hit him with the shovel.

"Is he alive?" I ask, even though I know I won't be satisfied with any possible answer to that question.

Agent Byrne shakes his head. "No. Landon Wexford is dead."

My hands shoot to my mouth, and tears again find their way down my face. Not because I mourn him, but because I know I am the reason he is dead, and I can't imagine killing the son of the Mayor of Chicago goes without punishment.

"Am I going to go to jail?" I ask in a whisper. The thought is so terrifying that saying it aloud makes me want to throw up.

"No. You will not go to jail. There is more than enough evidence that you acted in self-defense."

"But the Mayor—he can sway the police," I protest.

"Not anymore. Your case, as well as your father's, now fall completely under the FBI's oversight."

I sit up at the mention of my father. "My father's case?"

"Yes. We have some updates…" Remy's hand juts out and grabs Agent Byrne by the arm, stopping him mid-sentence. Remy gives him a shake of the head—an obvious effort to tell him not to share whatever he was just about to.

"Remy…" Byrne sighs. "She can either find out from us or find out from the news."

"Find out what?" I demand.

Both men are silent for what feels like an eternity, and then finally, Remy begins to speak.

"Connor Wilder has been arrested for evidence tampering, obstruction of justice, and blackmail, among other things."

I stare at him wide-eyed, waiting for him to continue, but it's Byrne who picks up where Remy leaves off.

"A day after Landon abducted and attacked you, Connor's apartment was raided, and the FBI found video surveillance Connor was using to blackmail the Ryland family for years."

Already knowing the answer, I ask, "What was on the video surveillance?"

Byrne looks to Remy, but Remy doesn't say a word. Instead, he stares at the floor with his fists clenched at his sides.

I suddenly lose my patience. "What the fuck was on the video, Remy?" I say, raising my voice. My throat feels like it's on fire, but I'm too worked up to notice the severity of the pain.

Remy looks up at me with glassy eyes. "The video shows Clive Ryland murdering your father."

The air is sucked out of my lungs. This is not news to me—Landon already told me that Clive was responsible for my father's death—but for there to be a video of him committing the act is too much for me to wrap my head around.

"I want to see it."

The words leave my mouth, and it feels like someone other than myself is speaking.

"You don't want to see it, Cosette. I can spare you the trauma of that experience and tell you exactly what happened," Remy says, and it sounds like a plea.

I know why he doesn't want me to see it—he's grown quite protective of me over the months. I know there is a cloud of guilt still floating over his head for what happened to my uncle, and I wouldn't be surprised if he's been blaming himself for my aunt and me being attacked by Landon. A piece of me almost wants to give in to him and let him save me from the harm watching the video is surely to cause me, but this isn't about Remy.

"No. I need to see it, Remy," I say matter-of-factly.

He opens his mouth to protest again, but I cut him off.

"I have spent the last five years going to bed every night wondering what happened to my father and waking up every morning having to remember I live in a world where he no longer exists. Over the past months, I have been lied to over and over again—the police, the mayor, the people that are supposed to protect us, to bring us justice, have lied. Please don't take offense when I say I'm tired of taking people at their word. I'd rather trust my eyes to tell me exactly what happened that night, not another investigative report."

Remy lets out a defeated sigh and runs a hand down his face. He shakes his head as if not understanding my justification.

"Please…I need to see it. I need to know what they did to him." This time, I'm not looking directly at either of the men in the room. My eyes are closed as I whisper the three words that have been haunting me.

"I need to know… I need to know… I need to know."

Tears roll down my face, and the pain I feel in my chest makes the physical pain of my injuries seem unremarkable. How can a heart break so many times? And how do you fix it when the broken pieces are so fine they are nothing but dust?

When I open my eyes, I see Remy—with his arms crossed over his chest—give a nod to Agent Byrne. The agent lifts a tablet that I didn't notice he'd been holding the entire time he's been in here and starts swiping on the screen. Once he has located whatever he was looking for, he walks to my bed and places the tablet on my lap.

I fight the pain in my face and lift my head to peer down to find an eighteen-minute video of black-and-white surveillance footage waiting for me to hit play.

My hand lifts to hover over the device, and there's no hiding the shake in it. I can see Remy out of the corner of my good eye making a step toward me, and I lift my hand to stop him.

I can do this. I can do this.

I close my eyes, and I can see him perfectly—standing in the kitchen of our old home. He was making coffee, and I was giving him a hard time about drinking too much of it. I'm a hypocrite for it now, but at the time, I thought I was saving him from an inevitable caffeine-induced heart attack.

"Cosette, what would you have me do? Drink coffee or lose my job because I've fallen asleep at work?"

"I'd rather you lose your job. At least then I'd be able to see you more," I snap at him. I know the words hurt him, and I meant them to.

I throw my chair back while simultaneously grabbing his cup of coffee. I walk to the sink and dump it down the drain. Turning to look back at him, I cross my arms in accomplishment and wait for the retaliatory punishment he's about to bestow upon me.

He clutches at his eyes with his fingers, and it's only then that I know I've crossed a line. My father is the most patient human I know, but even he has his limits. Limits I've tested every day since my mother died.

"Do you think I like working sixty hours a week, Cosette?" The calm in his voice is more unnerving than if he was screaming at me. It stuns me into silence. "Do you think I like knowing that my daughter spends so much time alone in this house?" He walks toward me, eyes widening, waiting for me to respond, but whatever words I had earlier die on my tongue.

"If you think the answer to either of those questions is anything other than a resounding no, you are out of your damn mind." He stands directly in front of me and grabs my hands in his. They're dry and calloused—the hands of a blue-collar man—hands that have endured and evolved to handle the harshest of conditions. And in that moment, I recognize that his hands are not the only things that have calloused over time, but my heart as well.

"I know you're mad, Cosette, and you're allowed to be. I'm mad too. I miss her too, you know?"

"I know…" I whisper as a tear falls down my cheek.

"I didn't want to sit around and watch her die, but God had other plans, and I loved her too much to leave her to do it alone." He pulls me into his chest and wraps his arms around me as I fight everything in me not to fall apart.

"Sometimes we have to do things that hurt in the moment if we want to avoid the lifetime of regret we are surely to feel if we don't."

I open my good eye and stare down at the screen. I don't want to watch this video, but I know if I don't, I will regret not getting the justice of witnessing the truth of my father's death. A justice I owe him—and a justice that no one's money can rob from me.

So, I do something I don't want to do, because I love him too much not to. With a now steady hand, I press play.

CHAPTER THIRTY-SIX

The video plays with no sound, and for the first forty seconds or so, you only see an empty lobby. I've been in that lobby—it's the one on the fourth floor of the Ryland Corp. building, where my father's office was. Less of an office and more of a broom closet, but I suppose that aligns for someone in charge of maintenance.

A petite woman with long dark hair walks quickly into view, and within seconds, a familiar figure emerges from the right side of the screen, grabbing her arm harshly.

Landon pulls the woman into him, and she attempts to fight him off. You can see her become more frantic as she realizes her efforts are unsuccessful and reaches her hand up to slap him across the face. The force of it throws them both off balance, and Landon throws her to the floor.

Before she can scurry away, he grabs her by the hair and slams her face into the floor—a pain I am all too familiar with—and the sight causes me to suck in a breath. I don't need to continue watching to know where this is going, as Landon rips at the woman's blouse and roughly palms her breast. Although the video is silent, I can almost hear the woman's cries for help as her face contorts when she screams.

Another excruciating minute of the video has gone by, and Landon has worked the woman's pants down to her knees and has her flipped over on her stomach. She's gone limp, but you can still see her sobbing.

A hand is covering my mouth now, and I feel like I'm about to be sick. Suddenly Landon stops and peers behind him. He makes to get off the woman, but before he can, a large male comes into view and rips him off her body.

"Dad." I choke on the word as I watch my father wrestle with Landon in the video. They begin to brawl, trading blows, and my father seems to be getting the best of him—but I know how this ends.

Watching this video is like watching a horror movie for the second time when you know that a character is about to die—only this time, that character is my father. I let out a heavy breath as I suck in more air, my mind forgetting to breathe as the panic of what I am about to witness sets in.

Another figure appears and rips my father off Landon, landing a punch to his face that knocks my father to the ground. Blood is pouring from his face while Landon yells something at Clive, frantically pointing at the woman and then back to my father.

Clive is staggering, appearing to be intoxicated, and screams something toward my father. I watch in horror as Clive Ryland stalks over to my father, mounts his body, and beats him to death. He delivers blow after blow after blow for what feels like an eternity.

It's not until Remy wraps his arms around me that I realize I'm screaming.

"Why? Why? Why?" I scream over and over again until the nurse and Doctor Sheila come running in, yelling things at Remy and Agent Byrne.

I see one of them move to the side of my bed and administer something into my IV. Within seconds, I feel my panic subside, and I come back into my body. I'm no longer screaming and can hear a conversation being had between Remy and the doctor. She's telling him to leave, and suddenly the panic starts to come back. He can't leave—I have so many questions. Questions that will drive me to the brink of insanity if I don't get answers now.

"No!" I yell. "Please…let them stay. I'm okay, I promise I'll be calm."

"As your doctor, I strongly advise that they leave you to rest. They have caused enough stress on you as it is," she says with a pointed look in the two men's direction.

"No, I need them to stay. I'll be more stressed if they leave."

Doctor Sheila's mouth flattens to a straight line, and she crosses her arms over her chest in a sign of disapproval.

"Fine. Visiting hours are over in fifteen minutes. I'll be waiting outside."

I turn to Remy, who is breathing heavily enough that I can see his shoulders bobbing up and down, and Agent Byrne is standing calm in the corner of my room.

"Where is Clive?" I ask calmly, to no one in particular.

"Clive has been arrested and will most likely be denied bail due to his access to funds and international connections. He has been charged with murder and is cooperating," Agent Byrne says pragmatically.

Kind of hard not to cooperate when you are on video.

"We've also made contact with the woman from the video. We're working to sort out her visa status in return for her cooperation as a witness."

Immediately it dawns on me that the woman in the video must have been the intern that is being housed in Evanston. It brings me a small comfort to know I was so close to getting answers.

"And what about all the people that helped cover this up? The mayor, the police department? What happens to them?" I demand.

"That is a little more complicated and will require further investigation before charges are brought forward," Byrne replies without a hint of emotion. "But rest assured, there is a money trail, and we will follow it."

"Right…" My reply is drenched in skepticism, and no doubt is felt by both men standing in my room.

"Cosette, I know you want justice. We just have to make sure we cross all our T's and dot the I's. The last thing we want is to bring charges when we don't have enough evidence to convict. Believe me when I tell you, I know the prosecutor that will be handling these cases, and he won't move forward unless he's confident in a conviction."

Agent Byrne is beginning to sound like a salesman. I'm not sure who he's trying to convince now—me or himself. As much as I would like to tell him all the reasons why I don't trust anything will happen to the mayor or his Chicago PD lackeys, I nod and tell him I need to get some rest instead. His mouth forms into a tight line, and I know he's aware he's being dismissed.

He leaves the room without another word, and now it's just Remy and me staring silently at each other. I don't have the energy to maintain this stare-down we have found ourselves in, so I close my eye and lay my head back on the pillow.

With my eyes still shut I say, "If you're going to stay, at least tell me something better than the 'it's complicated' bullshit your buddy just tried selling to me."

Remy huffs out a noise akin to a laugh, and I open my eye to a view of him shaking his head with a subtle smirk.

"Jesus Christ, Remy, what could you possibly find funny about any of this shit?" I click the button on my pain medication remote and realize most of my irritation is probably coming from the discomfort I'm feeling from my injuries and less about Remy. "I know you're old, but don't tell me you're going senile on me."

"It's not funny. I just…" He sighs, knowing there's not much to say that will save him from being my emotional dartboard . "I'm just glad you're awake, even if your attitude resurfaced with your consciousness."

If it wouldn't cause me pain, I would roll my eyes. "How is Billie?" I ask.

"She's doing really well. They moved her out of the ICU a few days ago, and she should be cleared to go home once they can get a home health nurse set up for her," he explains, and knowing she's going to be alright is the silver lining I needed.

"Does she know?"

He nods. "She knows you're here. We didn't give her the exact details, but she knows it was bad. She wanted to come see you, but with the two of you in different hospitals, her doctors didn't advise her leaving in her condition."

"I don't imagine she was pleased about that."

He shakes his head. "Not at all. She's been calling up here round the clock, every day."

He walks over to my side table that is host to a phone and my water cup to scribble some numbers down on a pad of paper. "Here. This is the number to call and her room extension. When you're feeling up to it, I'm sure she'd be relieved to hear your voice."

I nod in appreciation.

"You're probably exhausted. I'm not going further than the waiting room, but I'm afraid if I don't let you get some rest, your doctor is going to kick me out of the hospital completely."

He makes his way to the door and pauses to look me over once more.

"I know it doesn't make it any easier, but Clive is claiming that he attacked your father because he thought he was the one who assaulted the intern. Apparently, she was Clive's girlfriend at the time."

I instantly remember what Landon said to me in the woods—*He did it because I told him to.*

Remy is right. It doesn't make it easier. It makes it more heartbreaking. Of course, Clive would never believe Landon could be the assailant—a wealthy, privileged kid with everything to lose. No, it's a much more convenient truth to believe the maintenance man who fixes their toilets and makes a fraction of their weekly salary in an entire year would commit such a heinous act. The man with a name they don't remember and a life they never cared to ask about.

I shake my head. "No… No, it doesn't."

CHAPTER THIRTY-SEVEN

I don't know when I dozed off, but when I wake, the sun is no longer shining through the sterile white blinds of my hospital room window. With my good eye, I see my sleeping best friend, curled up like some sort of contortionist in a very stiff-looking chair. My mouth tips up with the slightest hint of entertainment when I truly take her in. Her mouth is dropped open, causing her to emit a subtle snore, and her hair looks like she hasn't run a brush through it in days. I only wish I had a camera to capture this moment for later teasing.

I reach my arm out to grab my water cup off the side table, but as I stretch, I feel a sharp pain in my side and release an audible groan loud enough to stir Esther awake. She blinks her eyes a few times while keeping her eyes on me, almost like she can't tell if she's awake or dreaming.

"Hi," I say, lifting a hand in an awkward excuse of a wave. "Mind helping me out with my water cup?"

My voice must snap her out of her sleepy stupor. "Oh my God, Cosette! You're awake!"

Instantly, she's up and standing next to my bed with a hand

gripping my arm like if she were to let go, she'd never see me again.

A tear slips down her face and, from the contorted muscles between her eyebrows, I know she's doing everything she can to not fall apart.

"I came as soon as I heard what happened. Stayed every day until they would tell me visiting hours were over." She starts to hiccup little sobs in between the last few words. While I had been unconscious, unaware of the outside world, my friend was sitting here tortured day after day. That alone makes my rage bubble up inside toward Landon, and for a split second, I don't feel remorse for killing him.

Of course, the split second is gone, and I'm back to square one, feeling sick to my stomach for taking someone's life—even if it was to save my own.

"It's ok. I'm ok," I console her with a soft voice, repeating the line over and over again.

Esther sniffles and then straightens. "How can you say that? You are anything but ok right now, Cosette."

Maybe from a physical standard I'm not ok—I'm still in a lot of pain, and I can't imagine what my face looks like. Bad enough to have Esther eyeing me like I'm on my deathbed. But I'm alive, and that surely counts for something.

"I know, but…it looks worse than it is."

She clicks her tongue, indicating that she's not buying my bullshit.

She expectedly asks about what happened, and I tell her almost all the details, only sparing her the parts that I know would terrify her more than she already is. Even though it was short-lived, she still had an intimate relationship with Landon.

"Your dad saved that woman from something terrible." She's looking down at the floor now. I know it's probably hard for her to look me in the eyes and see the pain this causes me. "I mean, he's a fucking hero for what he did. And Landon… Oh God."

She places her head in her hands and sobs silently. I only know she's crying because her shoulders move up and down, and her breaths are coming out staccato-like. I don't say anything because I honestly don't know what there is to say about all this. There are no words that can change what has already happened, and I fear that telling her it's ok would only serve to invalidate the emotions she's feeling right now. So, I allow my silence to stretch through the minutes she takes to pull herself back together.

"I let him in my home… Oh my God, I fucking slept with him." She runs over to the corner of the room and vomits in the small cream-colored plastic trash bin.

My sweet, happy-go-lucky Esther, so full of life and optimism, will never be the same after this.

We will never be the same after this.

As a woman, there's no moment more disturbing, none more terrifying than when you're hit with the cold reality of how dangerous men are—and how little we can do to stop them when they mean to hurt us. It's an irrevocable change in the way you live your life, the way you make decisions, the way you interact with strangers.

Not all men are bad men—my father wasn't. But not all men are good men, and ones with money, with power—those can be the most dangerous of them all.

Once Esther has calmed down, she tells me about how my aunt is doing. She tells me how she's taken the last week off so she could split her time between being here waiting for me to wake up, and at the other hospital where Billie is, to give her updates on me.

"You know, I'm not the only one who has been in the waiting room every day."

Initially, I don't follow what she's trying to say.

"Who, Remy?" I say as more of a statement than a question. "Yeah, I already saw him earlier."

Esther looks at me with an expression that I know means she's about to tell me something that will make her uncomfortable.

"Umm…no. Not Remy." She clasps her hands in front of her.

"Oh, for the love of God, Esther, nothing can be worse than the situation I'm in right now. Spit it out already."

She blows out a breath that lifts a lock of hair hanging in her face.

"Dylan… Dylan has been here every day." She spits out his name like it tastes spoiled on her tongue.

"Oh… Well, I don't want to see him."

"No fucking kidding, that's why he hasn't been allowed back here. Remy and I both made sure the entire hospital staff knew he wasn't allowed in to see you… But he's sitting out there as we speak."

Dylan… Of course, Dylan is here. I'm not sure why his name didn't come to mind earlier. I have no words for the feelings that are running through me right now because I'm not sure what those feelings are. Anger, grief, fear… the list goes on and on. All I know for certain is I don't want to see him. I can't trust him, even if I wanted to.

"Why is he still here if he's been told he can't see me?"

"He said he wasn't going to leave until you woke up and made the decision for yourself that you didn't want to see him." Esther makes a conscious effort to lace every word with annoyance.

"Well, feel free to tell him I'm awake and I don't want to see him. Honestly, I'm shocked he wasn't legally advised to steer clear of here." I lay my head back on the pillow and close my eyes. Even though I just woke up a little over an hour ago, I feel exhausted. This entire situation feels surreal, like I'm living in a nightmare.

"On second thought, why hasn't he been arrested? He was in the building when his brother…" I trail off because I can't bring myself to speak the words.

"I take it you haven't watched the news yet?"

"No, Esther, I haven't watched the news. I wouldn't even know how to get the TV on in here." I gesture to the black screen of the television mounted on the wall across from me.

Esther's mouth draws into a straight line.

"Go on… Tell me." I have a feeling this will not be the last time someone fills me in on what has happened in the days I've been lying in a coma.

Esther talks, and I, with my last ounce of mental energy, listen.

Over the next hour, I learn that Dylan's claims of being passed out in another room that night have been confirmed by not only his brother but the unnamed witness—who I know to be the intern who lost her visa. Dylan hasn't been arrested, but he's been advised not to leave the state and is cooperating with the authorities.

Clive has admitted to murdering my father and claims his father was the one to coordinate the disposal of the body—which aligns with Landon saying Mr. Ryland was the only one to know where my father's body is.

Disposal. The word makes my stomach sink. Disposal of the body, like my father was nothing but trash to be taken out to the street once the life was taken from him.

"Are they saying that? Disposal?" I ask Esther as she trails off with the rest of her retelling of this morning's news.

"Yeah. I'm sorry, Cosette. I should have paraphrased it better for you. The news can be so callous sometimes, like they forget they are talking about actual human beings who have friends and families mourning them."

Esther continues to tell me what they aren't saying on the news—the DA offered Clive a deal if he informs them where they can find the remains of my father. But he is sticking to his claim of his father being the only one who knows.

Mr. Ryland has been questioned multiple times by authorities and is currently under state supervision until his case is tried in court. I think it's safe to say the location of my father will likely die with the old man, whenever that day comes.

There have been three times in my life where I have experienced so much grief that I reached a point where I could no longer cry, could no longer feel that pit of emotion digging its way into my chest. Almost as if my mind switched into survival mode and knew one more ounce of emotion would break me.

The first was the day my mother died—by the time my father took me home, I couldn't muster another tear even if I wanted to. The second was the day I accepted my father was never coming back, and the third is right now.

As I watch Esther use a tissue to pat her wet eyes, it's not lost on me that mine are as dry as a bone. All I want to do is sleep, and maybe tomorrow I'll be healed enough for my mind to allow me some emotions.

"Are you going to be ok?" Esther asks.

She's careful not to ask if I'm ok, because the obvious answer to that is no.

No, she is asking if I'm going to be ok, and instead of curiosity motivating her question, it's fear I can hear in her words. The fear that I might not ever be ok after all this. It's a valid fear, but much like my mother's beloved lilac, I too am resilient.

CHAPTER THIRTY-EIGHT

Six months later...

"I'll have an Americano, black. Hot, please," I say to the wide-eyed barista behind the counter. Her eyebrows are practically touching her hairline as she slowly gazes down at her register screen to key in my order.

She looks back up at me and searches my face like she's trying to figure out how she knows me. It's not the first time I've had this encounter. Since Clive Ryland's arrest and swift conviction, my face has been plastered all over the news.

MISSING RYLAND CORP. EMPLOYEE'S DAUGHTER FINALLY GETS JUSTICE.

Justice would be having a body to bury, a grave to visit. But that's not what the people want to hear.

"Uhh… Can I get a name for the order?" the barista asks, waiting for me to confirm what she's finally figured out.

"Cassie," I say, and I watch her eyebrows scrunch in confusion.

I take a seat and wait for my pseudonym to be called and pull out my phone. I have a few messages from Billie asking me what I want for dinner tonight. After she was well enough to leave the hospital, I subleased my apartment and moved in with her to help get her back on her feet.

She's still going through intense physical therapy and hasn't been able to work. Luckily, between her disability checks and what I manage to bring home from The Lonely Olive, we've been able to make ends meet. It's not the most sustainable solution, but for now it will have to do.

Remy has offered, on multiple occasions, to help us with bills, but I refuse to take charity from him. So instead of trying to shove money in my pocket every other week, he switched his efforts to convincing me to bring a lawsuit against Ryland Corp.

His efforts were successful, and he set me up with "the best lawyer in the Midwest"—his words, not mine. My lawyer's name is Alan Blackwood, and he took on the case *pro bono*, meaning I don't have to pay him a dime. It felt a little fishy to me, but Remy insisted it's because the publicity alone from winning a case like this will land him any client he wants.

I don't fully understand how the legal system works, but according to Alan, we either win the case or Ryland Corp. will try to settle to avoid a lengthy trial. I'm personally willing to settle if it means I get to put this all behind me sooner rather than later.

I send a quick text back to Billie letting her know I'll stop by the grocery store on my way home from work.

I hear the name Cassie called a few times before remembering that's the name I gave for my coffee and quickly rush to the counter to grab it.

When I arrive at The Olive, I'm greeted by a bright-eyed redhead named Abigail. She's our new bartender and my first official new hire since taking on the permanent position of bar manager. I still don't make nearly as much in tips, but the consistency of a salary, health insurance, and paid time off make it worth it. Plus, Chrissy calls out often enough for me to make a little side cash when I cover for her.

"Hey Abigail, how's the day been?"

With a nod of her head, she directs my attention to one of our regular drunks sleeping at the end of the bar. "It's been great, other than the snoring coming from that one."

"Please tell me you didn't serve him."

She scrunches her nose at me, annoyed I'd ask. "Of course not, he came in like that. I already called a cab for him, but they're not going to take him again if we don't pay them up front."

I pull out two twenties from my apron and hand them to her.

"Here, I'll cover it this time. Greg's good for it. I'll get it back next time he comes in with a clear mind."

I don't usually pay for our customers' cabs, but I've got a soft spot for Greg. He lost his daughter last year in a car accident. Up until then, he'd been what most would call a functioning alcoholic, but since the accident, it's been a little less functional and a lot more sleeping on the bar.

"You sure?" Abigail asks, a hand on her hip, and I nod.

She shoves the money into her pocket and turns to walk toward a woman who just sat down in front of us, then stops mid-step and turns to face me again.

"Oh, I almost forgot!" She shoves her hand into the pocket of her apron and pulls out an envelope. "Some guy came in earlier, told me to give this to you."

I look at the envelope she holds out to me and see my name written on the front. The last time I got a mysterious letter, I was sent on some wild goose chase to find answers no one intended to give me.

"Well, take it already." Abigail's soprano voice jolts me out of my stupor, and I snatch the envelope out of her hand.

"Hopefully the guy left his number in there. He was *super* hot." She simultaneously flips her hair and turns to take the woman's drink order without giving me another thought.

I clutch the letter to my chest and feel my heart beating in tandem with my breathing. I know I can't open this here. I have no idea what's in it, and I won't risk having a breakdown at work.

I head to the back to find Chrissy grabbing her purse from a locker.

"Hey, I need you to cover for me tonight. I had something urgent come up," I say, hoping for once in our entire time working together, she helps me out.

"What? No, I'm not covering for you. I was literally just about to leave." She holds her bag up in front of my face to prove her point.

"Please, Chrissy, I never ask anything of you. Please, just this once—cover for me." I can't believe I've stooped low enough to beg, but my panic is rising, and I need to get the hell out of here.

"Sorry, can't help you." She sidesteps to walk past me, and I snap, putting my arm in front of her.

She halts and looks at me like I'm a crazy person. "What the fuck are you doing, Cosette? Get out of my way."

"Listen." I keep my tone level. "I have covered for you, no questions asked, more times than I can count. If you don't help me out tonight, I will never cover for you again. So, the next time you can't make it to work, whatever the reason, good luck finding anyone to help you out."

She stares at me, trying to gauge if I'm being serious.

"And you and I both know you are one call-out away from Jeremy firing your ass," I add.

She lets out a dramatic "Ugghhh" and throws her bag back toward the lockers.

I quickly grab my things and head for the door. Before I can make my escape, I hear Abigail ask where I'm going.

I throw my hand up without looking at her. "Something came up. Chrissy is covering for me."

I know without having to see her face she's silently cursing to herself. No one likes working with Chrissy.

Two train connections and a short taxi later, I make it back to my aunt's house. I enter through the back door and see her sitting in a La-Z-Boy recliner watching an old episode of *Seinfeld*.

"Cosette?" she calls. "What are you doing back so early?"

"I had my shifts mixed up. I don't work tonight!" I call back to her as I shimmy my way down the hall into the guest room that I've had to makeshift into my living quarters.

I sit on the bed and stare down at my name. I can tell by the handwriting the letter is from Dylan—a man I can't seem to forget no matter how much I try to leave him in the past.

Slowly, I open the envelope and pull out the folded letter. The papers are stationery from an assisted living residence.

Cosette,

It's been one hundred and ninety-two days

since my brother was arrested and told me my father was the only person that knew where yours was.

Since then, I have consistently done two things every single day. The first is think of you. You are a ghost that haunts my every moment. A ghost I will often welcome but will never escape. What my family has done to you is unthinkable and unforgivable, and I will spend the rest of my life thinking of ways to atone for their actions.

The second is sit with my father and wait for moments of lucidity. In one hundred and ninety-two days, my father has been lucid for five.

I know nothing can bring your father back,

but I hope this brings you and your family some closure.

—Dylan

I set the letter down next to me and look at the second page. It's a printout of a satellite image map with a circle around what looks to be a property. Inside of the circle, there is a small body of water where an X is drawn.

Shakily, I set the map down and stare at the markings, slowly running my finger over the X. I haven't cried since the day I woke up in the hospital, and I'm startled when I feel the warmth of a tear slide down my face. Over the years, my tears have held a spectrum of emotions, but today they only hold hope. It's finally time to bring my father home.

EPILOGUE

Even though the sun shines bright enough to sting my eyes, the cold snap of early spring air cools the weather enough to need a heavy sweater. There's always a smell that hints to winter officially being over, when the ground is moist and the humidity in the air carries the earthy scent of plants sprouting for the first time.

It was my mother's favorite time of year, and she used to say she wished she could bottle up the smell of new beginnings. It's not lost on me that the day my father will finally be laid to rest next to my mother happens to be the first gorgeous day of the year. It's as if the universe finally feels like some poetic justice has been served.

I stand outside the black car that drove my aunt and me to the cemetery. There are five others behind us that look just like it, all carrying distant relatives I haven't seen in years. My aunt has already made her way up to a group gathered around the wooden box that houses what's left of my father's body.

It took less than four days for the FBI to locate my father in a man-made lake on a piece of land owned by a shell company linked to Mr. Ryland. I don't know whether to believe Dylan truly got his father to reveal the location or if he knew all along. The latter hurts the most, so I've accepted the former to spare myself the added heartbreak that one more person was complicit in my father's tragic ending.

Clive Ryland already sits in jail, so finding the body didn't make a difference in his fate, but according to the state prosecutor, it does make a difference in Landon's father's case. The former mayor resigned shortly after the FBI found evidence of bribery and mysterious so-called donations from multiple shell accounts. He was also linked to paying money to Connor in his efforts to blackmail the Rylands and the Wexfords with the security footage they thought was erased.

As happy as I am that the piece-of-shit mayor is getting the justice he deserves, he's only a symptom of the disease. Another politician will take his place, and maybe that one won't be corrupt, but the opportunity to be corrupt will always exist when you give any one person that much power.

I look down at my phone and note it's six minutes past the time the funeral is set to begin. I know everyone up there is waiting on me, but I can't seem to make my feet move to bring me to my final goodbye. After we buried my mother, I never returned to her grave. I know everyone has their own way of coping with the loss of a loved one, but I never saw the point in revisiting a door you already closed. And what a heavy door that was.

I said my goodbyes to my mother the day as I tossed a handful of wet earth on her casket. It was one of the hardest things I've ever had to do, and at the time, I had no intention of saying a goodbye that final ever again.

Little did I know I would be waiting for that moment of closure with my father for years. And now that it's finally here, I'm terrified to do it again.

My phone pings with a text from Esther asking if I need her to come down to walk up with me. She's already joined the latter group because I told her to go on without me. As much as I love her for supporting me through all this, I can't handle the heartbreak I see in her eyes whenever she looks at me. I already know my story is a sad one—I don't need additional reminders today. I pocket my phone and lean back against the car. Closing my eyes, I focus on taking a few deep breaths to calm my nerves. Before I open them, I hear the ground crunch under someone's foot. When I finally look, I see Remy standing just a few feet away from me, staring up at the group. He holds two coffee cups in his hands, and I pray one of those is for me.

"Would you like some company?" he asks, handing me the cup, and in solidarity, leans against the car with me.

"Everyone is waiting on me," I say without looking at him.

"They waited years to do this. I think they can manage a few more minutes, kid." He speaks so casually that it calms my nerves and allows me to turn to look at him, making eye contact with someone for the first time today. He looks tired, but I don't see an ounce of pity when he looks back at me—a comfort I don't think he knows he's providing.

"Allan told me the good news."

And with that comment, I look away from him because I'm not sure if it is good news.

"That was quite the settlement. Does that make you the new owner of Ryland Corp.?" he teases, but the joke falls flat.

I blow out a puff of air. "God, I fucking hope not. I don't want to hear the name Ryland Corp. ever again in my life."

"Yeah, I don't blame you." He sips from his cup and runs a hand through his hair, and it dawns on me that he's also nervous to walk up.

"What are you going to do after all this?" He raises an arm to gesture to the crop of people waiting for us, but I know he doesn't just mean after the funeral—he means now that my father's been found.

"I don't know. That's a tomorrow question."

He nods, and with another sip of his coffee, holds an arm out. "Shall we?"

I nod and slowly weave my arm through his.

Looking up at the sky, I allow the warmth from the sun to kiss my face as I take my first step toward closing yet another heavy door. The harsh winter is finally over, the lilacs will bloom once again, and life will go on.

The End

AUTHORS NOTE

Thank you for reading my debut novel, *Lilac*. Since I can remember, I've always had a love for storytelling, and to be completely honest, I'm slightly embarrassed it took me thirty-four years to put that love into a piece of literary work.

Cosette's story manifested one night while I was on the road, suffering from a restless mind, alone in a hotel room. That night I sat in the dark, cross-legged, with the light of my laptop illuminating a sleep-deprived face and wrote what would be the scene where Cosette finds out who Dylan is.

There's something about a romantic tragedy that sits with me long after I've set the book down, and I thought how tragic it would be to find someone who finally makes you feel alive, only for them to be the one person your grief will never allow you to trust. Although *Lilac* isn't necessarily a love story, it is a tragic one. After all, love isn't the only thing grief can rob us of—and therein lies the heart of Cosette's story. I continued to work on *Lilac* for two years until, finally, it bloomed into something I deemed worthy enough to share with the world.

I never could have written this novel without my incredible family and friends, who supported me through bouts of imposter syndrome and gave me the honest feedback I needed to keep going.

To my amazing husband, my cheerleader from day one—thank you for tolerating my late-night writing sessions and for being the very first reader of *Lilac*.

To my sister Nicol, my literary partner in crime, who pulled me back into the world of literature after a long hiatus of missing out on the many adventures fiction can take you on. Your constant support and excitement about this novel kept me going. You saved *Lilac* more times than you probably realize from becoming just another forgotten file in my disorganized laptop.

To my mother, thank you for raising me with the courage to try something new and the persistence to keep going when it's harder than expected.

To my beta readers, my editor, and everyone who touched this story along the way: your insights and dedication helped shape *Lilac* into its best version.

I will forever cherish the journey this novel took me on. While *Lilac* is my first novel, I promise—it won't be my last.